SEPTIMUS HEAP

✚ BOOK THREE ✚

Physik

SEPTIMUS HEAP

☩ BOOK THREE ☩

Physik

ANGIE SAGE

ILLUSTRATIONS BY MARK ZUG

KATHERINE TEGEN BOOKS
An Imprint of HarperCollins*Publishers*

Septimus Heap Book Three: Physik

Text copyright © 2007 by Angie Sage

Illustrations © 2007 by Mark Zug

All rights reserved. Printed in the United States of America. No part of this
book may be used or reproduced in any manner whatsoever without written
permission except in the case of brief quotations embodied in critical articles
and reviews. For information address HarperCollins Children's Books, a divi-
sion of HarperCollins Publishers, 1350 Avenue of the Americas, New York,
NY 10019.

www.harpercollinschildrens.com

Library of Congress Cataloging-in-Publication Data

Sage, Angie.

    Physik / Angie Sage ; illustrated by Mark Zug. — 1st ed.

     p.   cm. — (Septimus Heap)

    "Book Three."

    Summary: Septimus Heap is pulled back through time and becomes an
apprentice to an alchemist.

    ISBN-10: 0-06-057737-1 (trade bdg.)

    ISBN-13: 978-0-06-057737-7 (trade bdg.)

    ISBN-10: 0-06-057738-X (lib. bdg.)

    ISBN-13: 978-0-06-057738-4 (lib. bdg.)

    [1. Magic—Fiction.] I. Zug, Mark, ill. II. Title.

PZ7.S13035Phy 2007   2006019858

[Fic]—dc22   CIP

                                                     AC

Typography by Karin Paprocki

1 2 3 4 5 6 7 8 9 10

❖

First Edition

For Rhodri—
my Alchemist,
with love

✛ CONTENTS ✛

Physik

tHE
CASTLE

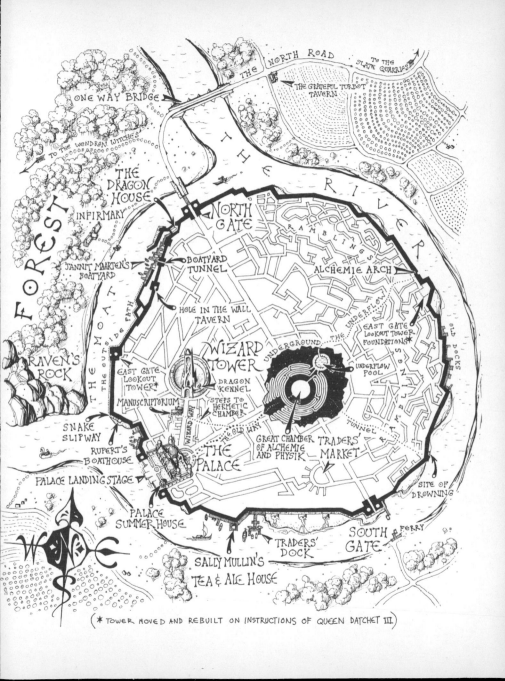

TO THE SLATE QUARRIES

THE NORTH ROAD

THE GRATEFUL TURBOT TAVERN

ONE WAY BRIDGE

TO THE WENDRON WITCHES

THE RIVER

FOREST

THE DRAGON HOUSE

INFIRMARY

NORTH GATE

JANNIT MAARTEN'S BOATYARD

BOATYARD TUNNEL

RAMBLINGS

ALCHEMIE ARCH

HOLE IN THE WALL TAVERN

THE OUTSIDE PATH

THE MOAT

UNDERFLOW

THE UNDERGROUND

EAST GATE LOOKOUT TOWER FOUNDATIONS*

RAVEN'S ROCK

EAST GATE LOOKOUT TOWER*

WIZARD TOWER

DRAGON KENNEL

STEPS TO HERMETIC CHAMBER

UNDERFLOW POOL

MANUSCRIPTORIUM

WIZARD WAY

THE RAMBLINGS

SNAKE SLIPWAY

RUPERT'S BOATHOUSE

THE OLD WAY

GREAT CHAMBER OF ALCHEMIE AND PHYSIK

TRADERS' MARKET

THE PALACE

TUNNEL

OLD DOCKS

PALACE LANDING STAGE

SITE OF DROWNING

PALACE SUMMER HOUSE

TRADERS' DOCK

SOUTH GATE

FERRY

W N S E

SALLY MULLIN'S TEA & ALE HOUSE

(* TOWER MOVED AND REBUILT ON INSTRUCTIONS OF QUEEN DATCHET III.)

attics are best left
peculiar. Anyw
find a new C
they'll sta
"T
Sila

2

*S*ilas Heap and Gringe, *the* North Gate Gatekeeper, are in a
dark and dusty corner of the Palace attic. In front of them
is a small door to a **Sealed** room, which Silas Heap, Ordinary
Wizard, is about to **UnSeal**. "You see, Gringe," he says, "it's
the perfect place. My Counters will never be able to escape
from there. I can just **Seal** them in."

Gringe is not so sure. Even he knows that **Sealed** rooms in

lone. "I don't like it, Silas," he says. "It feels
ay, just because you've been lucky enough to
lony under the floorboards up 'ere doesn't mean
here."

ey jolly well will stay if they're **Sealed** in, Gringe," says
, clutching his box of precious newfound Counters, which
e has just caught. "You're just being funny because you
won't be able to entice this bunch away."

"I did not *entice* the last bunch either, Silas Heap. They came
of their own accord. Weren't nothing I could do about it."

Silas ignores Gringe. He is trying to remember how to do
an **UnSeal Spell**.

Gringe taps his foot impatiently. " 'Urry up, Silas. I got a
gate to get back to. Lucy is most odd at the moment and I
don't want to leave 'er there alone for long."

Silas Heap closes his eyes so that he can think better.
Under his breath, so that Gringe cannot quite hear what he is
saying, Silas chants the **Lock Incantation** backward three
times, finishing it off with the **UnSeal**. He opens his eyes.
Nothing has happened.

"I'm going," Gringe tells him. "Can't 'ang around like a
spare part all day. Some of us 'ave work to do."

Suddenly with a loud bang, the door to the **Sealed** room slams open. Silas is triumphant. "See—I *do* know what I'm doing. I *am* a Wizard, Gringe. Oof! What was that?" An icy gust of stale air rushes past Silas and Gringe, dragging their breath right up from their lungs and causing them both to subside into fits of coughing.

"That was cold." Gringe shivers, with goose bumps running up and down his arms. Silas does not reply—he is already in the **UnSealed** room, deciding on the best place to keep his Counter Colony. Curiosity gets the better of Gringe and he tentatively enters the room. It is tiny, little more than a cupboard. Apart from the light of Silas's candle, the room is dark, for the only window that it once had has been bricked up. It is nothing more than an empty space, with dusty floorboards and bare, cracked plaster walls. But it is not—as Gringe suddenly notices—entirely empty. In the dim shadows on the far side of the little room a large, life-size oil painting of a Queen is propped up against the wall.

Silas looks at the portrait. It is a skillful painting of a Castle Queen, from times long past. He can tell that it is old because she is wearing the True Crown, the one that was lost many centuries ago. The Queen has a sharp pointy nose and wears her hair coiled around her ears like a pair of earmuffs. Clinging to her skirts is an Aie-Aie—a horrible little creature with a ratty face, sharp claws and a long snake's tail. Its round, red eyes stare out at Silas as though it would like to bite him with its one long, needle-sharp tooth. The Queen too looks out from the painting but she wears a lofty, disapproving expression. Her head is held high, supported by a starched ruff under her chin and her piercing eyes are reflected in the light of Silas's candle and seem to follow them everywhere.

Gringe shivers. "I wouldn't like to meet 'er out on me own on a dark night," he says.

Silas thinks that Gringe is right, *he* wouldn't like to meet her on a dark night either—and neither would his precious Counters. "She'll have to go," says Silas. "I'm not having her upsetting my Counter Colony before they've even got started."

But what Silas does not know is that she has already gone. As soon as he **UnSealed** the room, the ghosts of Queen Etheldredda and her creature stepped out of the portrait, opened the door and, pointy noses in the air, walked and scuttled out—right past Silas and Gringe. The Queen and her Aie-Aie paid them no attention, for they had more important things to do—and at long last they were free to do them.

╫ I ╫

SNORRI SNORRELSSEN

*S*norri Snorrelssen guided her trading barge up the quiet waters of the river toward the Castle. It was a misty autumn afternoon and Snorri was relieved to have left the turbulent tidal waters of the Port behind her. The wind had dropped but enough breeze caught the huge sail of the barge—named *Alfrún*, after her mother who owned it—to enable her to steer the boat safely around Raven's Rock and head for the quay just beyond Sally Mullin's Tea and Ale House.

Two young fishermen, not much older than Snorri herself,

had just returned from a day's successful herring catch and were more than happy to catch the heavy hemp ropes that Snorri threw to shore. Eager to show their skills, they tied the ropes around two large posts on the quay and made the *Alfrún* secure. The fishermen were also more than happy to dispense all kinds of advice on how to take the sail down and the best way to stow the ropes, which Snorri ignored, partly because she hardly understood what they were saying but mainly because no one told Snorri Snorrelssen what to do—*no one*, not even her mother. Especially not her mother.

Snorri, tall for her age, was slim, wiry and surprisingly strong. With the practiced ease of someone who had spent the last two weeks at sea sailing alone, Snorri lowered the great canvas sail and rolled up the vast folds of heavy cloth; then she heaved the ropes into neat coils and secured the tiller. Aware that she was being watched by the fishermen, Snorri locked the hatch to the hold below, which was full of heavy bales of thick woolen cloth, sacks of pickling spice, great barrels of salted fish and some particularly fine rein-deer-skin boots. At last—ignoring more offers of help—Snorri pushed the gangplank out and came ashore, leaving Ullr, her small orange cat with a black-tipped tail, to prowl the deck and keep the rats at bay.

Snorri had been at sea for more than two weeks and she had been looking forward to stepping onto firm land again, but as she walked along the quay it felt to her as if she were still on board the *Alfrún*, for the quay seemed to move beneath her feet just as the old barge had done. The fishermen, who should already have gone home to *their* respective mothers, were sitting on a pile of empty lobster pots. "Evening, miss," one of them called out.

Snorri ignored him. She made her way to the end of the quay and took the well-trodden path that led to a large new pontoon, on which a thriving café was built. It was a very stylish two-story wooden building with long, low windows that looked out across the river. The café looked inviting in the chill early-evening air, with a warm yellow light coming from the oil lamps that hung from the ceiling. As Snorri walked across the wooden walkway that led onto the pontoon she could hardly believe that, at long last, she was here— at the fabled Sally Mullin's Tea and Ale House. Excited, but feeling very nervous, Snorri pushed open the double doors to the café and nearly fell over a long line of fire buckets full of sand and water.

There was always a general buzz of friendly conversation in Sally Mullin's café, but as soon as Snorri stepped over the threshold the buzz suddenly stopped, as though someone had thrown a switch. Almost in unison, every customer put down their drink and stared at the young stranger who wore the distinctive robes of the Hanseatic League, to which all Northern Traders belonged. Feeling herself blushing and wishing furiously that she wasn't, Snorri advanced toward the bar, determined to order one of Sally's barley cakes and a half-pint mug of the Springo Special Ale that she had heard so much about.

Sally Mullin, a short round woman with an equal dusting of freckles and barley flour on her cheeks, bustled out of the kitchen. Seeing the dark red robes of a Northern Trader and the typical leather headband, her face took on a scowl. "I don't serve Northern Traders in here," she snapped.

Snorri looked puzzled. She was not sure that she understood what Sally had said, although she could tell that Sally was not exactly welcoming.

"You saw the notice on the door," Sally said when Snorri showed no sign of leaving. "No Northern Traders. You are not welcome here, not in *my* café."

"She's only a lass, Sal," someone called out. "Give the girl a chance."

There was a general murmur of assent from the other cus- tomers. Sally Mullin gave Snorri a closer look and her expres- sion softened. It was true; she was only a girl—maybe sixteen at the most, thought Sally. She had the typical white-blond hair and pale, almost translucent blue eyes that most of the Traders had, but she did not have that hard-bitten look that Sally had come to remember with a shudder.

"Well . . ." said Sally, backtracking, "I suppose it's getting on to nightfall and I'm not one to be turning out a young girl into the dark all on her own. What will you have, miss?"

"I . . . I will have," Snorri faltered as she tried hard to remember her grammar. Was it, I *will have* or I *shall have*? "I shall have a slice of your very fine barley cake and a half-pint of the Springo Special Ale, if you please."

"Springo Special, eh?" someone called out. "There's a lass after me own heart."

"Be quiet, Tom," Sally chided. "You'd best try the ordinary Springo first," she told Snorri. Sally poured out the ale into a large china mug and pushed it across the counter toward the girl. Snorri took a tentative sip and her face wrinkled in disgust. Sally was not surprised. Springo was an acquired taste and most youngsters thought it was revolting; indeed there were some days when Sally herself thought it was pretty foul. Sally poured a mug of lemon and honey for Snorri and put it on a tray with a large slab of barley cake. The girl looked like she could do with a good meal. Snorri gave Sally a whole silver florin, much to Sally's surprise, and got back a huge pile of pennies in change. Then she sat down at an empty table by the window and looked out at the darkening river.

Conversation in the café started up again and Snorri breathed a sigh of relief. Coming into Sally Mullin's café on her own had been the hardest thing she had ever done in her life. Harder than taking the *Alfrún* out to sea on her own for the first time, harder than trading for all the goods now in the *Alfrún*'s hold with the money she had saved up for years, and much, much harder than the crossing over the great northern sea that separated the land of the Northern Traders from the land of Sally Mullin's Tea and Ale House. But she had done it; Snorri Snorrelssen was following in the footsteps of her father, and no one could stop her. Not even her mother.

Later that evening, Snorri returned to the *Alfrún*. She was met by Ullr in his nighttime guise. The cat emitted a long, low welcoming growl and followed his mistress along the deck. Feeling so full of barley cake that she could barely move, Snorri sat in her favorite place at the prow, stroking the NightUllr, a sleek and powerful panther, black as the night with sea-green eyes and an orange-tipped tail.

Snorri was far too excited to sleep. She sat with her arm draped loosely over Ullr's warm, silky-smooth fur, looking out across the dark expanse of river to the shores of the Farmlands on the opposite banks. Later, as the night grew chill, she wrapped herself in a sample length of the thick woolen cloth that she planned to sell—and for a good price, too—in the Traders' Market, which started in two weeks' time. Balanced on her lap was a map of the Castle, showing how to get to the marketplace; on the reverse of the map were detailed instructions on how to obtain a license for a stall and all manner of rules and regulations about buying and selling. Snorri lit the oil lamp she had brought up from her small cabin below and settled down to read the rules and regulations. The wind was still now, and the fine drizzle of the early evening had died down; the air was crisp and clear, and Snorri breathed in the smells of the land—so different and foreign from the one she was used to.

As the evening drew on, small groups of customers began to leave Sally's café, until just after midnight Snorri saw Sally extinguish the oil lamps and bolt the door. Snorri smiled happily. Now she had the river to herself, just her, Ullr and the *Alfrún*, alone in the night. As the barge rocked gently in the outgoing tide, Snorri felt her eyes closing. She put down the tedious list of permitted weights and measures, pulled the woolen cloth more tightly around her and gazed out across the river for just one last time before she went down to her cabin. And then she saw it.

A long, pale boat outlined in a greenish glow was coming around Raven's Rock. Snorri sat very still and watched the boat make slow, silent progress up the middle of the river, steadily drawing closer to the *Alfrún*. As it drew near, Snorri saw it shimmering in the light of the moon, and a shiver ran down her spine, for Snorri Snorrelssen, Spirit-Seer, knew exactly what she was looking at—a Spirit Ship. Snorri whistled under her breath, for she had never seen a boat quite like this one. Snorri was used to seeing wrecks of old fishing boats steered by their drowned skippers, forever seeking safe harbor. Every now and then she had seen the ghost of a warrior longship, limping home after a fierce battle, and once she had seen the ghostly tall ship of a rich merchant, with treasure pouring from a gaping hole in its side, but she had never seen a Royal Barge—complete with the ghost of its Queen.

Snorri got to her feet, took out her Spirit eyeglass, which the wise woman in the Ice Palace had given her, and focused it on the apparition as it drifted noiselessly by, propelled by eight ghostly oars. The barge was decked out in flags that fluttered in a wind that had died long ago; it was painted in swirling patterns of gold and silver and was covered in a rich red canopy, strung from ornate pillars of gold. Beneath the canopy sat a tall, erect figure staring fixedly ahead. Her pointed chin rested on a high, starched ruff, she wore a simple crown and sported a decidedly old-fashioned hairstyle: two coiled plaits of hair tightly wound around her ears. Next to her sat a small, almost hairless creature that Snorri took to be a particularly ugly dog until she saw its long, snakelike tail curled around one of the gold pillars. Snorri watched the ghost boat drift by, and she shivered as a chill ran through her—for there was something different, something *substantial*, about its occupants.

Snorri put away her eyeglass and climbed through the hatch to her cabin, leaving Ullr on guard on the deck. She hung her lamp from a hook in the cabin roof, and the soft yellow light from the lamp made the cabin feel warm and cozy. It was small, for most of the space on a Trader's barge was taken up with the hold, but Snorri loved it. The cabin was lined with sweet-smelling applewood that her father, Olaf, had once brought home as a present for her mother and was beautifully fitted out, for her father had been a talented carpenter. On the starboard side was a built-in bunk that doubled up as a seat in the day. Under the bunk were neat cupboards where Snorri stowed all the cabin clutter, and above the bunk was a long shelf where Snorri kept her charts rolled up. On the port side was a drop-down table, an expanse of applewood drawers and a small potbellied iron stove from which a chimney ran up through the cabin roof. Snorri opened the door to the stove and a dull red glow came from the dying embers of the fire.

Feeling sleepy, Snorri climbed into her bunk, pulled her reindeer-skin coverlet around herself and snuggled down for the night. She smiled happily. It had been a good day—apart from the sight of the ghost Queen. But there was only one ghost that Snorri wanted to see—and that was the ghost of Olaf Snorrelssen.

⊹⊱ 2 ⊰⊹
THE TRADERS' MARKET

The next morning Snorri was up bright and early, and Ullr, back in his daytime mode of scrawny orange cat with a black-tipped tail, was eating a mouse for breakfast. Snorri had forgotten all about the ghostly Royal Barge, and when she did remember it over her own breakfast of pickled herring and dark rye bread, Snorri decided that she had dreamed the whole thing.

Snorri pulled out her sample bag from the hold, heaved it over her shoulders and set off down the gangplank into the bright morning sunshine, feeling happy and excited. Snorri liked this strange land that she had come to; she liked the green water of the slow river and the smell of autumn leaves and wood smoke that hung in the air, and she was fascinated by the tall Castle walls that reared up before her, behind which was a whole new world to explore. Snorri walked up the steep path that led to the South Gate and breathed in deeply. There was a chill in the air, but it was nothing like the frosts that Snorri knew her mother would be waking up to back home in their dark little wooden house on the quay. Snorri shook her head to get rid of any thoughts of her mother and followed the path up to the Castle.

As Snorri walked through the South Gate she noticed an old beggar sitting on the ground. She fished out a groat from her pocket, for her people considered it good luck to give to the first beggar you saw in a strange country, and pressed it into his hand. Too late, as her hand went through his, Snorri realized that this was a ghostly beggar. The ghost looked surprised at Snorri's touch, and in a bad temper at being **Passed Through**, he got up and walked away. Snorri stopped and dropped her heavy bag onto the ground. She looked around and her heart sank. The Castle was *packed*, stuffed full to overflowing with ghosts of all descriptions, which Snorri, as a

Spirit-Seer, had no choice but to see—whether the ghosts had chosen to **Appear** to her or not. Snorri wondered how she was ever going to find her father in such a crowd. She very nearly turned around right there and went home again, but she told herself that she had also come to Trade, and as the daughter of a renowned Trader, Trade she would.

Keeping her head down and avoiding as many ghosts as she could, Snorri followed her map. It was a good map, and very soon she was walking through the old brick archway that led into the Traders' Market Palace, where she made straight for the Traders' Office. The office was an open hut with a sign above it saying HANSEATIC LEAGUE AND NORTHERN TRADE ASSOCIATION INCORPORATED. Inside the hut were a long trestle table, two sets of scales with assorted weights and measures, a large ledger and a wizened old Trader counting the money in a large iron cash box. Suddenly Snorri felt nervous, almost as nervous as when she had entered Sally Mullin's. This was the moment when she had to prove that she had a right to Trade and a right to belong to the Association. She swallowed hard and, head held high, strode into the hut.

The old man did not look up. He carried on counting out the strange coins that Snorri had not yet become used to:

pennies, groats, florins, half crowns and crowns. Snorri coughed a couple of times but still the old man did not look up. After a few minutes, Snorri could bear it no longer. "Excuse me," she said.

"Four hundred and twenty-five, four hundred and twenty-six . . ." said the man, not taking his eyes off the coins.

Snorri had no choice but to wait. Five minutes later the man announced, "One thousand. Yes, miss, can I help you?"

Snorri put a crown on the trestle table and said fluently, for she had rehearsed this moment for days beforehand, "I wish to buy a license to Trade."

The old man looked at the girl in her rough woolen Trader dress standing before him, and he smiled as though Snorri had said something foolish. "Sorry, miss. You have to be a member of the League."

Snorri understood the man well enough. "I *am* a member of the League," she told him. Before the man could object, Snorri took out her Letters of Charter and put the roll of parchment with its red ribbon and great blob of red sealing wax in front of the man. As if humoring her, the old man very slowly pulled out his glasses, shaking his head at the impudence of youngsters today, and slowly read what Snorri had

given him. As his finger moved along the words, his expression changed to one of disbelief, and when he had finished
reading, he held up the parchment to the light, searching for
signs that it was a forgery.

It wasn't. Snorri knew it wasn't and so did the old man.
"This is most irregular," he told Snorri.

"Ir-regular?" asked Snorri.

"*Most* irregular. It is not usual for fathers to pass their
Letters of Charter on to their daughters."

"No?"

"But all appears to be in order." The old man sighed and
rather unwillingly reached under the table and pulled out a
stack of licenses. "Sign here," he said, pushing a pen over to
Snorri. Snorri signed her name and the old man stamped the
license as though it had said something extremely personal
and rude.

He pushed it across the table to Snorri. "Stall number one.
You're early. The first one here. Market starts at dawn two
weeks from Friday. Last day is MidWinter Feast Day Eve.
Clear out by dusk. All trash to be removed to the Municipal
Rubbish Dump by midnight. That will be one crown." The
man took the crown from where Snorri had laid it on the table

and threw it into another cash box, where it landed with an empty clatter.

Snorri took the license with a broad smile. She had done it. She was a Licensed Trader, just as her father had been.

"Take your samples to the shed and leave them for quality control," the old man said. "You may collect them tomorrow."

Snorri left her heavy bag in the sample bin outside the shed, and feeling as light as air, she danced out of the market-place and bumped straight into a girl wearing a red tunic edged with gold. The girl had long dark hair and wore a gold circlet around her head like a crown. Beside her stood a ghost dressed in purple robes. He had a friendly expression in his green eyes and wore his gray hair neatly tied back in a pony-tail. Snorri tried not to look at the bloodstains on his robes just below his heart, for it was impolite to stare at the means by which the ghost had entered ghosthood.

"Oh, sorry," the girl in red said to Snorri. "I wasn't looking where I was going."

"No. I am sorry," said Snorri. She smiled and the girl smiled back. Snorri went on her way back to the *Alfrún*, wondering. She had heard that the Castle had a Princess, but surely this could not be her, walking around just like anyone else?

The girl, who was indeed the Princess, continued on her way to the Palace with the purple-robed ghost.

"She's a Spirit-Seer," said the ghost.

"Who is?"

"That young Trader. I did not **Appear** to her but she saw me. I've never met one before. They're very rare, they are only found in the Lands of the Long Nights." The ghost shivered. "Gives me the creeps."

The Princess laughed. "You are funny, Alther," she said. "I bet *you* give people the creeps all the time."

"I do not," replied the ghost indignantly. "Well . . . only if I want to."

Over the next few days, the autumn weather closed in. The north winds blew the leaves from the trees and sent them skittering down the streets. The air grew chill and people began to notice how early it was getting dark.

But to Snorri Snorrelssen, the weather felt good. She spent her days wandering around the Castle, exploring its highways and byways, looking with amazement into the windows of all the fascinating little shops tucked away underneath the arches in The Ramblings and even buying the odd trinket. She had gazed up at the Wizard Tower in awe, caught a glimpse of what appeared to be an extremely bossy ExtraOrdinary Wizard, and been shocked at the great piles of manure that the Wizards kept in their courtyard. She had joined the crowd watching the old clock in Drapers Yard strike twelve noon and laughed at the faces that the twelve tin figures had made as they sauntered out from behind the clock. Another day, she had walked down Wizard Way, taken a tour of the oldest printing press, and then peered through the railings at the beautiful old Palace, which was smaller than she had expected. She had even talked to an old ghost called Gudrun at the Palace Gate, who had recognized a fellow countrywoman, even though they were divided by seven centuries.

But the one ghost that Snorri had hoped to see in her wanderings eluded her. Although she only knew what he looked like from a picture that her mother kept at her bedside, she was sure that she would recognize him if she saw him. But despite constantly scanning the crowds of ghosts that wandered by, Snorri caught not so much as a glimpse of her father.

Late one afternoon, after exploring some of the darker alleyways at the back of The Ramblings where many of the Traders took lodgings, Snorri had had a fright. It was getting near sunset and she had just bought a hand torch from Maizie Smalls's Takeaway Torch Shop. As she walked back along Squeeze Guts Alley to the South Gate, Snorri had the uncomfortable feeling that she was being followed, but every time she turned around, there was nothing to see. Suddenly Snorri had heard a scuffling behind her, she spun around and there they were—a pair of round red eyes and one long needlelike tooth glinting in the light of her hand torch. As soon as the eyes saw the flame, they melted into the twilight and Snorri saw no more of them. Snorri told herself that it was only a rat, but not long after, as she walked briskly back to the main thorough-fare, Snorri had heard a shrill scream coming from Squeeze Guts Alley. Someone who had ventured down the Alley with-out a torch had not been so lucky.

Snorri was shaken and in need of some human company, so that evening she had supper at Sally Mullin's. Sally had warmed to Snorri because, as she had said to her friend Sarah Heap, "You can't blame a young girl just because she's got the misfortune to be a Trader, and I suppose they're not *all* bad. You've got to admire her, Sarah, she's sailed that great barge all on her own. Don't know how she did it. I used to find *Muriel* difficult enough."

The café was strangely empty that evening. Snorri was the only customer. Sally brought Snorri an extra piece of barley cake and sat beside her. "It's terrible for business, this Sicke-nesse," she complained. "No one dares stay out after dark even though I tell them that rats run a mile when they see a flame. All they have to do is carry a torch. But it's no good, everyone's scared now." Sally shook her head gloomily. "They go for your ankles, see. And quick as greased lightning they are. One bite and that's it. You're gone."

Snorri was having some trouble following Sally's rapid stream of words. "Yorgon?" she asked, catching the end of the sentence.

Sally nodded. "As good as," she said. "Not dead exactly but they reckon it's only a matter of time. You feel fine for a while, then you get a red rash spreading up from the bite, feel dizzy and bang—next thing you know you're flat out on the floor and away with the fairies."

"Fairies?" asked Snorri.

"Yes," said Sally, springing to her feet at the welcome sight of a customer.

The customer was a tall woman with short spiky hair. She held her cloak close around her. Snorri could see little of the woman's face, but there was an angry look to the way she stood. A murmured conversation ensued between her and Sally, then the woman left as swiftly as she had come.

Smiling, Sally rejoined Snorri at her seat overlooking the river. "Well, it's an ill wind that blows no one good," she said, much to Snorri's bemusement. "That was Geraldine who just came in. Strange woman, reminds me of someone, though I can't think who. Anyway, she asked if the RatStranglers can meet up here before they go out, er, rat strangling."

"Ratstrang-gling?" asked Snorri.

"Well, rat *catching*. They reckon if they get rid of all the rats, they'll get rid of the Sickenesse, too. Makes sense to me. Anyway, I'm very pleased. A load of hungry and thirsty rat catchers is just what the café could do with right now."

No one else came into the café after the spiky Geraldine left, and soon Sally started noisily putting up the benches on the tables and began to mop the floor. Snorri took the hint and bade Sally good night.

"Good night, dear," said Sally cheerily. "Don't hang around outside now, will you?"

Snorri had no intention of hanging around. She ran back to the *Alfrún* and was very glad to see the NightUllr prowling the deck. Leaving Ullr on guard, Snorri retreated to her cabin, barred the hatch and kept the oil lamp burning all night.

✠ 3 ✠
AN UNWELCOME VISITOR

That evening, while Snorri Snorrelssen was barricading her cabin door, Jenna, Sarah and Silas Heap were finishing supper at the Palace. Although Sarah Heap would have much rather had supper in one of the smaller Palace kitchens, she had long ago given in to the Cook's insistence that royalty most definitely did *not* eat in the kitchen. No, not even on a quiet wet

Wednesday, no way, not while *she* was Cook—"and that, Mistress Heap, is final."

And so in the vast Palace dining room, marooned at the very end of a long table, three figures sat in a pool of candle-light. A log fire spat and spluttered behind them, occasionally landing a spark on the wiry and somewhat mangy coat of a large dog, who lay snoring and grunting in front of the fire, but Maxie the wolfhound did not notice. Beside the wolfhound hovered the Supper Servant, glad of the warmth but longing to clear the food and get away from the smells of singed dog hair—and worse—that floated up from Maxie.

But supper was taking an age. Sarah Heap, adoptive mother of Jenna, the Princess and heir to the Castle, had a lot to say. "Well, I don't want you leaving the Palace *at all*, Jenna, and that is that. There's something nasty out there biting people and giving them the Sickenesse. You are to stay here where it is safe until this whatever-it-is is caught."

"But Septimus—"

"No buts. I don't care whether Septimus needs you to clean out his disgusting dragon or not, though, if you ask me, it would be a whole lot better if he didn't clean it out quite so often—have you seen the mess down by the river? I don't know what Billy Pot is thinking of, the piles of dragon drop-pings must be ten feet high at least. I used to enjoy walking by the river but now—"

"Mum, I don't mind not cleaning out Spit Fyre, not one bit, but I *have* to go see the Dragon Boat every day," Jenna said.

"I'm sure the Dragon Boat will manage without you," Sarah told her. "It's not as if it knows you're there anyway."

"*She* does, Mum. I'm sure she does. It would be awful for her to wake up and find no one there, no one for days and days . . ."

"Far better than finding no one there ever again," said Sarah sharply. "You are *not* to go out until something has been done about this Sickenesse."

"Don't you think you're making a fuss about nothing?" Silas asked mildly.

Sarah did not think so. "I do not call having to open up the Infirmary *nothing*, Silas."

"What, that old dump? I'm surprised it's still standing."

"There's no choice, Silas. There are too many people sick for them to go anywhere else. Which you would have realized if you didn't spend so much time up in the attic playing silly games—"

"Counter-Feet is not a silly game, Sarah. And now I've found what must be the best Colony in the Castle—you should have seen Gringe's face when I told him—I am *not* going to let the Counters go. They won't be getting out of a **Sealed** room in a hurry."

Sarah Heap sighed. Ever since they had moved into the Palace, Silas had practically given up his day-to-day Ordinary Wizard job and had taken up a succession of hobbies—the board game of Counter-Feet being the latest and most long-lasting, much to her irritation. "You know I don't think it's a good idea to go opening **Sealed** rooms, Silas," Sarah chided. "They are usually **Sealed** for a reason, especially if they're hidden away up in the attic. We had a talk about it at the Herb Society only last month."

Silas was scathing. "And what do those Herbs know about Wizard stuff, Sarah? Nothing. Huh."

"Very well, Silas. I suppose you're safer up in the attic with your daft Counter Colony for now anyway."

"Quite," said Silas. "Is there any more pie?"

"No, you've got the last piece." A strained silence followed, and in the silence Jenna was sure she could hear a distant clamor.

"Can you hear that?" she asked. She got up and looked out one of the tall windows that overlooked the front of the Palace. Jenna could see down the drive, which, as ever, was lit with burning torches, and through the great Palace Gates that were locked at night. But on the other side of the gates was a mob, shouting and banging trash can lids and yelling, "Rats, rats, get the rats. Rats, rats, *kill* the rats!"

Sarah joined Jenna at the window. "It's the RatStranglers," she said. "I don't know what they're doing *here*."

"Looking for rats, I suppose," said Silas, his mouth full of apple pie. "Plenty of 'em around here. I think we had one in the soup tonight."

The chanting of the RatStranglers picked up speed. "Rat trap, rat trap, splat, splat, *splat*! Rat trap, rat trap, splat, splat, *splat*!"

"Poor rats," said Jenna.

"It's not rats that are spreading the Sickenesse anyway," said Sarah. "I was helping at the Infirmary yesterday and the bites are definitely not rat bites. Rats have more than one tooth. Oh, look, they're off up the road to the servants' quarters. Oh, dear me."

At that, the Supper Servant sprang into action. She scooped

up the plates, wrestled Silas's last piece of apple pie from his grasp and rushed out of the room. There was a crash as she dropped the plates down the garbage chute to the kitchens below. Then she fled back to her quarters to check on Percy, her pet rat.

Supper didn't last long after that. Sarah and Silas went off to Sarah's small sitting room at the back of the Palace, where Sarah had a book to finish and Silas was busy writing a pamphlet entitled *Top Ten Counter-Feet Tips*, for which he had high hopes.

Jenna decided to go to her room and read. Jenna liked her own company and she loved wandering around the Palace, especially at night when candles cast great shadows across the corridors and many of the Ancient ghosts woke up. At night the Palace lost the rather empty feeling that it had during the day and became a busy, purposeful place once again. Most of the Ancients chose to **Appear** to Jenna and relished the chance to talk to the Princess, even if many could not remember which Princess she actually was. Jenna enjoyed her chats, even though she had soon discovered that each ghost tended to say the same thing every night, and she soon knew most conversations by heart.

Jenna wandered up the wide sweeping stairs to the gallery that ran above the hall, and stopped to talk to the ghost of an old governess of a pair of young Princesses who spent most nights wandering the passageways looking for her charges.

"Good eventide, Princess Esmeralda," said the governess, who wore a permanently worried expression.

"Good evening, Mary," replied Jenna, who had long since stopped telling Mary that she was actually called Jenna, as it had no effect whatsoever.

"I am glad to see you are still safe and well," said the governess.

"Thank you, Mary," said Jenna.

"Be careful, my dear," said the governess as she always did.

"I will," Jenna replied as ever, and went on her way. Soon she turned off from the gallery into a wide candlelit corridor at the end of which were the tall double doors that led to her room.

"Good evening, Sir Hereward," Jenna greeted the Ancient Guard of the Royal Bedchamber, a disheveled and very faded ghost who had been at his post for some eight hundred years or more and had no intention of retiring. Sir Hereward was missing an arm and a good deal of his armor, as his entry into ghosthood had been the result of one of the last land battles between the Castle and the Port. He was one of Jenna's favorites and she felt safe with him on guard; the old knight had a jovial manner and a liking for jokes and, unusual for an Ancient, generally managed not to repeat himself too often.

"Good evening, fair Princess. Here's a good one: What is the difference between an elephant and a banana?"

"I don't know." Jenna smiled. "What *is* the difference between an elephant and a banana?"

"Well, I won't send you out to do *my* shopping then. Hurr hurr!"

"Oh . . . very funny. Ha-ha!"

"Glad you liked it. Thought you might. Good night, Princess." Sir Hereward briefly bowed his head and stood to attention, pleased to be back on duty.

"Good night, Sir Hereward." Jenna pushed open the doors and slipped into her room.

It had taken some time for Jenna to get used to her huge Palace bedroom, having slept in a cupboard for ten years, but now she loved it, especially in the evenings. It was a large, long room with four tall windows that overlooked the Palace gardens, and caught the evening sun. But now, in the cold autumn night, Jenna drew the heavy red velvet curtains across the windows, and the room was suddenly filled with deep shadows. She went over to the great stone fireplace beside her four-poster bed and lit the pile of logs in the grate, using the FireLighter Spell that Septimus had given her for her last birthday. As the warm light from the dancing flames filled her room, Jenna sat on her bed, wrapped her feather quilt around her and picked up her favorite history book, *Our Castle Story*.

Engrossed in her book, Jenna did not notice a tall, thin ghostly figure emerge from behind the thick curtains that hung around her bed. The figure stood very still, staring at Jenna with a disapproving expression in her bright beady eyes. Jenna shivered in the sudden chill cast by the ghost and pulled her quilt closer, but she did not look up.

"I wouldn't bother reading all that rubbish about the Hanseatic League," a high-pitched voice drilled into the air behind Jenna's left shoulder. Jenna leaped up like a scalded cat, dropped her book and was about to yell for Sir Hereward when an ice-cold hand was placed across her mouth. The ghost's touch sent freezing air down into her lungs and Jenna subsided into a fit of coughing. The ghost seemed unperturbed. She picked up Jenna's book and placed it on the bed next to where

Jenna sat, trying to catch her breath.

"Turn to Chapter Thirteen, Granddaughter," the ghost instructed. "There is no need to waste your time reading about common traders. The only history worth bothering about is the history of Kings and Queens—preferably the history of Queens. You will find me there on page two hundred and twenty. Generally a good account of my reign although there are one or two, er, misunderstandings, but it was written by a commoner, so what can one expect?"

Jenna finally stopped coughing enough to take a good look at her uninvited visitor. She was indeed the ghost of a Queen, and an ancient one too, which Jenna could tell by the old-fashioned look of her tunic and the starched ruff that she wore around her neck. The ghost, who looked surprisingly substantial for one so ancient, stood straight and erect. Her iron-gray hair was scraped back into two coiled plaits that were fastened behind her rather pointed ears, and she wore a simple, severe gold crown. Her dark violet eyes fixed Jenna with a disapproving stare that immediately made Jenna feel she had done something wrong.

"Wh-who are you?" stammered Jenna.

The Queen tapped her foot impatiently. "Chapter *Thirteen*,

Granddaughter. Look in Chapter Thirteen. I have told you before. You *must* learn to listen. All Queens must learn to listen."

Jenna could not imagine this Queen listening to anyone, but she said nothing. What bothered her was why the ghost had called her *granddaughter*. It was the second time she had used that word. Surely this horrible ghost could not possibly be her grandmother? "But . . . why do you keep calling me Granddaughter?" asked Jenna, hoping that she might have misheard.

"Because I am your great-great-great-great-great-great-great-great-great-great-great-great-great-great-great-great-great-great-Grandmother. But you may call me Grandmama."

"Grandmama!" said Jenna, aghast.

"Indeed. That will be entirely suitable. I do not expect my full title."

"What *is* your full title?" asked Jenna.

The ghost of the Queen sighed impatiently and Jenna felt her icy breath ruffle her hair. "Chapter Thirteen. I shall not tell you again," she said severely. "I can see I have not come a moment too soon. You are in grave need of guidance. Your own mother has much to account for in her neglect of your royal teaching and good manners."

"Mum is a really good teacher," Jenna objected indignantly.

"She hasn't neglected *anything*."

"Mum . . . Mum? Who is this . . . *Mum*?" The Queen managed to look both disapproving and puzzled at the same time. In fact, over the centuries she had perfected the fine art of mixing every possible expression with disapproval, until, even if she had wanted to, she would no longer have been able to untangle them. But the Queen did not want to. She was quite happy with disapproval, thank you very much.

"Mum is my mum. I mean, my mother," said Jenna edgily.

"And what is her *name*, pray?" asked the ghost, peering down at Jenna.

"It's none of your business," Jenna replied crossly.

"Would it be Sarah Heap?"

Jenna refused to reply. She stared angrily at the ghost, willing her to go away.

"No, I shall not *go away*, Granddaughter. I have my duty to consider. We both know that this Sarah Heap person is not your real mother."

"She is to me," muttered Jenna.

"What things are to *you*, Granddaughter, is of no consequence. The truth is that your real mother, or the ghost of her, sits in her turret and neglects your royal education, so that you do appear to be more a lowly serving girl than a true

Princess. It is a disgrace, an absolute disgrace, which I intend to rectify for the benefit of this poor benighted place that my Castle—and my Palace—has become."

"It is not your Castle or your Palace," Jenna objected.

"That, Granddaughter, is where you are mistaken. It was mine before and soon it will be mine again."

"But—"

"Do not interrupt. I shall leave you now. It is well past your bedtime."

"No, it's not," said Jenna indignantly.

"In my day *all* Princesses retired to bed at six o'clock until they became Queen. I myself went to bed at six o'clock every night until I was thirty-five and it never did *me* any harm."

Jenna looked at the ghost in amazement. Then, suddenly, she smiled at the thought of how relieved everyone else in the Palace must have been, all those years ago, when six o'clock came around.

The Queen misinterpreted Jenna's smile. "Aha, you are seeing sense at last, Granddaughter. I will leave you now to go to sleep for I have important business to attend to. I will see you in the morrow. You may kiss me good night."

Jenna looked so horrified that the Queen took a step back

and said, "Well, then, I can see you are not yet used to your dear Grandmama. Good night, Granddaughter."

Jenna did not reply.

"I said, *Good night, Granddaughter*. I shall not leave until you bid me Good night."

There was a strained silence until Jenna decided that she could stand looking at the ghost's pointy nose no longer. "Good night," she said coldly.

"Good night, *Grandmama*," corrected the ghost.

"I will *never* call you Grandmama," said Jenna as, to her great relief, the ghost began to fade away.

"You will," came the ghost's high-pitched drill of a voice out of thin air. "You will. . . ."

Jenna picked up a pillow and, furious, threw it at the voice. There was no response; the ghost had gone. Taking Aunt Zelda's advice, Jenna counted to ten very slowly until she felt calm, then she picked up *Our Castle Story* and quickly turned the thick yellow pages to Chapter Thirteen. The title of the chapter was "Queen Etheldredda the Awful."

✛4✛
THE HOLE IN THE WALL

While *Jenna sat reading* Chapter Thirteen, Septimus Heap, Apprentice to the ExtraOrdinary Wizard, had just been caught reading something he was not meant to have read. Marcia Overstrand, ExtraOrdinary Wizard of the Castle, had been temporarily defeated by a squabble in her kitchen between the coffeepot and the stove. In exasperation she had decided to leave them to it and go

check on her Apprentice. She had found him in the Pyramid
Library immersed in a pile of tattered old texts.

"What exactly do you think you are doing?" Marcia
demanded.

Septimus jumped guiltily to his feet and shoved the papers
under the book he should have been reading. "Nothing," he
said.

"That," said Marcia sternly, "was exactly what I thought
you were doing." She surveyed her Apprentice, trying—but
not entirely succeeding—to keep her stern expression.
Septimus had a startled look in his brilliant green eyes and his
curly, straw-colored hair was tangled from the way Marcia
knew he twisted it when he was concentrating. "In case it has
escaped your memory," she told him, "you are meant to be
reviewing for your Prediction Practical Examination tomorrow morning. Not reading a load of five-hundred-year-old
drivel."

"It's not drivel," objected Septimus. "It's—"

"I know perfectly well what it is," Marcia said. "I have told
you before. Alchemie is total twaddle and a complete waste of
time. You may as well go boil your socks and expect *them* to
turn into gold."

"But I'm not reading about Alchemie," protested Septimus. "It's Physik."

"Same difference," said Marcia. "It's Marcellus Pye, I presume?"

"Yes. He's really good."

"He's really *irrelevant*, Septimus." Marcia reached under the book Septimus had hastily placed on top—*The Principles and Practice of Elementary Prediction*—and drew out the sheaf of yellowed and fragile papers covered in faint jottings. "Anyway," she said, "these are only his notes."

"I know. It's a pity his book has disappeared."

"Hmm. It's time you went to bed. You've got an early start tomorrow. Seven minutes past seven and not a second later. Understand?"

Septimus nodded.

"Well, off you go then."

"But, Marcia . . ."

"What?"

"I'm really interested in Physik. And Marcellus did it the best. He had all sorts of medicines and cures worked out, and he knew all about why we get sick. Do you think I could learn about it?"

"No," said Marcia. "You don't need it, Septimus. **Magyk** can do everything that **Physik** can."

"It can't cure the Sickenesse though," said Septimus stubbornly.

Marcia pursed her lips. Septimus was not the first to have pointed this out. "It will," she insisted, "it will. I just have to work on it—what was *that*?" A loud crash came from the kitchen two floors below and Marcia shot off.

Septimus sighed. He put Marcellus's papers back in the old box he had found in a dusty corner, blew out the candle and went downstairs to bed.

Septimus did not sleep well. Every night for a week he had had the same bad dream about the exam, and this night was no exception. He dreamed that he had missed the exam, Marcia chased him, and he fell down a chimney that went on forever and ever. . . . He kept grabbing at the walls to stop himself but still he kept falling . . . falling . . . falling.

"Been having a fight with your blankets, Septimus?" A familiar voice echoed down the chimney. "Looks like you lost," the voice continued with a chuckle. "Not wise to take on a pair of blankets, lad. One, maybe, but two blankets always gang up on you. Vicious things, blankets."

Septimus forced himself out of his dream and sat up, gasping from the cold autumn air that Alther Mella had let in
through the window.

"You all right?" Alther asked, concerned. The ghost settled
himself down comfortably on Septimus's bed.

"Wh . . . errr?" Septimus mumbled, focusing with some
difficulty on the slightly transparent figure of Alther Mella, ex-
ExtraOrdinary Wizard and frequent visitor to the Wizard
Tower. Alther was not as difficult to see as some of the older
ghosts in the Castle, but at nighttime his faded purple robes
had a tendency to blend into the background, and the dimness
of the light made it harder to see the dark brown bloodstains
over the ghost's heart, which Septimus always found his eye
was drawn to, however hard he tried not to look. Alther had
a calm and kind expression in his old green eyes as he
regarded his favorite Apprentice.

"Same bad dream?" Alther inquired.

"Um. Yes," Septimus admitted.

"Did you remember to use your **Flyte Charm** this time?"
asked Alther.

"Er, no. Perhaps I will next time. Except I hope there isn't a next time. It's a horrible dream." Septimus shuddered and pulled one of the obstinate blankets up to his chin.

"Hmm. Well, dreams come to us for a reason. Sometimes they tell us things we need to know," mused Alther, floating up from the pillow and straightening himself out with a ghostly groan. "Now, I thought you might like a little trip down to a place I know not far from here."

Septimus yawned. "But what about Marcia?" he asked sleepily.

"Marcia's got one of her headaches," said Alther. "I don't know why she gets so upset over that contrary coffeepot. I'd get rid of it if I were her. She's gone to bed so there's no need to bother her. Anyway, we'll be back before she knows we're gone."

Septimus did not want to go back to sleep and get into the dream yet again. He tumbled out of bed and pulled on his green woolen Apprentice tunic, which was neatly folded on the end of his bed, just as he had been taught to do with his Young Army uniform every night for the first ten years of his life, and fastened his silver Apprentice belt.

"Ready?" asked Alther.

"Ready," replied Septimus. He headed for the window that

Alther had **Caused** to open when he had arrived. Septimus climbed onto the broad wooden windowsill and stood in the open window, looking down at the precipitous drop some twenty-one floors down, something that he never would have dreamed of doing a few months ago, given his fear of heights. But now Septimus had lost his fear, and the reason for this was held tightly in his left hand—the **Flyte Charm**.

Septimus carefully took the small golden arrow with its delicate silver flights and held it between his right finger and thumb. "Where are we going?" he asked Alther, who was hovering in front of him and absentmindedly trying to perfect a backward flip.

"Hole in the Wall," Alther replied, upside down. "Nice place. Must have told you about it."

"But that's a tavern," objected Septimus. "I'm too young to go into taverns. And Marcia says they're dens of—"

"Oh, you mustn't take any notice of what Marcia says about taverns," Alther told him. "Marcia has some strange theory that people go to taverns just to talk about her behind her back. I've told her that people have much more interesting things than her to discuss—like the price of fish—but she won't believe it."

Alther spun around and righted himself so that he was floating in front of Septimus. The ghost looked at the slight figure standing on the windowsill, his curly hair blowing in the wind that always played around the top of the Wizard Tower and his green eyes flashing with **Magyk**, as the **Flyte Charm** grew warm in his grasp. Although Alther had been helping Septimus practice the **Art of Flyte** for three months now—ever since Septimus had found the **Flyte Charm**—he still felt a flash of fear when he saw the boy standing on the edge of a sheer drop.

"I'll follow you," said Septimus, his voice almost blown away by a sudden gust of wind.

"What?"

"I'll follow you, Alther. Okay?"

"Fine. I'll watch you take off first though. Just to make sure you're nice and steady."

Septimus did not object. He liked Alther being with him, and once or twice during the early days of **Flyte**, he had been very glad of the ghost's advice, particularly one nasty time when he had nearly crashed into the roof of the Manuscriptorium. Septimus had, in fact, been showing off to his friend Beetle, but Alther had merely **Caused** a sudden uplift of air and set Septimus safely down in the backyard and had not mentioned the showing-off at all.

The Flyte Charm was beginning to feel hot in Septimus's grasp. It was time to go. Taking a deep breath, Septimus hurled himself into the night. For a brief moment he felt the leaden pull of gravity dragging him toward the earth, and then the thing that he loved happened: The downward drag disappeared and he was set free, free like a bird to fly and soar, to loop and swirl through the night air, supported and held safe by the Flyte Charm. At the moment the Flyte Charm kicked in, Alther relaxed and set off in front of Septimus, arms held out like the wings of a gliding eagle, while Septimus followed more erratically, trying out his new slalom skids.

They arrived at the Hole in the Wall Tavern with a bump— or rather, Septimus did. Alther shot straight through the wall, leaving Septimus to use a slalom skid for real and land with a crash in the bushes that grew across the tumbledown entrance to the tavern.

Alther came a few minutes later to find Septimus picking himself up out of the bushes. "Sorry, Septimus," Alther apologized. "Just saw old Olaf Snorrelssen. Nice chap. Northern

Trader, never got home to see his baby, you know. Sad, really. Goes on about it a bit but he's a good soul. I keep telling him he ought to get out and about the Castle, but there're not many places he can go apart from the Traders' Market and the Grateful Turbot. So he just sits here staring into his beer."

Septimus brushed a few leaves off his tunic, put the **Flyte Charm** back into his Apprentice belt and surveyed the entrance to the Hole in the Wall Tavern. It didn't look much like a tavern to him. It looked pretty much like a pile of stones dumped at the base of the Castle wall. There was no sign outside the door. In fact, there was no door, neither were there the usual steamy, lit windows that Septimus was used to seeing in taverns because, well, there were no windows either. As Septimus wondered whether Alther was playing some kind of complicated joke on him, a ghostly nun wafted by.

"Good evening, Alther," said the nun in her soft accent.

"Good evening, Sister Bernadette," Alther replied with a smile. The nun gave him a flirtatious wave and disappeared through the pile of stones. She was followed by a virtually see-through knight with his arm in a sling, who carefully tied up his limping horse to an invisible post and shuffled through the bush from which Septimus had just extricated himself.

"Looks like, being a busy night tonight, we've got quite a few visitors," mused Alther, nodding in a friendly fashion to the knight.

"But—they're *ghosts*," said Septimus.

"Well, of course they're ghosts," said Alther. "That's the whole point of the tavern. Any ghost is welcome; all others are by invitation only. And it's not easy to get an invitation, I can tell you. At least two ghosts have to invite you. Of course, we've had the odd gate-crasher over the years but it's still a pretty well-kept secret."

Three faded Ancient ExtraOrdinary Wizards had now arrived and were stuck at the entrance trying to decide who should go in first. Septimus nodded politely to them and asked Alther, "So who else has invited me?"

Alther, distracted by the sight of the three Wizards deciding to go in all at once to the accompaniment of much giggling, did not answer the question. "Come on, lad, follow me," he said, and disappeared through the wall. Some moments later, Alther reappeared and said, a little impatiently, "Come on, Septimus, best not keep Queen Etheldredda waiting."

"But I—"

"Just squeeze behind the bush and slip behind the pile of stones. You'll find the way in."

Septimus pushed through the bush, and feeling his way with the help of the light from the glowing Dragon Ring that he wore on his right index finger, he found a narrow passage-way behind the stones that took him deep into a broad, low space hidden within the Castle walls—the Hole in the Wall Tavern.

Septimus was astonished; he had never seen so many ghosts together in one place. Septimus was used to seeing ghosts around the Castle, as he had always been the sensitive kind of boy that ghosts liked to **Appear** to, and since he had been wearing the green robes of an Apprentice to the ExtraOrdinary Wizard, Septimus had noticed that even more ghosts chose to **Appear** to him. But there was something about the relaxed atmosphere in the Hole in the Wall Tavern—and the fact that he was with Alther, one of the most popular regulars —that meant most of the ghosts allowed Septimus to see them. It was an amazing sight: there were the usual ExtraOrdinary Wizard ghosts, all in purple but with many different styles of robe reflecting the fashions over the years; Septimus was used to seeing these around the Palace and the Wizard Tower. There were a surprising number of Queens and Princesses too. But there were other ghosts that Septimus was unused to seeing: knights and their pages, farmers and farmers' wives, sailors and

traders, scribes and scholars, tramps and tinkers and all manner of Castle inhabitants from the last few thousand years, all
holding on to their Hole in the Wall tankards, which they had
been given on their first visit and had never needed to refill.

A quiet hum of ghostly chatter pervaded the atmosphere as
conversations started many years ago continued their leisurely
way, but over in a far corner a regal figure heard the hesitant
footsteps of a living boy cut through the noise. She got up
from her seat beside the fire and glided through the throng, a
respectful sea of ghosts parting before her.

"Septimus Heap," said Queen Etheldredda. "Five and a half
minutes late, but no matter. I have been waiting five hundred
years. Follow me."

✛ 5 ✛
QUEEN ETHELDREDDA

Septimus soon found himself squashed between the two ghosts at a long table at the far end of the tavern. This was not what he had expected when he had gone to bed that evening, but after eighteen months as Apprentice to Marcia, Septimus had learned not to expect anything—except the unexpected.

Although Septimus knew he was not really squashed at all, he still *felt* squashed as he sat between Alther and Queen Etheldredda and tried not to touch either of them—but he could not shake the feeling that Queen Etheldredda's pointy elbows really *were* sticking into him. Septimus wriggled farther away from Etheldredda, for it was the height of rudeness to **Pass Through** a ghost and he suspected that the Queen would have something to say about it.

In fact, so far Queen Etheldredda had had something to say about pretty much everything. She sat tall and erect, and her dark violet eyes fixed Septimus with a stern gaze as she gave him the benefit of her opinion: "It's full of riffraff here, Apprentice, absolutely full. Look at that awful old tramp snoring under the table. Terrible place, terrible place. I shall most certainly have to do something about *this*. And the behavior of those young Queens over there—*most* unbecoming." A loud squeal of giggles had erupted from a table of four young Queens (all of whom had died in childbirth). Queen Etheldredda pursed her lips disapprovingly. "I don't know what Alther Mella is thinking of bringing you here. In my day the ExtraOrdinary Apprentice was not allowed out without a chaperone Wizard, and then it was only to come to the Palace on official business. And a boy your age should be in bed, not carousing in a den of iniquity like this."

Septimus was not bothered by Queen Etheldredda for she

reminded him a little of Marcia, but Alther looked irritated. "Your Majesty," Alther said huffily, "perhaps you might remember that it was on your express wish—*command* was the word you used—that I woke up this young Apprentice and brought him here. You had, you said, something of great importance to relate to him—a matter of life or death— although you refused to tell me what it might be. You yourself insisted on him coming to this tavern. I assure you, Madam Marcia Overstrand does not normally allow her Apprentice to frequent taverns at night or, indeed, at any time of the day."

Septimus held his breath. What was the Queen going to say?

Queen Etheldredda said nothing for some time. And then she leaned over to Septimus, and he felt an ice-cold breath across his cheek as she whispered in his ear, "Marcellus Pye, at Snake Slipway, midnight. Be there." With that, the Queen got up from the tavern bench as if rising from her throne. She swished her train into place behind her, walked, head held disdainfully high, into the fireplace and disappeared.

"Well," spluttered Alther. "Of all the nerve . . ."

"Marcellus Pye?" Septimus muttered, feeling a thrill of excitement.

Two nuns had sat down beside him in Queen Etheldredda's place. One of the nuns looked askance at Septimus. "Do not speak that name lightly, child," she whispered.

Septimus said no more, but his thoughts were buzzing. Why would the ghost of Marcellus Pye want to meet *him*— just a lowly Apprentice? After all, the ghost had never been seen before. Maybe . . . Septimus shivered at the thought . . . maybe the ghost had been **Watching** him read the notes that afternoon and had now decided to **Appear** to him. But why choose Snake Slipway? And why at *midnight*?

Alther noticed Septimus's preoccupied expression. "What did she say?" he whispered.

Septimus shook his head, not wanting to upset the nuns again.

Suddenly Alther felt weary. "Come on then, Septimus, let's go." He sighed. He got up and Septimus followed him, carefully squeezing past the nuns. Alther felt unsettled at the sudden appearance of Queen Etheldredda. She had not been seen around the Palace before, and while it was not unusual for ghosts to appear and disappear, especially the older ones who often fell asleep in a comfortable chair and did not wake for

many years, he had never known one to turn up so many centuries after her entry into ghosthood. It was very odd, and
there was, thought Alther, something particularly odd about
Etheldredda. He wished now that he had not brought
Septimus to see her.

Carefully Septimus followed Alther and made his way
toward the exit, which was indeed a hole in the wall, through
which he could now see moonlight shining. There was a lull
in the ghostly chatter as the living Apprentice to the
ExtraOrdinary Wizard slipped through the assorted throng.
Some stepped back to allow Septimus to pass and continued
their conversations; others stopped their chatter in mid-sentence and followed his progress with faded, ghostly eyes. Some
expressions were wistful, remembering what it had been like
to be a living, breathing eleven-year-old; others were vague,
lost in their ghosthood and seeing living beings as strange
creatures, unrelated to them. But not one of the ghosts was
Passed Through by Septimus as he negotiated his way
around them. At last he pushed his way through the bush and
reached the outside of the tavern with a feeling of relief.

"So what did she say?" Alther asked again. He and
Septimus were taking a shortcut through Drapers Yard, a

small courtyard around which was a cluster of old houses inhabited by families who worked with cloth. A few candles shone from the windows, which sported a strange variety of curtains and cloth remnants, but the doors were locked and barred, and the yard was so quiet that Septimus could hear the ticking of the Great Draper Clock in the clock tower above the central house.

"She said I should meet Marcellus Pye on Snake Slipway. Tonight," Septimus told him as the Draper Clock began to strike ten and its tinny bell echoed around the yard. *Pling, pling, pling . . .*

"You will of course be doing no such thing," declared Alther once the clock had stopped and the succession of comical tin figures had done their party pieces and filed back inside. "She's bonkers, Septimus, totally and utterly bonkers. Anyway, I've never even *seen* the ghost of Marcellus Pye. The trouble is, every now and then a ghost gets delusions of grandeur. Often happens to Royal ghosts. They think they can influence the living. Make things happen, just as they were used to doing when they were alive. Of course all they do is make a nuisance of themselves. Can be almost impossible to get rid of, that's the trouble. The best thing is to ignore them and hope they'll go away. Which is exactly what you must do, lad. I suppose you know who this Pye fellow was?"

"Yes," said Septimus.

Alther nodded approvingly. "Thought you would. It's good to read about the subject. Best not to let on to Marcia though. She has a thing about Alchemie."

"I know," Septimus sighed.

"He wasn't just an alchemist, Marcellus; he was a good physician, too," said Alther. "Pity we've lost some of the things he knew back then. We could use them now."

They were now walking briskly along Brindle Byway, which would lead them to Wizard Way. Brindle Byway was a narrow street with tall drying lofts for yarn and fabric on either side. The drying lofts were dark and quiet at this time of night and a chokingly unpleasant smell of dye hung in the still air. Septimus was too preoccupied with holding his nose and breathing through his mouth to hear, some way ahead, the scrabble of claws and the click of a needle-sharp tooth as it flicked down, ready to bite.

Neither Septimus nor Alther noticed two round red eyes emerging from a drain, blinking and shrinking from the light from the silver torch post outside Number Thirteen Wizard

Way. But they did hear something altogether louder and more insistent: hurried footsteps echoing off the walls of the byway, coming toward them.

Alther glanced at Septimus and gestured to a small opening between two drying lofts. In a moment both he and Septimus were hidden in the shadows, listening to the approaching footsteps.

"Probably some pickpocket up to no good," whispered Alther. "He'd better not try anything, I'm not in a good mood this evening."

Septimus did not reply. The footsteps had slowed down now; they sounded almost hesitant as they approached the gap where Alther and Septimus were hidden. Then the footsteps stopped.

Suddenly, to Alther's horror, Septimus jumped out.

Sarah Heap gave a piercing scream and dropped her basket with a crash. Bottles and jars tumbled out and rolled in all directions.

"Mum!' said Septimus. "Mum, it's only Alther and me."

Sarah Heap stared at them in disbelief. "What on earth are you doing here? Really, Septimus, you nearly gave me a heart attack. And what does Alther think he's doing bringing you down these ghastly alleyways at this time of night?"

"It's all right, Mum. We're on our way back now. We only went to the Hole in the Wall Tavern," Septimus explained, chasing after the dropped bottles and jars and putting them back into Sarah's basket.

"A *tavern?*" Sarah Heap looked horrified. "Alther took you to a tavern—at night? Alther"—this was addressed to the ghost who had just floated out of the alleyway, looking resigned to the evening rapidly going from bad to worse— "Alther, what *do* you think you are doing? And with all this Sickenesse about?"

Alther sighed. "I'll explain tomorrow, Sarah. Although I could ask the same of you. What exactly are *you* doing scurrying down a back alley with all your potions?"

Sarah did not answer. She was too busy checking whether any of her potion bottles had broken. "Thank you, Septimus," she said as he handed her the last bottle.

"But where are you going, Mum?" asked Septimus.

"Going?" Sarah Heap looked as if she had come down to earth with a bump. "Oh, heavens, I'll be late. I don't want to keep Nicko waiting—"

"Nicko?" asked Septimus, confused.

"Sarah," said Alther, "what is going on?"

"I've been called to the Infirmary, Alther. I must have had the last Message Rat in the Castle. They've had so many people brought in this evening they can't cope. Nicko's going to row me over. Now I *must* get going."

"Not on your own," said Alther. "We'll come with you."

Sarah looked as though she was about to protest but then she changed her mind. "Thank you, Alther," she said. "I—oh my goodness!" Sarah stifled a scream. "Look . . ." she whispered, pointing into the darkness.

Septimus looked. At first he saw nothing and then, as he shifted his gaze, he saw them—the red eyes, moving toward them, dodging from side to side. At first glance Septimus thought it was a rat, but there was something about the way the eyes were set, both looking forward, that looked wrong for a rat's eyes. Quickly Septimus reached into his pocket, took out a pebble and sent it spinning through the darkness toward the red pinpoints. A high-pitched yelp was followed by the sound of scuffling leaves, and the eyes disappeared into the night.

"Come on, Sarah," said Alther, "let's get you down to the boatyard."

✳   ✳   ✳

Nicko was waiting anxiously beside a rowboat tied up to the quay in Jannit Maarten's boatyard. Jannit had recently taken Nicko on as Junior Apprentice, and he now slept in a small cabin at the back of Jannit's ramshackle hut. An hour ago, Nicko had tumbled into bed, tired out after a long day helping Rupert Gringe repair the huge rudder belonging to the Port barge. He had only just fallen asleep when an insistent knocking on his window had jarred him awake—it was the Message Rat that Sarah had forwarded to him.

Quickly Nicko had found the rowboat that Jannit sometimes used to ferry people over the river; unfortunately he had woken Jannit, who even in her sleep could hear any unusual sound in the boatyard. Jannit had only just grumpily gone back to bed when she was woken again by the clinking of Sarah's bottles in her basket as she hurried through the boatyard.

Septimus helped Nicko steady the rowboat while Sarah clambered in. "You'll make sure Mum gets to the Infirmary okay, won't you, Nik?" he asked, looking doubtfully across the Moat, which was wide and deep by the boatyard, to the dim lights of the Infirmary, almost hidden under the outlying trees of the Forest some distance away. It was a dangerous walk from the ferry landing stage to the Infirmary at night.

"Of course I will." Nicko took up two long oars and waited for Sarah to get settled.

"Don't worry, *I'll* see Sarah to the Infirmary door," Alther said to Septimus. "I can still get rid of the odd wolverine if I have to. I'll have to whiz around by the North Gate, but I'll be there waiting for her."

"See ya later, Sep," said Nicko as he pulled away from the boatyard landing stage.

"No, you won't, Nicko," Septimus heard Sarah chide. "Septimus is going straight back to Marcia's."

As Septimus watched Alther fly toward the North Gate, a wonderful sense of freedom and exhilaration suddenly swept over him. He could go anywhere, do anything. There was no one to stop him. Of course he *should* go back to the Wizard Tower, but he was not sleepy. Septimus felt restless, as if somehow the night was unfinished. And then he realized why. Queen Etheldredda's words came back to him: "Marcellus Pye, at Snake Slipway, midnight. Be there."

Suddenly, Septimus knew why Queen Etheldredda had asked him to meet the ghost of Marcellus Pye: to give him the formula for the antidote to the Sickenesse.

It was only about half past ten. He still had time to get to Snake Slipway before midnight.

⊹6⊹

THE OUTSIDE PATH

Septimus decided to take the Outside Path along the Castle walls, just in case Marcia had been suddenly called out on **Magykal** business, headache and all—it would be just his luck to bump into her. With mounting excitement, he picked his way through the boatyard, careful not to make any noise that might disturb Jannit. Soon he reached the upside-down hull of an old river barge, and squeezing behind the barge, he found what he was looking for—the steep steps that led up to the Outside Path.

The Outside Path was a narrow and crumbling ledge just a few feet above the dark water of the Moat. It had not been built as a path, but was the point at which the huge foundations of the Castle walls finished and the slightly narrower walls, which were built from smaller, more finely cut rock, began. When Septimus had been in the Young Army, many of the older boys had run along the Outside Path for a dare, but it was not something that Septimus had ever wanted to do—until now. Now, with the confidence of a year and a half as the ExtraOrdinary Apprentice and the knowledge that if he slipped and fell he could always use his **Flyte Charm**, Septimus climbed the steps up to the Path.

The Path was narrower than he had expected; Septimus walked slowly, placing one foot in front of the other and feeling for loose stones as he went. He was grateful for the light of the waning full moon, which reflected off the Moat and shone on the pale stone of the Castle walls, making it easy to find his way. The air was calm in the lee of the east wind, and although Septimus could see the tops of the trees swaying, it was still and quiet beside the water.

Far away on the other side of the Moat, frighteningly near the Forest, the lights of the Infirmary flickered as the branches of outlying Forest trees moved in front of the long line of tiny, candlelit windows. Septimus stopped and watched the steady progress of Sarah Heap's lantern across the Moat as Nicko rowed toward the Forest bank. The lantern seemed such a small pinpoint of light against the great expanse of dark trees. He hoped that Alther would be waiting for her when they reached the Forest side.

Some minutes later, the lantern reached the far bank and Septimus saw Alther's shape illuminated in the glow. Relieved, he set off once more. Soon the curve of the Castle wall took him out of sight of the Infirmary, and a long empty stretch of the Outside Path lay before him. Septimus was a little surprised that he could see no sign of Snake Slipway. He had not realized how much the Castle walls curved. He was used to taking the direct route to the Slipway, but he pressed on, the thought of being able to talk to Marcellus Pye keeping him going.

As Septimus continued—more slowly than he would have liked, for the Path was very uneven—he could feel the chill coming off the Moat and smell the dankness of the water as it flowed by sluggishly. A layer of mist was beginning to form just above the Moat, and as Septimus watched, it grew thicker until he could no longer see the surface of the water. A soft silence came with the mist, which was broken only by the occasional moan of the wind in the tops of the trees on the outskirts of the Forest.

His enthusiasm for seeing Marcellus Pye began to wane, but Septimus kept going. He had no choice, for the Outside Path had now become so narrow that it would have been treacherous to turn around. After slipping twice on some loose stones and very nearly tumbling into the Moat below, Septimus decided that he was being foolish trying to walk along the Outside Path. He stopped, leaned back against the walls to try to keep his balance and fumbled in his Apprentice belt for his **Flyte Charm**. His hand got stuck in the small pocket in which he kept the **Charm**, and as he tried to pull it out, Septimus felt himself falling forward. In a panic, he grabbed at the stones behind him and only just managed to pull himself back up.

By now Septimus knew that taking the Outside Path was a stupid mistake, but he made himself concentrate on the way ahead and tried to pay no heed to the thoughts that clamored for his attention. These were:

His warm and comfortable bed, which was waiting for him at the top of the Wizard Tower.

The moaning of the wind in the tops of the trees.

Why did the moaning sound so weird?

His bed.

Did wolverines come down to the Castle walls at night?

Could wolverines swim?

They *could*, couldn't they?

His bed.

Why did the mist seem so spooky?

What was under the mist?

Do wolverines especially like swimming underneath mist?

His bed.

Hang on . . . didn't Marcellus Pye's writings say he had found the secret of eternal life?

Suppose Marcellus wasn't just a normal old ghost?

Suppose he was a five-hundred-year-old man?

Wouldn't he just be a skeleton with bits of skin hanging off?

Why hadn't he thought of this before?

It was then that a large storm cloud covered the moon and Septimus was plunged into darkness. He stopped dead, his heartbeat pounding in his head, and pressed himself against the wall. As his eyes got used to the dark he found he could still see the tops of the Forest trees, but he could not, for some reason, see his feet, however hard he stared. And then he realized why. The mist had risen and was covering his boots; he could smell its dampness. The Dragon Ring on the index finger of his right hand was shining with its comforting soft yellow light, but he took the ring off and put it in his pocket, for suddenly the glow of the Dragon Ring felt like a large label saying, "Come and get me."

It was probably only about half an hour later—although by now Septimus was sure it was at least three nights strung together by a **Reverse Enchantment**—when he heard footsteps behind him. Heart in his mouth, Septimus stopped, but he did not dare turn around for fear of falling into the Moat. The footsteps continued toward him and Septimus set off again, stumbling along the Path, peering into the night, desperate for the sight of Snake Slipway, but storm clouds kept piling in and the moon stayed hidden.

The footsteps were light and sounded agile, and Septimus knew they were gaining on him, for every two steps he managed to take, the **Thing**—and he was sure it was a **Thing**—

took three. Desperately, Septimus tried to pick up speed, but still the footsteps kept coming.

Suddenly Septimus heard a noise behind him. "Ssss . . . sssss. . ." The **Thing** was hissing at him. *Hissing.* It must be a **SnakeHead Spectre** . . . or even a Magog. Magogs sometimes hissed, didn't they? Maybe one of DomDaniel's Magogs had got left behind, maybe it lived in the Castle walls and then it came out at night when some idiot decided to go for a stupid walk along the Outside Path.

"Sssss!" A loud hiss sounded in his ear. Septimus jumped in fright. His right foot slipped from the narrow, crumbling Path and he slid off, hands clutching frantically at the stones as he went. His right boot was already in the Moat and Septimus was about to follow it when *something* grabbed his cloak.

┼┼7┼┼
SNAKE SLIPWAY

"Look, *just keep still*, will *you?*" said an exasperated voice. "You'll have us both in the Moat if you're not careful."

"Wh-what?" gasped Septimus, wondering why the **Thing** was pretending to be a girl. **Things** usually had very low, threatening voices that made your blood feel cold, not girls' voices. This one must have got it wrong somehow. Maybe it was a young **Thing**, thought Septimus, with

a glimmer of hope. A young **Thing** might be persuaded to let him go. Septimus decided he had to face whatever it was that had hold of him so tightly. He struggled to turn around, and as he did, he was hauled back up onto the Outside Path.

"Stupid boy. Lucky I didn't drop you. Would have served you right," said Lucy Gringe, breathless from heaving Septimus up.

Septimus suddenly felt weak and trembly with relief. "Lucy!" he said. "What are you doing here?"

"I could ask you the same thing, Apprentice boy," said Lucy.

"Um, well, I just felt like going for a walk," Septimus replied lamely.

"Weird walk," muttered Lucy. "Could think of better places to go. Well, get a move on, get on with your walk—or are you stopping here for the night? I hope not because you're blocking my way and I've got things to do."

With no alternative, Septimus carried on with his slow shuffle along the Outside Path. Lucy's impatient breath sounded behind him. "Can't you speed up a bit? We'll take all night at this rate."

"I'm going as fast as I can. Anyway, what are you in such a hurry for? And where are you going? Aargh!" Septimus's foot slipped but Lucy grabbed him and set him going again like a clockwork toy.

"None of your business. None of anyone's business," Lucy replied. "The Path gets wider now, so you can go a bit faster, can't you?"

To Septimus's relief, his boots found a firmer hold as the Outside Path did indeed widen. "You've done this before, haven't you?" he asked.

"Might have," said Lucy. "Can't you go any faster?"

"No, I can't. So why are you on the Outside Path . . . it's because you don't want Gringe—I mean, your father—to know where you're going, isn't it?" asked Septimus, a suspicion forming.

"It's none of his business what I do or where I go," said Lucy huffily. "Oh, just *hurry up*, will you?"

"Why?" asked Septimus, deliberately slowing down. "*Why* don't you want Gringe to know where you're going?"

"Gosh, you're irritating. I can see why Simon says you're an awful little—" Lucy halted in mid-sentence, but too late.

Septimus stopped dead and Lucy walked into him with a bump. "You're going to see Simon, aren't you?" he said.

"What are you doing? Stupid boy. You nearly had us both in the Moat."

"You *are* going to see Simon, aren't you?" Septimus repeated. "That's why you've come this way. So that no one sees you go. You know where he is, don't you?"

"No," said Lucy sullenly. "Now get going, will you?"

"I'm not going anywhere until you tell me where Simon is," said Septimus, stubbornly holding his ground.

"Well, we'll be here all night then," said Lucy, equally stubbornly.

Lucy and Septimus stood with their backs to the huge Castle wall, which reared up into the night. Neither was willing to back down. The standoff had lasted for some minutes when they both heard a low scuffling sound some ways behind them. This was followed by the sound of a stone being dislodged and falling with a quiet plop into the water.

"Look, Septimus," Lucy said in a hoarse whisper, "it's not safe out here. **Things** use the Path—I've seen them. Let's just get to Snake Slipway. We can talk then, okay?"

Septimus needed little persuading. "Okay," he agreed.

Ten minutes later, Septimus and Lucy had negotiated a particularly treacherous part of the Path below the East Gate

Lookout Tower and were nearing Snake Slipway when Septimus stopped unexpectedly. Lucy crushed the backs of his
heels with her heavy boots. "Ouch!" Septimus said under his
breath.

"Oh, do stop dithering about," Lucy hissed, exasperated.

"But I thought I saw a light. On the Slipway," Septimus
whispered.

"Good," Lucy hissed back. "At least we'll be able to see
where we're going."

Septimus set off again, only to hear a quiet splash a few seconds later and see the light disappear. He nearly stopped again
but thought better of it. "Did you hear a splash?" he whispered.

"No. But there'll be an irritating-boy-size splash in a
minute if you don't stop twittering on, Septimus Heap." Lucy
gave Septimus a sharp poke in the back. "Now *hurry up.*"

Thinking how lucky he was not to have a sister like Lucy,
Septimus hurried on.

Soon Septimus and Lucy were clambering down the narrow
flight of stone steps that led to Snake Slipway. As they stepped
onto it, the muffled sound of the Courthouse clock striking

one o'clock reached them through the still night air. Septimus looked around, but it was as he expected—there was no sign of Marcellus Pye.

Septimus yawned, and suddenly he felt very tired. Lucy caught his yawn and shivered in the chill. She took a large key from one of her many pockets and drew her cloak around her. Septimus thought that he had seen the cloak somewhere before, but he could not remember where. It was, he thought, a surprisingly nice cloak for Lucy to have. The Gringes were not a well-off family and Lucy usually made her own clothes and stomped around in a stout pair of brown boots that looked a size too big for her—even her long brown plaits were always tied up with a scruffy assortment of homemade ribbons and bits of string. But her dark blue cloak hung gracefully from her shoulders and had an air of luxury about it.

Lucy was, however, still wearing her big brown boots. She clomped over to a wide door, which Septimus knew went into the boat shed where Lucy's brother, Rupert, kept the paddle-boats that he rented out in the summer. With a practiced air, Lucy turned the key in the lock, pushed the door open and disappeared. Septimus ran after her.

It was dark in the boat shed. Septimus put on his Dragon

Ring and soon the shed was filled with a dull yellow glow. He could see Lucy in the shadows, struggling to put a paddleboat onto a small trolley.

"Go away," hissed Lucy when she realized that Septimus had followed her in.

"You're going to see Simon, aren't you?" asked Septimus.

"Mind your own business," Lucy replied, trying to heave the surprisingly heavy paddleboat onto the trolley. Septimus took the other end of the boat and together they managed to lift it. "Thanks," puffed Lucy as Septimus took hold of the trolley handle and helped her pull the boat out of the boat shed.

Together they trundled the paddleboat, painted a garish pink, down the Slipway to the lapping waters of the Moat, unaware that a ghostly figure with a pointy nose and a disapproving expression was standing in the shadows watching their efforts. As Septimus pushed the trolley into the water and allowed the paddleboat to float free, Queen Etheldredda's ghostly foot tapped the ground soundlessly in exasperation.

Septimus gave Lucy the boat's rope to hold, then he pulled the trolley up the Slipway and trundled it back into the boathouse. As he passed by the ghost, she glared at him and hissed under her breath, "Punctuality is a virtue; lateness is a vice, boy," but Septimus heard nothing above the squeak of the trolley's wheels.

He returned to Lucy and there was an awkward silence as Septimus took the rope and steadied the boat for Lucy while she stepped into it. Lucy settled herself down and then, to his surprise, looked at Septimus with a wry smile. "You're not a bad kid really," she said grudgingly as she took up the handles that turned Rupert's bizarre paddles.

Septimus said nothing. There was an air about Lucy that reminded him of his great-aunt Zelda, and Septimus had learned that if he wanted Aunt Zelda to tell him something, he had to be patient, for Aunt Zelda was as stubborn as Lucy Gringe appeared to be. So Septimus waited patiently, sensing that something was on Lucy's mind.

"Simon and I nearly got married," Lucy suddenly blurted out.

"I know," said Septimus. "Dad told me."

"No one wanted us to get married," said Lucy. "I don't know why. It's just so unfair." Septimus could not think of anything to say. "And now everybody hates Simon and he can never come back home, and that's so unfair too."

"Well, he did kidnap Jenna," Septimus pointed out. "And then he tried to kill me and Nicko and Jenna, and he almost destroyed the Dragon Boat. Not to mention Marcia—he practically finished her off with that **Placement**, and then he—"

"All right, all right," snapped Lucy. "There's no need to be so *picky* about everything."

There was another awkward silence and Septimus decided that there was no point trying to get Lucy to tell him anything more. He let go of the boat and pushed it out into the Moat.

"If you do see Simon," he said, "you can tell him from me he's not welcome here."

Lucy stuck her tongue out at Septimus, then she took up the paddles and started turning them. It looked strange to Septimus, for these were summer boats used for fun, and to see Lucy out in one on a misty, dank autumn night seemed odd. "Safe journey," he told her, "wherever you're going."

Lucy looked back. "I don't know where Simon is," she said, "but he wrote me a note and I'm going to find him. *So there.*"

Septimus watched Lucy paddle off in her pink paddleboat until she rounded the bend and disappeared from view. He stood on the Slipway for a while, listening to the clunky sound of the paddles turning as Lucy made her determined way toward the river.

It was when he at last turned to go home that Septimus saw it—fire under the water.

✛ 8 ✛

FIRE UNDER THE WATER

I t *made no sense*—how can fire burn underwater?

The water was dark and the flame flickered in the under-water currents as a candle does in the breeze. As Septimus watched, it moved steadily away from the Slipway, keeping close to the foot of the Castle wall. Indeed, it seemed to him that the flame was held by someone walking along the bottom of the Moat. The Moat was about twenty feet deep and the light was, Septimus figured, about fourteen feet below him. Entranced by the idea of a flame burning underwater, Septimus knelt down on the cold stone of the Slipway and stared into the depths of the Moat.

Slowly and surely, the flame was walking away from him. Septimus felt oddly upset, as though he was losing something precious. He leaned forward to take one last look.

Behind him the ghost of Queen Etheldredda stepped out of the shadows, a thin smile on her lips. So intent was Septimus on seeing what was under the water, he would not have noticed the ghost even if she had chosen to **Appear** to him— which she most definitely did not. He stepped right to the edge of the Slipway and leaned out. If he just got a little closer to the water he would be able to see—

Etheldredda gave Septimus a vicious shove.

There was a loud splash and suddenly Septimus was in the water, tumbling to the bottom of the Moat, gasping with shock from the cold. The tide had turned and an icy current was running in from the river; it was swift and strong, and although Septimus was a good swimmer, it quickly dragged him away from the Slipway and out into the center of the Moat.

Septimus surfaced at last, shivering uncontrollably. He was beginning to lose the strength from his arms and legs, and there was more to struggle against than just the swift current. Now he could feel a strong undertow beneath his feet, as though someone had suddenly pulled a plug and the water around him was swirling down the drain.

A moment later, Septimus's head disappeared below the inky waters for a second time. The undertow took him down fast, and within seconds his feet touched the bottom of the Moat. Struggling to keep his eyes open in the murky water and with his lungs feeling as if they were about to burst, Septimus kicked himself up from the muddy bed and swam straight into a thick patch of sticky Moat weed. In moments, the tendrils of the weed were wrapped around him, and Septimus felt his remaining strength drain away. A dark mist fell in front of his eyes, and Septimus began to lose consciousness; yet, as he did so, he had the strangest sensation of an ice-cold grip on his arm, pulling him up . . . up . . . up through a dark tunnel toward a bright light.

"Ouch, Sep—that hurt!" Jenna's voice reached Septimus from the other end of the tunnel. Coughing, spluttering,

Septimus gulped frantically for breath.

"Oh, stop making such a fuss, boy," an irritable ghostly voice snapped. "Here, Granddaughter, take him now, for I have no wish to be **Passed Through** yet again—it is most unpleasant. No manners, young Apprentices nowadays."

"Sep, Sep, you're okay now," Jenna's voice whispered in his ear, and Septimus felt as if she was guiding him through the darkness and—at last—into the light.

"Aaaah!" Septimus suddenly sat bolt upright and took the deepest breath he had ever taken in his life. And then he took another, and another, and another.

"Sep, Sep, are you okay?" Jenna thumped him on the back. "Can you breathe now? Can you?"

"Aah . . . aah . . . aah . . ." Septimus grabbed a few more lungfuls.

"It's okay, Sep. You're safe here."

"Ah . . ." Septimus focused his eyes and looked around. He was sitting on the floor of a small sitting room at the back of the Palace. It was a cozy room; a fire was burning in the grate and a mass of thick candles burned brightly on the mantel, their wax dripping steadily onto the hearth. The room had once been a favorite of Queen Etheldredda's, who would sit there every afternoon and take a small glass of mead and read morality tales. It was now Sarah Heap's sitting room, where she too sat in the afternoon, except she would drink herb tea and read romantic novels lent to her by her good friend Sally Mullin. Queen Etheldredda did not approve of Sarah Heap's taste in furnishings and she most definitely did not approve of romantic novels. As for the general clutter and untidiness that pervaded the sitting room, Queen Etheldredda considered it a disgrace, but there was little she could do about it yet, for ghosts must put up with the bad habits of the living.

Queen Etheldredda wore her usual disapproving expression as she looked at the sodden Septimus. He sat in a puddle of muddy Moat water, steaming beside the fire and giving off a dank Moat-water smell. The ghost sat on the only chair that remained in the room from her time as Queen; it was an uncomfortable wooden chair with a straight back that Sarah had been meaning to throw out. Silas had left the remains of a bacon sandwich on it a few days earlier, and Queen Etheldredda was now perched precariously on top of it.

"I trust you have learned your lesson, young man," Queen Etheldredda said, fixing Septimus with a severe stare.

Septimus coughed up some tendrils of slimy Moat weed and spat them out on the rug.

"Punctuality is a virtue," pronounced Queen Etheldredda. "Lateness is a vice. Farewell." Still remaining in the sitting position, Queen Etheldredda rose a few feet up from the chair. She glanced at the bacon sandwich with a look of horror, and then floated away through the ceiling. Her feet, clad in richly embroidered, extremely pointy shoes, hovered above Jenna and Septimus for two or three moments until, slowly, they faded away.

"Do you think she's gone now?" Jenna whispered to Septimus after a safe interval had passed. Septimus stood up to get a better look at the ceiling, but the floor came up to meet him with a crash and he found himself lying on Sarah Heap's favorite rag rug. Jenna looked concerned. "You'd better stay here tonight. I'll send a Message Rat over to tell Marcia."

Septimus groaned. *Marcia.* He had forgotten about Marcia until now. "Perhaps you'd better not wake her up, Jen. Anyway you'll be lucky to get a Message Rat. Best tell her in the morning," he said, thinking that it was not beyond Marcia to come over to the Palace right there and then and demand to know just what Septimus thought he was doing. It wasn't, Septimus thought, a question that he could easily answer right then.

"You feeling okay, Sep?" asked Jenna.

Septimus nodded and the room began to spin. "What happened, Jen?" he asked. "How did I get *here*?"

"You fell into the Moat, Sep—at least that's what Queen Etheldredda said. She said it was your own fault and that you were late. She said you were lucky that she happened to be on the Slipway, and she rescued you. Well, **Reclaimed** you, is what she said. Whatever that means."

"Er . . . I learned it last week. But I can't remember it. Brain's not working."

"No, I shouldn't think it is. You almost drowned."

"I know. But I want to remember. Sometimes when you nearly drown your brain doesn't work so well afterward. Suppose that's happened to me, Jen?"

"Don't be ridiculous, Sep. Your brain seems fine to me. You're just tired and cold."

"But . . . oh, I *do* remember. It was in the latest edition of the *Spirit Guide*," he said suddenly. "That's it. **Reclaime**: Ghostly transportation of living creatures in order to ensure they remain as such, i.e., living. Um . . . may involve removing from imminent life-threatening danger or longer term planning, such as ensuring that they do not encounter approaching danger. Most commonly reported occurrence is being pushed from path of runaway horse by ghostly hands. There, brain's okay." Septimus closed his eyes and looked pleased.

"Of course it is," said Jenna soothingly. "Now look, Sep, you're soaked. I'm going to get you some dry things. Just rest while I go find the Night Housekeeper."

Jenna tiptoed out, leaving Septimus dozing on the rug. Queen Etheldredda was waiting for her outside the door.

"Ah, Granddaughter," she said in her high, piercing voice.

"*What?*" asked Jenna irritably.

"How is your dear *adoptive* brother?"

"My *brother* is fine, thank you. Now would you mind getting out of the way? I want to get him some dry clothes."

"Your manners are sorely lacking, Granddaughter. You know I saved the boy's life."

"Yes. Thank you very much. It was . . . very nice of you. Now, please, may I get past?" Jenna tried to duck to one side of the ghost, having no wish to **Pass Through** Queen Etheldredda.

"No, you may *not*." Queen Etheldredda stepped in front of Jenna and barred her path. The ghost's features took on a stony look. "I have something to tell you, Granddaughter, and I suggest you listen well. It will be greatly to your *adoptive* brother's disadvantage if you do not."

Jenna stopped—she recognized a threat when she heard one. The Queen leaned down toward Jenna and a deep chill filled the air. Then she whispered in Jenna's ear, and Jenna had never felt so cold in all her life.

✢9✢
PREDICTION PRACTICAL

Alther, what do you mean, he spent the night at the Palace?" Marcia demanded very early the next morning. "Why?"

"Well . . . er, it's a little complicated, Marcia," Alther replied uncomfortably.

"Isn't it always, Alther?" snapped Marcia. "You do realize that if he doesn't get back right away he's going to miss his Prediction Practical?"

Marcia Overstrand was sitting at her desk in the Pyramid Library at the top of the Wizard Tower. The Library was dark and gloomy in the early morning light, and the few candles that Marcia had lit flickered as she thumped Septimus's Prediction Practical Papers down on the desk in exasperation. Her green eyes flashed crossly as Alther Mella floated along the book stacks peering at some of his favorite titles.

"This is very bad, Alther. I spent all day yesterday setting up the Prediction Practical and it's got to begin before 7:07 A.M. Any later than that and all the stuff will have started to happen—and then it's just Telepathy and Cognizance, which is *not the point*."

"Give the lad a break, Marcia. He fell into the Moat last night and—"

"He did *what*?"

"Fell into the Moat. I really think you should postpone—"

"How come he fell into the Moat, Alther?" Marcia asked suspiciously.

Eager to change the subject, Alther wandered over to Marcia and sat down companionably on the corner of her desk. He knew he would regret it, but he could not resist saying, "Well, perhaps you should have predicted this would happen, Marcia, and scheduled the Prediction Practical for later in the day."

"That's not funny," snapped Marcia, checking through the papers. "In fact, you are getting horribly predictable yourself. Predictably childish. You are spending far too much of your time flying around with Septimus and generally showing off when at your age you should know better. I shall send Catchpole down to the Palace to fetch Septimus right now. *That* will wake him up."

"I imagine you'll have to wake up Catchpole first, Marcia," Alther commented.

"Catchpole's on night duty, Alther. He's been awake all night."

"Funny habit he's got, that Catchpole," said Alther pensively, "of snoring while he's awake. You'd think he'd find it irritating, wouldn't you?" Marcia did not deign to reply. She got up from her desk, drew her purple robes around her and stormed out, slamming the Library door behind her.

Alther floated through the hatch that led onto the golden Pyramid roof and wandered up to the top of the Pyramid itself. The autumn morning air was cool and a fine drizzle fell. The base of the Wizard Tower had disappeared into a thick white mist. A few roofs of the taller houses were visible as they broke through the white blanket, but most of the Castle was lost to view. Although as a ghost, Alther did not feel the cold, he felt like shivering in the wind that eddied around the top of the Wizard Tower. He drew his faded purple cloak around him and looked down at the hammered-silver platform that surmounted the Pyramid. Alther had always been fascinated by the hieroglyphs inscribed in the platform, but he had never deciphered them, as indeed no one else had. Many hundreds of years ago one ExtraOrdinary Wizard had been brave enough to climb to the top of the Pyramid and taken a rubbing of the hieroglyphs, which now hung in the Library. Every time Alther, as ExtraOrdinary Wizard, had looked at the old gray piece of paper framed on the Library wall, he had felt a horrible sense of vertigo, for it reminded him of the time when, as a young Apprentice, he had been forced to chase his Master, DomDaniel, up to that very place.

But now, as a ghost, Alther was fearless. He experimented with standing on the platform first on one leg and then the other; then he threw himself off, tumbling and turning through the air. As he fell, he tried to imagine what it must have felt like to fall as a human being, as DomDaniel had once done. Just above the mist he leveled out and set off for the Palace.

Catchpole was having a bad dream and it was about to get worse. He hated being on night duty down in the old spell cupboard beside the huge silver doors to the Wizard Tower. It wasn't so much the lingering smells of decaying spells that upset Catchpole; it was the fear of being asked to do something by a more senior Wizard. Catchpole was only a sub-Wizard and he was not progressing as fast as he had hoped—he had had to retake his Primaries twice and still had not passed—which meant that all Wizards in the Tower were senior to him. After years of being deputy to the fearsome Hunter, Catchpole hated being told what to do, especially when he always seemed to do it wrong. So when Marcia Overstrand strode into the old spell cupboard and demanded to know just what he thought he was doing, sitting there with his eyes closed and looking about as useful as a dead sheep, Catchpole's heart sank. What was she going to ask him to do? And what was she going to say when, as usual, he made a mess of it? Catchpole was incredibly relieved when all Marcia did was tell him to get down to the Palace *at once* and bring her Apprentice back with him. Well, he could manage that—and it would get him out of the cramped cupboard. What was more, thought Catchpole, as he ran down the marble steps and into the misty Wizard Tower courtyard, it seemed that that upstart Young Army boy who had inveigled his way into becoming the ExtraOrdinary Apprentice was, for once, in the wrong. He would enjoy that, he thought with a smirk.

Catchpole had now reached a large kennel-like structure. It was built of great granite blocks, was the height of a small cottage and was at least twice the length. There was a line of tiny windows just below the eaves to provide much-needed ventilation and for the occupant to look out if he wanted. At the front of the kennel was a hefty wooden ramp leading to a barn door that was made of thick oak planks. The door was firmly closed and had three iron bars holding it in place. Above the door someone had written in neat handwriting, SPIT FYRE. As Catchpole trotted by, something inside the kennel hurled itself against the door. There was a loud splintering sound and the middle iron bar on the door bent a little, but not enough for the door to give way. Catchpole's smirk vanished. He shot off at high speed and did not slow down until he was halfway along Wizard Way and could see the light from the palace torches glimmering through the mist.

After dispatching Catchpole, Marcia took the silver spiral stairs back up to her rooms at the top of the Wizard Tower. Something was bothering her. It was so unlike Septimus to miss an exam; something felt wrong. Still on nighttime mode, the silver stairs slowly corkscrewed their way to the top of the Wizard Tower, and Marcia, who was never at her best early in the morning, began to feel queasy with the movement of the stairs and the smells of bacon and porridge, which were competing with the incense that drifted up from the hall below. As Marcia rose past the fourteenth floor, still puzzling over Septimus, something occurred to her. Something important.

"Come on, hurry up," Marcia snapped impatiently at the spiral stairs. Taking her at her word, the stairs sped up to double daytime speed, and Marcia shot up through the rest of the Tower, surprising three elderly Wizards who were up early for a fishing trip. The stairs stopped with the same enthusiasm with which they had obeyed Marcia's earlier command; in one seamless movement the ExtraOrdinary Wizard exited at

the twentieth floor and hurtled through the heavy purple door
that led to her rooms. Luckily the door saw her coming and
flung itself open just in time. Moments later Marcia was racing up the steps to the Pyramid Library.

With a worried frown, Marcia swiftly leafed through the
Prediction Practical Papers until she came across what she
was looking for: a series of closely written formulae and inter-
pretations that Jillie Djinn, the new Chief Hermetic Scribe,
had provided from the *All-Seeing Almanac*. Marcia pulled out
the piece of paper, and taking her illuminating pen from her
pocket, she ran it over the formulae. As the pen moved across
the page, the numbers began to rearrange themselves. Marcia
stared at them in disbelief for several minutes.

Suddenly she threw down her pen and ran to the darkest
corner of the Library, which housed the **Sealed** shelf.
Trembling, Marcia tried three times until she clicked her fingers loud enough to light the massive candle that was set
beside it. The flame illuminated the two thick **Sealed** silver
doors that covered the shelf and opened only with the touch
of the Akhu Amulet, which passed from one Extra-
Ordinary Wizard to the next. Marcia removed the lapis lazuli
and gold amulet from around her neck and pressed it against

the long purple wax **Seal** that covered the crack between the doors. The **Seal** recognized the amulet, the wax rolled itself up into a coil and, with a soft hiss, the doors swung open. Behind them was a deep, dark shelf from which the smells of stale air from hundreds of years ago drifted out. Marcia sneezed.

Marcia had never opened the **Sealed** section before. She had never had cause to until now. Alther had once shown her how to do it after he had decided that he wanted her to suc-ceed him as ExtraOrdinary Wizard. Marcia remembered how encouraging Alther had been to her when she had been his Apprentice, and a twinge of guilt stabbed at her for being so short-tempered with the ghost.

With some trepidation, Marcia shoved her arm into the recesses of the shelf, for one never knew what might lurk in a **Sealed** place or what might have grown there since it had last been opened. But it did not take her long to find what she was looking for, and with a sense of relief, Marcia pulled out a solid-gold box. She checked the box in the light of the candle, **ReSealed** the doors and took it down to the desk. Taking a small key from her ExtraOrdinary Wizard belt, Marcia opened the box and lifted out a decaying leather book. As she cradled it in her hands, Marcia could see that it had once been beautiful. The small, thick book was tied with a faded red ribbon and covered in the fragile remains of soft leather on which intricate gold-leaf designs were visible—as was the title: *I, Marcellus.* Gently Marcia placed the book on the table, and as she did so the ribbon fell to pieces, a scattering of fine red dust covered her hands, and the black seal that had bound its two ends fell to the floor and rolled away into the shadows. Marcia did not bother to pursue the seal, for she was anxious—and yet afraid—to open the *I, Marcellus.*

Heart beating fast, Marcia gingerly lifted the cover, sending a shower of leather dust into the air.

"Atchoo!" she sneezed. "Atchoo, atchoo, *atchoo!*" and then, "No, oh, *no!*" for the pages of the book had fallen prey to the dreaded Pyramid Library paper beetle. Marcia took a pair of long-nosed tweezers from a pot on the desk, and one by one, she lifted the delicate lace-wing pages, inspecting them closely with a large magnifying glass. The *I, Marcellus* was divided into three parts: Alchemie, **Physik**, and the Almanac. The first two sections, and much of the last section, were unreadable. Shaking her head, Marcia moved swiftly through the book until she came across a very fat, squashed paper beetle wedged under some astronomical calculations. With an air of triumph, Marcia lifted up the beetle with her pliers and dropped it into a glass jar on the desk, which already contained a collection of squashed paper beetles. Flipping faster now through the undamaged pages of the rest of the Almanac, Marcia soon came across the present year. Scanning down the cryptic entries, and occasionally consulting some tables at the back that were covered in ink blots, Marcia at last found the date she was looking for, the day of the Autumn Equinox—which was oddly out of sequence—and drew out an ancient piece of paper with familiar spidery writing scrawled over it.

Marcia's expression as she read this piece of paper changed from initial puzzlement to one of dawning horror. Shaking and deathly pale, the ExtraOrdinary Wizard staggered to her feet, gently placed the scrap of paper in her pocket and set off for the Palace as fast as she could.

✢ 1 0 ✢
THE QUEEN'S ROBING ROOM

Over *at the Palace, in* Sarah Heap's small sitting room, Septimus was beginning to stir. His head felt fuzzy as he opened his eyes, wondering where he was. A dull grayish light filtered through Sarah's flowery curtains and Septimus could feel the dampness from the river in the air. It was not the kind of morning that made him want to get up.

Jenna yawned, still sleepy. She pulled her crocheted blanket up over her head and wished the day would go away. A strange feeling of foreboding was weighing her down, although she could not remember why. "Morning, Sep," she said. "How are you?"

"Wherrr . . ." Septimus mumbled blearily. "Where am I?"

"Um . . . Mum's sitting room," Jenna mumbled sleepily.

"Oh, yes, I remember . . . Queen Etheldredda—"

Jenna was wide awake all of a sudden, remembering what her sense of foreboding had been about. She wished she hadn't.

Suddenly Septimus remembered something else: his Prediction Practical. He sat up, his straw-colored curls standing on end, a look of panic in his bright green eyes. "I gotta go, Jen, or I'll be late. I *knew* I was going to mess this up."

"Mess what up?"

"My Prediction Practical. I *knew* it."

"Well, then, that's all right, isn't it?" Jenna sat up and grinned. "I guess you've passed."

"Don't think it works like that, Jen," said Septimus gloomily. "Not with Marcia, anyway. I'd better go."

"Look, Sep," said Jenna. "You can't go back yet. You have to come see something first. I promised."

"Promised? What do you mean, *promised*?"

Jenna did not reply. Slowly, she stood up and carefully folded the crocheted blanket. Septimus saw a dark and anxious look in her eyes and decided not to push things any further. "Well, don't worry," he said, reluctantly crawling out of his makeshift bed, "I'll come see whatever it is first and then I'll go back. If I run fast I might just make it."

"Thanks, Sep," said Jenna.

As Jenna and Septimus closed the door of Sarah Heap's sitting room behind them, the ghost of Queen Etheldredda descended through the ceiling with a look of satisfaction on her sharp features. She settled herself down on the sofa, picked up the small book that Sarah had left on the table and, with fascinated distaste, began to read *True Love Never Lies*.

Septimus and Jenna made their way along the Long Walk, the wide passageway that ran the length of the Palace like a backbone. It was deserted in the dim light of the morning, for the Palace servants were quietly employed elsewhere getting things ready for the day, and the various Ancients who haunted the Long Walk at night had fallen asleep in the early-morning light. Some were propped up in doorways, others were contentedly snoring in some of the moth-eaten chairs that were scattered along the Walk for the benefit of those who found the distance too far to travel in one trip.

A threadbare red carpet that covered the old stone flags ran like a broad path in front of Jenna and Septimus. The Long Walk always felt to Jenna as though it went on forever, although now it was more interesting than it had been, since her father, Milo Banda, had brought back all kinds of strange and bizarre treasures from the Far Countries and set them up in its empty niches and alcoves. In fact, Milo had been so pleased with what he had called "brightening up the place" that he had soon set off on another voyage to bring back even more treasures.

When they passed by what Jenna thought of as a particularly weird section—the area where Milo had displayed some shrunken heads from the Cannibal Islands of the South Seas—Septimus lingered, fascinated.

"Come on, Sep," Jenna chided. "Don't stop here, this is a really creepy part."

"It's not the heads that are creepy, Jen. It's that picture. Isn't that old Etheldredda?"

It was an imposing, full-length painting. Queen Etheldredda's sharp features gazed down at Jenna and Septimus with her usual expression, accurately caught by the artist. The Queen was posed haughtily against a backdrop of the Palace.

Jenna shivered. "Dad found it in a **Sealed** room in the attic," she whispered as though the portrait was listening to them. "He took it out 'cause he said it was frightening his new Counter Colony. I'm going to ask him to put it back."

"The sooner, the better," said Septimus. "Before it scares the shrunken heads."

A few minutes later, Septimus and Jenna were outside the Queen's Room on the top floor of the turret at the end of the Palace. A tall golden door with beautiful emerald-green patterns glinted in the dusty shafts of the early-morning sunshine. Jenna unclipped a large emerald and gold key from the leather belt that she wore over her gold sash. Carefully, she placed the key in the keyhole that was in the middle of the door.

Septimus stood back and watched Jenna put the key into what appeared to him to be a completely blank and rather cracked wall. This did not surprise Septimus, for he knew he could not see the door to the Queen's Room. Only those who were descended from the Queen could see it.

"I'll wait for you here, Jen," Septimus said.

"No, you won't, Sep. You're coming with me."

"But—" Septimus protested. Jenna said nothing; she turned the key and leaped to one side as the door came crashing down like a drawbridge. Then she grabbed hold of Septimus's hand and pulled him toward what looked to him like an extremely solid and very hard wall.

Septimus resisted. "Jen, you *know* I can't go in there."

"Yes, you can, Sep. I can bring you in. Now keep hold of my hand and follow me." Jenna pulled Septimus forward. He saw her disappear through the wall until only her hand, stretched out behind her and clasping his, remained visible. It was one of the strangest things that Septimus had ever seen, and instinctively he held back, unwilling to be dragged through a wall, even by Jenna. But an impatient tug pulled him so that his nose was right up against the wall—no, it was *in* the wall. Another insistent tug followed and suddenly Septimus found himself in the Queen's Room.

At first Septimus could see little, for there were no windows and the Room was lit only by a small coal fire. But once his eyes became used to the dimness, Septimus was surprised. The Room was much smaller than he had expected; in fact, it was rather cramped. It was furnished simply, with just one comfortable chair and a worn rug laid in front of the fire. The only thing of interest that caught Septimus's eye was an old cupboard set into the curve of the wall on which was written in familiar gold letters: UNSTABLE POTIONS AND PARTIKULAR POISONS. It was identical to the cupboard that Aunt Zelda had in her cottage in the Marram Marshes, and it gave Septimus a sudden longing for one of Aunt Zelda's cabbage sandwiches.

What neither Septimus nor Jenna could see was the occupant of the fireside chair—the ghost of a young woman. Turning to look at her visitors, the young woman gazed at Jenna with a rapt expression. Around her long, dark hair, the ghost wore a gold circlet, identical to the one that Jenna wore. She had the red and gold robes of a Queen, which were heavily bloodstained over her heart. Having looked her fill at Jenna, the Queen turned her gaze toward Septimus, taking in his green Apprentice tunic and cloak, his brilliant green eyes and, in particular, his ExtraOrdinary Apprentice silver belt. Seemingly satisfied that Septimus was a suitable companion for her daughter, the young woman relaxed back into her chair.

"Feels funny in here," Septimus whispered, looking at the apparently empty chair.

"I know," Jenna replied in a hushed voice. Remembering what Etheldredda had said, she looked around the room, half hoping to see the ghost of her mother. She thought there was a faint glimmer of something in the armchair, but when she looked again there was nothing. And yet . . . Jenna shook the thoughts of her mother out of her head.

"Come on," she told Septimus.

"Come on where, Jen?"

"Into Aunt Zelda's cupboard." Jenna opened the door to the cupboard and waited for Septimus.

"Oh, great, are you taking me to see Aunt Zelda?"

"Stop asking questions, Sep," said Jenna a little sharply. Septimus looked surprised, but he followed her into the cupboard and Jenna closed the door behind them. The young woman in the chair smiled, happy to think that her daughter was going through the Queen's Way to see the Keeper in the Marram Marshes. She would, thought Jenna's mother, make a good Queen. When the Time was Right.

But, unknown to her mother, Jenna was not going to the Marram Marshes. As soon as she had closed the door behind Septimus, Jenna whispered, "We're not going to see Aunt Zelda."

"Oh." Septimus sounded disappointed. And then he said, "Why are you whispering?"

"Shhh. I don't know. Now there's a trapdoor here somewhere. Can you see it, Sep?"

"Don't you know where we're going either?" he asked.

"No. Look, can you shine your ring down here? I expect it's in the same place as Aunt Zelda's trapdoor."

"You're being very mysterious, Jen," said Septimus, shining his Dragon Ring so that the glow lit up the floor. Sure enough, the trapdoor in the Queen's Unstable Potions and Partikular Poisons cupboard was indeed in the same place as it was in Aunt Zelda's. Jenna lifted a carefully concealed thick gold ring (Aunt Zelda's was only brass) and pulled. The trapdoor lifted easily and silently, and Jenna and Septimus peered warily into the hole.

"What now?" whispered Septimus.

"We've got to go down," Jenna replied.

"Where to?" asked Septimus, beginning to feel uneasy.

"To the Robing Room. It's the room below. Shall I go first?"

"No," said Septimus, "let me go first. Just in case . . . and, well, I've got the light from my ring." Septimus lowered himself through the trapdoor, and instead of the rickety old wooden ladder that led down from Aunt Zelda's trapdoor, he found a flight of fine silver steps with open filigree treads and a polished mahogany banister on either side. Climbing down backward, for the steps were steep like a ship's ladder, Septimus called up to Jenna, "It's okay, Jen. I think."

Jenna's boots appeared through the trapdoor, and Septimus went down the steps and waited at the bottom. As Jenna jumped from the last silver step and her feet touched the fine marble floor, two large candles at the foot of the steps burst into flame.

"Wow," said Septimus, impressed. "It's a bit nicer than upstairs, Jen."

The Queen's Robing Room was more than nice—it was opulent. It was larger than the upstairs room, for the turret widened on the lower floor. Its walls were lined with a burnished gold leaf that, although it had dulled over the centuries, glowed deep and rich in the candlelight. On the wall facing the silver steps was an old looking glass in an ornate gold frame, but it seemed to be of little use, for much of the reflective silvering was gone after years of dampness. The glass was dark and showed only a blurred reflection of the candlelight.

All along the walls were solid silver hooks, each one a different, intricately cast shape. One was shaped like a swan's neck, another like a snake; another was cast from intertwined initials of some long-dead Queen and her soul mate. Some hooks were empty and some had robes or cloaks hanging from them, reflecting the different styles popular through the previous centuries, but all in the traditional red and gold that the Queens of the Castle had always worn. What amazed Jenna—although Septimus did not notice—was that not one of the robes had any dust upon them. All looked as new and fresh as if they had just been made by the Palace seamstress.

Enthralled, for she loved rich cloth, Jenna wandered around the room, running her fingers over the robes and exclaiming, "These are so soft, Sep . . . oh, feel this one, the silk is so fine . . . and look at this fur trim, that's even better than Marcia's winter cloak, isn't it?" Jenna had lifted a fine woolen cloak from a silver hook embedded with emeralds and twisted into the shape of a J. She slipped it over her shoulders; it was a beautiful cloak, soft and flowing, edged with a dark red fur trim. It fit her perfectly. Unwilling to put it back on its lonely hook, Jenna fastened the gold clasp and wrapped the cloak around her. It reminded her of Lucy Gringe's blue cloak that Jenna had worn not so long ago, and had recently given to a very surprised Lucy.

"Look, it fits me perfectly. It's as if it were made for me. And see, Nicko's present is just right." Jenna had fastened the cloak with her gold pin, also in the shape of a J, which Nicko had bought from a merchant in the Port and given to her for her last birthday.

"Very nice, Jen," said Septimus, who did not find clothes the least bit interesting and thought the Robing Room a little oppressive. "Look, hadn't you better show me whatever it was you wanted to?"

Jenna came back to earth with a jolt. For a few moments she had forgotten all about the wretched Queen Etheldredda. She pointed at the dark looking glass. "That's it, Sep. Now you have to look in it. That's what I promised."

Septimus looked wary. "Promised who?"

"Queen Etheldredda," Jenna whispered miserably. "Last night. She was waiting for me outside the door."

"Oh," Septimus muttered, "I see. But weird things can happen with looking glasses, Jen. Especially old ones. I don't think I should do this."

"Please, Sep," Jenna pleaded. "Please look in it. *Please*."

"Why?" Septimus saw a look of panic on Jenna's face. "Jen—what's the matter?"

"Because if you don't, she'll . . ."

"She'll what?"

Jenna looked white. "She'll **Reverse** the **Reclaime**. At midnight. You'll drown at midnight tonight."

✠ I I ✠
THE GLASS

S eptimus *stood warily in front* of the looking glass, deliberately avoiding it by staring at his boots. He remembered
Alther telling him how he had once looked in a Glass and seen
a **Spectre Waiting** for him. He was afraid he might be about
to see the same thing. "How does she know whether I've
looked into the Glass or not?" he asked.

"I don't know," Jenna said, unhappily twisting the red fur

trim on her new cloak. "I didn't ask. I was so scared that she would reverse the **Reclaime** that I just told her I would make sure you did it."

"Did she say why I had to?"

"No. She wouldn't say. She was just so . . . threatening. It was horrible. Can she really do what she said, Sep? Can she really reverse the **Reclaime**?"

Septimus angrily scuffed his boots on the marble. "Yes, she can, Jen. Within twenty-four hours, if she's skilled at it, which I bet she is. I bet she's done it lots of times before. Rescued some poor person and then held them ransom."

"She's horrible," muttered Jenna. "I hate her."

"Marcia says you shouldn't hate anyone," Septimus said. "She says first you should stand in their shoes before you judge them."

"Marcia wouldn't stand in anyone else's shoes," Jenna said with a wry smile, "unless they were pointy purple python skin with dinky little gold buttons."

Septimus laughed and then fell silent. So did Jenna. Both felt their gazes drawn toward the Glass but neither looked at it. Suddenly Septimus blurted out, "I'm going to look in it now, Jen."

"Now?" Jenna's voice rose up a pitch.

"Yes. Get it over with. After all, what's the worst that can happen? I might see a horrible old **Spectre** or **Thing**, but that's all. What you see can't hurt you, can it?"

"No. I suppose not. . . ." Jenna sounded unconvinced.

"So I'll do it now. You go back up to the cupboard and I'll be up in a moment. Okay?"

"No, I'm not leaving you here on your own," protested Jenna.

"But if there is a **Spectre Waiting** for me, Jen, you mustn't see it. It will **Haunt** you too. I know what to do about **Spectres** and you don't."

"But—" Jenna hesitated.

"Go on, Jen. Please." Septimus flashed Jenna a smile. "Go *on*."

Jenna reluctantly started up the silver stairs to the potions cupboard. Once she was safely out of the Robing Room, Septimus took a deep breath to steady his nerves.

Then he looked into the Glass.

At first he could see nothing. The Glass was dark, like a deep marsh pool. Septimus leaned closer, wondering why he could not see his own reflection and, despite doing his best not to, imagining all kinds of horrible **Spectres** at his shoulder, **Waiting** for him.

"Are you okay? Have you looked into the Glass yet?" Jenna's voice came from the cupboard.

"Um . . . yes. I'm looking now. . . ."

"What can you see?"

"Nothing . . . nothing . . . it's just dark . . . oh, wait . . . I can see something now . . . it—it's weird . . . an old man . . . staring at me. He looks kind of surprised."

"An old man?" asked Jenna.

"Oh, that's odd. . . ."

"What?" Jenna sounded worried.

"Well, if I raise my right hand he does too. And if I frown, he frowns too."

"Like your reflection would?"

"Well, yes. Oh, I know what it is—it's one of those Yet-to-Come Glasses. They were very popular in the old days. Traveling fairs used to bring them. They show you what you're going to look like just before you die."

"That's horrible, Sep," Jenna called down.

"Yeah. Don't ever want to look like that. Ugh. Oh, look, if I stick out my tongue, he—*hey!*"

"What?" Jenna could bear it no longer. She hurtled down the steps and arrived in the Robing Room just in time to see Septimus spring back from the Glass, slip on the shiny marble floor and fall. As he scrabbled to get up and away, Jenna screamed. Reaching out of the Glass were two old, wizened hands. With long bony fingers and curved yellow nails, they snatched at Septimus's tunic, grabbed hold of it, then wrapped themselves around his Apprentice belt, dragging him toward the Glass. Frantically Septimus tried to pull away, kicking out at the clutching talons.

"Jen! Help, Je—" he yelled, and then there was silence. Septimus's head had disappeared into the Glass as though sinking into a pool of ink.

Jenna ran down the steps and skidded across the floor, horrified at seeing Septimus's shoulders rapidly disappearing into the Glass. She leaped forward, grabbed his feet and pulled with all her strength. Slowly, slowly Septimus began to come out of the Glass. Jenna hung on like a dog with a bone, determined never, *ever*, to let go of Septimus. Little by little, as if emerging from one of the black Marram Marsh pools, Septimus's head broke free. He twisted around and yelled, "Careful, Jen! Don't let him get you!"

Jenna glanced up and saw a face that stayed with her for the rest of her life. It was the face of an old man—an *ancient* man—with a great long nose and sunken, staring eyes that looked at Jenna with surprise, as if he knew her. Long wisps of yellowish white hair hung down and caught over his enormous old ears. His mouth, which contained three great tombstone teeth, was fixed in a wide grimace of concentration as he tried to pull Septimus away from her. Then, suddenly, with a tremendous heave, he succeeded. Septimus shot through the Glass and Jenna was left alone in the Robing Room, staring in disbelief at all that was left of Septimus—his old brown boots, empty in her hands.

With toes stubbed from kicking the Glass and her throat sore from screaming at it to *give Septimus back*, Jenna fled up the steps, clutching Septimus's boots. Once she was safely in the Unstable Potions and Partikular Poisons cupboard, she slammed the trapdoor closed and opened the bottom drawer under the empty shelves. She heard the familiar metallic click, and then, trying to catch her breath, Jenna waited impatiently until something in the cupboard shifted and she smelled the familiar scent of cabbages cooking.

Jenna pushed open the door and stepped out into Aunt Zelda's cottage.

"Oi!" A startled voice came from the rug beside the fire. A boy with long matted hair, wearing a simple brown tunic fastened with an old leather belt, leaped to his feet with a look of alarm. On seeing Jenna, Wolf Boy relaxed and said, "Hey, it's you again. Can't keep away, huh?" And then, noticing Jenna's expression: "Jenna, what's the matter?"

"Oh . . . 409," gasped Jenna, who had picked up Septimus's habit of addressing Wolf Boy by his old Young Army number. "Where's Aunt Zelda—I've got to see Aunt Zelda. *Now.*"

Wolf Boy needed no excuse to leave his early reader potion book by the fire and come over to Jenna. He had never mastered the art of reading, having been completely terrified of his reading and writing instructor in the Young Army. And now, no matter how hard he tried and how patient Aunt Zelda was with him, the way the letters stuck together to make words— or not—still made little sense to Wolf Boy. "She's not here, Jenna," he explained. "She's out gathering marsh herbs an' stuff. Hey, aren't those 412's boots?"

Jenna nodded miserably. She had been sure that Aunt Zelda would know what to do, but now . . . She leaned against the cupboard door, suddenly exhausted.

"Can I help?" Wolf Boy asked quietly, a concerned look in his dark brown eyes.

"I don't know. . . ." Jenna almost wailed and then stopped. She must keep calm, she told herself. She must think what to do. She *must*.

"412's in trouble, isn't he?" asked Wolf Boy.

Jenna nodded again, not trusting herself to say anything. Wolf Boy put his arm around Jenna's shoulders. "Then we'd better get him out of trouble . . . yeah?"

Jenna nodded.

"I'll come with you. Wait, I'd better leave a note for Aunt Zelda and tell her where we've gone." Wolf Boy rushed over to Aunt Zelda's desk, which looked faintly ridiculous with duck feet on the ends of its legs and a pair of arms to help with the paperwork, both courtesy of Marcia Overstrand. Aunt Zelda hated these additions but Wolf Boy had learned to use them to his advantage.

"Piece of paper, please," he asked the arms. The rather clumsy hands on the ends of the arms scrabbled around in the desk drawer, took out a crumpled piece of paper, smoothed it out and put it neatly on the desk.

"Pen, please," asked Wolf Boy.

The right hand picked a quill pen from a tray on top of the desk and held it surprisingly delicately, hovering above the paper.

"Now write: Dear Aunt Zelda—what's the matter?" The left hand was impatiently drumming its fingers on the paper. "Oh, sorry. Ink, please. Now write: Dear Aunt Zelda, Jenna and me have gone to rescue 412. With love from 409. Oh, and Jenna. Love from Jenna too. That's it, yes, thank you. Thank you, you can stop now. Put the pen away. No, you don't need to blot it, just leave it on her desk and make sure she sees it." The hands rather fussily put away the pen, and then the arms folded themselves somewhat crossly, as if dissatisfied with being asked to write so little.

"Let's go," said Jenna, stepping back through the door of the Unstable Potions and Partikular Poisons cupboard.

"Coming," said Wolf Boy, and then remembering something, he dashed back to the fire and picked up an uneaten cabbage sandwich.

Jenna eyed the sandwich warily. "Do you really like those?" she asked.

"No. Can't stand 'em. But 412 does. Thought he'd like this one."

"He's going to need a whole lot more than a cabbage sandwich, 409." Jenna sighed.

"Yeah, well. Look, I'll follow you and you can tell me about it. Okay?"

Wolf Boy and Jenna emerged from the cupboard in the Queen's Room with Wolf Boy in a somber mood. Jenna had told him what had happened. They walked past the Queen's chair, unaware of her shocked expression at the apparently sudden change that Septimus had undergone—from neatly dressed Apprentice to a half-wild-looking boy. As Wolf Boy passed the ghost, he felt the hair on the back of his neck rise; he looked around like a wary animal and a low growl rose from the back of his throat. "Something funny in here, Jen," he whispered.

Jenna shivered, unnerved by Wolf Boy's feral growl. "Come on," she said. "Let's get out of here." She grabbed Wolf Boy's hand and pulled him through the door.

Jillie Djinn, recently **Chosen** Chief Hermetic Scribe, was waiting for them.

✢ 12 ✢
JILLIE DJINN

M iss *Djinn!*" *gasped* Jenna, taken aback at the unexpected sight of the Scribe's indigo robes with their impressive gold flashes. How did Jillie Djinn know where she had been? And how come the Scribe knew where the Queen's Room was? Even Marcia did not know that.

"Your Majesty." Jillie Djinn sounded a little breathless. She inclined her head respectfully, her new silk robes rustling as she moved.

"Please don't call me that," Jenna said angrily. "Call me

Jenna. Just Jenna. I am not Queen yet. And I don't ever want to be either. You just end up being a horrible person doing horrible things to everyone. It's awful."

Jillie Djinn looked at Jenna with a concerned expression and was not sure how to reply. The Chief Hermetic Scribe had no children and, apart from a very solemn and precocious Temple Scribe in a Far Country some years ago, Jenna was the first girl of eleven that Jillie had spoken to since she herself was eleven. Miss Djinn had devoted her life to her career and had spent years traveling in the Far Countries learning the arcane secrets of the many and varied worlds of knowledge. She had also spent some years researching the hidden secrets of the Castle, which she was pleased to see had not been wasted.

"Jenna," Jillie Djinn corrected herself, "Madam Marcia wishes to see you. Her Apprentice is missing and she fears the worst." Jillie Djinn's gaze alighted on Septimus's boots, which hung by their laces from Jenna's right hand. "I assume that I am right that something of that nature has occurred?"

Puzzled, Jenna nodded. She wondered how Marcia could possibly already know what had happened. And then she sniffed. And sniffed again. A strange smell of dragon poo was

in the air. Jillie Djinn sniffed too. She scraped her right shoe—
a neat black lace-up—vigorously on the floor, inspected the
sole, then scraped it again.

"Would I be right also, Princess, if I were to say that there
is a Glass in the Queen's Room?" Jillie Djinn's bright green
eyes fastened onto Jenna expectantly. Jillie had many theories
about many things and she was excited to think that one of
them might be working out right now.

Jenna did not answer, but she did not need to. The Chief
Hermetic Scribe was not the best person in the Castle at reading people's expressions, but there was no mistaking the look
of astonishment on Jenna's face.

"You may not be aware, Princess Jenna, but I have made
an extensive study of Alchemical Glasses—*extensive*—and
we actually have a specimen in the Hermetic Chamber. This
morning, I saw a disturbance in that Glass. I made haste to the
Wizard Tower to report the disturbance, which we are duty-
bound to do by our Charter, and I met Madam Overstrand
leaving in a distressed state. I have drawn my own conclusions
and now respectfully ask if you will consent to accompany me
to the Manuscriptorium," said the Scribe, as if addressing a
lecture hall of particularly slow scholars. "I have also asked

Marcia Overstrand to meet us there."

Marcia was about the last person Jenna wanted to see just then, as she knew she would have to tell her that *she* had caused Septimus's disappearance. But Jillie Djinn's mention of another Glass in the Manuscriptorium had raised her hopes. Could it be possible that the old man in the Glass was just one of those weird old scribes from their spooky Spell Vault that Septimus used to talk about? Maybe he had just pulled Septimus through to the Manuscriptorium? Maybe Sep was waiting for her there right now, and then he'd spend the rest of the day telling her all about it until she was completely fed up? Maybe . . .

Anxious now to get to the Manuscriptorium, Jenna followed the bustling, bright-eyed Scribe down the narrow winding steps. Wolf Boy, who had been hanging around in the shadows, blending into the background like the Forest creature that he was at heart, joined them, causing Jillie to jump in surprise. At the foot of the steps, Jillie scraped her shoe once more and then took the side door out of the turret.

"I must say," said Jillie self-importantly as she strode along the path around the back of the turret, "it is most gratifying when a theory is proved right. I had narrowed the whereabouts of the Queen's Room down to two positions. The first was down there—" Jillie Djinn waved her hand toward the old summer house by the riverbank, whose octagonal golden roof was just visible above the early-morning river mist. "Of course, Princess Jenna, I knew that your key would open both, but nothing else about the summer house made sense, although I did wonder whether its legend of the Black Fiend had been put about by the various Queens to keep people away. But naturally, by looking at all the facts and giving them due consideration, I chose the right place. *Most* interesting."

"Interesting?" muttered Jenna under her breath, wondering if Septimus's disappearance was no more than a diverting academic exercise for the Scribe.

With Wolf Boy and Jenna in tow, Jillie Djinn rounded the base of the turret and emerged at the front of the Palace. She set off across the lawns toward the Gate, and as their feet made dark footprints in the dew, the Chief Hermetic Scribe continued to expound on various pet theories, for Jillie had a captive audience and she was not about to waste it. Her audience was not, however, appreciative; Jenna was too preoccupied with worrying about Septimus to listen and Wolf Boy gave up after the first sentence. The way that Jillie Djinn talked made his head ache.

Despite her diminutive size, Jillie kept up a fast pace and they were soon rushing along Wizard Way, which was beginning to stir. Wizard Way was one of the oldest streets in the Castle. It was a broad, straight avenue lined with beautiful silver torch posts. It ran from the Palace Gates at one end to the Great Arch of the Wizard Tower at the other. The houses and shops were built from the oldest yellow limestone from quarries emptied long ago. They were weathered and crooked but had a friendly feeling to them that Jenna loved. The Way was lined with countless small shops and printers, selling all manner of printed papers, inks, books, pamphlets and pens, plus an assortment of spectacles and headache pills for those who had spent far too long reading in dark corners.

As the shopkeepers and printers peered through their misty windows and decided against putting out their wares in the damp air, the first thing they saw was the Chief Hermetic Scribe striding down the Way, accompanied by an odd-looking boy with tangled hair and the Princess, who was carrying an old pair of boots.

Two-thirds down the Way, the trio stopped outside a small purple-painted shop with its window stacked so high with papers and books that it was impossible to see inside. On the door was the number 13, and over the window was the inscription: **Magykal** MANUSCRIPTORIUM AND SPELL CHECKERS INCORPORATED. Jillie Djinn, her ample figure almost filling the narrow doorway, regarded Jenna and Wolf Boy with a solemn air.

"The Hermetic Chamber is not to be entered by anyone who has not been inducted into the tenets of the Manuscriptorium," she informed them ponderously. "However, in these difficult circumstances I will make an exception for the Princess, but the Princess only. Indeed there is a possibility of precedence as I have reason to believe that some of the more ancient Queens have been admitted to the Chamber." With that, the door to the Manuscriptorium opened with a little *ping* and Jillie Djinn stepped inside.

"*What* did she say?" Wolf Boy asked Jenna.

"She said you can't come in," said Jenna.

"Oh."

"Well, not into the Hermetic Chamber anyway."

"The what?"

"The Hermetic Chamber. I don't know what it is, but Sep told me a bit about it. He's been in there."

"Maybe he's there now," said Wolf Boy, brightening.

"Well, I—I suppose he could be," said Jenna, hardly daring to hope.

"You go in and have a look. I'll wait outside like she said, and I'll see you and 412 in a minute. How about that?"

Jenna grinned. "Sounds good," she said, and she followed Jillie Djinn inside.

⊹⊹13⊹⊹
THE NAVIGATOR TIN

As Jenna walked into the front office of the Manuscriptorium, she heard a strange noise, rather like the stifled squeak of a distressed hamster, coming from behind the door. She peered around and saw the shadowy figure of a slightly chubby boy with a shock of black hair wedged behind the door handle. "Beetle?" she asked. "Is that you?"

The distressed hamster, who was indeed Beetle, holding the door open for his Chief Hermetic Scribe, replied with another squeak, which Jenna decided to take as a yes.

Jenna glanced about the Manuscriptorium with some trep-idation, but to her relief there was no sign of Marcia.

"This way, please, Jenna. We shall have to proceed without Madam Marcia." Jillie Djinn's voice came from somewhere at the back of the office and Jenna hurried toward it, skirting a large desk at the far end. She joined the Scribe beside a small door in a half wood, half glass partition wall. Jillie Djinn pushed open the door, and Jenna followed her into the Manuscriptorium itself.

A hushed silence hung over the Manuscriptorium, broken only by the sound of the scratching of pens and the occasional twang of a broken nib. Twenty-one scribes were hard at work copying out **Incantations** and **Invocations**, **Chants** and **Charms**, **Summonses** and **Spells** and even the occasional love letter for those who wanted to make an impression. Each scribe was perched at a high desk, laboring under a small pool of yellow light cast by one of the twenty-one oil lamps, which were suspended on long and sometimes dangerously frayed ropes from the vaulted ceiling.

The Chief Hermetic Scribe beckoned Jenna to follow her. Jenna found herself tiptoeing through the tall banks of desks while each scribe turned to look at the Princess, and wondered what she was doing and why she was carrying a pair of old boots. Twenty-one pairs of eyes watched Jenna follow Jillie Djinn into the narrow passageway that led to the Hermetic Chamber. Surprised glances were exchanged and a few eyebrows were raised, but no one said anything. As Jenna disappeared around the first corner of the passageway, the scratching of nibs on paper and parchment resumed its normal level.

The long, dark passage that led into the Hermetic Chamber turned back on itself seven times to cut short the flight of rogue spells and anything else that might try to escape from the Chamber. It also cut out the light, but Jenna followed the rustling sound of Jillie Djinn's silk robes and before long she stepped into a small, white, round room. The room was virtually empty; in the center was a simple table on which was placed a lit candle, but it was not the candle that drew Jenna's eye, it was the Glass—a horribly familiar, tall, dark Glass with an ornate frame propped up against the roughly plastered wall of the Hermetic Chamber.

Jillie Djinn saw Jenna's hopeful expression fade. There was no Septimus, just the sight of another Glass, which was the last thing she wanted to see again.

"From my studies," the Scribe said, "I understand that the early Glasses were simple, one-way-only openings. And from my calculations, I would say that this Glass is an early model and was made at the same time as the Glass in your room. I suspect this one actually comes *back* from that place."

"The place where Septimus is?" asked Jenna, her hopes rising yet again.

"Indeed. Wherever that may be. So tell me," Jillie said, "does this look the same as the Glass in the Queen's Room?"

"Well, it wasn't exactly in the Queen's Room," said Jenna.

"Oh." The Scribe sounded surprised. "Then where was it?" She picked up a pen and a notebook from the table and stood poised to write down the information. It was not forthcoming.

"I cannot say," said Jenna, adopting the Scribe's officious tone. She felt grumpy at the intrusive questions—the secrets of the Queen's Room were none of the Scribe's business.

Jillie Djinn looked cross but there was nothing she could do. "But this Glass does look the same as the other Glass—*wherever* that may be?" she persisted.

"I think so," said Jenna. "I can't remember all the details of the other one. But it's got the same black glass and . . . the same horrible feeling."

"That is not entirely illuminating," said Jillie Djinn, "for a Glass will, to some extent—depending on your susceptibility to such manifestations that may or may not be apparent—reflect your own expectations."

Jenna had an inkling of how Wolf Boy had felt earlier. "They do what?" she asked.

"You see what you expect to see," said Jillie Djinn briskly.

"Oh."

The Scribe sat down at the table and opened a drawer. She drew out a large leather-bound notebook, a sheaf of papers covered in columns of figures, a pen and a small bottle of green ink. "Thank you, Jenna," she said without looking up. "I believe I have enough information. I will now proceed."

Jenna waited patiently for a few minutes and then, when the Scribe showed no sign of stopping her scribbling, she asked, "So . . . Septimus—he'll come back here, will he?"

The Chief Hermetic Scribe looked up, already lost in another world of calculations and conjunctions. "Maybe yes. Maybe no. Who can say?"

"I thought *you* might," Jenna muttered crossly.

"I may," said Jillie Djinn sternly, "be able to say when my calculations are done."

"When *will* they be done?" asked Jenna anxiously, feeling that she could hardly wait another minute to see Septimus again and ask him what had happened.

"This time next year, if all goes well," replied the Scribe.

"This time *next year*?"

"If all goes well."

Jenna walked back into the front office in a bad mood. At the sight of the Princess, Beetle jumped up from his seat behind the desk. His ears suddenly turned bright red; he gave a hamster-style squeak and said, "Hey."

"What?" snapped Jenna.

"Um. I wondered . . ."

"*What?*"

"Um . . . Sep okay?"

"No, he's not," Jenna replied.

Beetle's black eyes looked worried. "I guessed not."

Jenna shot Beetle a glance. "How did you know?"

Beetle shrugged. "His boots. He's only got one pair of boots. And you've got them."

"Well, I'm going to give them back to him," said Jenna, making for the door. "I don't know how I'm going to find him, but I will—and I'm not waiting a whole year to do it either."

Beetle grinned. "Well, if that's all you need to do, it's easy."

"Oh, ha-ha, Beetle."

Beetle gulped. He didn't like making Jenna cross. "No, no, you don't understand. I'm not being funny. It's *true*. He's easy to find—now that he's **Imprinted** a dragon."

Jenna stopped, hand on the doorknob, and stared at Beetle. "How do you mean?" she asked slowly, not daring to hope that Beetle might have the answer that his Chief Hermetic Scribe did not.

"I mean that a dragon can always find his **Imprintor**," said Beetle. "All you have to do is a **Seek** and then, whizz bang, off he goes. Easy-peasy. You could go with him if you wanted, seeing as you're the Navigator. Just got to do a **Locum Tenens**, that's all. Problem solved." Beetle folded his arms with an air of satisfaction.

"Beetle, could you . . . um, could you say all that again? A bit slower this time, please?"

Beetle grinned at Jenna. "Wait a minute," he said. Beetle hurled himself through the door and vanished into the back of the Manuscriptorium. Just as Jenna was wondering what could have possibly happened to him, the door burst open and

Beetle was back, clutching a bright red and gold tin.

He held the tin out to Jenna. "Yours," he said.

"Mine?"

"Yep."

"Oh, well, thank you," said Jenna. A silence ensued while she looked at the tin and read the words LOKKJAW TOFFEE COMPANY FINEST TREACLE TOFFEES, printed in thick black letters on the lid. "Would you like a toffee, Beetle?" asked Jenna, trying to pry open the tin.

"Not toffees," said Beetle, coloring.

"Oh?"

"Here, let me get the lid off for you."

Jenna handed Beetle the tin. He struggled with it for a few seconds; then the lid popped off, and a flurry of what appeared to be bits of very thin leather, most of them either singed, crumpled or torn, tumbled to the floor. A strong smell of dragon filled the air. Flustered and hot, Beetle knelt to retrieve the pieces of sloughed dragon skin.

"Not toffees," muttered Beetle as he collected them.

"No, they're not," agreed Jenna.

"Navigator stuff," Beetle elaborated. He picked out a long piece of green leather and held it up, saying, **"Seek."** Then he found a charred red scrap and said, **"Ignite."** Lastly he found what he was looking for—a much-folded sheet of thin blue papery material—and said triumphantly, **"Locum Tenens!"**

"Oh. Well, thank you, Beetle. That's really nice of you."

Beetle went a deeper red. "It's okay. I mean . . . um, you see, after you became Sep's Navigator on Spit Fyre, I collected all the stuff I could find about Navigators and put it in my toffee tin. The one that my auntie gave me for MidWinter Feast Day. I hope you don't mind," he said a little sheepishly. "I mean, I hope you don't think I was being nosy or anything."

"No, of course not. I always meant to find out about being a Navigator but I never did. I think Sep thought—I mean, *thinks*—that being a Navigator means cutting Spit Fyre's toenails and cleaning out the dragon kennel."

Beetle laughed and then stopped as he remembered that something horrible had happened to Septimus. "So . . . would you like me to show you the **Locum**?" he asked.

"The what?"

"The **Locum Tenens**. It will let you take over from Sep, and Spit Fyre will do everything you ask after that—or, well, he'll do everything that he would have done for Sep."

"Not *everything* then." Jenna smiled.

"No. But it's a start. Then you can do the **Seek** and off you go to find Sep. Easy—well, it should be. Here it is." Beetle carefully took the thin blue piece of sloughed skin, unfolded it and flattened it out on the desk. "It's a bit complicated, but I reckon it will work okay."

Jenna stared at a mass of confusing symbols, which were written in a tight spiral that wound its way up to a burned corner. Complicated was putting it mildly. She had no idea where to start.

"I can translate it if you like," Beetle offered.

Jenna brightened. "Could you really?"

Beetle's ears went deep crimson again. "Yeah. Of course I could. No problem." He took a large magnifying glass from the drawer and squinted at the skin. "It's quite simple, really. You just need something belonging to the **Imprintor**—" Beetle stopped and glanced at Septimus's boots. "Which . . . um . . . you've got. You lay it . . . them in front of the dragon, I mean Spit Fyre, and then you put your hand on the dragon's nose, look into his eyes and tell him—look, I'll write this down so you don't forget." Beetle reached into his pocket and pulled out a crumpled card, then, taking his pen from its inkstand, he wrote a long string of words with great concentration.

Grateful, Jenna took the card. "Thank you, Beetle," she said. "Thank you so much."

"'S all right," said Beetle. "Anytime. Except. I mean. I hope there isn't any other time. I mean. I hope Sep's okay and . . . if you need any help . . ."

"Thanks, Beetle," said Jenna, a little tearfully. She ran for the door and wrenched it open. Wolf Boy was leaning up against the window, looking extremely bored. "Come on, 409," said Jenna, and she ran off toward the Great Arch at the end of Wizard Way. Soon she and Wolf Boy had disappeared into the blue shadows of the lapis lazuli archway.

Back at the Manuscriptorium, Beetle sat down and ran his hand over his forehead. He felt hot, and he knew it was not just because he always went red whenever he saw Jenna. As Beetle leaned back in his seat, a cold sweat ran over him from top to toe and the office began to spin.

The scribes inside the Manuscriptorium heard the crash as Beetle fell off his chair. Foxy, the son of the disgraced former Chief Hermetic Scribe, rushed out to find Beetle sprawled on the floor. The first thing that Foxy noticed was a single punc-ture mark, from which spread a brilliant red rash, in the gap of flesh between the top of Beetle's boots and his leggings.

"He's been bitten!" Foxy yelled to all the shocked scribes. "Now *Beetle's* got it!"

✢I4✢
MARCELLUS PYE

Marcellus Pye hated mornings. Not that you could easily tell when it was morning in the depths where he lurked. Night or day, a dim red light suffused the Old Way under the Castle. The light came from the globes of everlasting fire, which Marcellus now considered to be his greatest, and certainly most useful, achievement. The Old Way itself was lined with the large glass globes, which

Marcellus had placed there some two hundred years ago when he had decided he could no longer live above the ground, among the mortals of the Castle, for it was far too noisy, fast and bright, and he no longer had any interest in it whatsoever. Now he sat damp and shivering by a globe at the foot of the Great Chimney, feeling sorry for himself.

Marcellus knew it was morning because he had been out the night before on one of his nighttime walks under the Moat. Nowadays, Marcellus only needed to breathe every ten minutes or so, and it did not particularly bother him if he did not take a breath for thirty minutes. He enjoyed the feeling of weightlessness under the water; it took away the terrible pain of his old fragile bones for a while. He liked to wander through the soft mud, picking up the odd gold coin that someone had thrown into the Moat for luck.

When he returned, squeezing through a long-forgotten Moat inspection chamber, Marcellus had taken a tall candle, marked the hours off down its length and stuck a pin into the fourth mark as an alarm. Not because he was afraid he might fall asleep, for Marcellus Pye slept no more—indeed he could not remember when he had last slept—but because he feared that he would forget the Appointed Hour, which he had promised his mother faithfully he would not miss. The thought of his mother made Marcellus grimace as if he had just eaten an unexpectedly rotten piece of apple with a fat maggot sitting in it. He shuddered and huddled up inside his threadbare cloak for warmth. He placed the candle in a glass, then sat on the cold stone bench under the Great Chimney and watched the candle burn all through the night, while old Alchemical formulae drifted in and out of his mind in their usual haphazard and useless way.

Above him the Great Chimney rose like a pillar of darkness. Cold wind swirled inside it and howled the way the Creatures in Marcellus's flasks once used to howl to get out— now he knew how they had felt. As the candle steadily burned down, Marcellus cast the occasional anxious glance at the pin and stared up into the blackness of the Chimney. As the flame approached the pin he tapped his foot nervously and started to chew his fingernails, an old habit that he soon thought better of. They tasted disgusting.

To pass the time and take his mind off what he would soon have to do, Marcellus thought about his escapade the previous night. It had been many years since he'd been out in the open air and it had not been so bad. It had been cloudy and dark and there was a pleasant mist that had muffled any sounds. He had sat for a while on Snake Slipway and waited, but Mother had been wrong. No one had arrived. That hadn't bothered him too much for he liked the Slipway; it held happy memories of when he had lived there, next to the house where they now kept those silly paddleboats. He had sat at his old place by the water and checked that his gold pebbles were still there. It had been good to see a bit of gold again, even though they had been hidden under a coating of mud and were badly scratched, presumably by those stupid boats. Marcellus frowned. When he'd been a young man he had had a *real* boat. The river was deep then, not the silted-up and lazy waterway that it was now. True, the waters had been fast and treacherous, but in those days, boats were big with long and heavy keels, great swaths of sail and beautiful woodwork painted in gold and silver. Yes, thought Marcellus, boats were boats in those days. And the sun always shone. Always. Never a rainy day that he could remember. He sighed and stretched out his hands, looking with distaste at his withered fingers, the parchmentlike skin stretched tight and transparent across every lump and hollow of the old bones inside, and at his thick yellow fingernails that he no longer had the strength to cut. He grimaced again; he was completely and utterly revolting. Would nothing release him? A faint memory of hope came to him and then slipped from his mind. He was not surprised—he forgot everything nowadays.

There was a sudden *ping* as the pin fell from the burning candle and hit the glass. Wearily Marcellus got to his feet, and feeling inside the Great Chimney, he clutched at a rung and swung himself onto an iron ladder that was bolted to the old brick of the inside walls. Then, like a misshapen monkey, the Last Alchemist began the long climb up the inside of the Great Chimney.

It took Marcellus longer than he had expected to reach the top of the Chimney. It was more than an hour later when, exhausted and weak, he pulled himself onto the broad ledge that ran around the top. And there he sat, eyes shut tight, pale and wheezing, trying to catch his breath and hoping that he wasn't too late. Mother would be angry. After a couple of minutes Marcellus made himself open his eyes. He wished he hadn't. The faint light from his candle way down at the foot of the Chimney made him feel dizzy and sick with the thought of how far he had climbed. He shivered in the dank wind and drew his feet up under his cloak; his cracked old toes felt like blocks of ice. Maybe, thought Marcellus, they *were* blocks of ice.

It was then that Marcellus heard voices—young voices— echoing through the walls of the Chimney. Creaking like a rusty gate, the Alchemist pulled himself to his feet and shuffled toward what, at first, seemed to be a dark window in the wall of the Chimney. As he approached, it became clear that the window was no ordinary window, but more like a deep pool of the darkest water imaginable. Fumbling, Marcellus Pye took a large gold disc from underneath his tattered robes and touched it against an indentation at the top of the Glass. He peered into the darkness of the first Glass he had ever made and, for a moment, looked surprised. As if in a dream he raised his left hand and then frowned. After a few moments, Marcellus stuck out his tongue, and then he pounced.

With a speed that startled his old bones, Marcellus Pye threw himself toward the Glass and pushed his arms through it, his fingers clawing into empty space. The Alchemist cursed, he had missed. *Missed*. The boy—what *was* his name?—had escaped. With one last stretch he pushed farther through the Glass and, to his relief, grabbed hold of the boy's tunic. After that it was easy; he wrapped his fingers around the Apprentice belt—this was where the curved nails came in handy—and pulled. The boy put up a fight, but that was to be expected. What he had not expected was the sudden appearance of Esmeralda. His old brain was playing cruel tricks on him nowadays. But Marcellus pulled with all his strength, for this was a matter of life or death to him, and suddenly the boy's boots came off in Esmeralda's hands, and Septimus Heap—*that* was his name—came hurtling through the Glass.

✝I5✝
THE OLD WAY

Septimus *came through fighting.* He landed three punches on the Alchemist and numerous kicks that were of little use without his boots, but gave Septimus some satisfaction. He twisted and struggled and at one point he broke free of Marcellus's bony grasp and hurled himself back at the Glass, only to bounce off as though it were a wall of stone.

"Careful, Septimus," said Marcellus. He grabbed hold of Septimus's tunic and pulled him away. "You'll hurt yourself."

"Let go of me," Septimus yelled, frantically twisting and turning.

Marcellus Pye kept his grip on Septimus. "Look, Septimus," he said. "You'll want to be cautious up here. It's a long way down, you know. You don't want to fall, do you?"

Septimus stopped at the sound of his name. "How do you know who I am?" he asked.

Marcellus Pye smiled—pleased that he remembered now. "We go back a long way, Apprentice," he said.

Septimus wasn't sure if he liked the sound of that, but the old man's smile calmed him a little. He stood still for a moment and took stock. He was, as far as he could tell, in a dark cave with a very old man. It could be worse, but then again, it could be better. He could have his boots on for a start. And then Septimus's right foot found the edge of the ledge and he realized it could be a whole *lot* better.

"How high up are we?" Septimus asked, feeling along the edge with his foot, the familiar feeling of vertigo shooting through him.

"I couldn't rightly say, Apprentice. 'Tis a long climb, *that* I know. 'Tis a long climb down too, so we'd best be going."

Septimus shook his head and pulled away. "I'm not going anywhere," he said. "Not with you."

"Well, that be true, for you won't go anywhere if you don't come with me." Marcellus chuckled. "There surely is nowhere else to go up here."

"I'm going back through the Glass. Back to Jen. I am not going with *you*." Septimus pulled away from Marcellus's grasp and threw himself against the Glass again. And again he bounced straight off and staggered back, losing his balance.

"Steady now," said Marcellus, catching him just before he reached the edge of the ledge. "You will never return through the Glass," he told Septimus. "I made the Glass. Only I have the **Keye**."

Septimus was silent. He was terribly afraid that the disgusting old man was telling the truth. He looked at his Dragon Ring, which was glowing with its usual reassuring yellow light, but it gave him little comfort.

Marcellus Pye shuffled over to the edge of the ledge and eased himself onto the top rung of the ladder. Septimus heard Marcellus moving. He held up his ring to see what the old man was doing, and Marcellus smiled at him, his three long teeth shining yellow with spittle. "Come now, Septimus. Time to see where you'll be spending your Apprenticeship. No need to look so gloomy. There were not many who got the chance to be *my* Apprentice."

"Apprentice! I will *never* be your Apprentice. I am already Apprenticed. To the ExtraOrdinary Wizard. And she'll be here soon to get me back," said Septimus, sounding more certain than he felt.

"I doubt that very much," Marcellus replied. "Now, it's time you came down."

"I'm not going anywhere," Septimus said.

"Don't be foolish. You'll be cold and hungry after a few days up here and you'll be begging to come down. Either that or you'll fall off and be smashed to pieces. Not nice, believe me. Now, come, won't you?" Marcellus's voice took on a wheedling tone.

"No," said Septimus flatly. "Never."

For the second time that morning Marcellus's claw flashed out and grabbed hold of Septimus's tunic and pulled him. The strength of the old man surprised Septimus and caught him off guard. He lost his balance and toppled toward the ledge. "Careful!" shouted Marcellus, suddenly afraid that his prize might be short-lived.

But Septimus had learned from his dream. In his left hand he now clutched the **Flyte Charm**. Holding it between finger and thumb, he pointed the ancient golden arrow down the chimney, and taking a deep breath, he hurled himself into the darkness.

As Marcellus Pye watched in horror as his potential

Apprentice plummeted down, he saw the golden glint of something he remembered well. It was something that he himself had once possessed and indeed loved almost more than anything else in the world, apart from his dear wife, Broda. "The **Charm!**" he yelled. "You have my **Charm!**"

But Septimus was gone, deep into the depths of the Chimney.

It was not an easy **Flyte**. Although Septimus had practiced regularly with Alther, it had always been in open spaces. The cramped conditions in the Chimney were much more difficult—and frightening. But Septimus soon discovered that the secret to controlling his **Flyte** was to drop through the air as slowly as possible. Several minutes later, Septimus landed lightly at the foot of the Chimney.

Septimus took a few deep breaths and looked around. Behind him was the solid brick wall of the Chimney, but in front of him stretched what Septimus knew must be an ancient tunnel. The Castle had many layers of tunnels built at different times, but the brick-lined ones were the oldest. Septimus had a map of known tunnels on his bedroom wall, but this one was not on it. This was another one to add to the map when he got back—*if* he got back.

The flames in the lines of globes on either side of the

passageway gave a dull red glow and cast flickering shadows across the walls. Septimus whistled under his breath. This must be the **Everlasting Fyre** of the Alchemists that he had read about but had never believed was possible. One of these globes was at Septimus's feet and he could not resist having a closer look at it. He knelt and touched the globe. The thick green glass was cool, even when the flame came up to meet his hand and danced before it, like a small excitable dog wanting attention.

Septimus was shaken from his fascination by the rattle of the ladder, as far above him, Marcellus Pye heaved himself onto it and began the long climb down. With each step Marcellus took, the ladder shook.

Septimus panicked. He ran, his thick woolen socks slipping and sliding along the smooth limestone floor of the Old Way, and as he ran he scanned the featureless walls for any sign of a doorway or tunnel that might hold out some chance of escape. But there was nothing, no escape and nowhere to hide once the old man finally reached the ground—as Septimus knew he surely must soon.

The Old Way meandered along, roughly following the route of the ancient Alchemie Way far above it. Soon Septimus had rounded the first bend and was, to his great relief, out of sight of the Chimney. Breathless, Septimus slowed his pace and took more care to look around him. It was not long before he was rewarded with the welcome sight of a small archway set a few feet up the wall. Quickly Septimus scrambled up into the archway and found himself at the foot of a flight of shallow, twisting lapis lazuli steps.

Feeling hopeful at last, Septimus rushed up the steps. They twisted and turned, snaking ever upward. After some minutes Septimus slowed down to catch his breath. He listened for the sound of pursuing footsteps but, to his relief, he heard nothing. Taking the steps more slowly now, Septimus headed on, his dragon ring lighting the lapis lazuli, which stretched in front of him and behind with no end in sight. Septimus was just beginning to get the feeling that the steps went on forever when he rounded the last shallow bend and found himself face to face with another Glass. It stood dark and mysterious at the top of the steps. Septimus saw a dim reflection of himself, wide-eyed and scared, staring back. He took a deep breath and told himself to calm down.

Praying that the surface would sink beneath his fingertips as the last one had, Septimus pushed his hand against the Glass. It was as he had feared—the old man had told the truth. The Glass would not let him pass. It was as solid as a rock. Desperately, Septimus threw himself against it, pushing with all his strength. But it held firm, as unyielding as ever. Knowing that it would do no good, but unable to stop himself, Septimus hammered on the Glass with his fists, until his hands were bruised and his arms were sore. On the other side of the Glass, Jillie Djinn looked up from her notes and smiled. It was always satisfying when one's calculations worked out. She placed her pens in a neat row, folded her papers and briskly set off for the Palace.

Septimus aimed one last, despairing kick at the Glass and stubbed his toe. Feeling horribly close to tears, he raced back down the steps. The descent was easier, and soon Septimus saw the little archway ahead and the red glow of the globes of everlasting fire beyond. He jumped down from the arch only to hear, "Well met, Apprentice." The old man's quavering voice echoed along the tunnel as he shuffled doggedly toward him. "We are nearly at our destination."

The confidence in the old man's voice told Septimus that he was already trapped, but there was one last thing Septimus could do that would keep him out of the old man's clutches for just a little longer. Septimus reached into his Apprentice belt for his **Flyte Charm**. *It wasn't there.*

Septimus raced off. "There is nowhere to run," his slow

but relentless pursuer called out, and as Septimus rounded the last bend in the tunnel he knew the old man was telling the truth. He had reached the end. In front of him, the Way was barred by two tall golden doors. Two huge globes of **Everlasting Fyre**, almost as big as himself, were placed on either side of the doors. Septimus sat down between them and watched the flames dance toward him as though meeting an old friend. He could go no farther. All that was left for him was to listen to the halting footsteps, steadily shuffling closer.

"Ah, Apprentice," puffed the old man, smiling his tombstone-toothed smile. "I believe this was yours." He waved the **Flyte Charm** tantalizingly at Septimus. "One must be ever vigilant to keep the **Flyte Charm**, for it is a flighty thing and delights in eluding those who think they possess it. But now, once again, it appears to be mine."

"The **Flyte Charm** belongs to no one," said Septimus sulkily.

The old man chuckled. "A good answer, Apprentice, and a true one. I can see we will work well together. My congratulations—for you have passed your entrance examination. You have found the entrance . . . ha-ha. 'Tis my little joke. Ah, now where did I put my key?"

Septimus panicked and turned to run, but Marcellus's

practiced hand reached out, his bony claws wrapped around Septimus's Apprentice belt and hauled him back. Breathing laboriously with the effort, the old man pulled out his gold disc and placed it in a circular indentation in the center of the golden doors. Then he dragged Septimus away, saying, "Step back, Apprentice, this is dangerous work we do today."

The doors slowly opened to show a deep, mirrored blackness beyond. Septimus stared before him, unable to understand what he was seeing. Suspended within the blackness, gazing out at Marcellus Pye and Septimus, stood a young man with dark curly hair wearing black and red robes embroidered with a golden circle rather like the disc that the old man held in his hand. The expression on the young man's face was an odd mixture of shock and expectation.

With a look of infinite longing, for Marcellus knew he was face to face with something he could never be again—himself as a young man of thirty years—the old man gave Septimus a powerful shove and sent him sprawling into the icy blackness.

Silently the great doors closed behind him and Septimus was gone.

✢✢16✢✢
THE EMPTY PALACE

As *Septimus was being* pushed through the great gold doors, Gringe, the North Gate Gatekeeper, was crossing the low wooden bridge that led to the Palace.

"Mornin', miss," said Gringe to Hildegarde, the sub-Wizard on duty at the door that morning.

"Good morning, Mr. Gringe," Hildegarde replied.

"Say, you know

my name!" exclaimed Gringe.

"Well, of course I do, Mr. Gringe. Everyone knows the North Gate Gatekeeper. Can I help you with anything?"

"Well, see . . . it's a delicate matter and I can't be long, seein' as I left Mrs. Gringe on the Gate and she's in a bit of a state and she don't like countin' the money at the best of times so I got to get back sharpish and, well . . ."

"So what can I do for you?" asked Hildegarde.

"Oh. Yes, well, I've come to see Silas Heap. If you don't mind."

"No, I don't mind at all, Mr. Gringe. If you'd like to take a seat over there I'll send a messenger to find him." Hildegarde went over to the Long Walk and rang a small silver handbell that sat on an ancient ebony chest. The tinkling sound echoed down the empty corridor.

Gringe felt a little overawed by the Palace; he could not quite believe that Silas Heap actually lived there. He eyed the line of fragile-looking gold chairs with little red velvet seats that Hildegarde had waved him over to and decided they looked troublesome, so he scuttled off to the darkest corner of the hall, where he had spied a comfortable-looking armchair. The armchair was almost hidden in the shadows and sitting on it, unseen by Gringe, was the Ancient ghost of Godric, ex-doorkeeper, slumbering peacefully.

"No!" Hildegarde's voice rang out sharply. "Not that seat, Mr. Gringe!"

Gringe, who had been about to sit down, jumped up as though something had bitten him.

"There's someone sitting on that one," explained Hildegarde.

Gringe, who had never seen a ghost in his entire life and had no intention of starting now, shook his head sadly. It was true what they said; they were all bonkers up at the Palace. That was, of course, why it suited Silas Heap so well.

Gringe was relieved when Silas arrived with Maxie trailing behind him. Silas was a little flustered; he had been glad of an excuse to get away. He had left Marcia searching the Palace for Septimus, who appeared to have skipped an exam, much to Silas's admiration. At last his son was settling down and acting like a normal boy.

Gringe jumped up like a terrier after a rabbit. "Where is he?" he demanded.

"Not you as well," said Silas. "I've just told Marcia, I don't know. Anyway, it's perfectly normal. Personally, I don't blame the boy for missing the odd exam."

"What exam?" asked Gringe, taken aback.

"Well, it's not one I remember doing, that's for sure. Can't be that important. Anyway, what do *you* want him for? Has he been playing chicken on the drawbridge? That's boys for you." Silas chuckled indulgently, remembering the times when he and a gang of friends would run up the drawbridge as it was being raised and see who could jump at the very last moment and not fall in the Moat.

"Chickens?" asked Gringe, who was getting the usual disconnected feeling of living on a different planet from Silas Heap. "'As Simon been pestering chickens now? Not that I'm surprised, mind. He'll cause trouble wherever he goes, that boy will."

Now it was Silas's turn to be taken aback. "Simon?" he asked. "*Chickens?*"

Gringe was not to be put off. "Look 'ere, Heap. I just want to know where your Simon is."

"Well, wouldn't we all?" snapped Silas.

"Yeah. My Rupert would be after him, that's for sure. He's very attached to 'is little sister, is Rupert, and now she's run off again with that good-for-nothin'—"

"Run off with Simon?" asked Silas, who was beginning to share Gringe's opinion of his eldest son as a good-for-nothing. "How?"

"I dunno *how*. If I knew *how* I would've stopped her."

"Well, I'm sorry, Gringe," said Silas, who was tired of being blamed for Simon's misdeeds, "but I don't know where Simon is. And I'm sorry that your Lucy is still mixed up with him. She's a nice girl."

"Yeah, she is," said Gringe, the wind taken out of his sails. Gringe and Silas stood awkwardly in the Palace Hall for a moment. Then Gringe said, "Well, I'll be gettin' along then. Make sure you keep an eye on your Jenna, if that Simon's around."

"Jenna . . ." said Silas. "That's funny, I haven't seen her this morning. . . ."

"No? Well, I'd go look for 'er if I was you. I'll be off then. See you later for a game, if you like. I can lend you a set of Counters."

"I have my own set now, Gringe. No thanks to you," said Silas, sniffing. And then, remembering Sarah's instructions, he said, "Look, why don't you come up here? Make a change."

"Me? Up at the Palace twice in one day? Well, well." Gringe chuckled. "Thank you, Silas."

Silas walked Gringe to the Palace door. "See you later then," said Gringe. And then after a moment's thought: "We don't have no chickens on the drawbridge. Not even *one*."

"No. Of course you don't," said Silas, soothingly. He waved Gringe good-bye; then he and Maxie set off in search of Jenna.

Silas had as little luck finding Jenna as Marcia was having. Marcia strode down the Long Walk with Alther in tow. She threw open each door in turn, yelling, "Septimus? *Jenna!*" and then slammed the door with a crash, until Alther felt he could stand it no longer.

"There's something going on here, Marcia," he told her.

"Too right, Alther. Septimus? Jenna?" *Crash!*

"It's odd that Jenna is not around either."

"Quite. *Very* odd. Septimus? Jenna?" *Crash!*

"Well, Marcia, I'll be off for a while. There's someone I want to talk to about it."

"Talking is not going to do any good, Alther. I had enough talking this morning from that wretched Hermetic Scribe to last me a lifetime—and it's all a load of rubbish. I have to find

Septimus *now*. Septimus? Jenna?" *Crash!*

Alther left Marcia to her doors and flew off along the Long Walk. When he got to the end, he floated through to the turret on the east end of the Palace; then he wound himself around the spiral stairs and stood for a quiet moment on the top-floor landing, gathering his thoughts. Alther looked a little nervous. He brushed down his robe, which of course made no difference to its appearance at all, and tugged at his beard. Then he took a deep breath and, in an unusually respectful manner for Alther, he walked slowly through the wall into the Queen's Room.

The Queen jumped up.

"Please excuse me, Your Majesty," said Alther, rather formally, bowing his head slightly.

"I might do, Alther, I suppose," replied the Queen with a half smile. "If you tell me what it is that brings you here. And for goodness' sake don't call me Your Majesty. Just Cerys will do. I am only a Spirit like yourself. No more majesty for me, Alther." She sighed.

"I am wondering if you have seen your daughter this morning, Cerys?" asked Alther.

The Queen smiled fondly. "Yes, I have indeed," she replied.

"Ah. So she went to Zelda's, did she?"

"So you know about the Queen's Way too, Alther? It is no longer the secret it was."

"Your secret is safe with me. Did Jenna take the young ExtraOrdinary Apprentice with her by any chance?"

"He was with her. A nice-looking boy. How much you know, as ever. I always was in awe of you. You seemed to understand . . . well, everything."

"So she *did* take Septimus with her? Well, that explains it. Thank you, Cerys. I shall go tell Marcia to stop driving everyone mad."

"Dear, dear Marcia," mused the Queen. "She saved my Jenna, you know."

"I know," said Alther. They were both silent for a moment, remembering the day when they both entered ghosthood, until Alther shook himself out of his reverie. "I'll be off then. Thank you."

Alther turned to go and then said, "You know, Cerys, you should get out more. It's not good for you being stuck in this turret all the time. And you could think about **Appearing** to young Jenna. I know it's a big decision but . . ."

"I shall **Appear** when the Time is Right, Alther," the

Queen said, a little severely. "It is important for a Princess to discover things for herself and to prove herself worthy of becoming Queen—just as I had to. Meanwhile, I stay here to guard the Queen's Way from harm, as my mother did for me. And as Jenna will do for her own daughter."

"Goodness, Cerys. That's a little way off, I hope."

"I hope so too. But one must be eternally vigilant. Goodbye. Until we meet again . . ." The Queen drifted back to her chair by the ever-burning fire, and Alther knew that the audience was over. He floated through the wall with a vague feeling of dissatisfaction—but it was only later that Alther realized that the Queen had not given a straight answer to any of his questions.

Alther went to find Marcia to tell her to stop slamming doors because Jenna had taken Septimus to see Aunt Zelda. He found her arguing with Sir Hereward outside Jenna's room.

"If you don't stand aside, Sir Hereward," Marcia was telling the ghost angrily, "I shall be forced to **Pass Through**, make no mistake about it."

The old knight shook his head regretfully. "I do apologize, Your ExtraOrdinariness, but the Princess specifically instructed me not to let anyone into her room. Which, unfortunately, includes yourself. I only wish it were otherwise, but . . ."

"Oh, do stop dithering, Sir Hereward. I need to speak to her urgently. Now stand aside!"

"Oof!" Sir Hereward gasped as the sharp point of Marcia's purple python shoe poked through his armor-plated instep.

"Marcia!" said Alther sharply. "Marcia, there is no need for that. No need at all. Sir H does a very good job. Jenna is not in her room, she has taken Septimus to see Aunt Zelda."

"*What?*" Marcia stopped, her foot still firmly placed in Sir Hereward's. The knight pulled his foot away; then he drew his sword, placed it across the door and gave Marcia a withering look.

Marcia stepped back from the ghost. "But—but why on earth has she taken Septimus to see Aunt Zelda? Alther, this is terrible. Septimus must not leave my side today, he is in grave danger. And as for Jenna, you know as well as I do that she should stay in the Castle. Anything could happen to them traveling all that way across the Marshes. What *are* they thinking of?"

Alther glanced at Sir Hereward, unsure if he should say anything in the presence of the old knight, but the ghost was diplomatically staring at his feet. Sir Hereward knew when to blend into the background. All the same, Alther took Marcia by the elbow and led her away from the old ghost. As they walked up the corridor, Alther noticed to his dismay that Marcia was trembling.

As soon as he was sure they were out of earshot, Alther said, "Um, they haven't gone across the Marshes, Marcia. There is another Way." Alther felt awkward. The Queen's Way was a secret kept by the Queens and their descendants. Many years ago, when he himself was ExtraOrdinary Wizard, Alther had stumbled across the Queen's Way at Keeper's Cottage when he had been looking for Aunt Zelda's predecessor, Betty Crackle. Betty had left the Way open, and Alther had, to his shock, found himself in the Queen's Room in the company of Queen Matilda, Cerys's fearsome grandmother. He had soon made his way back to Keeper's Cottage, but not before Queen Matilda had extracted a terrible promise from him never to divulge the secret of the Way.

"Well, going through the Port is no better, Alther."

"It's not through the Port, Marcia. It is much quicker— and safer—than that."

Marcia knew her old tutor well enough to tell when he was

keeping something from her. "You know something, don't you?" she asked. "You know something and you're not telling."

Alther nodded. "I am sorry, Marcia, I swore I would never tell. It is a secret of the Queens."

"It's obviously not a secret from Septimus," Marcia said.

"No. Well, Septimus seems to be different," said Alther.

"That's the trouble, Alther," replied Marcia, her voice rising in what sounded to Alther suspiciously like a panic. "He *is* different. He's different enough to have written me a note *five hundred years ago.*"

✛ 17 ✛
PALACE GHOSTS

With great relief, Sir Hereward had watched Marcia and Alther set off down the wide corridor, take a right turn at the end and disappear from sight.

Behind the doors of Jenna's bedroom, another, altogether more unpleasant ghost took her ear from the door, a smile playing across her thin lips. So the troublesome young Princess had run off to the Marram Marshes with the Apprentice, had she? And not done what she had promised by the sound of it. She would pay for this, and the Apprentice need not think he had gotten away with anything either.

Quickly the ghost of Queen Etheldredda crossed the floor to a small roughly made box where Jenna kept all her treasures. The ghost perused the box and then **Caused** the lid to silently open. Poking a long and bony finger through Jenna's possessions, Etheldredda found what she was looking for and then did something that no ghost should be able to do—she picked up the object, a small silver ball inscribed with the letters *I.P.*—and placed it in her pocket. Then, with a knowing smile, the ghost of Queen Etheldredda walked through the door and **Passed Through** the much put-upon Sir Hereward.

The ghost of Queen Cerys gave every appearance of dozing in her fireside chair, so when the ghost of Queen Etheldredda sidled in and headed straight for the potion cupboard, she was most surprised to suddenly find her way barred by a very determined descendant.

"You may *not* pass," Cerys told Etheldredda coldly.

"Don't be ridiculous, child. I have every right to walk the Queen's Way. And I intend to do so. Stand aside."

"I will not."

"You will!" The angry Etheldredda pushed her way through. Cerys, who gasped—not only from the shock of being **Passed Through**, but also from the surprisingly solid feeling of Etheldredda—recovered just in time to **Cause** the potion cupboard door to jam shut.

"Two may play at that game," snapped Etheldredda, **Causing** the door to reopen.

"But only one may win," replied Cerys, **Causing** the door to close.

"Indeed, child. I am glad you see sense." Etheldredda **Caused** the door to open.

"I intend to protect my daughter. You shall not stop me," Cerys declared angrily, and **Caused** the door again to slam shut. Then, before Etheldredda could retaliate, Cerys began to spin. Faster and faster she turned, like a whirlwind, revolving the air in the turret with her until, despite herself, Etheldredda was caught up in the currents and whirled around the small circular room like an autumn leaf caught up in a windy corner.

"Go!" yelled Cerys. With that, Queen Etheldredda was

hurled from the room, out of the turret and across the lawns toward the river, where she landed in the middle of one of Billy Pot's careful arrangements of dragon droppings. Angrily, she picked herself out of the mess and haughtily floated toward the riverbank, where the ghostly Royal Barge awaited her.

Head held high and without a backward glance, Queen Etheldredda walked up the gangplank. As she took her place upon the dais, the ghostly barge began to move. Silently it glided away from the Palace gardens and headed for the middle of the river, where it drifted downstream, **Passing Through** a blockade of boats, which for some reason seemed to be on fire. Queen Etheldredda tutted to herself at the lawlessness of the Castle and comforted herself that it would not be so for much longer. She would see to that.

With a satisfied smile, Queen Etheldredda sat back to enjoy the journey. There was, thought the ghost, more than one way of getting to Keeper's Cottage.

As Queen Etheldredda was being hurled from the turret, Alther was leading Marcia down one of the many flights of back stairs that led to the Long Walk. "What exactly do you mean, Marcia—he wrote you a note nearly five hundred years ago?"

"This morning, Alther . . . I opened the **Sealed** shelf."

"You did *what?*"

"You know, you showed me once how to do it. There was something there I had to see."

"Not the *I, Marcellus?*" Alther had become increasingly pale over the previous half hour. Now he went almost translucent.

Marcia nodded.

"You opened the *I, Marcellus?* But it's been **Sealed** since before the Tunnels were **Frozen**."

"I know, I *know*, but it was a risk I had to take. I saw . . . I saw something in Jillie Djinn's calculations for Septimus's Prediction Practical."

"Huh. That woman's always calculating something," said Alther. "I caught her working out the percentage of wear on her new shoes yesterday. Wanted to know exactly how long they were going to last."

"That does not surprise me, Alther. Personally, she drives me nuts. I'm meant to be at the Manuscriptorium now listening to more of her tedious theories. Oh, what a *mess*."

"Marcia," said Alther, "what exactly did you find in the *I, Marcellus?*"

"I found . . ." Marcia started, and then ground to a halt as her voice choked up. "Oh, it was *awful*."

"What did you find?" asked Alther gently.

"I found a note from Septimus. It was addressed to me."

"Marcia, are you *sure*?"

"Yes. You know how Septimus always signs his name with that complicated squiggle at the end—I think it's meant to be a number seven?"

"Yes," said Alther. "It's terribly affected, but the young do have the most peculiar signatures nowadays. I just hope he settles on something more down-to-earth when he gets a bit older."

"He can have the weirdest signature he wants, Alther. He can sign his name in strawberry jam standing on his head if he wants to—I really don't mind. But I doubt we'll ever see him get older . . . not in this Time anyway."

Alther was silent. He was stunned, for he knew that Marcia was not one to exaggerate. Marcia was silent too, because she had just realized that what she had said was probably true.

"What did the note say?" asked Alther quietly. They had reached the foot of the stairs and stopped in the curtained darkness of the doorway. A brief squall of chill rain battered a

skylight high above them, and Marcia shivered as she brought
out a scrap of very fragile old paper. Carefully, for the paper
was threatening to disintegrate into a pile of dust, Marcia
unfolded the note, and squinting in the dim light, she read
aloud the words that Septimus had written all those years ago.

> *Dear Marcia,*
>
> *I know that one day you will find this note*
> *because when I don't come back I know you will*
> *look everywhere in the Library and through all*
> *the Alchemie things that are there. I've never seen*
> *Marcellus's book in the Library but I bet you*
> *know where it is. It is probably in that **Sealed***
> *shelf. I hope you find it soon after I have gone so*
> *that you do not worry about me too much and*
> *you can tell everyone where I am. I am going to*
> *put it in the Almanac section of Marcellus's*
> *book. He is writing it for our Time—I mean,*
> *your Time. It is not my Time anymore. I will put*
> *it in the day that I went so you will know where*
> *to look for it. I hope the paper beetles don't eat it.*
>
> *I want to say thank you as I really liked*

*being your Apprentice and I wish I still was, but
I am Apprenticed to Marcellus Pye now. You
must not worry as it is not so bad, but I miss
you all and if you can by any chance come get
me (but I don't know how you can), I would be
SO happy.*

   I have to go now, Marcellus is coming.

   *I came here through a Glass. Jenna will
tell you.*

Love,

Septimus xxx

"Oh," whispered Alther.

✛ 18 ✛
THE DRAGON KENNEL

Jenna and Wolf Boy *were* outside Spit
Fyre's kennel. Although the kennel
was only a couple of months old, the
door had already acquired a battered
look and was showing some serious
splits that had been repaired by
metal ties.

"You take one side of the
bar and I'll take the other,"
Jenna told Wolf Boy. "They're
really heavy. Sep . . . well, Sep
always gets someone to
help him. Usually
me." The door was

barred with three broad iron bars, and it was the top one of these that Jenna and Wolf Boy were about to lift off.

Septimus had not liked keeping Spit Fyre locked up at night, but he had been forced to give in after a deputation of Wizards had refused to leave Marcia's rooms until something was done. Up until then, Spit Fyre had been allowed the run of the Wizard Tower courtyard, but the combination of a free-range young dragon and two-foot-high piles of dragon droppings had led to trouble. Soon there was scarcely a Wizard who, late at night, had not inadvertently walked into one of these piles and lost a boot or, even worse, fallen in headfirst and had to be pulled out. Spit Fyre had also developed a taste for the blue woolen cloaks worn by the Ordinary Wizards, and the dragon enjoyed nothing more than a quick chase around the courtyard in pursuit of a tasty-looking cloak to work up an appetite.

The kennel was reverberating to the sound of the young dragon's snores, for Spit Fyre, who had reached the dragon equivalent of a teenager, had recently begun to sleep late in the mornings. But as Wolf Boy and Jenna lifted the bar and placed it carefully on the ground, Spit Fyre woke up. With a great crash, his tail smashed against the rafters of the roof, and a loud crack of splintering wood resounded through the air. Wolf Boy jumped back in shock, but Jenna, who had heard worse noises by far coming from Spit Fyre's kennel, stood her ground.

"Sorry, Jenna," said Wolf Boy, a little shamefaced. "Wasn't expecting that. Here, I can do the other two." To Jenna's surprise, Wolf Boy heaved off the badly bent middle bar and the lowest bar all by himself and dropped them onto the ground with a clang. Inside the kennel came an answering smash as Spit Fyre thumped his tail with excitement at the prospect of being let out.

Now all Jenna had to do was unlock the kennel door. She fetched the large key that hung on a hook and placed it in the big brass keyhole. "The door opens outward," she told Wolf Boy. "So you have to be careful it doesn't smash into you when Spit Fyre comes out. And keep your feet out of the way too, as he likes to tread on your toes. Sep always said—says— he does it by accident, but I reckon Spit Fyre does it on purpose. He thinks it's a game, he likes the way people hop around yelling and holding their feet." Jenna turned the key, the door crashed open and Spit Fyre hurtled forward, neck outstretched to catch the cool morning air, claws clattering down the ramp. At the foot of the ramp the young dragon stopped and looked around as if puzzled. He tilted his head to one side and then, seeming a little dejected, he sat down unusually quietly.

Spit Fyre was growing into a handsome young dragon. Although he was still only about fifteen feet long—half his eventual adult size—he already looked large and powerful. His brilliant green scales shone in the early-morning drizzle and rippled across his huge shoulder muscles as he shifted position slightly. His leathery greenish-brown wings were neatly folded on either side of the row of thick black spines that ran along his backbone, from just behind his ears to the very tip of his tail. Spit Fyre's emerald-green eyes flashed and his wide nostrils flared as he sniffed the air, searching for the scent of Septimus Heap, his Imprintor.

Keeping a tight hold on Septimus's boots, Jenna approached Spit Fyre with some caution, careful not to make any sudden movements, for he could be unpredictable in the mornings. But the dragon did not react as Jenna walked slowly up to him and laid her hand on the cool scales of his neck. "Septimus is not here, Spit Fyre," she said gently. "I'm here in his place."

Spit Fyre regarded Jenna suspiciously and sniffed the boots. Then he snorted and blew out a large greenish-gray blob of dragon snot, which shot straight across the courtyard and landed with a resounding *splat* on one of the second-floor windows of the Wizard Tower. A moment later the window was thrown open and an angry Wizard poked her head out. "Hey!" she yelled. "Can't you keep that beast under control? It took me three days to scrape the last stuff off," and then, seeing that it was Jenna rather than Septimus with the dragon, "Oh. Oh, dear. Sorry, Your Majesty," and slammed the window closed.

"*Don't* call me that," Jenna muttered, and then, seeing Wolf Boy's quizzical look, she said, "I'm *not* Queen. They shouldn't call me that. And I don't ever want to be Queen either." Wolf Boy looked surprised but he said nothing, which is generally what Wolf Boy did when things became a little tricky.

"I've got to do the **Locum Tenens** now, 409," said Jenna, looking a little anxious. "I hope it works."

"'Course it'll work," said Wolf Boy, who was of the opinion that Jenna could do anything that she wanted to. He watched Jenna take Beetle's scruffy card of instructions from her tunic pocket and read them slowly, then open an old toffee tin, draw out a fragile sheet of blue dragon skin, and carefully unfold it. Jenna sat down quietly beside Septimus's boots and Wolf Boy saw her lips move as she read the words on the dragon skin over and over, painstakingly memorizing them. He was surprised at how long it took—almost as long as he had taken to read one of Aunt Zelda's potion recipes. Wolf Boy knew there wasn't much he could do to help Jenna with the **Locum Tenens**, but he thought he could try out the skills he had learned when he had lived with the wolverines in the Forest.

And so Wolf Boy sat down about ten feet in front of Spit Fyre and very deliberately fixed his gaze on the dragon, willing him to stay calm and quiet. Spit Fyre caught Wolf Boy's glance and quickly looked away, but it was enough. The dragon knew he was being **Watched**. He shifted about uncomfortably, but he did not move away. Spit Fyre sat unusually still in the soft drizzle, hoping that soon his **Imprintor** would appear and put an end to the unnerving two-legged wolverine who would not stop staring at him.

At last Jenna was sure that she could remember the **Locum Tenens**. She picked up Septimus's boots and laid them at Spit

Fyre's feet. Still quiet, Spit Fyre sniffed the boots. Then he reared up his head and blew out a long, hot breath. Wolf Boy felt sick. He was not used to the smell of dragon breath, which is best described as a combination of the stench of burning rubber and the stink of old socks, with overtones of a hamster cage in dire need of a cleaning.

Jenna stood on tiptoe and rested her hand on Spit Fyre's nose. "Look at me, Spit Fyre," she said. Spit Fyre looked at his feet, he looked at the sky, he looked at his claws and then, twisting his head back, he suddenly found the tip of his tail extremely interesting. "Spit Fyre," said Jenna, insistent, "look at me—*please.*"

Something in Jenna's voice caught Spit Fyre's attention. He put his head to one side and looked at her. Jenna kept her hand firmly on the dragon's wet and sticky nose. Her hand was trembling. This was her only chance of finding Septimus and it all depended on Spit Fyre, who was not the most dependable of creatures. Spit Fyre regarded Jenna warily. Did she have his breakfast with her? he wondered.

Jenna held Spit Fyre's gaze. Then she took a deep breath and slowly began. "Spit Fyre, look at me and I will tell you the five things you must understand. First: Spit Fyre, in good faith

I tell you that your Imprintor is lost." Spit Fyre cocked his head and hoped it wasn't porridge for breakfast again.

"Second: Spit Fyre, in good faith I bring you that which belongs to your Imprintor." Spit Fyre closed his eyes and decided a couple of chickens would be very tasty.

"Open your eyes, Spit Fyre," said Jenna sternly. Spit Fyre opened his eyes. What was all the fuss about?

"Third: Spit Fyre, in good faith I tell you that I am your Navigator." Spit Fyre thought that he wouldn't mind chickens *and* porridge that morning. Preferably all mixed together in a big bucket.

"Fourth: Spit Fyre, in good faith I ask you to accept me as your Locum Imprintor." Spit Fyre wondered if they might give him three chickens with his porridge, since breakfast was late.

"Fifth: Spit Fyre, in good faith I beseech you to find your true Imprintor, through fire and water, earth and air, wherever he may be." Jenna held Spit Fyre's gaze for the required thirteen seconds and then looked away. Spit Fyre wondered if he had to find Septimus before or after breakfast. He hoped it was after. Then he picked up Septimus's boots—and ate them.

"Spit Fyre!" yelled Jenna. "*Give them back!*" She grabbed at a fast-disappearing bootlace and pulled. Spit Fyre pulled his head back. He liked tug-of-war games and this seemed like a good one. He had always thought that Septimus's boots looked tasty. Jenna tugged hard, there was a *snap* and she was left holding nothing more than the damp, frayed end of a bootlace. Spit Fyre swallowed, gave a satisfied burp and then jumped in surprise.

A deafening clanging and banging had just started up outside the Great Arch, along with some loud and threatening whoops and screams. Wolf Boy leaped to his feet in consternation. He did not like sudden loud noises—they reminded him too much of the Young Army's midnight wake-up call.

"It's the RatStranglers," said Jenna. "They must have found a rat. Poor creature. Doesn't stand a chance now. You'd think people would have something better to do than run around the Castle all day banging trash can lids and killing rats."

The noise became louder as the RatStranglers started up their chant. "Rats, rats, *get* the rats. Rats, rats, *kill* the rats! Rat trap, rat trap, splat, splat, *splat!*" It echoed around the Wizard Tower courtyard, and numerous Wizards threw open their windows to see what the noise was. Then, with a roar, the assorted mob of RatStranglers surged through the Great Arch in pursuit of their quarry: two desperate rats in full flight, one dragging the other behind it.

Why the rats headed for the dragon kennel. Jenna did not know, but they scooted across the courtyard, ignoring the relative safety of the well and two convenient drains. They dived between Spit Fyre's feet, shot up the ramp of the kennel and hurled themselves deep into the pungent straw covering the kennel floor.

In a moment the RatStranglers had surrounded the kennel, banging their lids and chanting. Spit Fyre snorted in dismay. No dragon likes to be surrounded, especially by a raucous mob banging lids and screaming. Dragons generally have a surprisingly subtle ear for music and enjoy the finer kinds of classical music and plainsong; indeed, many an isolated monastery has been surprised to find a dragon regularly turning up to listen to the evening's Gregorian chant. Spit Fyre was no exception. The banging made his delicate dragon ears hurt and the chanting was not even in tune. With a roar he rounded on the RatStranglers, breathing hot dragon breath over them.

Most people would have given up at this point, and some of

the hangers-on who had just come along for a laugh and a bit of fun took off, but the bulk of the RatStranglers stayed. They had never yet lost a rat and they did not intend to start now.

Jenna was furious. "How dare you?" she yelled. "How dare you come in here chasing two poor rats and frightening a young dragon. How *dare* you?" The noise subsided as the RatStranglers, who in their excitement had not noticed the Princess, put down their lids. The chant petered out into an embarrassed silence.

The leader of the RatStranglers, an earnest-looking young man sporting a badge showing a fearsome rat with huge yellow fangs dripping with blood, stepped forward. "We are doing our civic duty, Your Princessness. Rats are filthy vermin, they spread disease—"

At this Jenna laughed. "That's ridiculous. They're as clean as you or I. And it's humans that spread disease, not *rats*."

"We beg to differ, Princess," said the young man. "The Sickenesse that has come to the Castle has been brought by the rats. They must be destroyed."

"That's crazy," said Jenna, shaking her head in disbelief. "You're just chasing rats because you like killing defenseless animals. It's horrible."

"*You* should be grateful to us," a thin, reedy voice piped up from the back of the crowd.

"Why?" asked Jenna, catching the threat in the voice.

"Because some people say that *you* have brought the Sickenesse, Princess."

"*Me?*" Jenna was incredulous.

"They say it came on your Dragon Boat. They say it's a pity that that *mutant* ship wasn't left on the bottom of the Moat where it belongs." This was accompanied by a general muttering of agreement from the back of the throng, but no one near Jenna dared say anything.

Jenna was shocked into silence and the RatStranglers took her silence for permission to invade Spit Fyre's kennel. They swarmed up the ramp, and in no time at all they were raking through the straw, searching for the rats. Jenna and Wolf Boy were overwhelmed by sheer numbers and there was nothing they could do—but Spit Fyre decided otherwise. As the RatStranglers crowded past him, he swung his tail angrily and sent the owner of the reedy voice flying into a pile of dragon droppings at the back of the kennel. Then with a loud creaking as the tough dragon skin stretched out from its creases— accompanied by the smell of stale dragon sweat—Spit Fyre unfurled his wings and raised them high into the air, casting a shadow across the dragon kennel. The RatStranglers stopped their hunt and watched in amazement as Spit Fyre bowed his head toward Jenna, as if inviting her to sit where Septimus always sat—just behind his neck between his shoulders.

Afraid that Spit Fyre might change his mind any minute, Jenna scrambled up into Septimus's place and hauled Wolf Boy up behind her, into the Navigator's position where she usually sat. Then, remembering the instructions that Alther had given Septimus on Spit Fyre's **FirstFlyte**, she gave the dragon two kicks on the right side. They worked; Spit Fyre beat his wings slowly, once, twice, and on the third stroke, Jenna felt the dragon's muscles tense as he rose just a few inches off the ground, keeping himself steady and controlled in the close confines of the Wizard Tower courtyard. Then, as Spit Fyre hovered for a brief moment and prepared to accelerate, a yell came from one of the RatStranglers: "There they are! Catch 'em!"

As Spit Fyre left the ground, he was carrying more passengers than he had bargained for. Hanging from the barb on the tip of his tail were two terrified rats.

✦ 19 ✦
THE RATSTRANGLERS

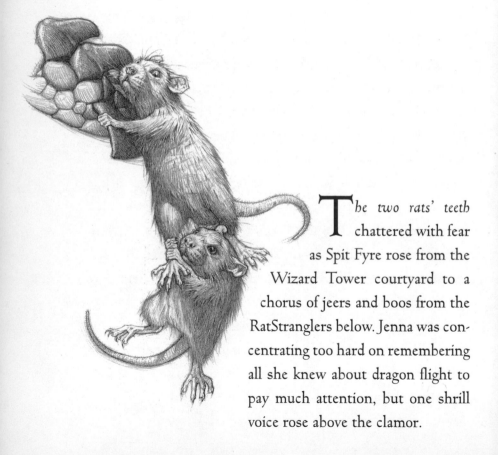

The two rats' teeth chattered with fear as Spit Fyre rose from the Wizard Tower courtyard to a chorus of jeers and boos from the RatStranglers below. Jenna was concentrating too hard on remembering all she knew about dragon flight to pay much attention, but one shrill voice rose above the clamor.

"She's in league with them. Didn't I tell you? It's her and that boat she brought here. Come on, boys." Although the voice belonged to a tall, spiky-looking woman, the Rat-Stranglers were mostly men and boys. "Come on, let's go sink it once and for all." There was an answering howl from the rest of the RatStranglers.

Spit Fyre flew higher, and Jenna and Wolf Boy saw the mob surge through the Great Arch and head off along the narrow lane that led to the boatyard. Underneath the dragon, the rats swayed perilously.

"Dawnie," gasped the larger rat that was hanging on to Spit Fyre's tail, while the shorter, more rotund rat clutched on to his ankles. "Dawnie, your claws are *killing* me. Do you have to hold on quite so tight?"

"Do you think I am doing this for the fun of it, Stanley? What do you suggest I do? Let go and get killed by those fiends down there? Is that what you want?"

"Ouch. No. Don't be silly, dear. I just wondered if you could loosen your grip a little. I can't feel my feet."

Spit Fyre swooped down low over the mob members, one of whom let fly a well-aimed trash can lid. It skimmed toward the rats, spinning in the air like a flying circular saw. Stanley shut his eyes. This was it, he thought. What a way to go, seen off by a flying trash can lid.

But Spit Fyre had seen the missile hurtling toward them, and the last few weeks of avoidance training with Septimus, which he had hated, as it had involved Beetle throwing all manner of things at him, paid off. Like a true professional, Spit Fyre dodged the lid and for good measure gave it a hefty swipe with his tail.

"Aargh, Stanley! We're going to dieeeeeee . . ." Dawnie screamed. Wolf Boy, who was feeling quite sick, felt some sympathy for Dawnie.

Jenna took Spit Fyre at full speed to the boatyard. They flew over the RatStranglers and Jenna reckoned they had about five minutes before the mob arrived at the boatyard. Five minutes in which Jenna had to land Spit Fyre, get over to the Dragon House and somehow make it secure.

Jannit Maarten was not at all pleased when she saw Spit Fyre heading toward her boatyard. The last time the dragon had turned up had been a complete disaster, brought about by the Heaps, as usual. And now here it was again, no doubt with one of the Heap clan on board. As Spit Fyre flew low into the boatyard Jannit tried to direct the dragon to an empty space recently occupied by the Port barge that Jannit and Rupert

Gringe had just launched. Spit Fyre ignored Jannit. He didn't like people waving their arms at him and shouting, "Over here, over *here*! Oh, gunwales and gimlets, what *is* the idiot creature doing?"

Spit Fyre flew right over Jannit's head, missing her by a hairbreadth, and landed on the pilothouse of an old trawler, which was in a rather delicate state. The pilothouse could just about withstand the odd seagull landing on it, but it had no chance against a dragon whose total weight in seagulls was exactly 764. With a loud crack, the pilothouse collapsed, and Spit Fyre and his passengers found themselves in a pool of stagnant water in the trawler's hull.

"Up, Spit Fyre, up!" yelled Jenna, giving Spit Fyre a hefty kick on the right. With some difficulty, accompanied by a lot of squeaking from the end of his tail, Spit Fyre flapped and clawed his way out of the hull in a rather undignified fashion and landed beside the trawler.

"Look what you've done!" protested Jannit, arriving breath-less beside the wreckage. "We could have repaired that. Rupert was going to make a start on it tomorrow. *Now* look at it."

"I'm sorry, Jannit," Jenna apologized as she slipped down from Spit Fyre's neck. "I really am. But the RatStranglers are on their way to smash up the Dragon Boat."

"Whatever for? She's not a rat."

"I know," said Jenna rather curtly. Leaving Wolf Boy to keep hold of Spit Fyre, Jenna ran off toward the Dragon House.

Jannit set off in pursuit. "Jenna!" she called out to her. "*Jenna!*" But Jenna did not stop. Jannit was annoyed; she didn't like the sound of this. It was true that she had not been exactly thrilled when the half boat, half dragon had turned up unannounced in the middle of the night a few months back. But now that the Dragon Boat was in her boatyard, Jannit considered it to be her responsibility, and no one messed around with Jannit Maarten's boats, especially not a bunch of thugs calling themselves RatStranglers. Jannit liked rats.

"Rupert," said Jannit, waylaying Rupert Gringe, who was busy sawing wood, "take as many yard hands with you as you can find and close the tunnel gates. Put the bar across. Quick!" Rupert Gringe dropped what he was doing and went to do Jannit's bidding at once. He knew when Jannit meant business.

The Dragon Boat lay at the end of the Cut, until recently a dead-end piece of water that lay to the side of the boatyard, which had ended at the blank cliff face of the Castle wall. Ever since Jannit had had the boatyard she had wondered what the point of the Cut was. Three months ago she had found out. She had woken in the middle of the night to find that a huge cavern had opened up deep into the wall at the end of the Cut. Not just any old cavern either, but a towering lapis lazuli hall, covered in golden hieroglyphs. Jannit did not go in for opu-lence and thought the whole thing was a bit of an embarrass-ment, but she could not help being impressed all the same. She doubted that any other boatyard in the world had such a place—or such a boat—and that made her proud.

What dismayed Jannit was that although she, Rupert Gringe and Nicko had repaired the Dragon Boat beautifully—so that you would never know the dragon had been hit by two **ThunderFlashes** and had sunk to the bottom of the Moat—the creature itself was still unconscious. The dragon lay with her head resting on the cool marble walkway on the side of the Dragon House, her great green eyes closed, her breathing quiet and slow. Her tail had been carefully placed on a marble ledge at the back of the Dragon House, neatly coiled by Jannit and Nicko, like a huge piece of green rope, and it had not moved since.

A great clang reverberated through the yard as Rupert put the bar in place across the doors to the tunnel. A moment later an even louder clanging and banging started up. The RatStranglers had arrived just in time to see the doors closed against them.

"I'm not having that unruly mob in here wrecking my boats." said Jannit, catching up with Jenna. They squeezed around a large stack of planks piled up against the great Castle wall, then they ran along a narrow path between two tall-masted boats in need of new rigging and quickly reached the entrance of the Dragon House. With angry shouts and the sound of battering on the boatyard doors echoing across the yard, Jenna and Jannit entered the quiet shadows of the Dragon House.

The Dragon Boat lay still, with her great head resting on Jannit's one and only Persian rug, now somewhat charred, which was laid on the marble walkway along the side. Jenna knelt down and placed her hand on the creature's head, but the dragon, as ever, did not move. Her smooth scales felt cool to the touch and the emerald eyes under her thick dark green eyelids did not flutter as Jenna gently stroked them.

Jannit stood back and watched Jenna. Even at a time like

this, Jannit did not like to interrupt whatever was going on between Jenna and the Dragon Boat. She was used to Jenna's moments with the dragon, but usually she kept well out of the way, for she felt as if she would be intruding if she came too near. Jannit had noticed that the boatyard often fell silent when Jenna put her hand on the dragon, but not today. The sounds of the RatStranglers systematically ramming the boatyard door filled the air. Jannit wondered what Jenna thought she was doing, wasting time stroking the dragon when they ought to be setting up some kind of barricade in front of the Dragon House. But she did not say so, for Jannit had, over the last few months, become a little in awe of Jenna and her determination to wake the Dragon Boat.

Suddenly Jenna sprang to her feet. "I think I heard her," she said, her eyes bright with excitement.

"What?" asked Jannit, distracted by some inventive insults that Rupert Gringe was hurling at the RatStranglers.

"The *dragon*. She was very faint, but I'm sure I did. We have to **Seal** the Dragon House."

"How, exactly?" snapped Jannit, worried now, realizing that the mob was not going to go away and was unlikely to stop at smashing up just the Dragon Boat.

"The way it was opened. With **Fyre**—Dragon **Fyre**." And then Jenna's face fell as she remembered. "Oh," she said. "Spit Fyre can't do **Fyre**."

"Yes, he can," said Jannit, who had heard all about Spit Fyre's hatching from Nicko. "Did it when he hatched."

"That's just Infant **Fyre**. All dragons do that when they're first hatched."

The noise of splintering wood echoed through the boatyard.

"They're nearly through the doors," said Jannit in her matter-of-fact tone. "Not much time left. Excuse me, I'm going to go get my ax. If they're looking for trouble, they're going to find it."

Jenna knew that there was nothing else to be done; she must try to **Ignite** Spit Fyre. Taking her Navigator's toffee tin from her tunic pocket, Jenna opened it and fished out the red piece of dragon skin. She unfolded it and, to her surprise and dismay, there was only one word on it: **Ignite**. How could that possibly be enough?

But Jenna knew she had to try. She raced back to Spit Fyre.

"Excuse me, 409," said Jenna, breathless, clambering back onto Spit Fyre. Wolf Boy began to climb up too, but to his relief Jenna said, "I've got to do this on my own. I've got to make Spit Fyre breathe **Fyre**."

Spit Fyre pricked up his ears. **Fyre**? Now? But what about breakfast?

A chorus of yells rose from behind the boatyard door, and Rupert's voice could be heard shouting, "If you want rats, Matey, you've got 'em. Great big ones with axes. Come on then!"

As if in response to Rupert Gringe's kind invitation, the RatStranglers gave one massive heave at the door. There was a splintering crash and the mob surged through. A tremendous noise erupted as a fight broke out at the gate. Rupert, Jannit and the yard hands put up a good fight and seemed to be winning, but a few of the RatStranglers evaded the hail of blows.

Led by the tall, spiky woman, they broke away, and brandishing an assortment of makeshift weapons, they headed toward the Dragon House, yelling, "Get the dragon, kill the dragon, kill, kill, *kill!*"

✢ 2 0 ✢
FYRE AND SEEK

Jenna and *Spit Fyre* were airborne.

As the breakaway party of RatStranglers headed across the boatyard below them, Jenna guided Spit Fyre toward the small golden plaque set into the wall above the arch at the entrance of the Dragon House. Spit Fyre was flying beautifully, his wings beating against the air slowly and with great control; he responded to Jenna's every command. Soon the dragon was hovering in front of the plaque, nice and steady, as though he understood exactly what Jenna wanted him to do. In front of him the disc of gold was dull in the chill, damp air, but below him the RatStranglers were now running single file between the two tall-masted ships. They were nearly to the Dragon House.

"Ignite!" Jenna yelled at the top of her voice. "Ignite, Ignite, Ignite!"

Nothing happened. Afraid that there was indeed more to the Ignite, Jenna was horrified to see the spiky-woman RatStrangler emerging from between the tall ships, brandishing a large plank studded with nails. She was heading toward the sleeping head of the Dragon Boat.

"Please, Spit Fyre, *please*. Ignite!"

And then Jenna felt Spit Fyre shudder. From deep within the dragon, a subterranean rumble began. It started in the pit of his fire stomach, gathering force until it burst through the fire valve and shot into his great, thick dragon windpipe. Jenna felt the wave of it travel up his neck. Spit Fyre coughed as if in surprise, instinctively flared his nostrils and a great rush of gas came shooting out.

"Ignite!" yelled Jenna at the top of her voice. With a tremendous *whoosh*, the gas Ignited. The jet of flame leaped forward and enveloped the golden disc, and for one awful

moment Jenna was afraid that the heat of the flame would melt
the gold, for the disc glowed and shimmered so that it looked
almost liquid in the red light. And then, far below her, Jenna
heard a great yell of surprise from the RatStranglers. She
glanced down to see if they had reached the Dragon Boat, and
to her amazement, all she could see was the great expanse of
stone of the Castle wall.

Spit Fyre had done it! The Dragon House had disappeared
as though it had never existed. Once again it was **Sealed**
behind the Castle wall as it had been ever since the time of
Hotep-Ra.

Jenna threw her arms around the dragon's neck. It was
hot, almost too hot to touch, but she did not care. "Thank
you, Spit Fyre, *thank you*. I will never, *ever* complain about
cutting your toenails again. I promise." Spit Fyre snorted,
coughed out more superheated gas, and another great plume
of **Fyre** sent the RatStranglers diving for cover. It also set fire
to a pile of paddleboats that Rupert Gringe had brought in for
repair.

Jenna and Spit Fyre flew back to the collapsed trawler.
Jenna guided Spit Fyre down beside the smashed-up remains
of the boat, and keeping his wings outstretched for a quick

takeoff, the dragon waited for Wolf Boy to take his place behind Jenna.

"Excuse me, Your Majesty," came a familiar voice beside Jenna's left foot, "could you budge up a bit? Then Dawnie and I can squeeze in behind you."

Jenna knew that voice. It always seemed to turn up when she least expected it. She looked down and there, as she had guessed, was Stanley—ex-Message Rat, one-time Secret Rat. Current position: fugitive from the RatStranglers.

"Come on then, Stanley, quickly, before the RatStranglers see you." Jenna leaned down to help Stanley up.

"I'm not getting back on that—that *thing*," said the small fat rat who was with Stanley.

"But, Dawnie dear, it's our only hope."

Suddenly the clamor of the RatStranglers changed.

"She's over there," said the shrill voice of the spiky woman. "*She* did this. She should answer for it. *Now*."

"Now, now, *now!*" the chant began. "Now, now, *now!*"

"They're coming this way," said Wolf Boy. "Quick, Jenna. Leave the rats if they don't want to come. We've gotta go."

Jenna reached down to grab Stanley's paw.

"Don't leave me, Stanley!" wailed Dawnie. She launched

into a superb tackle and brought Stanley down by the ankles.

"Dawnie, *let go!*"

Jenna hauled up the two squabbling rats, one in each hand, and placed them firmly between two large spines behind her, one behind the other. A moment later Spit Fyre was airborne, followed by a hail of trash can lids and a nasty-looking plank with nails stuck in it.

Two hundred feet above the Castle, the squabbling continued. "I hope you realize you nearly had us both killed, Stanley."

"Me? *I* nearly had us both killed? That's rich, that is, coming from you. If you'd had your way, Dawnie, which may I say you usually do, we'd have both been strangled by now and hung up on the tally board."

"Sometimes you say the cruelest things, Stanley. My mother was right."

"There's no need to bring your mother into it, Dawnie. No need at all."

"Well, it's nice to see that you got back together," said Jenna cheerily, trying to change the subject.

Both rats were unusually silent.

Taking advantage of the silence, Jenna passed the Navigator's tin back to Wolf Boy. "Can you fish out the green piece of, er . . . stuff?" she asked. "It's got **Seek** written on it. That's the one I need to get Spit Fyre to find Sep."

"**Seek**?" asked Wolf Boy in a panic. "What does **Seek** look like?"

"S-E-E-K," Jenna spelled out, shouting above the whoosh of the dragon's wings. "Big black letters. Can't miss it."

"*I* can," Wolf Boy muttered to himself. "What's the . . . *S* thing look like?" he yelled back.

"Like a snake! *S* for snake, see?"

Jenna was guiding Spit Fyre so that the dragon kept following the Castle walls. She had decided to take him around in circles until she could do the **Seek** properly. It was also an excuse to look at the Castle, which, spread out far below like a map with ants moving slowly across it, fascinated her. It reminded her of a much-treasured map that Simon had given her one MidWinter Feast Day. It had shown every rooftop, tree, roof garden, alleyway and secret hideaway in the Castle. In fact, as Spit Fyre flew leisurely toward the old Message Rat headquarters, the East Gate Lookout Tower, Jenna wondered if the mapmaker had not had his own dragon, so like the map was the vista spread below her.

Wolf Boy was having trouble finding the **Seek**. It was quite enough, he thought, to be hundreds of feet up in the air, feeling sick and trying not to fall off a flying dragon, without having to look at letters as well. Spit Fyre did not exactly fly smoothly. With every downbeat of the dragon's wings, a great rush of dragon-smelling air passed Wolf Boy's face. Then the dragon shot up in the air, where he hung for a few seconds until the upbeat of his wings. There was another rush of smelly underwing air, and then down he went again. These were not ideal conditions in which to look for a snaky kind of letter-thingy.

As he rifled through the toffee tin, trying not to lose any precious bits of dragon skin, something occurred to him that would explain his troubles finding the **Seek**. "But not all snakes begin with S, do they?" he shouted forward to Jenna. "I mean, there's python and adder and Big Green Forest Snake and—"

Jenna leaned back and saw the look of puzzlement on Wolf Boy's face. "Tell you what," she shouted, "why don't you just pass me all the green pieces?"

"Hey, I've got it!" yelled Wolf Boy, triumphant, as the dragon wings swept down. "I was confused because . . . aargh"—the dragon wings swept up—". . . there are two

snakes on this one. But none of the others . . . oof"—the
dragon wings swept down again—". . . have any snakes at all
so this must be it. Here, oops"—the wings swept up—". . .
you are." He passed Jenna a piece of crackly green leather. On
the front of it was written **Seek and Ye Shall Find**.

"Great!" said Jenna. With some difficulty—it was like
reading on a roller coaster—and hanging on tight to the scrap
of green dragon skin so that it did not blow away, she read out
the words of the **Seek**:

"Faithful dragon Seek the One
Whom you be Imprinted on.
Let this Seek show in your Mind
The Way to your Imprintor—*Find!*"

At once Spit Fyre banked sharply to the right. Jenna was
caught by surprise. She had taken both hands off Spit Fyre's
spines while she read out the **Seek**, and in one swift and ter-
rifying movement, she slipped from her place behind Spit
Fyre's neck, grabbed at the spines she should have been holding on to—and missed.

"Jenna!" yelled Wolf Boy. "*Jenna!*"

There was no reply. Jenna was gone.

✠ 21 ✠
RIDER RETRIEVE

Jenna *was too shocked to scream,*
she knew that there was
nothing but thin air between
her and Raven's Rock far below.
But, as Spit Fyre felt the
weight behind his neck disappear, something instinctive kicked
in. Something that, unknown to Spit Fyre, all human-
Imprinted dragons possessed: Rider Retrieve. As Jenna fell,
Spit Fyre dropped like a rock and grabbed her with his feet.

Two seconds later he was carrying Jenna in his talons, as an eagle carries its prey.

Wolf Boy was frantic. He could not see Jenna dangling below. All he knew was that she was no longer there.

"Jenna!" he yelled. "*Jenna!*"

" 409!" came an answering voice, or so he thought.

"Where's she gone, Stanley?" asked Dawnie peevishly. "I do think that's a bit much, just getting off like that. I mean, who's going to fly this thing now, I'd like to know?"

"Oh, do be quiet, Dawnie!" snapped Stanley. Dreading what he was going to see, the rat peered out over the great black spines of the dragon, but all he could see was Spit Fyre's fat stomach.

"409!" came Jenna's voice, almost blown away by the wind.

"Jenna?" Wolf Boy twisted around to see if she was behind him but there was nothing. He looked down to see if she was clinging on below him but he saw nothing except Spit Fyre's belly.

"409 . . . I'm *here.* . . ." Wolf Boy began to wonder if he was imagining it. Where *was* she?

Spit Fyre had turned back toward the Castle and was descending now, slowly and carefully. Wolf Boy looked down, scanning the ground, fearing the worst. They flew over Raven's Rock, across the new boat blockade, which spanned the river and stopped any Sickenesse-infested boats from arriving at the Port, and now they were heading toward the quay below Sally Mullin's Tea and Ale House. Customers were running from the café, and Wolf Boy could see people milling around, looking up and pointing excitedly. As Spit Fyre came in lower, Wolf Boy could hear what they were saying.

"It's the Princess!"

"That Wizard dragon's taken the Princess!"

"Look at her—just hanging there . . . oh my, oh my . . ."

"Dead."

"Don't say that. She can't be. She *can't*."

"Well, she ain't doin' much."

"Ain't much she can do, stuck in them claws like that. I always said that that dragon would turn. They all do."

"Look! Look—she's moving. She's alive, *look* . . ."

"He's comin' down. He's going to squash her."

"Aargh! I can't look—I *can't*!"

Spit Fyre was now hovering no more than ten feet off the ground. Wolf Boy's relief at realizing that Jenna had not fallen was replaced by a horrible thought: How was Spit Fyre going to land without crushing her?

Slowly, slowly, Spit Fyre came lower until he was so near to the quay that Wolf Boy could easily make out the complicated patterns on top of the fishermen's hats. The beating of Spit Fyre's wings—and quite possibly the strong smell of dragon—pushed the crowd back; Wolf Boy watched their astonished faces as the dragon hovered about five feet above the ground, uncurled his talons and let Jenna jump lightly onto the edge of the quay, running forward to keep her balance.

The crowd applauded and there were a couple of appreciative whistles, which seemed to go to Spit Fyre's head, for the dragon settled onto the quay, stuck out his neck and rumbled so that Wolf Boy felt it deep inside him. The crowd, fascinated by seeing Spit Fyre at such close quarters, especially after such a daring feat, was drawing near, pointing out the various strange bits and pieces that are part of any dragon.

"Horrible black spines he's got . . ."

"Look at the size of his tail . . ."

"Wouldn't fancy being stuck in them claws myself . . ."

And then, noticing Wolf Boy: "There's a kid on the back . . ."

"He's got quite a stare on him. Wouldn't want to come

across *him* on a dark night."

"Shh, he'll hear you."

"No, he won't. Listen, what's that?"

The rumble deep inside Spit Fyre was getting louder. Jenna jumped back, for she knew what was coming, missed her footing and fell off the edge of the quay into the water. Still intrigued by the dragon, the crowd paid no attention whatsoever to the *splash* as their Princess vanished below the flotsam. As if drawn by a magnet, people drew closer and closer to Spit Fyre, watching the dragon as he threw back his head and flared his nostrils, listening to the volcanic rumblings inside him. Unnoticed, Jenna surfaced, spat out a small, but disgustingly dead fish and swam toward the steps at the end of the quay.

Suddenly, with a jet-engine of a roar, a great plume of hot gas streamed from Spit Fyre's nostrils and **Ignited**. Ten, twenty, thirty seconds of fire shot into the air and across the water, where it torched the sails of two herring boats that formed part of the blockade across the river. At the end of the thirty seconds the crowd had gone. Many had taken refuge in Sally Mullin's café only to find themselves handed one of the large collection of fire buckets kept at the ready and told to "go and put that dragon out before we all go up in flames." The rest could be seen running up the hill toward the South Gate with a great story to tell in the taverns at lunchtime.

By nightfall, most people in the Castle had heard a version of how "the Princess was snatched by the Wizards' dragon, yes, she was, I'm telling you, she *was*. Great beast of a thing. Then it dropped her like a stone, it did. Yes, it *did*. No, she's all right. No, she didn't bounce. She fell in the river. She's a good swimmer, that girl. But then the dragon, see, he *turned*. They all do. Great fire spurting out of his nose right at me—singed my hair too, see? No, look, this bit here, no, *here*. Well, you need to get yourself a decent pair of glasses, that's all I can say."

Most people had also heard the other version too—how the Princess was to blame for bringing the Sickenesse in her pestilential boat, how she had tried to trap the RatStranglers in the Castle wall by means of some **Darke** trickery and— "Well, if you want *proof*, I'll give you proof. She rescued a couple of vermin. Not ermine, *vermin*. Are you deaf? Rats, you fool, *rats*. Took them away on her dragon. Now what do you have to say to *that*?" And the speaker would sit back, arms folded with a smug smile.

It was, people discovered, quite possible to believe both,

depending on who you were talking to at the time. But every-one agreed on one thing: There was more to this young Princess than met the eye. Much more.

Stanley and Dawnie had watched the crowd run away with a great feeling of relief. In the middle of all the excitement no one had paid them much attention as they cowered among Spit Fyre's thick spines. They sat up straight again, and Dawnie settled herself with the air of a rat much used to drag-on flight. "I hope we get going soon," she said. "I'm feeling quite famished. I rather fancy some lunch in the Port."

Stanley sighed, but he said nothing. He watched Jenna, dripping wet, clamber back onto Spit Fyre. "All right, Your Majesty?" he asked.

Jenna did not mind Stanley calling her Your Majesty. In fact, she rather liked it, for she knew Stanley meant it affec-tionately. "Yes, thank you, Stanley," she replied. "And are *you* all right?"

"Never been better," said Stanley brightly. "Lovely crisp morning, clouds clearing and off for a flight. What more could a rat want?"

"Lunch," said Dawnie under her breath.

✠ 22 ✠
THE *ALFRÚN*

*S*pit Fyre *had a confident* and purposeful air about him. He was flying at
a leisurely pace, following the river
south, toward the Port.

"I hope he's not going out to sea,"
said Jenna.

"Yeah," agreed Wolf Boy, who was
feeling quite dragon-sick and could think
of nothing worse right then. To take
his mind off things, Wolf Boy
gazed down at the silver thread of
the river that wound beneath them and tried to spot Sam's
Beach, where he and 412 had set off from the Forest a few
months ago. Wolf Boy smiled, remembering how thrilled he

had been to find his best friend again, even though 412 was nothing like his Young Army self. It wasn't just that 412's hair had grown, that he had acquired a family and a weird name to go with them, or that he was wearing a fancy Apprentice tunic and belt; it was more than that. 412 had become confident, funny and even more like . . . well, even more like the best parts of 412. And now . . . and now 412 was gone—maybe forever.

"Did you see that Quarantine notice on the quay?" Jenna's voice suddenly intruded on Wolf Boy's thoughts. He was glad it had.

"What notice?" he shouted above the noise of Spit Fyre's wings. Wolf Boy thought he wouldn't know one notice from another. And anyway, what was a Quarantine? Wolf Boy imagined a horrible monster, the kind of thing that was maybe, just at that moment, chasing 412 through the Forest, or wherever he was. Wolf Boy, even with all his tracker skills, was stumped. How can you track someone who is pulled through a looking glass?

"The one about the Sickenesse!" yelled Jenna across the two rats, who were following the conversation as if watching a tennis match. "And the barricade. That means no Northern Traders this year. It's going to be a miserable MidWinter

Feast without the Traders' Market!"

"Oh," said Wolf Boy. And then yelled, "What's a Northern Trader?"

"They've got very nice boats," ventured Stanley. "Go anywhere, those boats do. Mind you, when I was a Message Rat you had to be careful. The Traders ran a tight rat-free policy. Had to, you see, to comply with the Market Regulations. Some of the nastiest cats I've ever encountered have been on a Trader's barge. Had a terrible run-in with an ex-Trader cat on my last Message Rat mission." Stanley shook his head ruefully. "Should have realized then how things were going to turn out. Worst mission ever, that was—never met another rat who encountered anything like it. Did I tell you about Mad Jack . . ." And so Stanley rattled on, blissfully unaware that no one could hear him above the noise of Spit Fyre's wings, except for Dawnie, who always made a point of not listening to more than the first sentence of anything Stanley said.

"There's one down there!" Jenna shouted in reply to Wolf Boy's question. "Look!"

Wolf Boy peered at the river. Far below, he saw a long, narrow barge with a large white sail going downstream—and so did Spit Fyre. Wolf Boy felt the rhythm of the dragon's flight change and began to feel slightly less sick.

"We're going down!" Jenna yelled.

Spit Fyre slowed his wing beats and was losing height. Jenna glanced around to see where he was heading, and a feeling of excitement came over her. There was no doubt about it, Spit Fyre was homing-in on something. The **Seek** was working. Soon, very soon, perhaps, they would find Septimus.

"He's heading for the water!" shouted Wolf Boy.

"No, he's not. He's going for the Forest!" yelled Jenna.

Spit Fyre had wheeled around so that he was no longer above the river; he was still descending and was now heading over the Forest. Then, just as Wolf Boy and Jenna had resigned themselves to a Forest landing, the dragon began to turn back toward the river again.

"He's circling!" shouted Jenna. "I think he's trying to figure out where to land." Jenna was half right. Spit Fyre was circling but he knew exactly *where* to land—he just had to work out *how*.

After three more circuits Spit Fyre and his passengers were flying over the tops of the Forest trees almost close enough for them to reach down and grab at the leaves. A thin wisp of smoke drifted up from a campfire, and Wolf Boy felt a pang of homesickness for the Heap boys' camp.

Spit Fyre left the trees behind and suddenly dropped sharply down over the river. Dawnie screamed. Right in front of them was the Trader's barge, from which came an enticing smell of frying bacon.

Jenna did not think it was possible for a fifteen-foot dragon to land on a sixty-foot boat sporting a large sail. As Spit Fyre came in low and hovered directly above the barge, her opinion was clearly shared by the boat's skipper, who was waving her arms and yelling something in a language whose words Jenna did not understand but whose meaning she certainly did.

Spit Fyre neither understood nor cared. He was heading for the flat expanse on top of the barge's cabin and he could smell *breakfast*. Even a dragon on a **Seek** needed breakfast, *particularly* a dragon on a **Seek**.

They landed with a bump. Not a big bump by dragon-landing standards, but big enough to push the *Alfrún* down into the water almost up to her gunwales. The barge rebounded and then rocked from side to side, sending waves washing out to the banks of the river and her skipper running angrily toward them, brandishing a long boat hook.

"Go away! *Go away!*" yelled Snorri Snorrelssen angrily.

Snorri had had a bad day. She had been woken at dawn by the sound of heavy footsteps tramping across her cabin roof and an insistent hammering on the hatchway. Snorri was not easily frightened but this did frighten her. Over the previous few days the Castle had become an unwelcoming place for a foreigner. People were beginning to blame the Traders for the Sickenesse and Snorri had had numerous insults aimed her way as she had wandered around the Castle. The last few days had seen Snorri hiding in the *Alfrún*, waiting for the arrival of more Northern Traders. None came. Unknown to Snorri, the fishing boat blockade at Raven's Rock was already turning them away with a hail of abuse and rotten fish.

And so that morning Snorri had sailed away as the gray dawn broke, after being given ten minutes "to get out, or else." Snorri didn't like the idea of *else*—whatever it was—so she got out. And now, just as she was beginning to take stock, 764 seagulls' worth of dragon had landed on her cabin roof. It was definitely not a good day.

The *Alfrún* was made of sterner stuff than the rotten fishing boat in the boatyard. The deck creaked a little in protest but stayed put. The barge settled a little lower in the water, and continued her way downriver with her new cargo, which was not taking kindly to being poked in the ribs by a sharp boat hook. Beneath her feet, Jenna could feel a telltale rumble of fire starting up in Spit Fyre's fire stomach.

"No, Spit Fyre!" she yelled. "No!" Jenna scrambled down from the dragon, much to the amazement of Snorri, who had not noticed that the dragon was carrying passengers. The rumble continued to grow. Wolf Boy heard it and jumped off, and the two rats scurried up the mast and perched precariously on a narrow yardarm, roosting like an odd pair of seagulls.

Jenna grabbed Snorri's boat hook, which she was prodding at Spit Fyre. "Don't provoke him!" she shouted. "Please!" But Snorri, who was taller and stronger than Jenna, wrested the boat hook back. The rumble in the fire stomach grew louder until even Snorri noticed it. She stopped and looked puzzled.

"What . . . is . . . that?" she asked in Jenna's language.

"**Fyre!**" yelled Jenna. "He's making **Fyre!**"

Snorri, as any boat skipper would, understood the word *fire* well enough. She grabbed a couple of buckets with rope tied to their handles and thrust one into Jenna's hands. "Water!" yelled Snorri. "Get water!"

Jenna followed Snorri's example and, holding on to the

rope, she threw her bucket over the side of the barge into the river, pulled it up brimming with murky green water and threw it. It landed on a surprised Wolf Boy, who was quickly feeding Spit Fyre Snorri's breakfast of bread and bacon. It was then that Jenna realized that the rumble had stopped.

Wolf Boy grinned. "I figured he couldn't eat and make Fyre at the same time," he said.

Snorri watched Spit Fyre gulp down the last of her bacon, siphon up the rest of the water from the fire bucket and finish by swallowing the wooden plate whole. This, thought Snorri, is going to be trouble. You didn't need to be a Spirit-Seer to see that.

┿┾2 3┿┾
SPIRIT·SEER

S *pit Fyre was asleep* and Snorri had an empty space in her tightly packed hold where one of the barrels of salted fish used to be. The *Alfrún* was tied up to a large willow tree that overhung the bank on the Farmlands side of the river, for the skipper felt it was too dangerous to continue the journey with an unpredictable dragon on board.

Snorri and Jenna were sitting in the cockpit at the stern of the barge, trying not to listen to Spit Fyre's snores and snuffles. Wolf Boy, who was still queasy after his dragon flight, and wanted to feel solid ground beneath his feet, was exploring the apple orchards planted along the riverbank.

Snorri had never expected to meet the Princess for a second time, let alone have her land on her boat on a *dragon*. She was a little overawed. She had provided Jenna and Wolf Boy with a welcome breakfast of bread, cake, pickled fish and apples, which they had eaten hungrily. Wolf Boy regretted that he had fed all the bacon to Spit Fyre, particularly as it had hardly dented the dragon's appetite, and Snorri also had to feed him a whole barrel of salted fish.

"I am really sorry, Snorri," said Jenna yet again after Wolf Boy had set off. "We were on our way to find Septimus, and Spit Fyre just decided to land. I didn't stop him because I thought Septimus was here . . . but he's not." Jenna lapsed into silence. She could not help wondering whether the **Seek** was going to work with Spit Fyre. He was such a young and impetuous dragon, and if he could be distracted by the smell of frying bacon, what else would send him off on the wrong course?

"Your brother Septimus. He . . . fell through some glass?" asked Snorri.

Jenna nodded.

"Then . . . surely you will find him in the Infirmary?"

Jenna shook her head. "It was a looking glass—you know, a mirror?" she explained.

"Ah . . ." said Snorri. "An Ancient Glass. Now I understand."

"You do?" said Jenna, surprised.

"My grandmother had one. But we are . . . we were never allowed to touch it. Her sister, Ells, fell through it when she was young."

"Did"—Jenna hardly dared ask—"did they ever find her?"

"No," said Snorri.

Jenna was silent. Suddenly Snorri leaped up and ran to the side of the barge, looking upriver. Jenna followed her gaze but she could see nothing. The river was empty and quiet. The drizzle had stopped a while ago and now the water was flat and sluggish, reflecting the heavy gray clouds that hung in the sky. Nothing, not even an adventurous fish popping up to the surface for a fly, disturbed it.

Snorri drew out her Spirit eyeglass from a pocket in the folds of her tunic and put it to her left eye. She muttered something under her breath.

"What is it?" asked Jenna.

"I do not like this boat," whispered Snorri.

"But it's a lovely boat," said Jenna. "I really like it, especially your little cabin. It's very cozy."

"No. Not *this* boat," explained Snorri. "*That* boat." Snorri put the eyeglass down and pointed upriver. Jenna followed Snorri's gaze, noticing now how her eyes were locked onto something, following its slow progress downriver toward them.

Snorri glanced at Jenna. "Ah," she said, "you cannot see the Spirit Ship?"

Jenna shook her head.

"It is coming this way," whispered Snorri.

Suddenly the air felt colder and the river seemed threatening. "*What* is coming this way?" Jenna asked.

Snorri did not reply. Squinting through the eyeglass, she was engrossed in watching Queen Etheldredda's Royal Barge draw near. Although the barge had been on the far side of the river as it rounded the bend, it was now crossing the river and heading straight for the *Alfrún*. Snorri shivered.

"*What?* What can you see?" Jenna whispered.

"I see a barge. It is with a high prow and it is built as they used to build many years ago. I see four ghostly oars on the port

and four on the starboard; they move but they make no disturbance on the water. I see a Royal red canopy covering the barge
on gilded posts, and I see the Queen who sits beneath it."

"Does . . . the Queen wear a high ruff around her neck and
have coiled plaits wound around her ears?" whispered Jenna,
who suddenly had a horrible feeling who the Queen was.
"Does she look as though she has just smelled something disgusting?"

Snorri turned to Jenna with a smile, the first smile that
Jenna had seen on Snorri's face.

"So you, my sister, are a Spirit-Seer too. I have so much
longed for a Spirit Sister. Welcome!" Snorri enveloped Jenna
in a hug but, desperate not to be seen by Queen Etheldredda,
Jenna wriggled out and fled to Snorri's cabin.

Snorri followed Jenna below. "I am sorry if . . . I offended
you," she said.

Jenna was sitting on the steps, white-faced and hugging
her knees. "You—you didn't offend me," she whispered. "I
mustn't let the Queen see me. She is the one who made me
show my brother the Glass. She's horrible, really *horrible*."

"Ah," whispered Snorri, not at all surprised, remembering
the chill that had run through her when she had first seen the

Royal Barge. "You stay here, Jenna. I shall go **See** this Queen. I will tell you what she is doing, for I think she has chosen not to **Appear** to you for a bad reason. Maybe she has your brother prisoner on board?"

"Sep!" said Jenna. "On a ghost boat. But that would mean that he's a ghost too. . . ."

"No, not always. It is possible to be **Taken** by a Spirit and still be Living. It happened to my uncle Ernold." With that, Snorri disappeared up on deck, leaving Jenna to reflect that Snorri's family was somewhat accident-prone when it came to the Spirit side of things.

The Royal Barge was nearing the *Alfrún*, and Snorri saw that it had once been a beautiful boat. It was a long, narrow barge painted with intricate gold and silver swirls. Ornate gold poles held up a luxuriant red canopy to keep the sun and the rain off the Queen and her courtiers, who would have lolled on the long cushioned seats on the dais at the stern of the barge. But now Queen Etheldredda sat alone, as she had also done for much of her lifetime, for her courtiers had found all manner of excuses to avoid being stuck on the Royal Barge without escape from the Queen. Belowdecks eight ghostly oarsmen sat on their narrow wooden benches, pulling their insubstantial oars to and fro, to and fro, while the river water remained undisturbed.

As the Royal Barge swung toward the *Alfrún*, Snorri put the Spirit eyeglass away and busied herself tidying the breakfast things. She had no wish to show the Queen that she was a Spirit-Seer and it was clear to Snorri that if Jenna could not see the Queen, then the ghost had chosen not to **Appear**. Queen Etheldredda rose from her cushions, walked over to the side of her boat and stared across the water at Snorri. The Queen sniffed disapprovingly. A servant girl, no doubt. The Queen's stare took in the remains of breakfast, which the servant girl was slowly clearing away—disgracefully slowly. Servants were so lazy in this Time; things would change once she became Queen again. Etheldredda's eyes were drawn back to Snorri herself. There was something odd about the girl, she thought. She didn't like the way the girl's eyes flickered from side to side like a lizard's and avoided looking anywhere. Very devious. No doubt her employer would be waking one night soon to find his entire cargo had been sold under his very nose. It would serve him right.

With a grim smile on her lips, Queen Etheldredda allowed the Royal Barge to drift toward the *Alfrún* while she perused the rest of the boat, searching for Jenna. The Queen was on her way to the Marram Marshes, but as soon as she had rounded the bend and seen the *Alfrún* moored alongside the riverbank, she had been overcome by a strong feeling that her errant granddaughter was nearby, which she did not understand, for surely the girl was at the Keeper's Cottage. Those two irritating ExtraOrdinary Wizards had said as much—she had heard them from behind the bedroom door. Queen Etheldredda was a great believer in information gained through eavesdropping; in her lifetime she had perfected it to the point where she never believed what anyone told her to her face unless she had also overheard it for herself.

As the Royal Barge drew alongside the *Alfrún*, Queen Etheldredda's feeling that Jenna was on board became even stronger, but she could see no sign of her. With a puzzled air, the Queen scrutinized the boat. It appeared to be nothing more than a typical Northern Trader's barge: It flew the official flag of the Hanseatic League and was, despite the slatternly servant girl, neat, shipshape and well maintained. All was peaceful, quiet and as it should be. The ropes were neatly coiled, its sail was expertly furled and—*it had a dragon on the deck.*

✠ 24 ✠
THE BOARDING PARTY

The dragon on the deck did not stir despite Queen Etheldredda's piercing stare. Spit Fyre lay snoring. A large bubble of gas floated to the top of his stomach and made a break for freedom with a loud *pop*. Queen Etheldredda recoiled as if struck, and the Royal Barge drew away from the noxious dragon fumes. Queen Ethel-dredda leaned over the side, staring at the *Alfrún* with nar-rowed eyes. Something, the ghost decided, was going on in that boat and she was going to find out. Delicately, like a heron picking its way through shallow water, the ghost of the Queen stepped from her Royal Barge and, as if walking across the Palace lawns, she sauntered over the surface of the water and stepped aboard the *Alfrún*.

"She is *here!*" Snorri gasped in her own language. Jenna, who did not understand what Snorri had said, but understood the tone well enough, dived under a large woolen blanket, dislodging Ullr, who had been sleeping after his previous night on guard. The cat darted out of the cabin and rushed up on deck, his tail a great sausage of indignant fluff. Ullr was not only a Night Creature, but he was also from a long line of Spirit-Seer cats, which are, of course, much more common than Spirit-Seer humans. As he emerged on deck he decided he did not like the look of the visiting ghost at all. He didn't like the look of the two rats up the mast either, but they could wait. They would make a good supper that evening.

At the sight of Queen Etheldredda advancing, Ullr threw himself at the ghost, yowling as only a Spirit-Seer cat can. It was a terrible sound, a mixture of banshee and Brownie with a touch of Marsh Moaner thrown in. Queen Etheldredda gasped at the shock of being **Passed Through** in such a violent way and collapsed onto the deck, coughing and spluttering, feeling as if she had swallowed a whole cat—fur, claws, screech and all.

Along the riverbank, Wolf Boy heard Ullr's yowl. He came running through the orchards to see what was going on. He arrived at the *Alfrún* to see the strangest sight: the Trader girl and her cat had gone crazy, totally and utterly crazy. The cat— a nasty, thin orange thing—was hurling himself backward and forward as though running through something over and over again. The girl was waving her arms and yelling something in her own language, which sounded to him like shouts of encouragement. And then suddenly the cat stopped. The girl punched the air in triumph, scooped up the cat and ran to the side of the boat where she gazed down at the river, laughing.

Wolf Boy jumped aboard and rushed down to the cabin. "Jenna? Jenna?" he said in a hoarse whisper.

"Yes?" came the reply from underneath the blanket.

"What are you doing under there?"

"Hiding," came Jenna's muffled reply. "Shh. She'll see you."

"It's no good hiding, Jen, she's nuts. Let's get out of here while we can. Quick, before she—oh, *bother*."

Snorri's grinning face appeared in the hatchway. "The UnQuiet One has gone," she announced. "She fell overboard and disappeared underwater. She is back on her barge now with riverweed on her crown." Suddenly Snorri's smile disappeared. She clambered through the hatchway and sat down at the top of the steps, shaking her head.

Wolf Boy shook his head too. Their escape route was blocked. They should have gone when they had the chance.

"There are things," muttered Snorri, "that I do not understand."

"What things?" asked Jenna, extricating herself from the extremely itchy blanket.

"One thing is that the Queen has not been on my boat in her Living Time—so why was she not **Returned**?"

"What?" asked Wolf Boy. Why did the Snorri girl talk in riddles?

"A ghost may only tread once more where, Living, he has trod before," Snorri recited.

"That's just a kids' rhyme," scoffed Wolf Boy.

"It is no kids' rhyme," retorted Snorri, offended. "It is a Rule of Ghosthood."

Wolf Boy snorted.

"It *is*. I *know*," Snorri insisted. "All Spirit-Seers know them."

"Huh," muttered Wolf Boy.

"Shh, 409," said Jenna, shooting Wolf Boy a warning glance. Jenna believed Snorri, for Snorri had clearly seen Etheldredda, and she wanted to hear more. "What are the other things you do not understand?" she asked.

"I do not understand why the riverweed stuck to her crown. A Spirit has no substance. It should not be possible."

Wolf Boy sighed; it was all too weird. Give him the Forest any day, where at least you knew where you stood with most of the inhabitants: potential supper.

"So—so what *is* she?" asked Jenna in a hushed voice, as though Queen Etheldredda was eavesdropping outside the cabin.

Snorri shrugged. "I do not know. She is Spirit and yet . . . she is more than Spirit—"

Thump . . . thump . . . thump. Someone—or some*thing*—was knocking on the hull. Snorri leaped to her feet. "What is *that*?" she gasped.

Jenna and Wolf Boy, who were both feeling rather spooked by now, went pale. The sound echoed eerily through the cabin, "*thump . . . thump . . .*"

"Etheldredda's come back," whispered Jenna.

Bravely, Snorri stuck her head out of the hatchway. "Hello?" she said, in her singsong Northern Trader accent.

"Hello!" replied a cheery voice. "Did you know you've got an escaped dragon on your deck?"

"Escaped? From where?" asked Snorri.

"The Castle. It belongs to my brother. He'll be looking everywhere for it."

"Your brother?" Snorri hurriedly scrambled up on deck and saw a boy with laughing green eyes tying up his boat to the *Alfrún*. She looked at his salt-stained seafaring tunic and his tangled, curly hair, which was almost as fair as her own, and she knew she could trust him.

"Yeah. 'Fraid so," said Nicko. "I'd offer to take him back with me but he's too big for my boat. Bit too big for yours too, if you ask me. Hey—*Jen!*"

"Nik!" Jenna emerged from the cabin and laughed. "What are you doing here?"

"Been sent out collecting Rupert's blasted paddleboats. Someone broke into his store last night and he figures he's lost loads. But I've only found one so far." Nicko indicated a small pink paddleboat that he was towing. "Waste of time if you ask me."

Jenna noticed Snorri's look of confusion. "It's Nicko. He's my brother," she explained.

"Your brother?" asked Snorri, who felt that the brother tally was stacking up a little too fast. "The one who fell through the Glass?"

"What glass?" asked Nicko.

"Oh," said Jenna, her feelings of excitement at seeing Nicko draining away, as if she had suddenly sprung a leak. "You don't know about Sep, do you?"

Nicko saw the tears now welling in Jenna's eyes. With a heavy heart, he clambered aboard the *Alfrún*.

Wolf Boy left Jenna and Nicko together and slipped away. There was someone he wanted to check up on. He found Lucy Gringe where he had left her, sitting on the riverbank under a willow tree.

"You again?" she said, grumpily. "I told you to *leave me alone*. I don't need the stupid paddleboat anyway." Lucy sat with her blue cloak wrapped around her, arms hugging her knees, her pink ribbon bootlaces soggy with the wet grass. She was holding a crumpled and much-folded and -unfolded piece of paper, her lips moving slowly as she read the words that she knew inside out and upside down. It was a note from

Simon Heap, and she had found it in the hem of her blue cloak
that Jenna had returned to her. It was headed simply with the
words The Observatory, and it read:

> *My own Lucy,*
>   *This cloak is for you. I will be back soon and*
> *we will be together at the top of the Tower. I*
> *shall make you proud of me. Wait for me.*
>   *Your only,*
>   *Simon*

But Lucy was tired of waiting, and she now knew that
Simon could never return to the Castle, so she had set out to
find him. And so far all she had done was fall asleep and wake
up to find her boat gone. It was not a good start. Wolf Boy's
voice broke into her thoughts.

"I found your boat," he said, breathless.

"Where?" asked Lucy, hastily folding the precious note and
jumping to her feet.

"Nicko's got it."

"Nicko *Heap*? Simon's brother?"

"Yeah. Suppose he is. He can't help that though." Wolf

Boy, who had been on the receiving end of one of Simon's **StunFlashes**, had a poor opinion of Simon Heap.

"What do you mean he can't help that, you rude boy!" Lucy's brown eyes flashed angrily.

"Nothing," said Wolf Boy, who could see that Lucy was trouble. He was beginning to wish that he hadn't bothered to ask her if she was all right earlier, when he had seen her tearfully searching the riverbank.

"So where *is* Nicko Heap?" demanded Lucy. "I shall go ask him just what he thinks he's doing stealing my boat. The *nerve* of it."

Knowing that he probably shouldn't, Wolf Boy waved an arm in the general direction of the *Alfrún* and watched Lucy stomp off along the riverbank toward the Trader barge. He followed at a safe distance, which, with Lucy Gringe, was a long one.

As Wolf Boy neared the *Alfrún* he heard the sound of raised voices.

"Give me back my boat!"

"It's Rupert's boat, not yours."

"Rupert says I can use his boats *anytime*, so there."

"Well, I—"

"And I'm using it *now*, Nicko Heap—got that?"

"But . . ."

"Excuse *me*. Get out of my way, *will you?*"

Wolf Boy arrived just in time to see Lucy Gringe running across the deck of the *Alfrún* and tripping over the sleeping Spit Fyre's tail. But nothing put Lucy Gringe off her stride for long. She picked herself up, held her nose as another bubble of gas erupted from Spit Fyre and lowered herself over the side of the *Alfrún*.

Nicko followed her. "Where are you going in that?" he asked, concerned.

"None of your business, nosy boy. Are *all* Simon's brothers such irritating busybodies?"

Snorri added Simon to the brother count. How many did Jenna have?

"That paddleboat is not safe on the river," Nicko persisted. "It's no better than a toy. They're only meant for fun on the Moat."

Lucy jumped into the paddleboat, which rocked alarmingly. "It got me this far and it'll get me to the Port, just you see."

"You can't go to the Port in that!" said Nicko, aghast.

"Have you any idea what the tide race is like at the mouth of the river? It will spin you around and drag you out to sea—and that's only if you haven't already been sunk by the waves that run in off the Great Sandbar. You're *crazy*."

"Maybe. I don't care," said Lucy sulkily. "I'm going anyway." She untied the rope, took up the paddle handles and began turning them furiously.

Nicko watched the little pink boat wobble its way out into the river until he could stand it no more. "Lucy!" he yelled. "Take *my* boat!"

"What?" Lucy shouted above the clattering din of the paddles.

"Take my boat—*please!*"

Lucy felt relieved, although she was not going to show it. She had a terrible feeling that Nicko was right about the paddleboat. With some difficulty—and only by rapidly turning one paddle and then another for at least five minutes—Lucy steered the boat around and arrived back at the *Alfrún*, breathless and hot and still in a bad mood.

Jenna, Snorri, Wolf Boy and Nicko watched Lucy Gringe set off once again, this time in Nicko's deep and seaworthy rowboat.

"But how are you going to get back now?" Jenna asked Nicko. "You're not going in that paddleboat, are you?"

Nicko snorted. "You must be joking. I wouldn't be seen dead in one of those, especially one *that* stupid color. I'm coming with you to find Sep, silly."

Jenna smiled for the first time since Septimus had disappeared. Nicko would make everything all right. She knew he would.

✢25✢
THE *I, MARCELLUS*

From the Diary of Marcellus Pye:

SunnDay. Equinox.

    Today has been a Wondrous yet most Fearfull day.

    Though I didst Forecast this Happening in mine Almanac (which will be the Laste Parte of my Booke, the I, Marcellus). Truly, I did not believe that it would come to Pass.

    At the Appointed Hour today, Seven minutes past Seven of the

*Clock this morning, my new Apprentice didst Come Through.
Though I was up betimes this morn and made sure that I was
beside the Great Doors to Await their Opening, great was my
surprise when they did part and Reveal my Glass. Beyond the Glass,
dimly didst I see a boy with Feare in his eyes. His garb was a
strange green tunic with a silver belt, he wore no shoes, and his
hair was ragged but he had a pleasant Face and I liked him well
enough at first sight. But what I didst not like, what indeed I
hated and feared, was the sight of the Creature behind him. For
this Creature I know to be none other but my Poore Self—in five
hundred yeares' Time.*

*The Boy came through the Glass well and is here in my House
now. I pray that his Despair will soon abate when he sees the
wonders of which he is destined to partake and the good that he
will do.*

Woden'sDay

*It is some three days since my new Apprentice hath Come
Through. He seems a promising boy, and as we are Approaching
the Conjunction of the Planets for which I have long waited, I do
begin to have hope for my new Tincture.*

I pray that it may be so, for yesterday I foolishly didst ask my

Apprentice, "How was the Ancient Dribbling Ghastliness, my Poore Self, who took you from your Time? Was he—was I—so very repulsive?" My Apprentice nodded but would not speak. I pressed him to tell me and, seeing my Concern, he did relent. How I wish that he had not. He has a strange way of speech, yet I Feare I didst Understand him all too well.

He didst tell me in much detail how my stench was most unbearable, that I shuffled like a Crabbe and cried out in pain at each step, cursing my fate. He didst Saye my nose was ridged and like unto the hide of an Elephant (though I know not what that Creature be but suspect it to be a most foul Toad) and my ears were like great cabbages and spotted also and full of slugs. Slugs—how can this be? My nails were long and yellow like great claws and filthy with hundreds of years of Grime. I do detest dirty fingernails—surely I will not come to this? But it seemeth so. I have Five Hundred Yeares of Decay and Mouldering to endure. I cannot Beare to think on it.

After this I didst detect a lightening in my Apprentice's Gloom, but an increase in mine Own.

Freya'sDay. The Conjunction of the Planets.
A day of Hope. Septimus and I didst mix the Tincture at the

Appointed Hour. Now it is set to Ferment and Stewe in the cabinet in the Chamber, and it is for Septimus to know when I may add the Final Part. Only a Seventh Sonne of a Seventh Sonne may tell this to the Moment, I know this now. It grieveth me that I didst drink of my first Tincture before Septimus Came Through. Mama was right, for hath she not always said, "Thy Hastiness and Haughtiness shall be thy Undoing, Marcellus"? Indeed, I was both too Hasty and too Haughty to think that I could make the Tincture perfectly without the Seventh of the Seventh. Alack, it is true (as Mama also do Saye) I am but a Poore Foole.

I pray that this new Tincture will work and give me not only Everlasting Life but Eternal Youth also. I have faith in my Apprentice; he is a most talented and careful Boy and has a great love for **Physik**, just as I did at his age, though I am sure I was not so given to Despondency and Silence.

Tir'sDay

It is some months now since we didst mix the new Tincture and still Septimus will not say that it is ready. I do grow impatient and afraid that something will happen to it while we wait. It is my Last Chance. I can make no more, for a Conjunction of these Seven Planets will not come for many hundreds of yeares hence, and I know that In my State to Come I will not be Fitte to make Another. Daily Mama grows insistent on her own Tincture. She wheedles from me all my doings and I cannot keep anything from her.

Loki'sDay

I write with some Excitement, for this Day we do **Seal** my most Precious Booke, my I, Marcellus. My young Apprentice, who hath now been here One Hundred and Sixty Nine days and hath worked so well, is completing the last few checks upon the final Pages. Soon I must away to the Great Chamber, for all there do Await me.

After I have **Sealed** my great Work, I shall yet again aske the Boy Septimus to look at my new Tincture. I pray it will be ready soon that I may drink of it. Mama doth grow impatient for she thinketh it is for her. Ha! To think that I shouldst desire Mama to live forever too. I wouldst rather die. Except that I cannot. . . . Oh woe.

Ah, the Bell sounds for Ten of the Clock. I must Tarry no more but make Haste to My Booke.

At the sight of Marcellus Pye arriving, Septimus quickly finished his letter to Marcia and put it in his pocket. He planned to sneak it into the *I, Marcellus* as soon as he could, before the book was **Sealed** that afternoon at the propitious hour of 1:33.

Septimus knew Marcellus Pye's book well; he had read it many times over the seemingly endless days he had now spent in Marcellus's time. The book was divided into three sections: the first was *Alchemie* which was, as far as Septimus could tell, completely incomprehensible—although Marcellus insisted that it gave clear and simple directions for transmuting gold and finding the key to eternal life.

The second part, **Physik**, was different, and Septimus understood it easily. **Physik** contained complicated formulae for medicines, linctuses, pills and potions. It had well-argued explanations of the origin of many diseases and wonderfully detailed drawings of the anatomy of the human body, the likes of which Septimus had never seen before. In short, it had everything anyone would ever need to become a skilled Physician, and Septimus had read, reread and then read it again until he knew much of it by heart. He now knew all about iodine and quinine, creosote and camomel, ipecacuanha and flea-seed, and many other strange-smelling substances. He could make antitoxins and analgesics, narcotics, tisanes, emollients and elixirs. Marcellus had noticed his interest and given him his own **Physik** notebook—a rare and precious thing in that Time as paper was very expensive.

The third section of the *I, Marcellus* was the *Almanac*, a day-to-day guide for the next thousand and one years. This was where he planned to hide his note—in the entry for the day that he had disappeared.

Septimus was dressed in his black and red Alchemie Apprentice robes, which were edged with gold and had gold Alchemical symbols embroidered down the sleeves. Around his waist he wore a thick leather belt, fastened with a heavy gold buckle, and on his feet, instead of his lost—and much-loved—brown boots, he wore the strange pointy-toed shoes that were fashionable and made him feel very foolish. Septimus had actually cut the ends off each point because he had kept tripping over them, but it did not exactly improve the shoes' appearance and made his toes cold. He sat huddled in his winter woolen cloak. The Great Chamber of Alchemie and **Physik** felt cold that morning, as the furnace was cooling after many days of use.

The Great Chamber was a large, circular vault underneath the very center of the Castle. Aboveground there was nothing to show but the chimney that rose from the great furnace and spouted noxious fumes—and often rather interestingly colored smoke—day and night. Around the edge of the Chamber were thick ebony tables, carved to fit the curve of the walls, on which great glass bottles and flasks filled with all manner of substances and creatures, alive, dead—and halfway between— were lined up and neatly labeled. Although the Chamber was underground and no natural light reached it, it was full of a bright, golden glow. Everywhere great candles were set burning and the light from these reflected off a sea of gold.

Set into the wall near the entrance to the Chamber was the furnace where Marcellus Pye had first transmuted base metal into gold. Marcellus had so enjoyed the thrill of seeing the dull black of the lead and the gray of the mercury slowly change to a brilliant red liquid and then cool to the beautiful deep yellow of pure gold that barely a day since had passed when he did not make a little gold just for the fun of it. Consequently, Marcellus had amassed a large amount of gold, so much that everything in the Chamber that could be made of gold was—hinges on the cupboard doors, drawer handles and their keys, knives, tripods, rushlight holders, doorknobs, taps—everything. But all these little golden knickknacks

paled into insignificance beside the two largest chunks of gold
that Septimus had ever seen—and wished he never had—
The Great Doors of Time.

These were the doors that Septimus had been pushed
through one hundred and sixty-nine days ago to the day. They
were set into the wall opposite the furnace, two ten-feet-tall
chunks of solid gold covered with long strings of carved symbols, which Marcellus had told him were the Calculations of
Time. The Doors were flanked by two statues brandishing
sharp swords, and they were **Locked** and **Barred**—Septimus
had found that out soon enough—and only Marcellus had the
Keye.

That morning, Septimus was seated at his usual place, the
Siege of the Rose, next to the head of a long table in the middle
of the Chamber, with his back to the hated Doors. The table
was lit with a line of brightly burning candles placed down the
center. In front of him was a pile of neatly stacked paper, the
results of his early morning's work that had involved the last,
laborious checking of Marcellus's astrological calculations,
which were the final touches on what he called his Great
Work.

At the other end of the table sat seven scribes, for Marcellus

Pye had a thing about sevens. Normally the scribes had little
to do and spent much of the day staring into space, picking
their noses and tunelessly humming strange songs. The songs
always made Septimus feel terribly alone, for their notes were
put together in an odd way and they were like nothing he had
ever heard before. Today, however, all seven scribes were fully
employed. They were scribbling furiously, copying out in
their very best script the last seven pages of the Great Work,
desperate to meet the deadline. Every now and then, one stifled a yawn; like Septimus, the scribes had been hard at work
since six that morning. It was now, as Marcellus reminded
everyone as he strode into the Chamber, ten o'clock, or ten of
the clock, as he put it.

Marcellus Pye was a good-looking, somewhat vain young
man with thick black curls of hair falling over his brow in the
fashion of the day. He wore the long black and red robes of an
Alchemist, which were encrusted with a good deal more gold
than those of his Apprentice. That morning there was even a
dusting of gold on his fingertips. He smiled as he looked
around the Chamber. His Great Work—the *I, Marcellus* that
he was sure would be consulted for centuries to come and
make his name live forever—was nearly finished.

"Bookbinder!" Marcellus snapped his fingers impatiently as he surveyed the Chamber in search of the missing craftsman. "Pray, you dullards and dolts, where hideth you the Bookbinder?"

"I hideth not, Your Excellency," a voice quavered from behind Marcellus. "For surely, I be here. Even as I have so stood upon these cold stones these last four hours or more. Indeed, I was here then and still I be here now."

Several of the scribes stifled giggles, and Marcellus spun around and glared at the hunchbacked elderly man who was standing next to a small bookbinding press. "Spare me thy twitterings," said Marcellus, "and bring the press to the table."

Seeing the man struggling to lift the press, Septimus slipped down from his place and went to help him. Together they heaved the press onto the table with a thud, sending ink flying from the inkwells and pens leaping to the floor.

"Take care!" shouted Marcellus as spots of deep blue ink landed on the last pages of his Work. Marcellus picked up the page, which the scribe had just finished. "Now 'tis Despoiled," Marcellus sighed. "But the Hour is against us. It must be bound as it stands. 'Twill show that, tho' Man may strive for Perfection, he will Ever fall short. 'Tis the Way of the Worlde. But a few Spottes of Ink will not divert my Purpose. Septimus, now is the time for your Task."

Septimus picked up the great bundle of parchment and, doing exactly as Marcellus Pye had instructed him earlier that morning, he took the first eight sheets, folded them and handed them to the nearest scribe. The scribe took out a large needle already threaded with thick linen thread and, with his tongue stuck between his teeth in concentration, he sewed the sheets along their fold. Then Septimus passed them to the Bookbinder. And so the process went on for the rest of the morning, all seven scribes sewing and cursing under their breath when the needle pricked their fingers or the thread snapped. Septimus was kept busy running from one scribe to another, for Marcellus Pye was most insistent on Septimus handling the pages himself. He believed that the touch of a seventh son of a seventh son could impart powers of immortality, even to books.

They were now working their way through the *Almanac* and as they approached the page for the date of his capture, Septimus grew nervous, although he tried his best to hide it. He desperately wanted to get a message to Marcia and to try to make contact with his own Time. Septimus had resigned himself to the fact that it was probably impossible for Marcia to help, for—and this is where his brain always turned to mush—if she *could* retrieve him from this Time, surely she would have already done so and he wouldn't still be here, over five months later . . . would he? But whatever Marcia could or couldn't do, Septimus wanted to tell her what had happened.

Suddenly Septimus realized that the next sheet of paper was *the day*. With shaking hands, he pushed it into the middle of a group of eight other sheets—slightly out of sequence, but that could not be helped—and then he passed it to the nearest free scribe for sewing. As soon as the scribe had finished sewing, Septimus took the folded sheets and slipped his note inside. Guiltily, he glanced around him, afraid that all eyes would be upon him, but the steady work of putting the book together continued. The Bookbinder took the sheets from him with a bored expression and added them to his stack of parchment. No one had noticed.

Trembling, Septimus sat down and promptly knocked over an inkwell.

Marcellus frowned and snapped his fingers at one of the scribes. "Go, thee, fetch a rag. I will not have this Work delayed."

At 1:21 the Bookbinder finished binding the *I, Marcellus*.

He handed it to Marcellus Pye, accompanied by a few low whistles from the scribes, for it was a beautiful book. It was covered in soft leather, the title was tooled in gold leaf and surrounded by various Alchemical symbols, which Septimus now understood, and wished he didn't. The Bookbinder had edged the pages with Marcellus Pye's very own gold leaf and had laid the book on a thick red silk ribbon.

At 1:25 Marcellus heated a small copper pot of black sealing wax over a candle flame.

At 1:31 Septimus held the book while Marcellus Pye poured black sealing wax onto the two ends of the ribbon to tie them together.

At 1:33 Marcellus Pye pressed his signet ring into the sealing wax. The *I, Marcellus* was **Sealed** and the whole Chamber breathed a sigh of relief.

"The Great Work be done," said Marcellus, reverentially holding the book in his hands, almost lost for words.

"My stomach rumbleth." The Bookbinder's petulant voice broke into Marcellus Pye's dreams of greatness. "For 'tis well past the time to break Bread. I shall tarry no more. I bid you Good day, Your Excellency." The Bookbinder bowed and left the Chamber. The scribes exchanged glances. Their stomachs

were not entirely silent either, but they dared not say anything. They waited while the Last Alchemist, lost in dreams
of greatness, cradled his Great Work in his arms, gazing at the
book as if at a newborn baby.

However, despite Marcellus Pye's great hopes, no one ever
looked at his book again. It was **Sealed** away after the Great
Alchemie disaster and never again opened—until Marcia
Overstrand ripped the seal off on the day her Apprentice was
snatched from his Time.

✢→26←✢
THE WIZARD TOWER

The scribes had gone to lunch, leaving Septimus behind. Marcellus approached his Apprentice with an anxious look.

"A moment of thy time, Apprentice," he said, sitting down on the stool beside Septimus, which was normally occupied by Septimus's personal scribe. "For surely the Tincture neareth completion and doth require thy attention." Marcellus nodded

toward a glass cabinet that stood on a golden plinth on one of
the ebony tables at the edge of the Chamber. Inside the cabinet, on a delicate three-legged stand of gold, was a small phial
filled with a thick blue fluid. Although Septimus was tired
from his morning's work he did not mind the chance to work
with Marcellus on some real **Physik**. He nodded and got up.

Next to the glass cabinet was a new oak chest with gold-
covered corners, bound with two thick gold bands. This was
Septimus's personal **Physik** Chest and he was very proud of
it. Marcellus had given it to him at the start of their work on
modifying the Tincture for Everlasting Life. It was the only
possession that Septimus had in that Time, and it contained
his carefully written notes on Mixtures, Linctuses, Remedies
and Cures. Most precious of all, it contained his copy of
Marcellus's Antidote to the Sickenesse, carefully folded at the
bottom. His **Physik** Chest was the only thing he would regret
leaving behind if he ever got a chance to try his escape plan—
and if it actually *worked*.

But though the chest belonged to him, Septimus did not
hold the **Keye**. Like all things in the Great Chamber of
Alchemie and **Physik**, it was opened by only one key—the
Keye that hung around Marcellus's neck on a thick gold

chain, securely fastened inside his tunic by a large gold pin. Keeping a wary eye on Septimus, Marcellus unpinned the **Keye** and pulled out the chain, the same thick gold disc embossed with seven stars surrounding a circle with a dot in the middle that the old Marcellus had worn. Septimus eyed the disc longingly, knowing it opened the Great Doors of Time and was the key to his freedom. But short of ambushing Marcellus and grabbing it—which was impossible given their difference in size—he could see no way of getting it. Marcellus placed the gold disc in a round indentation on the front of the chest and the lid swung open as if lifted by ghostly fingers.

Septimus selected a thin glass rod from the chest, his divining rod, which when dipped into a substance would tell him whether it was what Marcellus called **Entire**. Then he opened the door to the glass cabinet and took out the Tincture. He removed the cork, dipped the rod into the contents, turned it seven times and then held it up to a nearby candle flame.

"What thinkest thou, Apprentice?" Marcellus asked Septimus anxiously. "Are we yet ready for the venom?"

Septimus shook his head.

"When thinkest thou it may be so?" Marcellus asked anxiously.

Septimus said nothing. Although he had become used to the oddly circuitous way of speaking that Marcellus and indeed everyone in this Time used, he found it hard to speak like that himself. If he did say anything, people would look puzzled; if they thought about it for a few moments, they understood what he had said, but they knew there was something very odd in the way he had said it. Septimus had lost count of the number of times people had asked where he came from. It was a question he did not know how to answer and one that he did not wish to think about. The worst thing was that now, at the rare times he spoke, his accent and intonation sounded odd even to him, as if he no longer knew who he was anymore.

Normally Marcellus did not mind having such a silent Apprentice—particularly as the only subject that Septimus seemed willing to talk about was Marcellus's future decrepitude—but there were times when it could become irritating. This was one of them. "Oh Prithee, Apprentice, *speak*," he said.

The truth was, the Tincture had been ready almost immediately, but at the time Septimus had not had the skills to recognize it. But then, as is the way with complex tinctures and potions, it had quickly become unstable, and Septimus had spent the next few months patiently coaxing it back to being Entire, for he knew that Marcellus believed that his future depended on this.

Try as he might, Septimus could not dislike Marcellus Pye. Even though Marcellus had taken him from his own Time and was keeping him against his will, the Alchemist had always been kind to him and, more important, had taught him everything Septimus had asked about Physik—and more.

"Thou knowest how this is a matter of Life and Death to me, Apprentice," said Marcellus quietly.

Septimus nodded.

"Thou knowest also that this small amount of Tincture is all I have left. There is no more and none can be made, for the Planetary Conjunction will not come again."

Septimus nodded again.

"Then I Pray you think hard on this and answer me, for this is my only hope to Change my Terrible Fate. If I can drink of the Tincture which thou hast made I hope that I may not grow Old and Foul as I have seen."

Septimus didn't see how Marcellus could change things. He had already seen him as an old, decaying man and that was how it would be, but Marcellus was determined to cling to this one hope. "So Pray tell me when we may add the venom, Apprentice," said Marcellus urgently. "For I fear the Tincture will decay ere long."

Septimus spoke. Briefly, it is true, but he spoke.

"Soon."

"Soon? *How* soon? Tomorrow morn? Tomorrow eve?"

Septimus shook his head again.

"When?" asked an exasperated Marcellus. "*When?*"

"In forty-nine hours exactly. Not a moment before."

Marcellus looked relieved. Two days. He had waited so long already that he could manage another two days. He watched Septimus carefully place the phial back in the glass cabinet and gently close the door. Marcellus breathed out and smiled.

Relieved about his Tincture, Marcellus took time to notice his Apprentice. The boy was pale and thin, with dark circles under his eyes. Of course his appearance wasn't helped by his refusal to cut or comb his bird's nest of hair, but even so, Marcellus felt a pang of guilt.

"Apprentice," he said, "it is not good that thou sitteth here like a Mole beneath his Mound. Though it be chill and Snow still layeth upon the ground, outside the Sunne doth shine." Marcellus fished out two small silver coins and pressed them into Septimus's unwilling and inky palm. "The last Winter Faire is set up upon the Way. Take thee two groats for thy Pleasure and hie thee there."

Septimus looked at them without much interest.

" 'Tis true what they say, Septimus: *A Surfeit of Ink Maketh the Spirit to Sink*. Begone." Marcellus wandered back to the large table and picked up the pad of blotting paper that rested at Septimus's place, revealing a red rose carved into the wood—which Septimus stared at gloomily. "Go," insisted his master, shooing Septimus out.

Septimus took the scribes' exit from the Chamber. He made his way up a steep flight of steps and emerged into the network of tunnels that would take him to the Wizard Tower. This was the one treat that Septimus allowed himself: Every so often he would walk through the Great Hall of the Wizard Tower, as the Alchemie Apprentice was entitled to do. It was a bittersweet experience, but nevertheless it reminded him of home in a way that nothing else in that Time could. He knew the way well now and walked slowly along the rush-lit tunnels. Before long he reached a small underground archway through which could be seen a flight of steps.

"Good day, Septimus Heap," said the ghost sitting at the

foot of the steps—a fairly recent ghost of an ExtraOrdinary Wizard, judging by the brightness of his robes.

Septimus nodded, but he said nothing.

"Turn left at the top and say the password," instructed the ghost slowly and extremely clearly. Since Septimus had never spoken a word, the ghost had decided that he was not the brightest of Apprentices and made a point of loudly giving Septimus the same instructions whenever he saw him.

Septimus nodded again politely and headed for the steps with the usual strange feeling lurking in the pit of his stomach. At the top of the steps, he turned left as he always did and went through a small cloakroom, which he still thought of as the broom closet. This was the part that still raised his hopes, no matter how many times he told himself not to be so ridiculous. He pushed open the door and walked out into the Great Hall of the Wizard Tower.

The first time that Septimus had visited the Wizard Tower, he had stepped into the Great Hall and was convinced that he had somehow come back to his own Time. Everything was the same. The walls had their brilliant, fleeting **Magykal** pictures floating over them, the same air of **Magyk** permeated the atmosphere and made him feel dizzy with relief. Even the floor of the Great Hall had the same strange sandy feel as he had run across it, too excited to glance down at the welcome message it was writing him. He had jumped on the silver stairs and ridden to the top of the Tower, just as he had done every day for nearly two years. He had not noticed the confused glances of the Ordinary Wizards on the various landings; all he had wanted to do was see Marcia and tell her what had happened—and to promise her that he would never go along the Outside Path again. Never, ever, *ever*. On the twentieth floor he had leaped off the stairs and dashed toward the great purple door at the entrance to the ExtraOrdinary Wizard's rooms.

The door would not open.

Septimus had pushed it impatiently, feeling that he could not possibly wait another second to see Marcia, but the door had stayed firmly shut. He could not understand it. Maybe Marcia was in trouble. Maybe she had **Barred** the door . . .

As Septimus stood wondering what could possibly be the matter, the door had suddenly opened and a purple-robed figure stepped out.

"Marcia, I'm—"

The ExtraOrdinary Wizard had peered down at Septimus,

regarding him with a puzzled air, asking, "How did you get up here, boy?"

"I—I—" Septimus had stammered, staring uncomprehendingly at the ExtraOrdinary Wizard, a thin man with straight fair hair, which flopped over his green Wizard eyes. Around his neck hung *Marcia's* Akhu Amulet, and around his waist he wore *Marcia's* platinum and gold ExtraOrdinary Wizard belt. Suddenly Septimus realized the truth of what he was seeing.

"Be not afraid, child," said the ExtraOrdinary Wizard kindly, noticing Septimus's sudden gray pallor. "You are newly come, are you not?" The ExtraOrdinary Wizard looked Septimus up and down, taking in his black and red tunic with the planetary symbols embroidered in gold thread down the sleeves. "Surely, you are the new Alchemie boy?"

Septimus had nodded, utterly miserable for having had his hopes raised and then dashed.

"Come now, child. I will take you down to the Great Hall and show you the way out. Follow me." Septimus followed the ExtraOrdinary Wizard onto the silver spiral stairs, and they stood together in silence as the stairs slowly made their way down through the Wizard Tower.

Now Septimus knew that he no longer belonged in the Wizard Tower, or rather, as he had realized after the first few desperate days, he had *yet* to belong. But, even so, he found it hard to keep away.

As Septimus walked through the Great Hall, a message in shimmering red and gold saying, WELCOME, ALCHEMIE APPREN-TICE, flashed briefly around his feet before moving on to a more important message saying, WELCOME, EXTRAORDINARY APPRENTICE. A slim figure in a green tunic, wearing the sil-ver—*Septimus's* silver—ExtraOrdinary Apprentice belt, had just come in through the great doors to the Wizard Tower, the ones that he was no longer entitled to use. Septimus had taken an immediate dislike to the Apprentice, a girl not many years older than himself. He knew it was unfair to dislike her. She was friendly enough and nodded to him in a distant way when she saw him, but she had taken his place. Or was it, he asked himself, that *he* will have taken *her* place—eventually? At that point Septimus's brain refused to think anymore.

Not wishing to have to explain his presence, Septimus slipped into the shadows and headed down the crumbling stone steps at the back of the Wizard Tower. Then he skirted the great base of the Tower and set off across the snow-covered cobblestones of the courtyard toward the Great Arch. It was, as Marcellus had said, a beautiful day; the air was chill but the bright, low sunlight glinted off the gold streaks that ran through the lapis lazuli, which lined the Arch. However, Septimus paid it little attention as he wandered through and emerged into a thronged Wizard Way. He stood for a moment and pulled his thick red and gold woolen cloak around him against the frosty air, breathing in the strange smells and listening to the unfamiliar sounds. He shook his head in disbelief, he felt so tantalizingly near to home and yet so impossibly far away—five hundred years away, to be precise.

As Septimus stood in the chill winter sun, a realization stole over him. At last he had a few hours of freedom—he had time to try out his plan. It was a desperate plan but it might—just *might*—work.

✣27✣
HUGO TENDERFOOT

As Septimus walked along Wizard Way, his feet did not tread on the pale limestone that he had been used to in his own Time, but on snow-covered earth. The silver torchposts that Septimus had so often watched being lit from his bedroom window at the top of the Wizard Tower were still in the process of being erected in honor of the Queen's Silver Jubilee. The low, yellow stone buildings on either side of the broad avenue, although already old, had a less weathered appearance and showed fine details that Septimus had never seen before.

As he passed the Manuscriptorium at Number Thirteen

Wizard Way, Septimus glanced at the window—which looked odd to him, for it was almost empty and very clean—and a wave of longing to see Beetle swept over him. What would Beetle say now? Septimus wondered. Beetle usually had something to say about everything but he thought even Beetle would be lost for words.

Septimus shook away the memories of the fun he and Beetle had had and turned his thoughts to his destination. A network of tunnels, which Septimus knew from his own Time as the Ice Tunnels, linked all the old buildings of the Castle. In this Time the tunnels were still free of ice and were used by the Alchemists and Wizards to move around the Castle on their business, unseen and unremarked upon. Septimus traveled through one every day to get from Marcellus's house to his workplace at the Great Chamber. Recently he had been sent to the Palace to deliver some solid-gold bowls as a gift to the Queen—an apology for something that Marcellus had done wrong. It was this trip that had given Septimus the beginnings of his plan and it was to the Palace tunnels that he was heading now, except this time he was going aboveground, for he had no wish to bump into any nosy Alchemie scribes or Marcellus himself.

The last Winter Faire was in full swing at the end of the
Way, just in front of the Palace Gate. Great streams of smoke
rose from dozens of braziers cooking chestnuts, corn on the
cob, thick winter soup, sausages and potatoes. Septimus
pushed his way through the strange-smelling crowds, refus-
ing offers of "best crunchy pig's ear, Apprentice," or "tasty
hoof pie, who will buy my tasty hoof pie?" Trying to ignore
the strains of the hurdy-gurdy playing what he supposed was
festive music, Septimus wrenched himself free from a particularly insistent fortune-teller who offered to "reveal thy true
Destiny for one groat, young Master—for who knoweth
what Life doth have in store for us?" Who knoweth indeed?
thought Septimus grimly, as he shrugged away the clutching
hand.

Septimus sidestepped a pair of identical twin stilt-walkers,
ducked under a tightrope and narrowly avoided being hit by a
large piece of wood from an overenthusiastic participant in a
Whack-the-Rat stall. One final squeeze past two fat ladies
throwing crayfish and rice into a large vat of boiling water and
Septimus was out of the crowds. Quickly he turned off down
The Twitten, an alleyway that led to Snake Slipway. Soon he
was ringing the doorbell of the house that he still thought of
as Weasal Van Klampff's.

As Septimus waited to be let in, he remembered all the times that Marcia had sent him to the very same place to pick up the various pieces for her **ShadowSafe**. If he closed his eyes, he could easily imagine himself there, with the raucous insults of the boys on the pier echoing in his ears. Septimus never thought that he would long to hear the sound of *Hey! Caterpillar Boy!*

A small boy wearing the neat uniform of a house servant opened the door. He looked surprised to see Septimus, who usually came up through the tunnel, but he smiled and bowed to the Alchemie Apprentice. "Prithee, step inside, Septimus Heap," said the boy, who had earnest gray eyes and freckles, and whose sandy-colored hair sported the usual pudding-basin haircut that all the children had. Septimus had resolutely refused it, insisting on letting his curls grow ever longer and more tangled by the day.

The boy looked at Septimus expectantly, waiting to escort Septimus where he wanted to go. Septimus sighed; this was not part of his plan. He had forgotten about young Hugo Tenderfoot, who had an irritating tendency to follow him around like a lost puppy. Septimus was forced to say something. He cleared his throat and said, "Thanks very much, Hugo. You can go now."

"Prithee?" The boy's eyes widened, partly in surprise at hearing Septimus speak, but mainly because, although he did not *quite* understand what Septimus had said, he felt as if he should.

Septimus made an effort at what he thought of as Old Speak. "Um. Prithee, Hugo, begone."

"Bigoon?"

Septimus was saved from further efforts by the tinkling of a bell upstairs, which Hugo, after giving Septimus a small bow, ran off to answer.

Quickly Septimus walked to the back of the house and took the creaky steps down to the cellars, where he took the familiar tunnel that led out of the farthest end, along which he had first followed Una Brakket to the Laboratory. The tunnel was well swept and brightly lit with burning rushlights, unlike in Una's Time, but apart from that, it looked just the same. Septimus ignored the door to the Laboratory, which Marcellus used for the more delicate experiments, and took the side tunnel that he used every morning to get to work.

He soon reached the familiar trapdoor—but *where* was the ladder? Septimus knelt and opened the trapdoor. It looked like a long drop. He hunted around for the ladder, but he could find no sign of it. There was nothing else to do—he would have to jump. Septimus hesitated, trying to judge how far he would have to fall if he dangled full-length from the trapdoor. He told himself that if Simon could do it while wearing a pair of ice skates, then he could easily do it without.

In the tunnel, the sound of voices drew near and Septimus stepped back from the trapdoor. He watched a group of chattering Palace servants pass by below him. They were wearing the old-fashioned Palace uniform that he had seen on some of the ghosts in his own Time. The sight of the servants disappearing around the corner suddenly made up his mind, for it would be much easier to get into the Palace unnoticed in the middle of a gaggle of servants. Quickly Septimus slipped through the trapdoor. After dangling uncertainly for a few moments, he realized the reason why the floor of the tunnel seemed so far away—it actually *was* far away, for it was no longer covered in a thick layer of ice. But Septimus was committed now. He closed his eyes, took a deep breath and let go.

"*Oof!*"

The jarring from the drop took his breath away, and as Septimus lay winded on the tunnel floor he saw Hugo's worried face peering down at him through the trapdoor. A moment later Hugo had unclipped the ladder from where it hung from the ceiling and pushed it down to Septimus.

" 'Tis far to fall, Apprentice," said Hugo, scrambling down. "I beg a thousand pardons for leaving the trap unsecured. Prithee, give me your hand." Hugo hauled Septimus to his feet.

"Where was the ladder?" asked Septimus.

"Prithee? I pray you, Apprentice, ascend with care."

Septimus sighed. "Hugo," he said, "I don't want to ascend with care. Now buzz off."

"Buzzoff?"

"Yes, buzz off. Go away. Scram. Oh . . . begone with you!"

Hugo's face fell. He understood "begone with you." It was something his elder brother said regularly. And his two elder sisters. And his cousins who lived around the corner.

"Oh, come on then, if you want to," Septimus relented, realizing that if Hugo went back, he would very soon be telling everyone that the Alchemie Apprentice had gone off into the tunnels alone. Septimus had a feeling that Marcellus might get suspicious.

Hugo looked at Septimus quizzically. "Want to?" he said, copying Septimus's accent. "Want . . . to. I . . . want to!"

"Well, come on then," Septimus told him, impatient to catch up with the Palace servants whose chatter was fast fading away.

Hugo trotted after him. "Buzzoff!" said the boy, running behind Septimus like a small bee. "Buzzoff, buzzoff, buzzoff!"

Septimus half ran, half walked beneath the rushlights that lined the wide brick tunnel that branched off toward the Palace. The small bee running behind kept pace with him and, apart from the occasional "buzzoff," did not make any attempt at conversation. As the voices of the Palace servants became clearer, Septimus concentrated on maintaining some distance from them while still keeping them in sight, for as they approached the Palace, numerous small turns appeared and the tunnel began to resemble a rabbit warren.

After a few minutes, the servants took one of the small tunnels and Septimus was just in time to see them disappear through a narrow red door. He turned to Hugo. "You ought to get back now," he said, and then, seeing Hugo's puzzled look, he said, "Prithee, begone. I pray you do not disclose our journey, for I go about the Master's secret affairs."

Hugo put his head to one side like a parrot wondering whether it was worth repeating what he had just said. "Buzzoff?" he asked.

"Yes, buzz off. Hop to it. Go on, *shoo!*"

Hugo got the message. His face fell and he set off dejectedly back along the tunnel. Septimus felt a stab of remorse. No one else had shown the remotest interest in being with him ever since he had been stuck in this dump of a Time. "Oh, come on then," he called out.

Hugo's face lit up. "Not buzzoff?"

"No," sighed Septimus, "not buzzoff."

A few minutes later Septimus and Hugo were standing in the main kitchen corridor in the middle of what appeared to be frantic preparations for a banquet. A wave of servants swept past them while the boys stood like two rocks in the middle of a fast-moving stream, watching the great stacks of plates, trays of goblets and tubs of golden knives pass by. Two servants almost bumped into them as they staggered past with a massive silver tureen between them; they were followed by a swarm of girls, each carrying two small silver bowls. From each bowl, the head of a duckling poked out.

Septimus was amazed. He was used to the Palace being a quiet and almost empty place. He had expected to be able to sneak in and find his way to the turret that housed the Queen's Room unnoticed. His plan was to follow the Queen or Princess into the Room while the invisible door was still open. He would then sneak down to the Robing Room and try to go through the Glass once more. Septimus knew it was a desperate plan with little chance of succeeding but it was worth a try. But now he could see that if the Palace was this crowded everywhere, he had no chance, especially standing out as he did in his gold-emblazoned Alchemie tunic.

In fact, Septimus's strange attire was already attracting glances. Servants were slowing their pace and staring at him. Soon a jam of people began to build in the corridor, causing a large and impatient footman, who was trying to get out of a linen cupboard just behind Septimus and Hugo, to push his way forward and barge into them. Angrily, the footman grabbed Septimus's collar. "Thou art a Stranger here," he said suspiciously.

Septimus tried to pull away, but the footman held on tight. Suddenly Hugo piped up, "Sire, we are but Messengers, come with urgent tidings for the Pastry Cooke." The footman looked at Hugo's earnest expression and let Septimus go.

"Take you the third Turning and then the second Entrance. Madame Choux may be found therein. Treadst thou softly, for she did burne four dozen Pies but one houre past." The footman winked at Septimus and Hugo, stepped into the stream of servants and was carried away.

Hugo looked at Septimus, trying to understand what he wanted to do. Hugo liked him, for Septimus was the only person he knew who did not shout at him or order him around as if he were no better than a dog. "Buzzoff?" asked Hugo as three fat women bearing great baskets of bread rolls pushed past.

Septimus shook his head and glared at the women who had all turned to stare at him. "Not buzzoff," he replied. "There is something I have to do." In Old Speak, Septimus said, "I have . . . a Queste. Here, in the Palace."

Hugo understood Questes. All knights and pages had them and he didn't see any reason why an Alchemie Apprentice should not have one too. He had never heard of a Queste starting in a Palace, but anything was possible with the Alchemists. He took Septimus by the hand and pulled him into the flow of servants. Following the smells of hot water and soap suds, Hugo soon found what he was looking for: the laundry room.

Several minutes later—and two groats poorer—two new Palace servants, dressed in clean servants' attire, slipped out of the laundry room and set off, the small sandy-haired one trotting behind the taller one with tangled curly fair hair. They had gotten no farther than the corner when a large woman in a stained apron stepped out of the sauce-kitchen doorway carrying two ornate gold jugs. She thrust the jugs, which were full of hot orange sauce, into their hands, saying, "Make haste, make haste," and pushed them off to join a long line of other boys, each carrying an identical golden jug.

Hugo and Septimus had no choice. Under the eagle eye of the sauce cook, and followed by a large Palace footman carrying a crisp white cloth in case any boy might spill the sauce, they followed the line of boys up the long and winding back stairs and emerged into the gloom of the Long Walk. As they progressed slowly, the chatter and clatter of a banquet beginning in the Ballroom drifted toward them. Suddenly the great doors to the Ballroom were thrown open and a roar swept over them. The long line of boys began to file inside.

Septimus and Hugo trailed into the Ballroom at the end of the line and the footman closed the doors behind them. Open-mouthed, Hugo stared at the sight before him. He had never seen such a huge room packed full of so many people wearing such rich and exotic clothes. The hubbub was almost deafening and the rich smells of the food made the boy's head swim, for no one ever remembered to feed Hugo very much.

Septimus, who was more used to such occasions—Marcia was a generous hostess at the Wizard Tower—was also open-mouthed but for another reason. Sitting at the top table, a familiar figure surveyed all before her and, as ever, Queen Etheldredda wore her usual expression of disapproval.

✢✢ 2 8 ✢✢
IMPOUNDED

Snorri Snorrelssen's *Trader's barge had* just tied up at the Traders' Dock at the Port. Alice Nettles, Chief Customs Officer, stood on the quayside looking at it suspiciously. Alice was a tall, gray-haired woman with an imposing manner acquired during her time many years ago as Judge Alice Nettles. But now she wore the official blue robes of a Customs Officer with two gold flashes on the sleeves. People at the Port did not mess with Alice, or at least not more than once.

"I'd like a word with your skipper," Alice told Snorri.

This was not a good start to any conversation with Snorri. She glared at Alice and did not deign to reply.

"Do you understand what I'm saying?" demanded Alice, who was sure that Snorri did. "I want to speak to your skipper."

"I am the skipper," Snorri told Alice. "You will speak to me."

"You?" asked Alice, shocked. Surely the girl was no more than fourteen at the most. She was far too young to be skippering a Trader's barge on her own.

"Yes," said Snorri defiantly. "What do you want?"

Alice was nettled. "I want to see your Castle Inspection Papers."

Glowering, Snorri handed them over.

Alice perused them and then shook her head. "These are incomplete."

"They are all that I was given."

"You have failed to comply with the emergency Quarantine regulations. I am therefore impounding your boat."

Snorri flushed with anger. "You—you cannot do this," she protested.

"Indeed I can." Alice motioned to two Customs Officers who had been hanging around in the shadows in case of trouble. They produced a great roll of yellow tape and proceeded to cordon off the *Alfrún*.

"You must leave your boat immediately," Alice told Snorri. "It will be towed to a dock in the Quarantine area until the emergency is over. You may then reclaim it on full payment of dock dues and inspection fees."

"No!" said Snorri. "No! I will not let you!"

"Any more trouble and you will be spending time in the Customs House lock-up," Alice told her sternly. "I shall give you five minutes to pack a bag. You may bring your cat if you wish."

Five minutes later, Snorri Snorrelssen was homeless. From their perch up the mast, Stanley and Dawnie watched Snorri trudge off with her bag slung over her shoulders, Ullr trailing at her heels.

"That's a bit much," Stanley muttered to Dawnie. "Nice kid like that. What's she going to do now?"

"Well, at least we're in time for a late lunch," said Dawnie. "I fancy something from that nice pie shop over there."

Stanley didn't fancy anything, but he followed Dawnie

down the mast and scuttled off after her to the pie shop.

Snorri wandered away, lost in her thoughts. It had been one long disaster ever since she had arrived at the Castle. She must have seen nearly all the ghosts in the Castle—except for the one she had really wanted to see. She had been thrown out of the Castle just before the Market was due to start and nearly sunk by a dragon. She had only just got rid of the wretched creature and now *this* had happened. Snorri was so annoyed that she did not at first hear Alice Nettles calling after her. And when she finally did, Snorri made a point of ignoring the Customs Officer.

But Alice was not to be put off. "Wait—I say, wait a moment!" She ran after Snorri and caught up with her. "You are young to be alone in the Port," said Alice.

"I am not alone. I have Ullr," muttered Snorri, glancing down at her orange cat.

"It is dangerous here at night. A cat may be company but it will not protect you—"

"Ullr will," Snorri replied stonily.

"Here," said Alice, pushing a piece of paper into Snorri's unwilling hand. "This is where I live. Warehouse Number Nine. Top floor. There is space for you and Ullr to sleep comfortably. You would be very welcome."

Snorri looked unsure.

"Sometimes," explained Alice, "I have to do things in my job that I do not like to do. I am sorry about your barge but it is for the good of the Port. We cannot risk the Sickenesse spreading here. Boats bring rats and rats bring disease."

"Some say," said Snorri, "that it is not rats that spread the Sickenesse. They say it is another kind of creature."

"People say many things." Alice laughed. "They say that great chests of gold have mysteriously appeared on their ships without their knowledge. They say that barrels of water must have miraculously turned to brandy during the voyage. They say that they will return to pay the duty on their cargo. It does not mean that what they say is true." Alice was aware of Snorri's clear blue eyes under their pale, quizzical eyebrows. She met Snorri's gaze and said, "But what I said to you was true. I hope you will stay."

Snorri nodded slowly.

"Good. It is Warehouse Number Nine. You will find it on the fifth street on the left past the old dock. It is best to arrive before nightfall, for the old dock is not safe after dark. Go in the blue door set into the green, take a candle from the tub and walk through the lower warehouse. Take the iron steps at the back to the top. The door is always open. There is bread and cheese in the cupboard and wine in the jug. Oh—and my name is Alice."

"I am Snorri."

"I will see you later, Snorri." With that, Alice was off to a small boat waiting for her at the foot of the harbor steps. Snorri watched the oarsmen row Alice toward a large ship at anchor about a half mile out from the Port, and Ullr rubbed against her tunic and meowed. He was hungry—and so, Snorri realized, was she.

Tucked away between the Traders' Dock Customs House and an abandoned loft was the Harbor and Dock Pie Shop. A welcoming yellow light glowed from its steamed-up windows, and the wonderful smell of hot pies drifted out the open door. Neither Snorri nor Ullr could resist it. Soon they had joined a line of hungry workers waiting for their supper. The line moved slowly but at last it was Snorri's turn.

A boy came out of the kitchen carrying a tray of newly baked pies and Snorri pointed to them. "I shall have two pies," she said.

The young woman behind the counter smiled at Snorri.

"That will be four groats, please."

Snorri handed over four small silver coins.

Maureen—ex-kitchen maid, ex–Doll House skivvy and brand-new owner of the Harbor and Dock Pie Shop—wrapped up the pies and added some scraps from a broken pie. "For your cat," she said.

"Thank you," said Snorri, hugging the hot pies to herself and thinking that the Port was not such a bad place after all. As she left the shop she heard Maureen scream.

"Rats! Quick, Kevin, *Kevin!* Get them!"

Snorri and Ullr sat at the Traders' Dock harbor wall eating their pies. Ullr, who always got very hungry just before nightfall, quickly ate the scraps from Maureen and then finished off the pie that Snorri had bought for him. As the sky darkened and gray rain clouds began to blow in from the west, Snorri and Ullr watched a tug tow the *Alfrún* out of Traders' Dock and take it on its way to the Quarantine Dock, which was in a bleak marshy area on the other side of the river mouth. Despite the warmth of her pie, the company of Ullr and Alice Nettles's offer, Snorri felt desolate as she saw the *Alfrún* leave the protected waters of the harbor and pitch to and fro as she entered the black waters of the Port tidal race.

Her mother's words came back to her: "You are a fool, Snorri Snorrelssen, to think that you can Trade on your own—what makes *you* so special? It is no life for a woman, let alone a girl of fourteen. Your father, Olaf, rest his soul, would have been horrified—*horrified*, Snorri. The poor man did not know what he was doing when he left you his Letters of Charter. Promise me, for the love of Freya, that you will not go. Snorri—Snorri, come back here *right now!*"

But Snorri had not promised, she had not come back *right now*. And so here she was, stranded in a strange port, watching all her trading hopes be towed away before being left to rot in some pestilential dock in the middle of nowhere. Snorri got to her feet with a sigh. "Komme, Ullr," she said.

With the first few drops of a cold autumn rain falling, Snorri set off. Alice's directions should have been easy to follow, but Snorri was still preoccupied with her thoughts and soon found herself lost in a bewildering maze of derelict old warehouses and decrepit old ghosts. Snorri had never known such disreputable-looking ghosts. The streets were crowded with old smugglers and muggers, drunkards and thieves all jostling, cursing and spitting, just as they had done when they were Living. Most of them paid no attention to Snorri, for they were too busy fighting one another to notice the Living or to bother to **Appear** to them, but one or two, aware that Snorri could see them, began to follow her along the streets, enjoying the anxious look on her face as she turned to check if they were still there.

The rain began to fall heavily and Snorri's spirits sank even lower. She felt trapped. She had no compass, no chart, and everything looked the same to her: street after street of great black shapes looming overhead, blocking out the sky. Snorri would far rather have been adrift in the towering gray waves of the northern sea in the *Alfrún* than lost among these menacing old warehouses. Looking all around, desperately searching for a blue door in the green—or was it a green in the blue?— Snorri began to panic. She stopped to try to get her bearings, but the entourage of ghosts closed in and Snorri could no longer see where she was. She was surrounded by mocking faces sporting rotting teeth, broken noses, cauliflower ears and blinded eyes.

"Go away!" screamed Snorri, her shout echoing along the chasm of a street and bouncing back to her.

"You lost, sweetie?" said a soft voice nearby. Anxious to see who had spoken, Snorri **Passed Through** the circle of ghosts to a chorus of curses and protests. A young woman, dressed in various shades of black, stood in the shadows of a doorway a few yards away—a blue doorway within a big green warehouse door. Cut into the brick arch above the door was the number 9.

"No, I am not lost, thank you," said Snorri, heading gratefully for Alice's door. Seeing where Snorri was headed, the young woman stepped forward and put her arm across the little door, barring Snorri's way. With a stab of fear, Snorri saw the young woman's shining black eyes with their flashes of brilliant blue. She knew she was dealing with a **Darke** Witch.

"You don't want to go in there," the Witch told her.

"I *do* want to go in there," retorted Snorri.

The **Darke** Witch smiled and shook her head as though Snorri had not understood what she had meant. "No, sweetie. You *don't*. You want to come with me. Don't you?" A spark of blue flashed across the Witch's eyes and Snorri felt herself weakening. Why did she want to go into some horrible old warehouse anyway?

"That's right, you come back with Linda now. Come on." Linda, trainee Coven Mother of the Port Witch Coven, took hold of Snorri's hand, and Snorri felt her viselike grasp close over the bones in her hand and squash them together,

"Ouch," protested Snorri, trying to pull her hand away while Linda's grip tightened even more, rolling her bones across one another. "Ouch, you're *hurting.*"

"*Surely* not. A strong girl like you is no match for little ole me." Linda giggled, knowing that she had Snorri in her power. Linda had been out on what the Witches called a Twilight Trawl; she needed to replace their maid-of-all-work after the girl's irritating accident in the coven's cauldron earlier that day. They had eventually fished the girl out but it was too late. Now Linda was determined to bring back what looked like a promisingly strong maid who would probably last more than the usual couple of months.

However, Snorri was not being as cooperative as Linda had expected. The witch roughly tugged her away from the doorway and Snorri resisted. Linda crunched her hand hard. Snorri gasped with pain, but suddenly Linda loosened her grip and Snorri saw a flicker of fear in the Witch's black eyes. She followed Linda's gaze and almost laughed with relief.

Ullr was transforming.

The scrawny orange cat at which Linda had just surreptitiously aimed a kick was no longer scrawny or even particularly orange. As Linda stared, unwilling to release her catch, she saw the NightUllr beginning to appear. The black tip at the end of Ullr's orange tail was spreading over the cat like the darkness of an eclipse traveling across the land. Ullr's fur was becoming sleek, short and shiny; it covered his new muscles, which rippled under his skin, forming and reforming as he grew slowly and steadily, becoming a full-sized panther.

But still Linda kept her grip tightly on Snorri's hand. Enthralled, she stared at Ullr, a brilliant plan forming in her mind. With this great black beast at her side there would be no arguing about her rightful place as Coven Mother—not with a Familiar such as this. He would get rid of old Pamela with no trouble, not to mention any of the other Witches who gave her trouble and, come to think of it, that old nurse next door. The Coven could take over the nurse's place, which would pay old nursie back for setting fire to the bridge. Linda smiled. What fun this was going to be.

And then Ullr underwent his final nighttime transformation: His eyes became the eyes of the NightUllr. Linda looked into Ullr's night eyes and something inside her went cold. She knew she was no match for this creature. Something of the **Darke**, far **Darker** than Linda had ever known, stared out from Ullr. She dropped Snorri's hand as if it had bitten her and backed away, murmuring, "Nice kitty, nice kitty cat."

A long, low menacing growl rose from Ullr's throat; the great black cat's lips retracted in a snarl, baring his sharp white teeth. Linda turned and ran, racing through the throng of watching ghosts. She did not stop until she had reached the Port Witch Coven, where she had to hammer on the door for at least half an hour before anyone bothered to let her in.

Nursing her sore hand, Snorri pushed open the small blue door and she and the NightUllr stepped into Warehouse Number Nine.

✦29✦
WAREHOUSE NUMBER NINE

S *norri was fast asleep* when Alice Nettles returned much later that night. The Chief Customs Officer was cold, tired and wet after a rough crossing back from a particularly uncooperative ship, but as she pushed open the little blue door, Alice was smiling, for stepping through the door with her was the ghost of Alther Mella.

Alther had had a difficult day at the Palace. By the afternoon, Marcia had joined Jillie Djinn in the Hermetic Chamber with the words "No, Alther, I do not wish to see anyone—not even you. No, I *don't* know when I shall be out again. Not for months probably. Now go *away*." Alther had continued to search the Palace for Jenna and Septimus but there was no sign of them anywhere. There was, however, an endless supply of stories about what had happened to them. It seemed to Alther that Spit Fyre was definitely involved, especially since the dragon had disappeared too, but apart from that he could not make any sense of it. Alther could not bring himself to believe that the note Marcia had found was really from Septimus. He still hoped that Jenna and Septimus had gone to see Aunt Zelda, although as the day wore on and darkness began to fall, he realized that he was clutching at straws, for he knew that Aunt Zelda would not allow either of them to stay away so long.

Silas, meanwhile, grew ever more despondent. By nightfall, Alther finally admitted to himself that Septimus's letter was genuine. He had told Silas that he "still had a few leads to follow up" and would be back the next morning. Alther left Silas and Maxie, both sitting gloomily by the Palace door, awaiting the arrival of Gringe.

What Alther meant was he needed to talk to Alice Nettles.

And so, as Alice was being rowed back across the choppy dark seas toward the welcoming lights of the Port, she had seen the ghost of Alther Mella standing patiently on the harbor wall, as she had once seen Alther many years ago when he was still a Living ExtraOrdinary Wizard. On that memorable day, Alice had been returning from the Castle Court's annual Mystery Winter Picnic. Alther had found out where the picnic was— a windswept affair on Sandy Isle a few miles south of the Port—and had come especially to meet her. Alice had never before, or since, felt as happy as she had at the moment when she had recognized Alther's purple-robed figure gazing out to sea, waiting for her. Two weeks later Alther was dead, shot by an Assassin's bullet.

Alice picked up a candle from the tub, struck the flint and lit it. Alther followed Alice through the warehouse as she threaded her way through narrow canyons precariously carved out between the great teetering stacks of ancient cargo. The light from Alice's candle threw dancing shadows across the piles of old wooden chests, furniture, assorted junk and even an ornate carriage with huge red wheels and two stuffed tigers in the harness. Alther jumped at the sight of the tigers' glittering glass eyes, which seemed to stare reproachfully at him as if he was somehow responsible for their fate.

Alice's warehouse was one of many in the old part of the Port, stuffed full with the contents of ships long rotted, brought to the Port by seafarers long dead who had neglected, or refused, to pay the duty on their goods. Now it never would be paid, for much of it was centuries old and the interest on the duty amounted to many times the value of the items.

After many twists and turns, Alice and Alther arrived at the staircase at the back of the warehouse. Alice's clattering footsteps echoed on the steep iron steps as she climbed past the floors, each crammed to the ceiling with its dusty and cob-webbed mix of treasure and junk.

"Can't think why you live in this dump, Alice," said Alther, teasing, "when you could have the Chief Customs Officer's stately pile on Dock One."

"Can't think why either," said Alice, a little breathless, as they were now on the fifth floor and still climbing. "Must be something to do with an old ghost who insists on following me around." Alice stopped on the sixth floor landing to catch her breath, leaning for a moment against a frighteningly tall stack of Chinese willow pattern plates before thinking the bet-ter of it. "Pity you never went to the Customs House parties, Alther," she puffed. "It would have saved a lot of trouble."

"You wouldn't be in such good shape though," Alther replied, smiling. "You look good with all this exercise, Alice."

"Why, thank you, Alther. I do believe I get more compliments from you now than I ever did when you were . . . well, you know."

"Living, Alice. It's all right, you can say the word. Well, I was a fool then. Didn't realize what I had until it was too late."

Alice Nettles did not trust herself to reply. She turned and ran up the last flight of steps to the seventh floor, pushed open the door to her warehouse aerie and busied herself lighting the huge stove in the middle of the floor.

Alther floated in a few moments later, following in some of the footsteps that he had once taken many years ago, after Aunt Zelda had discovered some letters hidden behind the chimney in Keeper's Cottage. She had paid Alther a surprise visit, insisting that there was *something* important in Warehouse Number Nine and she wanted him to help her find it. When Alther had asked Aunt Zelda exactly what was so important, she would only say that she would know it when she saw it. After much arm-twisting from Aunt Zelda, Alther had reluctantly agreed to do a **Search**. The **Search** had taken him three weeks, during which he had become allergic to dust, fallen out with Aunt Zelda and found nothing important as far as he could tell, apart from a nest of rare and very bad-tempered tropical spiders behind the hot water pipes. By then Aunt Zelda had stopped speaking to him. Later, when they had made up their quarrel, Aunt Zelda had told him what she had been looking for. Alther had always meant to go back and search for it again, but like many things in his life, he had never quite gotten around to it.

And so Alther had considered the whole episode a complete waste of time until many years later, when Alice had tried to find somewhere in the Port to live, where the ghostly Alther could visit her. Alther had not frequented many places in the Port when he was Living, so when Warehouse Number Nine came up for sale, he and Alice were thrilled. Alice had bought Warehouse Number Nine, with contents included, and moved into the top floor. Now Alther could visit Alice and wander freely through the entire warehouse without any fear of being Returned, which he loathed.

Up in her aerie, Alice put her candle down on the big table beside one of the small windows looking out over the Port, Alther joined her and together they sat side by side in companionable silence. In a far, shadowy corner, Snorri stirred but she did not wake. Alice glanced at the small figure lying on a thick pile of Persian rugs, snugly covered in a large wolfskin, and smiled. She was pleased to see Snorri safe but . . . what was *that*?

Forgetting for a moment that Alther was a ghost, Alice grabbed his arm. "Alther," she whispered, as her hand clung to thin air. "Alther, there's something in here. An animal. It's big. Oh, my goodness, *look*."

Two green eyes were reflected in the candlelight. They stared at Alice and Alther.

"Good lord, Alice," gasped Alther. "You've got a panther up here."

"Alther, I do *not* keep panthers up here. Or anywhere. I don't even *like* panthers. Oh, no, listen to it. . . ." A low growl filled the top floor of Warehouse Number Nine as the Night-Ullr got to his four padded feet, the fur on the back of his neck bristling. Snorri woke up.

"Kalmm, Ullr," she murmured, seeing Alice and Alther silhouetted against the moonlight and knowing that she was safe. The NightUllr gave one last growl just to make a point. Then he lay down beside his mistress, rested his great black head on his paws and regarded Alice Nettles and her ghostly companion through half-closed eyes. Snorri laid her arm across his warm smooth back and fell into a deep sleep.

"I didn't know she had a panther as well as a cat," muttered

Alice. "She might have told me. These Traders are an odd bunch."

Alther looked at the Customs Officer with an affectionate smile. He loved the way Alice, who appeared so tough on the outside, was really nothing of the sort. If you were in trouble, then Alice Nettles was not one to stand aside and watch. "Another of your waifs and strays, Alice?" he asked.

"Just a girl whose boat I had to impound for Quarantine. I felt bad about it, but what could I do? The Sickenesse is spreading through the Castle like wildfire. We can't risk it coming here."

"Ah, yes . . . that reminds me." Alice's mention of the Castle brought Alther unwillingly back to reality, for he would have happily stayed sitting with Alice beside the little window, looking out at the lights of the Port, all night long.

"What is it, Alther? Why do I have the feeling this is not going to be a romantic evening spent talking in the moon-light?"

Alther sighed. "I'd really like it to be, but something has happened."

It was Alice's turn to sigh. "Really? Something always does, doesn't it?"

"Please, Alice. This is bad. I need your help."

"You know you don't even have to ask. What can I do?"

"I need to **Search** the warehouse from top to bottom. There is something in here that I need to find. Zelda and I never found it many years ago, but now I'm a ghost I think I can." Alther sighed. "I shall have to **Pass Through** everything."

Alice looked shocked. "But you *hate* **Passing Through**, Alther. And—well, you know how much stuff there is here. Mountains of junk and who knows what. It will be *horrible*. Goodness, this must be serious."

"It is, Alice—very serious. You see, this morning Septimus and Jenna—say, what *is* going on out there?"

A loud banging way down in the street was rattling Alice's windowpanes. As they listened, the noise became louder and more insistent, until it turned into a regular *thump, thump, thump* that shook the floor and reverberated through the table.

"Sometimes I worry about you living in such a rough neighborhood," said Alther.

"Just late-night revelers, Alther. I'll tell them to be quiet." Alice stuck her head out the window and said, "Oh. Goodness me. Well, at least it's not a panther, I suppose."

"What's not a panther?" asked Alther.

"A dragon."

"A dragon is not a panther?" Alther repeated slowly. He felt as though Alice was talking in code.

"Generally speaking, no. A dragon is a dragon and a panther is a panther. That's just the way things are. Don't ask me why. I suppose I had better go and let them in before it smashes the door to pieces."

"Who? What?"

"The *dragon*, Alther. I told you, there's a dragon at the door."

✢ 3O ✢
SACRED SHEEP

All right, all right, I'm coming!"
Alice yelled as the great
warehouse door shuddered under
the force of the blows. Alice,
watched by a frustrated Alther, who
longed to help her but could only
stand by, pulled back two great
iron bolts and, using all her
strength, pushed the huge
green warehouse door along
its rusty runners. The door
moved slowly but, with the
help of Jenna and Nicko
pushing from out-

side, it creaked and groaned its way open until there was enough room for a fifteen-foot dragon to squeeze in.

Spit Fyre galumphed inside. "Careful!" shouted Alice—too late. A great stack of boxes marked *fragile* crashed to the floor accompanied by the sound of tinkling glass. Spit Fyre was unconcerned. He sat down and looked around him expectantly as if he was waiting for someone to bring him supper, which was not far from the truth since Spit Fyre spent most of his time hoping for supper—or breakfast, mid-morning snack, lunch, tea, or dinner. Spit Fyre didn't mind what it was called as long as he could eat it.

"Jenna!" Alther gasped with relief. "What are *you* doing here?" The ghost smiled broadly as Jenna and Nicko, looking pale and tired, stepped inside. "Ah, and the master boatbuilder too. Hello, lad." Nicko gave Alther a brief smile, but did not seem to be his usual cheery self. More in hope than expectation, the ghost peered out at the dark, rainy street and said, "Septimus with you?"

"No," said Jenna—unusually curtly.

"You both look worn out," said Alice. "Come upstairs and get warm." Spit Fyre banged his tail with a loud crash.

"Quiet, Spit Fyre," said Jenna wearily, patting the dragon's neck. "Go lie down. Come on. Lie down. Sleep." But Spit Fyre did not want to sleep. He wanted dinner. The dragon sniffed the air. It did not smell promising, just dust, moldering cloth, wormy wood, rusting iron, sheep bones . . . mmm, *sheep bones*.

Spit Fyre pushed his nose into a tall tower of finely balanced wooden boxes, which stretched about twenty feet high into the darkness. The tower wobbled precariously.

"Out of the way, everyone!" Alice yelled, pushing Jenna and Nicko back out on the street with herself and Alther, who did not want to be **Passed Through** by a load of dead sheep. A deluge of boxes crashed to the ground, bouncing off Spit Fyre and landing all around him.

When Alice, Alther, Jenna and Nicko peered warily inside, the dragon was almost buried in boxes. He lifted his head, shook off a shower of dust and splinters and set about crunching open the first smashed box. A pile of yellowing bones and what looked like an old sheepskin rug fell out.

"Ugh!" said Jenna, who had recently developed a particular dislike of bones. "What has he got there?"

"Sheep," said Alice, raising her voice over loud crunching, cracking sounds as Spit Fyre bit into the contents of the first box. "It's sheep bones. He's eating one of the Sarn herd. Oh, well."

Gingerly, Alice, Jenna and Nicko stepped back inside and picked their way through the boxes. Jenna could just make out the words written on the side of one of the still-intact boxes in an old-fashioned scrawl that had turned brown with age: SACRED HERD OF SARN. BOX VII OF XXI. URGENT. FOR IMMEDIATE DELIVERY. They were almost obliterated by two more words stamped over them in a commanding, unfaded red: DUTY UNPAID.

"Spit Fyre!" Jenna shouted, pushing her way through to reach the dragon. "Stop it! Give that to me. *Now!*" Spit Fyre looked down at Jenna out of the corner of his eye and carried on crunching through sheep number VII. It was *his* food and he was not giving it to anyone else—not even to his **Locum Imprintor**. She could go and find something of her own to eat.

"It doesn't matter," puffed Alice as she and Nicko pushed the door closed and the warehouse became shrouded in darkness.

"But they're *sacred* sheep," said Jenna. Spit Fyre cracked another bone and gulped it down with a loud gurgle.

"That I doubt very much." Alice chuckled. "I reckon they're most likely part of the Sacred bones scam that the Customs Office stamped out about a hundred years ago. I wouldn't worry about it. Best use for them, if you ask me.

They've not been much good to anyone else. In fact, I did hear that a farmer from the High Farmlands had bought them thinking that they were a live flock. When he came down to pick them up and realized that he'd bought a load of boxes full of old bones he refused to pay the duty and threw the Customs Officer into the harbor. Spent thirty days in the Customs House lock-up for his trouble."

With firm instructions to Spit Fyre that he must behave himself and go straight to sleep when he had finished the sheep, Jenna and Nicko left the dragon crunching his way through the Sacred Herd of Sarn and followed Alice and Alther to the top of the warehouse.

The NightUllr growled as Jenna and Nicko walked in.

"Ouch!" Nicko gasped. At the sight of the panther's green eyes shining in the light of Alice's candle, Jenna had grabbed his arm hard. Which was, thought Nicko, unusually jumpy for Jen.

Snorri sat up, woken by Ullr's rolling growl. Her sleepy eyes focused with surprise on the two newcomers, "Kalmm, Ullr," she said.

"Snorri?" asked Jenna, recognizing the white blond hair in the dark.

"Jenna? It is you?" Snorri untangled herself from the wolf-skin and, with the NightUllr padding at her side, she stumbled across the rough wooden floor to greet Jenna.

"Hello, Snorri." Nicko's voice came out of the dark and gave Snorri a shock. "Nicko . . . I . . . I did not know you were coming to the Port also?" she said in her singsong accent that Nicko liked so much.

"Neither did we," said Nicko grimly. "Stupid dragon circled above the Port for hours. Thought we'd never land. Freezing cold up there."

"I would rather be in my boat." Snorri smiled.

"So would I," said Nicko. "Give me a boat anytime—even a paddleboat. I saw Wolf Boy paddling over to the Forest and I'd have swapped that dragon for one of those any day—even a pink one."

"I don't think Wolf Boy's right about Septimus being lost in the Forest," said Jenna.

Nicko shook his head in agreement. "He may as well look, though, since there was no way he was going to get back on Spit Fyre."

"Did he get to the Forest all right?" Jenna asked Snorri.

Snorri nodded. "He whistled and a boy came to meet him."

"That will be Sam," said Nicko. "He'd have been fishing."

"Sam?" asked Snorri.

"Yes, Sam. He's my—"

"Brother!" Snorri laughed.

"How did you know?" asked Nicko, puzzled.

"They always *are*," said Snorri, and just kept on laughing.

Alice returned with some blankets from a pile tumbling out of a chest marked PRODUCIA DE PERU. DUTY UNPAID. IMPOUNDED. "Well, well, so you all know one another," she said. "Here, Jenna, Nicko, wrap yourselves up in these and get warm, you're both shivering like a couple of jellyfish on a plate."

Wrapped in the brightly patterned blankets, which smelled strongly of goat as the damp from their tunics crept in, Jenna and Nicko stood steaming in the heat of the briskly burning logs inside Alice's stove. While they slowly warmed through, they watched Alice place a pot of water to boil, mix up some chopped oranges, cinnamon, cloves and honey in an earthenware jug and then pour the boiling water over the mixture. A warm spicy smell filled the air.

"You must be hungry too," said Alice. Nicko nodded. As he slowly became warm and forgot about the hours he and

Jenna had spent on Spit Fyre circling in the drizzle above the Port, he realized that he was ravenous. Alice disappeared into the shadows at the far end of the space that she called home and returned with a tray laden with a huge fruitcake, a large loaf of rough Port bread, great chunks of Port herb sausage and half a spiced apple pie.

"Now everyone, *eat*—you too, Snorri." Alice noticed that Snorri, unsure, was hanging back.

Snorri took her place at the table. She sat next to Alther and smiled at him. "I . . . I think I have seen you at the Castle," she said.

Alther nodded. "You are a Seer?" he asked.

Snorri blushed. "I do not always wish it, but it is so," she replied. "Like my grandmother."

"And like your mother?" asked Alther.

Snorri shook her head. She was *not* like her mother. No way.

After the fruitcake, bread, sausage and most of the pie had disappeared and Alice had made two more jugs of spiced orange, she looked at Jenna and said gently, "Would you like to tell us what happened today? Alther and I . . . well, we would like to know."

Alther smiled. He liked the sound of "Alther and I" and he liked the way Alice considered his concerns to be hers too. He reflected that just then he would have felt perfectly content if it had not been for the awful business of Septimus.

Jenna nodded. It was a relief to tell them. She took a deep breath and began her story, starting from when Queen Etheldredda had **Appeared** in her bedroom the previous night. Alice and Alther listened somberly, and when Jenna told them about Septimus and the Glass, Alther became almost transparent with concern.

Then it was Alther's turn to tell bad news. When Jenna heard what Marcia had found in the *I, Marcellus*, she gasped and put her head in her hands. Septimus was gone. Forever. And it was *her* fault.

Nicko put his arm around Jenna's shoulders. "You mustn't blame yourself, Jen."

Jenna shook her head. She did blame herself.

"Well, *I* think . . ." said Alther suddenly. Everyone looked at the ghost, who was sitting between Snorri and Alice, his purple robes becoming surprisingly substantial in the candle-light as a small ray of hope flickered in Alther's mind. "I think there might—just—be a way to find him. It's a long shot, of course, but . . ."

And so, on the top floor of Warehouse Number Nine, one Night Creature and four Living humans sat in the firelight, listening to a ghost as he began to explain how they might, *possibly*, be able to rescue Septimus.

On the ground floor of Warehouse Number Nine, the Sacred Herd of Sarn was slowly disappearing—gnawed, crunched and gulped down until there was nothing left but a few empty boxes and a long, satisfied sheepskin-smelling burp.

Not so very far from Warehouse Number Nine, a Royal Barge made its stately progress over the Marram Marshes, floating in on a ghostly flood from more than five hundred years before. It drew up at a long-gone landing stage and lay shimmering in the moonlight, rocking gently, while its occupant stepped ashore and, with a disapproving expression, picked her way up a muddy path that led to a little thatched cottage.

Queen Etheldredda **Passed Through** the door and the cottage's inhabitant—a comfortable-looking woman dressed in a large patchwork tent—looked up from her seat by the fire, puzzled at the **Disturbance** she had felt blow into the room. She shivered as Queen Etheldredda drifted by, sending the candle flames guttering. Aunt Zelda got to her feet and, through half-closed bright blue witch's eyes, she surveyed the cozy room, which suddenly no longer felt *quite* so cozy. But for all Aunt Zelda's **Looking**, she could not make out the ghost of Etheldredda as she drifted about, searching for Jenna.

Aunt Zelda was spooked. She could see a **Disturbance** pass across the walls of books and potion bottles as Etheldredda inspected them for signs of a hidden door, but found only a cupboard hiding a giant flask. And as Etheldredda ascended the steep stairs to the attic, her pointy nose leading the way, Aunt Zelda followed, though she did not know why.

Convinced that Jenna was there, Etheldredda searched the little attic room from top to bottom. Etheldredda **Blew** back the covers on all three beds, fully expecting to find Jenna hidden under one of them—but found nothing. Then she stuck her pointy nose under the beds—there was nothing— and looked in Aunt Zelda's closet, which was full of identical patchwork dresses—and still found nothing.

Aunt Zelda was, by now, frantic. She knew there was an UnQuiet Spirit in her cottage. She ran downstairs to find her **Expell Spell**, leaving Etheldredda poking around the attic. It was then that Etheldredda found something that Aunt Zelda had promised to keep safe for Jenna: her silver pistol. With a great effort of will, Queen Etheldredda picked up the pistol, while downstairs Aunt Zelda began to chant the **Expell**. In a rush of stale air—for Aunt Zelda's spell was old and had been kept in a damp cupboard—Queen Etheldredda was **Expelled** from the cottage and hurled into the low-tide mud of the Mott. Etheldredda picked herself up, and clutching the pistol, she reembarked on the Royal Barge.

Sitting in her cabin, away from the prying eyes of Aunt Zelda, Etheldredda inspected the pistol. Then she drew out the small silver ball that she had taken from Jenna's room. Holding the bullet in her increasingly Substantial hand, Etheldredda inspected it closely and smiled a grim smile. It was inscribed with the letters I.P.—short for Infant Princess—and had been Named for Jenna when she was a baby. It had been a stroke of luck, thought Etheldredda, bumping into the ghost of the spy who had betrayed the Heaps all those years ago. If the UnQuiet Spirit of Linda Lane had not crawled out of the river and hauled herself up onto the Royal Barge, Etheldredda would never have known about the power of a Named bullet. And luck was still on her side, because now she had the silver pistol to go with it—all she needed was the princess to point it at.

The ghostly Royal Barge drifted away from Keeper's Cottage,

leaving a very unsettled Aunt Zelda in its wake. Lounging on her cushions, rocked by the slight swell of an ancient storm, Queen Etheldredda closed her eyes and dreamed of the day soon to come when the Princess would be no more and the Castle would revert to its rightful Queen—Queen Etheldredda the Everlasting.

⊹ 31 ⊹
DRAGO'S HOARD

The pale light of a frosty autumn morning was trying to shine in through the high windows at the back of the ground floor of Warehouse Number Nine. It was not helped by the thick green glass in the tiny windows or by the layers of grime that covered them, but it did its best and eventually emerged as long shafts of feeble brightness swimming with great shoals of dust.

"*Where* did you say this wretched mirror was, Alther?" asked Alice crossly, as she negotiated her way out from underneath a stuffed elephant. Alther was sitting on an ebony chest, which was firmly bound with thick iron straps and secured with a huge lock. DUTY UNPAID: IMPOUNDED was stamped all over it in bright red, as though some past Customs Officer had lost his temper and taken it out on the chest.

Alther looked ill; he felt as if he had eaten a bucketful of dust and washed it down with the slime from a bag of moldy carrots. He had spent the last hour **Passing Through** the most dusty, mildewed and decrepit pile of junk it had ever been his misfortune to **Pass Through**. There were so many large objects tied up in sacks, sealed in trunks and stuck at the back of inaccessible stacks that the only way to check every single piece in the warehouse was for Alther to **Pass Through**. So far he had found nothing and he had only checked maybe one thousandth of the available junk and rubbish piled up in Alice's warehouse. Alther could not even think straight, for the loud snores and foul-smelling burps—and worse—that were emanating from Spit Fyre stopped his dusty, muddled thoughts from making any sense at all.

"It's a *Glass*, Alice, a Glass—not a mirror," Alther corrected grumpily. "And if I knew where it was, I wouldn't be sitting here feeling like I'd been trampled by a herd of Foryx, would I?"

"Don't be silly, Alther," snapped Alice. "Foryx don't exist."

"Are you sure, Alice? You've probably got a whole stash of 'em stored up here somewhere," said Alther testily.

"When I was little, I used to think Foryx existed," said Jenna, hoping to help things along. "Nicko liked to scare me with bedtime stories about them—all half-decayed and slimy, horrible warty faces, huge feet with great claws running forever around the world and crushing everything in their path. I used to have to watch the boats from my window for hours before I forgot about them."

"That's not a very nice thing to tell your little sister, Nicko," said Alther.

"Jen didn't mind, did you, Jen? You used to say that you wanted to be a Foryx."

Jenna gave Nicko a push. "Only so that I could chase you, you horrible boy." She laughed. Snorri watched the brother and sister together and wished that she had a brother like Nicko. She would never have left home and come to this crazy place if she had.

Alice clambered over a pile of sacks containing seventy-eight pairs of backward-pointing joke shoes. Her foot went through one of the sacks and a cloud of leather-beetle droppings rose into the air. She succumbed to a coughing fit and slumped down on the chest beside Alther. "Alther, are you quite sure—*cough*—that this Glass—*cough*—is actually—*cough, cough*—here?"

Alther felt too full of dust to reply. The ghost was sitting in a shaft of light, and Jenna could see that he was full of millions of minute swirling particles. The dust cloud inside him was so thick that it made Alther appear almost solid and strangely grubby.

"But you think it *could* be here, don't you, Uncle Alther?" asked Jenna, coming over to sit beside the disconsolate ghost.

Alther smiled at Jenna. He liked it when she called him Uncle Alther. It reminded him of happy times when Jenna was growing up in the Heap household in their chaotic room in The Ramblings.

"Yes, Princess, I do think it could be here."

"Maybe we should ask Aunt Zelda to come help?" Nicko suggested.

"Aunt Zelda had *no idea* where it was," said Alther grumpily, remembering his trying time with the White Witch in Warehouse Number Nine. "She just stood in the middle of the floor waving her arms like this"—Alther did an impression of a windmill in a hurricane—"and saying there, Over *there*, Alther. Oh, you *silly* man, I said *over there!*" Jenna and Nicko laughed; Alther did a surprisingly good imitation of Aunt Zelda.

"But I am *sure* that the Glass is here. Marcellus himself says so. One hundred and sixty-nine days after he had his first success with what he calls the True Glass of Time, which he made a great palaver about and had gold doors for it and all the works, he completed two more Glasses of Time. A matched pair this time, which would be portable. These worked very well, apparently. It's these I am looking for. I reckon one of them is here."

"Wow . . ." Nicko whistled under his breath and looked around as if expecting to suddenly see a Glass of Time looming out of the junk.

"Are you sure, Alther?" asked the ever-skeptical Alice.

The dust particles inside Alther were beginning to settle and the ghost was feeling better. "Yes," he said, more definitely now. "It's all in Broda Pye's letters, even though Marcia says they're a load of old claptrap."

"Sep told me about Broda once," said Jenna. "She was a Keeper, wasn't she? Oh, I *so* miss Sep, he used to tell me so much stuff about all sorts of useless things . . . and I used to tell him to stop going on like a dumb parrot . . . and I wish I hadn't. I really *do*." Jenna sniffed and wiped her eyes. "It's just the dust," she mumbled, knowing that if someone said anything remotely comforting to her she would burst into tears.

"Ah, well. I expect Septimus was interested in Marcellus's **Physik**," said Alther. "It worried Marcia sick. She got jumpy every time he went near the **Sealed** section in the Library. I wonder where he found out about Broda?"

"Aunt Zelda told him," said Jenna.

"Did she now? Well, well . . . and did she tell him about the stack of letters she found behind the fireplace when she was making the cat tunnel for Bert?"

Jenna shook her head. She was sure Septimus would have told her *that*.

"Well, those were the letters from Marcellus Pye to his wife, Broda."

"But Keepers aren't allowed to get married," said Jenna.

"Right," agreed Alther. "And this goes to show why."

"Why, Uncle Alther?"

"Because Broda told Marcellus all the Keeper's secrets. And when things got tough for Marcellus, she let him use the Queen's Way as a shortcut to the Port. He brought all sorts of **Darke Alchemical** stuff through there. There are still pockets of **Darkenesse** hanging around. You must always take care going through there, Princess."

Jenna nodded. She wasn't surprised. She always felt a little scared on the Queen's Way.

"So Marcellus told Broda that he'd put the Glass in this warehouse?" asked Nicko.

"No. He wrote and said he'd been swindled out of it. Apparently he had taken it through the Queen's Way, got it to the Port on a succession of stubborn donkeys and finally put it on a ship. He planned to take it to a small but power-ful group of Alchemists up in the Lands of the Long Nights, but he was double-crossed by the ship's captain. As soon as Marcellus was out of the way, the captain sold the Glass to a certain Drago Mills—a merchant in the Port who was in the habit of buying a load of old tat without paying too much attention to where it had come from. Anyway, some months later Drago fell out with the Chief Customs Officer over a small matter of unpaid duty for another cargo and got the whole contents of his warehouse impounded for his trouble. No one, not even Marcellus, could get into the warehouse without the say-so of the Chief Customs Officer, whom Marcellus referred to as an Officiouse Tubbe of Malice, and the Officiouse Tubbe never did give the say-so."

"So *this* was Drago Mills's warehouse?" said Nicko.

"You've got it, Nicko. Warehouse Number Nine. Even more junk has been added over the years, of course, but at the core of it is Drago's hoard. And somewhere, hidden away under all this stuff, there is a Glass that should take you through Time—one hundred and sixty-nine days after Septimus arrived."

There was silence as Nicko, Jenna and Snorri took this in.

"We have to find it," said Jenna. "It must be here somewhere. Come on, Uncle Alther."

Alther groaned. "Give an old ghost a rest, Princess; I still feel like the inside of a carpet sweeper. Just a few more minutes and then I'll get back to it. Aha . . . that dragon of yours is stirring. I'd see to it quickly if I were you. And you might want to take a shovel with you from that pile of old garden tools over there."

A pungent smell filled the air. "Oh, Spit Fyre!" Jenna protested.

Ten minutes later, a large pile of dragon droppings was steaming outside Warehouse Number Nine, and Spit Fyre was gulping his way through a barrel of sausages that Jenna had bought from a passing cart on its way to market. The dragon downed the last sausage, sucked up the contents of a bucket of water that Nicko had fetched and snorted, sending a great lump of dragon spit slamming into a pile of novelty fake brass candlesticks and melting the paint off them.

Spit Fyre was content—a fire stomach full of bones, a food stomach full of sausages. Now he just had to complete the Seek. With a purposeful air, the dragon thumped his tail down, sending a great cloud of dust up in the air, and closed his eyes, Seeking the way to his Imprintor.

Ever since Spit Fyre had been Seeking, he had felt drawn to the Port, and apart from the irresistible call of breakfast on Snorri's boat, he had not been deflected from his purpose. He had circled for hours above the Port, Seeking, until at last he had felt something. He had landed on the old dock and followed the faint callings of the Seek all the way to the great green door of Warehouse Number Nine. But now, with a full stomach, Spit Fyre could think clearly—and the Seek was stronger, much stronger.

Suddenly, with a loud snort, the dragon reared up and crashed his way into the depths of the warehouse, sending the pride and joy of Drago Mills flying in all directions. Jenna, Nicko, Snorri and Alice saw him coming, but Alther, pale and full of dust, did not. In a moment, the ghost was tossed into the air, **Passed Through** by a dragon on a mission and thrown to the ground, where he lay feeling worse than he had ever felt in his entire ghosthood.

As Alther lay dusty and trampled on the floor, Spit Fyre ripped into the ebony chest that the ghost had been sitting on. In seconds the iron bands were peeled off, the giant lock snapped and the lid of the chest flipped open by a large, sharp dragon claw.

Inside the chest, lying in soft velvet folds, was a Glass.

⊹⟶3 2⟵⊹
THE DARK POOL

A strange silence fell over Warehouse Number Nine. Even Spit Fyre stopped his excited snorting and became unusually still. Everyone stepped a little closer, gingerly peered into the black ebony chest and shivered. It had a ghastly coffinlike look to it. The Glass lay like a dead body within, held secure and cushioned from the world for the past five hundred years in dark red padded velvet, which was shaped perfectly to every little swirl and twirl of its gold frame. Silently, four people, one ghost, a dragon and a thin orange cat gazed into the depths of the chest, trying to see into the dark pool of Glass, over which a dim white mist hung suspended as though it lay over still water on a fall morning.

The Glass was horribly enthralling. Spit Fyre stared into it, his tail slowly swishing from side to side, clearing the way through the debris of ten dozen smashed novelty gnomes and a hundred pounds of crushed wax fruit like a great windshield wiper. Nicko wanted to jump in and see how deep it was, and Snorri wondered if she could **See** her great-aunt Ells. Alice wanted to see exactly what it was she had bought in the job lot of Warehouse Number Nine—for the Glass belonged to her now and she felt responsible for it.

Alther was fascinated to see the very thing that he had read about in Marcellus Pye's letters, written all those long years ago. It looked exactly as he had imagined it would. As Alther stared deep into its depths, he had the sensation of gazing into a bottomless pit, a pit into which he would love to lose himself forever. Stop it, you old fool, Alther told himself sternly. With some difficulty, he shook himself out of his reverie.

"Funny you didn't notice that you were sitting on the Glass all that time, Alther," said Alice.

"Not particularly funny, Alice," said Alther huffily, "since the chest is lined with solid gold. Soaks up most stuff, does gold. No wonder Marcellus was complaining to Broda about the weight of the Glass—what on earth did he expect?"

Jenna stared at the Glass, gathering her courage. If Alther was right, then here was the way to Septimus. Here was her chance to make amends for the harm she had done to him; all she had to do was jump into the Glass and find him, wherever he may be. She had no choice. Taking them all by surprise, Jenna scrambled onto the edge of the chest.

"Get back!" Alther shouted. Jenna jumped at the sound of alarm in the ghost's voice, lost her balance and fell toward the Glass.

Nicko was there in an instant. "Jen!" he yelled, but he was too late. Jenna tumbled forward, awkwardly, arms outstretched like those of a diver who has misjudged her dive, and plunged through the liquid blackness of the Glass. All that was left were a few ripples, which soon subsided, leaving the surface undisturbed as before.

A horrified silence was broken by Nicko yelling, "Jen, Jen!"

He threw himself into the chest, but was hauled out, just as his boot touched the Glass, by a hefty heave from Alice Nettles.

"No, Nicko, it's too dangerous," puffed Alice, keeping a tight hold on his arm.

"*I don't care,*" said Nicko fiercely, unable to take his eyes off the *thing* that had just swallowed his little sister. "Let go of me. Jen's in there on her own. Let me *go!*" Alice hung on like a ferret with a rabbit, but Nicko was very nearly as tall as she was, and three months' hard work in Jannit Maarten's boatyard had made him strong. With a desperate twist he wrenched himself away, and before Alice could do anything, Nicko threw himself forward once more. This time he succeeded.

It was cold going through the Glass. Nicko felt as though he was falling through liquid ice. The surface of the Glass passed over him like a tight, frozen band and let him go, as if it was no longer concerned with what happened to him. And then Nicko was in free fall, tumbling, twisting and turning like an autumn leaf on the still night air, until he was pulled into another sheet of coldness, which ran over him and let him go, leaving him to drop into a pile of old coats. Nicko got up, hit his head on something and was sent flying by the advent of a small orange cat with a black-tipped tail hurtling into his back.

"Ullr . . . Snorri?" asked Nicko, rubbing his head. He was sitting half in and half out of a large green cupboard, which was full of dusty old coats. As he twisted around to see where Ullr had come from, he saw Snorri tumble from an old looking glass—just like the one he had just jumped through—which was propped up at the back of the cupboard.

"Hello, Nicko." Snorri stepped out of the UnderCooks' coat cupboard—no longer used due to the UnderCooks having taken over the second footmen's coatroom after a bitter power struggle. Snorri looked at Nicko uncertainly. What would Nicko think of her following him like that? Her mother had always told her that a girl must never chase a boy. . . . Snorri shook her head to get rid of the thought of her mother. Well, she told herself, her mother never said anything about not jumping through a Glass after a boy. Never.

The UnderCooks' coat cupboard was in a deep recess at the junction of two passageways. Warily, Snorri and Nicko crept out and looked around. The place was pervaded with a strong smell of roasting meat, which immediately made Nicko feel hungry, but there was no sign of Jenna. None. The place was deserted. Nicko suddenly realized how stupid he had been. Jenna could be anywhere. Who was to know where the Glass would have taken her?

Something lying on the passage floor caught Snorri's eye. She bent down and picked up a delicate gold pin in the shape of a J. Nicko went pale. "That's Jen's," he said. "I gave it to her for her birthday."

"She was with this pin until a few minutes past," said Snorri. "I feel it. I *know* it."

Nicko smiled and held out his hand. "Come on, Snorri," he said. "Let's go find her. She can't be far."

Back in Warehouse Number Nine, Alice Nettles was readying herself to follow Jenna, Nicko and Snorri through the Glass. They could not, she told Alther, be left to face the dangers alone. Whatever might happen, she was determined to go.

Alther shook his head, horrified at the turn that events had taken. He had lost Jenna, Nicko and Snorri through the Glass, and now he was about to lose his beloved Alice. Alther held out very little hope of seeing any of them again. He would have given anything to be able to go with Alice, but he knew that as a ghost, he could not go.

Wretched, Alther watched Alice gingerly step into the chest. He saw her stand delicately on the frame of the Glass, gathering her courage for the plunge and resisting a strong urge to hold her nose, which Alice always did when she jumped into water. As Alther tried to fix the last sight of Alice in his mind, a sight that would have to last him forever, Spit Fyre finally located the **Seek**.

Spit Fyre, whose dragon nerve endings had yet to catch up with his growth spurts, had no idea what size gap he might or might not fit through. He flung himself at the Glass, expecting to go through, just as he had seen Jenna, Nicko and Snorri do. Alice Nettles was thrown back out of the chest and fell beside Alther, where she lay winded, unable to stop the dragon from smashing the Glass into a thousand dark, glittering fragments of nothingness.

PRINCESS ESMERALDA

Two *Palace Guards had just* come off duty and were making their way toward the kitchens, where one of their wives worked as a Stewer of Meates and the other as a Keeper of the Gravie Boate. The smaller guard, a chubby man with a stretched, shiny face and little piggy eyes, had been discussing exactly how many kidneys should go into a steak and kidney pie. His thinner, rather ratty companion, who was beginning to feel queasy, almost stepped on a dazed Jenna as she stumbled out of the UnderCooks' coat cupboard. In a moment she found herself grabbed by her arms.

"Well, well, well, what be here?" asked the piggy-eyed guard, whose eyesight was none too good in the dim light of the lower reaches of the Palace. "Where be thy Palace livery, my girl?"

Jenna stared at the guard. She had the oddest feeling that she *almost* understood what he had said.

"Thou'rt a Stranger here," the piggy man growled. "A trespasser upon the Royal Ground. 'Tis a grave offense. Thou wilt have to answer for this."

Jenna had the distinct feeling that it was better not to say anything just then. She was aware of the ratty guard staring at her. She glanced up at him and saw a look of panic in his eyes.

"Let her loose, Will. Do you not see she wears the garb of a Royal Princess?"

The piggy guard peered at Jenna so intently that his eyes became little slits in the rolls of fat in his face. Beads of sweat broke out on his forehead, and he let go of Jenna's tunic as if he had just had an electric shock. "Why didst thou not say?" he hissed angrily to the ratty one.

"Forsooth, I *have* said. If thou didst not prate on so with

Kidneys and Stewes and Gravies until my stomach revolts against me and my mouth fills with bile, then thou wouldst have seen with thine own tiny eyes."

Jenna's head was spinning. What were they saying? She had heard *Royal Princess* and she had an uncomfortable feeling that she had been recognized. She found herself taken firmly, but this time respectfully, by each elbow and propelled along the passageway.

Jenna listened to the guards' excited talk, catching some of the words and trying to make sense of it.

"There will surely be a reward for us, Will. To have found our lost Princess will be truly marveled at."

"'Tis true, John. And what a great joy for the Queen, to be reunited with the daughter she had feared drowned. Perchance we might see a queenly smile once more."

"Maybe. Though I do not know that we did ever see a queenly smile, Will, if truth be told."

Will grunted in agreement and Jenna was respectfully asked to climb the stairs, if she pleased, up to parts of the Palace "more Fitt for her Royal Person."

Soon they emerged into the Long Walk and it was only then that Jenna became sure that the Glass had not only transported her back to the Palace, but back through time as well. The Long Walk was just as Sir Hereward, one particularly talkative evening, had once described to her. It was full of ancient treasures—not the strange, exotic finds that Milo Banda had strewn along the Long Walk, but a rich array of history that belonged in the Palace and told its story. There were beautiful tapestries, finely detailed paintings of Princesses and their nurses, Palace dogs, visiting Magicians and Soothsayers, even a great bronze of a rare blue dragon, which had a look in its eye that reminded Jenna of Spit Fyre.

The Palace was not the quiet, hushed place that Jenna was used to; it was buzzing with activity. The Long Walk reminded Jenna of rush hour at The Ramblings. Hundreds of Palace servants—all immaculate in their Palace livery of a gray tunic or dress with a deep red stripe around the hem— were bustling to and fro on important business. Some were carrying trays of small covered silver dishes; some had stacks of documents. Many were clutching Palace message bags, which were small red folders with the Palace crest stamped upon them in gold. But the strangest thing was that the air was filled with the tinkling of bells, for outside every room a small bell was poised, ready to be rung by a higher servant to summon a passing lower servant to do their bidding. The bells rang incessantly, and generally their only effect was to cause the nearest servants to rush past and pretend not to notice.

Jenna's progress was slow. As each servant realized who was walking between the guards they stopped in surprise, causing others to bump into them. Some gasped in shock, others curtseyed or bowed, and many smiled and quickened their pace, anxious to be the first to tell the news that the drowned Princess was **Returned**.

It was some time later when the guards finally made it to their destination: the Throne Room. The Throne Room was the one room in the Palace that Jenna had never been in, and had no wish to go into either, for it was the room where her mother and Alther had been assassinated, and the room where she too had nearly lost her life—and would have done so had not Marcia Overstrand taken her to safety. When Jenna had returned to live at the Palace, she had decided that she wanted the Throne Room locked, and Alther, who had no love for the place either, had readily agreed.

At the sight of the drowned Princess, the two door pages' eyes widened in shock, and the smaller boy squeaked in surprise. Both pages bowed low, and in a well-practiced maneuver, they pushed open the great doors to the Throne Room and ushered Jenna in. The Knight of the Day, a rotund, friendly faced man who was the Queen's personal knight for that day, looked astonished at the sight of Jenna, then made a low and extremely elaborate bow, which involved a lot of arm waving and hat doffing.

While this was going on, Jenna's attention wandered to the Throne Room itself. The Throne Room was huge. It was the second biggest room in the Palace and took up the front five windows of the building, which looked out over the Palace Gate and straight down the old Alchemie Way. To the left was Wizard Way and in the distance, behind the Great Arch, Jenna could see the Wizard Tower soaring into the pinkish late-afternoon sky. The golden Pyramid at the top was almost lost to view in what Jenna recognized as a **Magykal** haze, which was drifting out the windows of the ExtraOrdinary Wizard's rooms and swirling up into the sky.

The Knight of the Day, having finally finished his bow, had been a little put out to find that the person it had been directed at was staring out the window. He gave a discreet cough. Jenna's attention snapped back to the Throne Room. It was richly hung with thick tapestries depicting the lives and adventures of various Queens. At one end, a blazing fire roared in the huge fireplace; at the other, on an ornate golden throne, sewing her tapestry with short, vicious stabs of her needle, sat the living, breathing, greatly disapproving Queen Etheldredda.

"Oh, *no*," gasped Jenna.

The Knight of the Day stepped forward and addressed the Queen, who had still not bothered to look up. "Your Majesty," said the Knight, who took hours to say what most people said in minutes, if they bothered to say it all. "Your most Gracious and Royal Majesty, may I present a Joy to Your Heart, a Succor to Your Mother's Grief, a Great Returning, the Wondrous Thing for which we all Hoped but yet did Fear may never come?"

"Oh, get on with it, man," snapped Queen Etheldredda, breaking a thread with her teeth and crossly tying a complicated knot.

"Your own drowned *daughter*, Your Highness," the Knight continued, allowing what Jenna thought was a slight air of disapproval to color his words. "Your very own Flesh and Blood, Madam. That Delicate Rose for whom the Castle has Pined these long months gone, those dark months of Grief and Pain are now but a painful Memorie—"

Queen Etheldredda flung her tapestry to the floor in exas-peration. "Oh, for goodness' sake, man, cease your brainless wittering, else I will have your head perched upon the Palace Gate this nightfall." The Knight of the Day turned ashen and subsided into a fit of coughing. "And cease your foul splutter-ings—*what is this?*" Queen Etheldredda had at last seen Jenna.

"I-It is your lost daughter, Your Majesty," the Knight of the Day ventured timidly, unsure whether this would be consid-ered brainless wittering or not.

"I can see that," said Etheldredda sourly, peering down the length of the Throne Room, seeming for once almost lost for words. "But . . . *how?*"

"These two fine guards, Your Majesty"—the Knight of the Day waved an expansive arm at the two Palace Guards who were now standing respectfully to attention on either side of Jenna—"found your Heart's Delight a-wandering, lost and a-wailing in the depths of the Palace."

Jenna was annoyed but said nothing. She most definitely had *not* been wailing.

"Then take them away to the dungeon!" Etheldredda barked. Two burly soldiers stepped from the shadows and grabbed the two guards. Before they had time to catch their breath, they were frog-marched from the Queen's presence, whisked down to the Palace basement and thrown into the dungeon—a nasty damp pit below the offal kitchens, dripping with rancid fat and filthy water from the wash-up overflow.

Without the strangely reassuring presence of Will and John, Jenna suddenly felt very alone. The physical presence of Queen Etheldredda as flesh and blood was horribly intimidating in a way that her ghost had not been. And the snake-tailed creature that clung to the Queen's skirts, staring at Jenna with its malevolent red eyes while it clicked its retractable single tooth in and out of its pointy jaw, made her want to turn and run. But there was no escape. Jenna could feel the meaty breath of the Knight of the Day on the back of her neck.

"And you," said Queen Etheldredda, addressing the anxious Knight, "*you* can take Esmeralda to her room and lock her in until suppertime tomorrow. She will know not to run away from her mama in the future."

The Knight of the Day bowed to the Queen; then he gently took Jenna by the arm, murmuring, "Allow me, Princess, to accompany you to your Chamber. I will instruct the Cooke to provide you well with victuals." Jenna had no choice but to let the Knight of the Day escort her along the corridor and take the familiar route to her own room.

The ghost of Sir Hereward was leaning against the wall gazing into space, looking bored and listless. At the sight of Jenna he looked amazed. He snapped to attention, bowed respectfully and then, smiling broadly, said, "Welcome home, Esmeralda. 'Tis a *most* Happy Outcome, for we did Fear thee Drowned. Now, I have some merriment for thee, for thou seemest to mine eyes a little pale and distressed. What, pray, be the difference betwixt the Griffin and the Pomegranate?"

"I don't know, Sir Hereward. What *is* the difference between a Griffin and a Pomegranate?" Jenna smiled.

"Ah, I shall not send *thee* forth upon my marketing. Hur hur!"

"Oh. Oh, I see. Very funny, Sir Hereward."

As the Knight of the Day ushered Jenna into her room, Sir Hereward peered at her. "Thou art changed, Esmeralda. Changed in thy speech. 'Tis the shock, no doubt. Rest well, Princess. I shall guard thee from harm. Thy mama shall not enter." The ghost bowed, the Knight of the Day closed the great doors to Jenna's room, and Jenna found herself alone in her room—or rather, alone in the drowned Esmeralda's room.

Princess Esmeralda's room had a creepy feeling to it. Not only was it cold, damp and growing interesting crops of furry green spots in various places, but there was a miserable, even malevolent, atmosphere about the place. Jenna wandered around the room, which was surprisingly decrepit for a Princess's bedchamber. The floors were rough and bare, with splintery pieces of wood coming off the boards. The meager curtains were threadbare and did not even reach to the bottom of the tall windows. Great chunks of plaster were missing from the ceiling. There was only one small candle beside the bed, and of course there was no fire in the grate.

Jenna shivered—and not just from the deep chill in the musty air. She sat on what she thought of as her bed, and discovered that it felt nothing at all like her own bed. But Jenna hardly noticed the lumps; she was too busy thinking about Septimus. How was she going to find him? She had somehow expected him to be waiting for her as soon as she had come through the Glass, but now she saw how foolish that had been. She was in a whole new world and Septimus could be anywhere in it, anywhere at all. He could even be much older—so much older that she would not recognize him. In fact, he could even be . . . dead. Jenna shook her head to try to get rid of such pointless thoughts. Alther had been quite clear about this—the Glass she had **Gone Through** was completed one hundred and sixty-nine days after the Glass that Septimus had **Gone Through**. One hundred and sixty-nine was an important Alchemical number, being thirteen times thirteen. Jenna was good at math and soon she had worked out that Septimus would already have been in this Time for about five and a half months—if Alther was right. But where *was* he?

She lay back on the bed and tried to figure out how to find Septimus while she watched a large spider rappel down one of the bedposts. Being the true Princess that she was, Jenna was quick to feel something sharp digging into her back, and she wondered how Princess Esmeralda had ever got any sleep at all in such a lumpy bed. What could possibly be causing it? Exasperated, Jenna tipped the mattress up to see if she could find the problem.

Underneath the damp old feather mattress, which smelled strongly of chickens, there was a large leather-bound book with sharp metal corners. On the cover was written: THE VERIE PRIVATE AND PERSONALLE DIARIE OF PRINCESS ESMER-ALDA. NOT TO BE OPENED OR READE BY ANY PERSON. ESPE-CIALLY MAMA.

Jenna picked up the diary and let the mattress go with a *thud*, sending up a cloud of dust and mold spores. "Atchoo!" she sneezed. "Atchoo, atchoo, *atchoo!*" Eyes streaming, Jenna sat down on the now considerably less lumpy bed and, ignoring the instructions on the cover, began to read Princess Esmeralda's diary.

⊹⊹34⊹⊹
PRINCESS ESMERALDA'S DIARY

P rincess Esmeralda's diary was written in the same flowing, old-fashioned script that adorned the cover. The ink was black and clear—as was the awful story it had to tell.

MoonDay
Today has been a most Foul and Fearful Day.
*   Upon the orders of Mama (who maketh me to toil in all the*

Lowly places of Our Palace so that "You will knowe, Esmeralda,
what it is to Work"), I didst go to the Meate Kitchens today. I was
set to work to pull all manner of Innards and Gizzards for the
Meate Cooke, who is a foul-mouthed Manne who doth sweat like
an overripe Cheese. He hath a Face like unto a Cheese also, the
kind that Mama doth eat: white and pitted with blue Veins upon
his Nose. Methinks that if Mama didst eat the Meate Cooke's Nose
she would not knowe the difference. And if she didst knowe it to be
the Meate Cooke's Nose, methinks Mama wouldst still eat of it. But
I must not write of Mama, for it is dangerous Business so to do.

When I didst return to my Chamber from the Meate Kitchens,
and the Servant had given me a Bowle of sweete cleene Water to
take the Blood and Gristle from under my Fingertips, then Mary
didst come a-knocking at my Door as frantically as if the
Wendron Witches of the Forest were hard upon her Heels. Mary,
whom I love dearly, near as much as I do love my little baby
Sisters, was in the most Distressed State.

I didst ask her, as I always do (for Mama does not allow me
to see my dear Sisters near as oft as I wouldst like), how fared my
little Cherubbs this day. Whereupon Mary didst wail like the Pigs
do wail when they see the Meate Cooke's Cleaver. I sat her down
beside my small Fyre (for which my Servant doth steal me a few

Coals upon frosty Nights) and I heated some Water over it, for poore Mary's Teeth were a-chattering like a loose Windowpane in the Winde.

I put my question about my little twinne Sisters once again with, I confess, some Feare in my Heart. "They are Gonne!" Mary didst cry with such heart-wrenching grief that deare Sir Hereward did come a-running (or a-floating, rather, I shouldst say) and didst aske of us "Wherefore the Teares?" For by the time the deare Ghoste was by our side I knew the true tale of my Sisters' Fate. They were Gonne.

Early this Morn, Mary didst take my baby Sisters to see our mama, for Mama had ordered that it be so. Mary was told by the Bumptiouse Barrelle of Larde to leave the Babies in the Throne Room to await Mama. They didst run after her, crying, "Mary, Mary," but the Bumptiouse Barrelle didst push her from the Chamber and barre the Door.

Now Mama and the Bumptiouse Barrelle do saye that Mary never brought the Babes to the Throne Room and that she hath loste them. Poore Mary's feet are like fat pigs' Bladders, swelled from a day walking the Palace to find them, and I believe she is losing her Mind. I fear 'twill fare ill for poore Mary. And how will it fare for my poore Sisters?

Tir'sDay

A most Dismal Day. My Spirits are low. There is no word on my little Sisters and of Mary there is no trace. I am alone in the Worlde.

Woden'sDay

I knoweth not myself today. My Mind is in Turmoil. I am returned to my Chamber from another foul day in the Meate Kitchens and something is wrong. I do not know what. I have a great Feeling of Dread.

Thor'sDay

At dawn Sir Hereward did go to fetch my deare Brother. All last night I didst heare a great lamenting and crying behind the Wainscoting at all hours. It was the Voices of my baby Sisters. I care not what my Brother or Sir Hereward may say, but I do know the Cries of my Sisters. I did beg my Brother to remove the Wainscoting and he, fearing for my Mind, did do so. There was nothing there, but even now I heare their little Voices crying for me to set them free.

Freya'sDay

My Brother came. I am to stay with him awhile. I am grateful, for I cannot bear to heare the Crying a moment longer. Mama would not allow it at first but he hath Gainsayed her. I leave this afternoon and I shall take my little Booke with me.

Loki'sDay

Today Mama didst call upon my deare Brother, for there is some Business between them. My Brother is uneasy on this count for he didst saye to me, "I will not do this, Esmeralda. Although I do wish Mama well, as I must for I am her Sonne, I do not wish for her to live Forever." Although I understood not what he meant— for how can any person live Forever?—I didst reply that most certainly I did not wish it either and we laughed. It is good to laugh with my Brother.

SunnDay

Mama didst call again today. My Brother locked his Chamber and didst saye to me, "Begone, Esmeralda, for this is not Business upon which you should thinke." But tho' I should have obeyed my deare Brother, I didst not. I didst listen at the Door, though I needed not to press my Eare so close, for Mama's voice did drille into my Eare through the great oake Door like a woodpecker's Beake. "I tell thee now, Marcellus, I shall not rest until I have *it!" Mama didst scream. I heard not my Brother's reply for Mama didst not stop her Torrent of Words.*

As she didst leave, her creature, which doth bite all who displeaseth her and cause them to Sicken and Die, didst bite my little cat. Tonight poore Puss doth aile and moan most piteously.

MoonDay

My Brother's Chambers are most darke and gloomy for there is a great Storm howling through the Castle, but I care not, for it mirrors my Mind. My poore little cat is no more.

Mama didst call yet again. When she had departed with her Retinue, which was the Bumptiouse Barrelle of Larde and Six Armed Guards, my deare Brother didst come to me and tell me all that has transpired. My Brother was forced to agree to provide Mama with a Potion for Eternal Youthe. She will Live Forever. I didst Remonstrate and ask, with what Dangers doth he sport? I DO NOT wish Mama to Live Forever, for I do wish to be Queen one Day and how shall I be Queen if Mama does not die, as all of us must do? And my deare Brother didst smile grimly and Saye that though there was a Potion, it was not for her, ha-ha! It was for him and he hath drunk of it many monthes past.

Tir'sDay

Why cannot I too have a Potion for Eternal Youthe? It is not fair.
I am most poorly used.

Woden'sDay

My Brother has today a new Apprentice. Though he hath a
pleasing countenance he is a most peculiar boy. When he didst
see me he laughed and shouted out some strange name that I
knew not. I spoke to him most Pleasantly even though he is but
a common Apprentice, yet when I didst speak, he ran away.
My Brother is still much troubled. He doth say over and over,
"I didst see myself in the future. I didst see my terrible fate. Oh,
Esmeralda, I am a fool. I wouldst not wait. What have I
done?" But I do not know what he hath done, for he will not
saye.

Freya'sDay

A Day of Great Foreboding. Mama did come for me today. I am
no more to stay with my deare Brother for she said, "He has
important work to do, Esmeralda, and with your great moanings
you do distract him from his task." I begged to stay—and my
Brother begged also, but to no avail. Now I sit in my Most

*Dismal Chamber. Mama is sending the Bumptiouse Barrelle of
Larde for me at dawn tomorrow. I am greatly afraid.*

And there the diary ended. Jenna slowly closed the book and
sat on the edge of Esmeralda's bed, trying to take it all in.
What had happened to Esmeralda? And what—now that
everyone thought that she was Esmeralda—would happen to
her?

✛35✛
KNIGHTS

*L*ater *that afternoon, Jenna* sat wrapped in a damp bedspread on Princess Esmeralda's lumpy bed. Beside her were the remains of a large pie, crusty bread, cheese, apples, cake and milk that the Knight of the Day, true to his word, had the Cooke bring to her. She had lit the small candle beside the bed, and as she sat warming her hands over the feeble candle flame, she heard a faint knocking on the wooden paneling of the room. The sound came and went in bursts, sometimes frenzied, sometimes weary and despairing. The hairs on the back of Jenna's neck rose: It was the little Princesses and they were *still alive.*

Jenna knew she shouldn't, but somehow she could not help but put her ear to the panel where the knocking was coming from. To her dismay she was sure she could hear the faint snuffling, hiccupping sounds of exhausted sobbing—*children's* sobbing. It was too much. Jenna ran to the door and hammered loudly with her fists, calling out, "Sir Hereward, Sir Hereward! They're here. I can hear them—we've got to get them out! Oh, Sir Hereward, *please* find someone to help!"

To Jenna's surprise, the ghost **Passed Through** the bedroom doors. Sir Hereward did not **Pass Through** doors for many people, but sometimes it had to be done. He stood next to Jenna, shaking his head to get rid of the unpleasant sensation of being full of wood.

"Princess," said the knight, leaning on his sword and regarding Jenna with a puzzled air, "forgive my confusion but it seemeth to my poor brain that though thou art most assuredly a Royal Princess, thou art not the poor Princess Esmeralda, e'en though thou hast her looks to a strange degree."

Jenna nodded. She knew she could trust Sir Hereward but she was not sure if he would understand what she was about to tell him. "I am Princess Jenna," she said very quietly, just in case anyone was listening. "I have come from a Time in the future. . . ." She trailed off, unsure if Sir Hereward would understand what she meant.

The old knight was quicker than Jenna expected. "Ah, so thy speech is that from times yet to come," Sir Hereward mused. " 'Tis a strange sound to be sure, so quick and sharp to the eare, like the rattling of a bird's beake upon the bars of its cage. What a cacophony must sound through *your* Palace, Princess Jenna."

Jenna was about to say that her Palace was quiet and empty compared with this one when the knocking inside the wall started up again. "Th-there it *is*," she whispered.

" 'Tis the poor baby Princesses, Princess Jenna." Sir Hereward sighed mournfully.

"But we have to get them out before they suffocate," said Jenna, frustrated by Sir Hereward's lack of action.

"They are already suffocated," murmured Sir Hereward, staring at his rusty feet.

"But—"

" 'Tis their UnQuiet Spirits that you do hear, Princess. As indeed didst poor Esmeralda. Perchance, if I had known the true nature of our Queen . . . I might have saved the Babes."

"But they were her *daughters*," said Jenna. "How could she . . ."

"Methinks it was for the very reason that they *were* her daughters," said Sir Hereward gravely. "I didst hear something most strange . . . but I dare not believe it to be so." The ghost shook his head as if to clear the thought away.

"What? *What* don't you believe?" asked Jenna. And then realizing that the way she spoke must sound almost rude to the knight, she added a little self-consciously, "Pray, tell me, if you will, Sir Hereward, what it is thou darest not believe."

Sir Hereward smiled. "Why," he said, "now thou seemest e'en more like Princess Esmeralda." Jenna was not sure if this was a particularly good—or safe—thing to seem like, but she took it as a compliment.

"It is said the Queen doth seek eternal life upon this Earth. That, indeed, she is close enough to it that she desireth no heirs, for she will hold the Queenship forever more." Sir Hereward heaved a sigh. "So it seemeth that throughout eternity our Queen will ever be Queen Etheldredda."

"No, she won't!" cried Jenna.

Sir Hereward looked at Jenna with a faint ray of hope in his eyes. "Will she not, fair Jenna? Methinks to make certain of such a thing, thou must escape thy many-times-great-grandmama," he said, "for thou art no safer here than the little Princesses and poore Esmeralda were. I am but a ghost but even a ghost may **Cause** a lock to open." Sir Hereward placed his only hand with its battered and rusty gauntlet on the door. After some minutes, and a great deal of huffing and puffing from the old ghost, Jenna heard the lock click open.

"Thou art free, fair Jenna. Fare thee well. I trust we will meet again."

"We will, Sir Hereward," said Jenna.

Jenna was free, but she knew she would never truly be free until she found Septimus. She decided to head for Wizard Way; there was a saying in the Castle that if you stood under the Great Arch long enough, all who lived in the Castle would pass by. It was as good a place as any to start looking, and the sooner she got there the better. With a wave to Sir Hereward—who raised his arm in a respectful salute—she set off.

The Palace corridors were bright and busy, much to Jenna's

surprise. She was used to the night being dark. In *her* Palace the night was lit only by a few candles, for Sarah Heap found it hard to leave her frugal habits behind. The candles were placed at long enough intervals from one another to provide plenty of deep shadows in which a fugitive Princess could hide. But *this* Palace was a different matter; Bertie Smalls, the Royal Candle Trimmer saw to that. Bertie, a tall thin man, waxen pale with a mop of flame-red hair, patrolled the nighttime corridors with great dedication. It was a matter of honor for Bertie that not one candle ever went out under his guardianship.

Although Jenna was tempted to take one of the myriad shortcuts and servants' passageways through the Palace, she decided it would be too risky, for a Princess would never dream of using them and she would quickly be noticed. Jenna decided that she would have to brazen it out; after all, who was to know that Queen Etheldredda had made a prisoner of her? And so, head held high, hoping that people would assume that Princess Esmeralda had a perfect right to walk the Palace corridors, Jenna set off.

She made good progress, and was even beginning to enjoy people curtseying and bowing to her and the excited whispers that followed in her wake, when she had the misfortune to see the Knight of the Day coming toward her. The good-natured knight smiled and bowed, and then to his horror remembered that he had been told to keep Princess Esmeralda locked in her room. With a sudden vision of his head stuck on the North Gate gatepost, the Knight of the Day stepped in front of Jenna to bar her way.

"Prithee, Princess Esmeralda, allow me to escort thee to your Chamber before thy deare Mama doth—"

"Sorry," muttered Jenna, "I've got to go." She ducked under the Knight of the Day's outstretched arm and ran.

Faced with what he was sure was a straight choice between letting Jenna go and keeping his head, the Knight of the Day chose his head. He chased after her, shouting out to passing servants and officials for help. Soon Jenna was being pursued by a long and ever-growing line of servants. Now was the time to use those shortcuts. Jenna dived behind a thick brocade curtain, which still hung, although in tatters, in her own Palace. She dashed down a short flight of steps, along a three-cornered passageway, threw herself inside a small doorway and stopped by a flight of spiral steps to catch her breath and listen for her pursuers. The great clattering of feet along the three-cornered passageway told her she had not escaped them.

Jenna knew what she had to do. She rushed up the steps, her legs burning with the effort, and hurtled across the small landing at the top, all the while fumbling to unclip the large emerald and gold key from her belt. Behind her, the thud of heavy boots on the steps made her hand tremble as she placed her key in the central keyhole of the emerald and gold door to the Queen's Room. Her pursuers arrived just in time to see the Princess apparently walk through a solid wall. A great cry of amazement came from the overcrowded landing.

The Knight of the Day sank to the floor with a groan and put his head in his hands, which only had the effect of reminding him of how very attached he was to his head—although not, he feared, for very much longer.

++36++
BRODA PYE

Jenna stepped into the Queen's Room with a feeling of relief. She knew she was safe, no one could follow her. The room was just as it always was, the same small fire burning in the grate, the same old armchair and rug beside it—except for the ghost sitting in the chair. Instead of the ghost of her mother, whom Jenna had yet to see, the chair was occupied by the ghost of Queen Etheldredda's mother. Queen Etheldredda's mother was as different from her daughter as it was possible to be. The elderly ghost had been slumbering in her chair, her crown slipped forward over her wispy white hair, and a contented smile on her face as she dreamed of the happy times she and her husband had had at the Palace and all the friends she had known. If a frown did occasionally flicker across her brow, it was when the teenage tantrums of the young Etheldredda intruded into her dreams, but they soon vanished, replaced by the many good memories the much-loved old Queen had stored up. As Jenna came into the Room, the Queen opened her eyes and, thinking she was seeing her granddaughter, smiled and returned to her reveries.

Jenna was about to sit down in the old chair by the fire and wait until everyone outside had given up and gone away, but there was something about the chair that told her that it was not hers to sit in—not yet. She wandered around the tiny room while the old Queen slumbered, oblivious to the pres-ence of her great-granddaughter.

Interested to see if the Unstable Potions and Partikular Poisons cupboard had changed in any way, Jenna peeked inside. To her surprise, instead of the bare shelves she was used to, the cupboard was full of exquisite little bottles in a hundred different shades of blue, green and red glass, which sparkled in the glow of the firelight. In each bottle was a gold-topped cork, and the long lines of gold corks twinkled like a precious golden chain.

Intrigued by the bottles, Jenna slipped inside the cupboard, and the door closed behind her. To Jenna's surprise, when the door closed, a line of tiny candles on the bottom shelf burst into flame and filled the cupboard with light. Jenna was curious to see what was now kept in the little mahogany drawers, so she opened the top drawer. It was full of what looked like thick gold coins, but they smelled like mint chocolates. Jenna picked one up, scraped away some of the thin gold leaf and tentatively licked the dark, bitter chocolate. Unable to resist, she popped the rest of the mint into her mouth. It melted in the most wonderful mix of mint and chocolate that she had ever tasted. Jenna closed the drawer before she was tempted to take another and, one by one, opened the rest of the drawers, which were neatly packed with yet more bottles lying on soft unspun wool.

Preoccupied by deciding whether to have just *one* more mint chocolate after all, Jenna opened the bottom drawer, and—too late—she heard the telltale *click* as the door to the cupboard locked itself and the Queen's Way was set in motion. Everything went black and then someone trod on her toe—and screamed. Very loudly.

"Aargh! Broda, Broda! Mama is in the closet. She hath **Come Through**. *Brodaaaaa!*"

The cupboard door was thrown open with a bang, and a girl rushed out, still screaming. Ears ringing, Jenna nervously peered out of the cupboard and was confronted by the bizarre sight of what appeared to be her twin hurling herself at a very beautiful young woman with long, dark curly hair and brilliant witch-blue eyes.

"There, there, Esmeralda," shushed the young woman, gently stroking Esmeralda's hair, "cease thy Din. Thou art safe now, and thy mama will not Dare to venture through the Way, for thou knowest thy grandmama will forbid it. Shh . . . there now. *Oh!*" Broda Pye gasped at the sight of another Esmeralda stepping out of the Unstable Potions and Partikular Poisons cupboard.

"Uh . . . hello," said Jenna uncertainly.

Esmeralda stared at Jenna, and Jenna returned the stare—unable to believe that she was not looking in a mirror and seeing her own reflection. They were the same height, their brown hair was the same length and they both wore identical gold circlets. Suddenly Esmeralda started sobbing. "My Time Is Come. I see my Doppelgänger. All is *lost*—aieeeeeeee!"

"Cease now, Esmeralda!" said Broda Pye, rather more sternly. "'Tis not your Doppelgänger—behold her boots, Esmeralda."

Esmeralda stared at Jenna's brown boots, and her nose wrinkled up disapprovingly in an expression that showed she was indeed her mother's daughter. "They are but common brown boots," said Esmeralda, as though Jenna was not there.

Jenna looked down at her boots. She *liked* her boots, and she didn't think that Esmeralda had any room to talk, considering the stupid shoes she was wearing: the weirdest shiny red things with points so long that two pieces of ribbon were fixed to the ends and tied to her ankles to stop her from tripping over them.

"Who art thou?" Broda interrupted Jenna's thoughts on Esmeralda's footwear.

"My name is Jenna," said Jenna.

"By thy golden circlet and thy red robes, thou dost appear a Princess, despite thy boots," said Broda. "But how can this be?"

"I *am* a Princess," said Jenna crossly. "And in my Time we wear boots."

Broda Pye was used to many strange things happening in her cottage, for the Marram Marshes were even more untamed than in Jenna's Time; all manner of Spirits and Creatures lived there and would sometimes wander into the Keeper's Cottage. Broda decided that Jenna was one of these—a Spirit of a long-dead Princess wandering the marshes, maybe searching for the Dragon Boat. Broda could see that Jenna was one of the more substantial Spirits with a bit of a temper and thought it would be wise to appease her by offering food and drink.

Broda disappeared into the kitchen, leaving Esmeralda and Jenna together. There was an awkward silence between them, and then Esmeralda, who was a practical person and had decided that Jenna looked far too solid to be a Spirit, said, "Thou art truly a Princess?"

Jenna nodded.

Esmeralda knew something of Marcellus's experiments. "Art thou from a Time Yet to Come?" she asked.

Jenna nodded again.

Esmeralda was thinking hard. "Tell me . . . is Mama Queen in thy Time Yet to Come?" she asked.

Jenna shook her head. "Not when I left," she said. "But last month her ghost suddenly **Appeared**. Now I am afraid that if I don't return, she will become Queen."

"Then thou *must* return," said Esmeralda as if that settled the matter. "See now, Broda hath brought forth her sweet-meats—thou art truly honored."

Broda had returned carrying a tray of tall glasses filled with a hot misty-looking drink and a gold plate of delicate pink and green squashy sweets covered in a dusting of soft sugar. She offered them to Jenna, who took a pink one. It was like nothing Jenna had eaten before—smooth and chewy at the same time, and it tasted of a wonderful aromatic mixture of rose petals, honey and lemon.

The misty drink was less wonderful. It tasted bitter, but it was hot, and Jenna was enjoying sitting beside Broda's fire. She felt safe and warm, just as she always did at Keeper's Cottage, but she knew she had to go. She would not find Septimus here.

"I must leave now," said Jenna, getting used to the more formal ways of speaking. "But I thank you for your hospitality."

Broda Pye bowed her head, relieved that the Spirit Princess

was satisfied. Then, as was considered prudent in Spirit visitations, she asked, "Prithee, fair Princess, do not depart from this house empty-handed. Ask of me what thee will and I will be honored to meet thine every desire," said Broda, hoping that Jenna would not ask for her nice new pearl necklace that Marcellus had recently sent her, which she wished she had tucked out of sight inside her tunic while she was in the kitchen. It was too late now, and Broda held her breath while she waited for the Spirit Princess's reply.

There was something that Jenna wanted more than anything else—apart from finding Septimus—and she knew this was the one place where she might be able to find it. "I desire . . ." she said slowly, trying to find the right words.

"Yes?" asked Broda Pye on tenterhooks, anxiously fingering her necklace.

"I desire to know how to **Revive** the Dragon Boat."

Broda Pye breathed an audible sigh of relief. "From death?" she asked.

"From half death, half life. She breathes but does not move."

"She speaketh?"

"But weakly. Like a whisper on the breeze," said Jenna, really getting into the old way of speaking and rather enjoying it.

"Stay thee a few minutes longer and I will fetch you the Remedie," said Broda, and before Jenna could change her mind, she rushed into the Unstable Potions and Partikular Poisons cupboard. Jenna heard her open the trapdoor and climb down the old ladder, on her way to the Dragon Boat in her dark and lonely underground temple.

There was a silence, and then Esmeralda said, "Mama liketh not the Dragon Boat, but *I* shall like her. I know that she will talk to *me*, when the Time Is Right, e'en though she will not speak to Mama, though Mama doth shout and cajole every MidSummer Day."

Jenna smiled; she knew that the Dragon Boat had good judgment.

Broda returned, breathless and smelling of the musty passageways below the ground. She placed a battered old box on her desk and beckoned Jenna over. On the box was written the words LAST RESORT. Broda muttered an UnLock over the box and then lifted the lid. Inside was a small leather pouch that Jenna recognized.

"That's the Transubstantiate Triple," she said, disappointed. "We tried that before."

Broda looked impressed. "Thou art a Wise Spirit for thy

tender Years," she observed, taking out the three small hammered gold bowls with blue enameling around their rims that Jenna remembered. Broda laid out the bowls on the desk, and then to Jenna's surprise, she also brought out a small green bottle.

Jenna picked up the bottle. On the label was written TX3 REVIVE. "I have not seen this before," she said.

"Then you have not seen the **Transubstantiate Triple**," said Broda simply. "It will not work without, though with strong **Magyk**, some may do good."

"May I take just the bottle?" asked Jenna.

Broda bowed her head. "Surely you may. There are many more in the Queen's cupboard to be had. You are most welcome, Princess."

"Thank you," she said.

Broda stood waiting for the Spirit Princess to depart. She was afraid that she might ask for something else; some Spirits could get greedy. Broda had once had a Spirit of a merchant who had taken her entire thimble collection, and then come back for her best needles.

Jenna knew Broda wanted her to go, but she said, "There is one more thing. . . ."

Broda's face fell. So this *was* a greedy one. She didn't look it, but you could never tell with Spirits. "What?" said Broda rather sharply.

"Do you have a Boggart?" she asked Broda.

Broda looked surprised. "You want a *Boggart?*" she asked in disbelief, but a Spirit Princess must not be denied. Broda threw open the cottage front door. The dank smell of the marshes drifted in, and Jenna breathed in the smell that she loved— then jumped with shock. At least a dozen little Boggarts were grouped on the doorstep watching her, their brown eyes and wet muddy noses glistening in the light of the lantern.

"Which Boggart do you want?" asked Broda.

"I don't want one, I just wanted to see one again," explained Jenna. "Aren't they lovely? Look at their great big eyes and their huge flippers."

Patience at an end, Broda shook her head at the craziness of Spirits. "Shoo!" she said, flapping her arms wildly at the baby Boggarts. "*Shoo!*" The Boggarts stared at Broda, unblinking, and showed no sign of even beginning to be shooed.

"They try my patience most unmercifully," said Broda, slamming the door. " 'Tis the breeding season, and I declare there must be a dozen litters upon the island."

"In my Time there is only one Boggart," said Jenna.

"Then in your Time, you are truly fortunate. Now, fare thee well, Princess," Broda said, holding open the door to the Unstable Potions and Partikular Poisons cupboard.

Jenna got the hint. "Fare thee well, Broda. Fare thee well, Esmeralda," she said politely, and stepped into the cupboard.

Broda Pye firmly closed the door.

Jenna slipped out of the Queen's Room and was relieved to find the landing empty. She tiptoed down the turret stairs and—

"Princess!" The Knight of the Day pounced.

The Knight of the Day had not quite given up all thoughts of keeping his head. He took hold of Jenna's arm and marched her off, saying, "Thy mama will worry, fair Esmeralda. Thou must *not* stray from thy Chamber. 'Tis past six of the clock and all Princesses should be abed. Come now."

Jenna could not escape the Knight's steely grip. At top speed, he propelled her along the corridor, and before she knew it, she was hurtling toward her bedroom doors—and a surprised Sir Hereward.

Sir Hereward was not alone. A short fat man with a bright red face and a bulbous nose was banging furiously on the bedroom door. The man was almost swamped in his gray silk Palace livery, which had five very long gold ribbons dangling from each sleeve, plus two large gold epaulettes, which had been added at his own request. "Open!" he shouted. "Open up in the name of her most Gracious Majesty, Queen Etheldredda. Open up, I say!"

The Knight of the Day saw his chance to hand over his troublesome charge. "Percy," he said loudly over the din of the banging, "cease thy bellowing. I have here Princess Esmeralda."

The red-faced man wheeled around in surprise. "Why is she not abed?" he demanded.

The Knight of the Day thought fast. "Princess Esmeralda is a most delicate flower, Percy. She didst have a Fitte of the Vapors and I, mindful of her *dear* mama's concerns for her Most Precious and now her *Onlie* daughter, did—"

"Oh, cease thy mitherings," snapped the beribboned man. He turned to Jenna and gave her a curt bow. "Princess Esmeralda, her most Gracious Majesty, your *deare mama*, requests your Royal Presence at a banquet held this night to Celebrate your Safe Return from the Cold Waters of the River. Follow me."

Jenna glanced in panic at Sir Hereward, who whispered, "It

be the Queen's Steward. He will not be gainsaid. Thou hast best obey."

"But, she—I mean, Mama—said that I must stay here," protested Jenna. The Steward shot Jenna a questioning look. Esmeralda had certainly changed for the worse since he last met her. She was far too daring, and he didn't like the way she spoke one bit.

"I do not think thou truly wishest to disobey thine own deare mama," said the Steward stonily. "I myself would not wish it, if I were in thy place."

"Thou best go," whispered Sir Hereward. "I will stay by thy side. He will not see, for I do not choose to **Appear** to this Bumptiouse Barrelle of Larde."

Jenna smiled gratefully.

With a horrible sinking feeling in her stomach, but with the faithful Sir Hereward by her side, she followed the Bumptiouse Barrelle of Larde along the candlelit passageways, cutting a swath through the bustle of servants and sweeping down the great stairs toward the ominous sounds of preparations for the banquet.

✢✢37✢✢
THE BANQUET

"Sit here!" Queen Etheldredda barked sharply at Jenna, pointing to a small, uncomfortable gold chair. The chair had been set next to Queen Etheldredda's generously upholstered throne, which dominated the top table set up on the dais of the banquet hall. Queen Etheldredda was not a generous hostess and gave as few banquets as possible. She considered them a waste of both good food and precious time, but sometimes they had to be done.

The Queen had been taken by surprise at the speed at which the news of the **Return** of the drowned Princess had

spread not only through the Palace, but also through the
entire Castle. However, along with the news, a certain opinion
put about by the Knight of the Day was gaining a worrying
foothold. Many thought that the Queen was displeased to
see her poor Returned daughter and had locked her away,
and what was *worse*, from the look upon her face when she
had first beheld her dear drowned one, anyone would have
thought that she had wished her daughter *dead*. Or, and this
was delivered in hushed tones after much looking over the
shoulder to check for eavesdroppers, people whispered that
the Queen had drowned the child *herself*. The imparting of
this news was invariably accompanied by gasps of dismay and
amazement followed by an overpowering wish to find someone else to tell it to and enjoy the dismay and amazement all
over again.

The gossip had spread faster than a forest fire and by nightfall Queen Etheldredda knew she had to do something—fast.
And so the Palace Scribes were set to work on writing the invi-
tations to:

> *A Magnificent Banquet, being*
> *A ThanksGiving for the Safe* Return

Of our Beloved Daughter,
Princess Esmeralda.
Bring your own plates.

The hastily assembled throng gathered outside the great doors to the Ballroom—the largest room in the Palace where all banquets were held. Jenna nervously perched on the wobbly gold chair and surveyed all before her. She shook her head, trying to get rid of the bizarre feeling she had had ever since she had jumped through the Glass, that she was actually at home in her own Time and in the middle of one of Silas's extended practical jokes. Jenna still remembered fondly her sixth birthday when she had woken to find that she was on board a ship bound for, as Silas had put it, Birthday Island. The whole room had been made to look like the inside of an extremely untidy ship. Her brothers were dressed as pirates and Sarah as the ship's cook. When Simon had shouted out, "Land ahoy," everyone had climbed down a rope ladder hung precariously from the window to a real boat waiting for them below in the river, which had taken them to a small sand spit upriver, where Jenna discovered a treasure chest with her birthday present inside it.

However, Jenna thought ruefully as she stole a look at the Queen, she could not imagine the mother of poor Esmeralda and the little Princesses pretending to be a ship's cook for a day. It seemed to be almost too much for her to pretend to even *like* her supposed daughter. Jenna turned around and stole a quick glance at Sir Hereward. She felt better seeing the old ghost standing behind her, still on guard. He caught Jenna's eye and winked.

Jenna watched Queen Etheldredda take her place on the throne. The Queen sat down as if she was expecting a nasty surprise to have been left on the chair. Sitting bolt upright, as though someone had tied her to a plank, Etheldredda settled herself onto the throne: a lavishly gilded chair upholstered in deep red velvet and dripping with gemstones. The Aie-Aie scuttled under the throne and curled its tail around one of the carved legs, flicking its tooth in and out and staring at the tasty ankles passing by. Stonily the Queen's hooded violet eyes stared at the great doors at the end of the Ballroom, which were still firmly closed against the rising hubbub outside. Jenna stole a glance at the living Etheldredda. She thought that the Queen looked remarkably like her ghost: the same steely gray plaits were coiled tightly around her ears, and the same pointy nose sniffed the air in the familiar disapproving manner. The only difference was that the living Etheldredda smelled of old socks and camphor. Suddenly, the unforgettable voice drilled out, "Let the rabble in!"

Two little boys, Door Pages for the night and up well past their bedtime, ran and heaved on the golden door handles, pulling the doors open in unison as they had practiced under the stern eyes of the Royal DoorKeeper for the last four hours.

A most exotic and highly polished group of people began to file into the Ballroom, two by two, each one clutching a plate. As each pair came through the doors, their gaze turned immediately to the **Returned** Princess, and even though Jenna had become used to being stared at during her walks around the Castle in her own Time, she began to feel very self-conscious. She flushed bright pink and could not help but wonder if anyone was going to notice that she was not Esmeralda.

But no one did. A few people thought that Esmeralda appeared in much better health than she had been, and looked, not surprisingly, much happier for her time away from her mama. Gone was the drawn look to her face, the anxious frown that always hovered over her eyes. She had filled out a little too, and no longer looked in need of a good meal or two.

For having sent an invitation with such short notice, Queen
Etheldredda had rustled up an impressive-looking group of
guests. Everyone wore their very best set of clothes; most
wore their wedding clothes, although the more scholarly ones,
particularly the Ordinary Wizards and the Alchemists, wore
their graduation gowns adorned with fur and richly colored
silks. The Royal courtiers and officials, noses in the air, strut-
ted importantly through the Ballroom doors in their ceremo-
nial robes. These were made from dark gray velvet edged in
red and were adorned with long gold ribbons that hung from
the sleeves, the number and length of which depended upon
the status of the officials. On the robes of important officials,
the ribbons reached the floor, and on the robes of *extremely*
important officials, the ribbons trailed along on the floor and
were often—accidentally on purpose—stepped on. It was not
unusual to see a long gold ribbon lying forlornly in the Palace
corridors, and some officials had even taken to carrying spare
ribbons with them, for the number of ribbons on one's sleeves
was highly significant, and it would not do for a five-ribbon
official to be seen with only four or, perish the thought, *three*.

Jenna watched the sumptuous stream of guests pour in and
find their places at the three long tables that were set down

the length of the Ballroom. After much fussing and treading on ribbons, all were finally seated. A small, nervous page was pushed onto the dais by the Steward; the boy ran to the middle, stood on his spot in front of the Queen and rang a small handbell. The tinkling sound immediately brought complete silence. Everyone stopped their chat in mid-sentence and looked expectantly at Queen Etheldredda.

"Welcome to this feast." Etheldredda's voice rang through the Ballroom like fingernails being dragged down a blackboard. Some people winced, others ran their fingernails across their front teeth to get rid of the nasty sensation. "Held in honor of the safe **Return** of my *deare* daughter, Princess Esmeralda, whom we all did think sadly drowned. Who was Much Mourned by her *deare mama* and who has been welcomed home with Most Great Rejoicing and Motherly Affection, for we have not been out of each other's sight since her **Return**, have we, my *Darling One?*" Queen Etheldredda gave Jenna a sharp kick on the shins under the table.

"Ouch!" gasped Jenna.

"*Have we,* my Darling One?" Etheldredda's eyes bored into Jenna and she hissed under her breath, "Answer *No, Mama,* you little fool—else it shall be the worse for thee."

With all eyes upon her, Jenna did not dare refuse. "No, Mama," she muttered sulkily.

"*What* was that, my most *Precious One?*" asked Queen Etheldredda silkily, with steel in her eyes. "*What* did you say?"

Jenna took a deep breath and said, "No, Mama. Indeed, the sight of you is . . . haunting." and then immediately she wished she hadn't, for all eyes were now upon her at the sound of her strange accent and her odd way of speaking. But Queen Etheldredda, who had made a habit of never listening to a word that Princess Esmeralda said, appeared not to notice. Bored with having to think about the wretched Esmeralda for longer than she had ever had to before, the Queen stood up.

With much scraping of chairs, everyone in the Ballroom rose to their feet and turned their respectful gaze away from the odd Esmeralda to their more familiar Queen.

"Let the banquet begin!" Etheldredda commanded.

"Let the banquet begin!" responded the guests. After making quite sure that the Queen was already seated, the throng sat down and an expectant buzz of chatter began again.

Jenna had been worried about the prospect of having to talk to Queen Etheldredda, but she need not have concerned herself, for the Queen did not look once in her direction for the rest of the banquet. Instead, she directed her attention to the dark-haired young man sitting to her left. The man, Jenna noticed, did not wear the Royal Red but wore a striking black and red tunic emblazoned with a dazzling amount of gold. He kept glancing at Jenna with a puzzled look, but with Queen Etheldredda between them, the young man seemed unwilling to say anything. With little else to do—for the Bumptiouse Barrelle of Larde sat on her right and, taking his cue from the Queen, was also ignoring her—Jenna occupied her time listening to the acrimonious conversation between Etheldredda and the young man and was amazed to hear him call the Queen "Mama."

A gong sounded.

An expectant silence fell upon the hungry crowd. This was the announcement of the first of fifteen courses. They licked their lips, shook out their napkins and, almost as one, tucked them under their chins. The little Door Pages heaved open the doors, and a long line of serving girls in pairs, each one carrying two small silver bowls, filed in. On entering the Ballroom, the girls divided up, one line to serve each table. In a tide of gray, the girls swept along the tables, each depositing a bowl in front of an eager diner. The last two girls to enter the

Ballroom made their way up to the dais, and soon Jenna too had a small silver bowl in front of her.

Curious, Jenna looked down at the bowl and gasped in horror. A young duckling, scarcely big enough to be out of the egg, lay in a puddle of thin brown broth. The duckling had been marinated in wine, plucked, and its little naked, goosebumpy body was slumped in the bowl. Its head rested on a small ledge that stuck out from the special duckling bowl and gazed with terrified eyes at Jenna. *It was still alive.* Jenna was nearly sick on the spot.

Queen Etheldredda, on the other hand, looked very pleased at the sight of her duckling. The Queen licked her lips, remarking to the young man on her left that this was one of her favorite dishes—there was nothing like a tender young duckling freshly scalded in hot orange sauce.

The gong sounded for the second time, announcing the arrival of a long line of boys carrying jugs of boiling hot sauce. Jenna watched the boys enter the Ballroom two by two, one line going to the right and one to the left, each boy stopping to pour some of the orange sauce into the waiting bowls of the diners. The two boys at the end of the line with the hottest jugs of sauce were ordered straight up to the dais. Quickly,

before the sauce boy reached her, Jenna picked the duckling
out of her bowl and thrust it into her tunic pocket, where the
tiny creature lay in the soft fluff at the bottom of her pocket,
rigid with terror.

Jenna watched the boys thread their way through the
throng. Eyes down, trying to avoid spilling the brimming jugs
of hot sauce, they stepped up onto the dais, where a burly
footman hissed in their ears, "Tarry not, serve the Queen and
Princess Esmeralda first." And so it was that when Jenna
looked up to politely thank the boy who had just poured
orange sauce into her duckling-free bowl, she found herself
looking into the haunted eyes of Septimus Heap.

Jenna looked away. She did not believe it. This boy with the
long straggly hair, thin in the face and somewhat taller than
she remembered, could not possibly be Septimus. Not in a
million years.

Septimus for his part had expected to see Princess
Esmeralda—so that was who he saw. He was annoyed with
himself for thinking for a few hopeful seconds that the
Princess could possibly be Jenna. He had already been fooled
like that once before when Princess Esmeralda had stayed

with Marcellus just before she disappeared. He wasn't going
to let it happen again. Carefully, Septimus poured the orange
sauce into her bowl, grateful that for some reason she did not
have a small, live duckling in there.

Suddenly there was a loud crash and a collective gasp of
horror mixed with glee rose from the Ballroom. At the sight
of the duckling in Queen Etheldredda's bowl, Hugo had
dropped the jug, and the boiling orange sauce had spilled into
the Queen's lap. Etheldredda leaped to her feet screaming,
the Bumptious Barrelle of Larde threw back his chair and
grabbed Hugo by the neck and lifted him bodily off the
ground, half throttling him. "You little fool!" yelled the
Barrelle of Larde. "You will pay for this. You will regret this
moment for the rest of your life—which will not be long, boy,
mark my words."

Hugo's eyes were wide with fear. He dangled helplessly
from the Barrelle of Larde's pudgy hands, which were tight-
ening around his neck. Septimus saw that his lips were turning blue, Hugo's eyes rolled up and a great expanse of white
began to show, Septimus leaped forward. Using more strength
than he knew he had, he pulled the boy from the pudgy hands,
yelling, "Let him go, you fat fiend!" The sound of Septimus's

voice rang through the Ballroom with more effect than he had intended.

Jenna jumped from her seat. She had been watching the Steward throttle Hugo with as much horror as Septimus had been, and now she knew. It *was* Septimus—it was *his voice*. She knew his voice anywhere. It was *him!*

At the same time, the young man sitting on the other side of Queen Etheldredda also jumped up. He too knew his Apprentice's voice—what was the boy doing here dressed as a Palace servant?

Jenna and Marcellus Pye collided in the melee on the dais. Marcellus slipped on the puddle of orange sauce and crashed to the ground. The Bumptious Barrelle of Larde lost his battle with Septimus and let go of Hugo, who dropped to the ground dazed from his grip. Seizing her opportunity, Queen Etheldredda, dripping with orange sauce, aimed a swipe at the boy; she missed and caught the Barrelle of Larde a stinging blow across his ear. The Barrelle of Larde, who was an aggressive man, automatically gave Etheldredda a slap in return—much to the glee of those assembled in the Ballroom, who were watching enthralled, ducklings poised midway to their gaping mouths.

The Barrelle of Larde suddenly realized what he had done and turned white, then ashen gray. He gathered up his sauce-stained robes and fled the banquet, tearing down through the tables, his ten precious gold ribbons flying out behind him. The Door Pages saw him coming, and thinking that this happened at every banquet, they ceremoniously opened the great doors for the fleeing Barrelle and bowed as he shot past them. As they pushed the doors closed, the pages grinned at each other. No one had told them a banquet was this much fun.

Hanging on to the dazed Hugo with one hand, Septimus grabbed Jenna by the other. "It *is* you, Jen, isn't it?" he asked, his eyes shining with excitement. A wonderful feeling of hope and happiness at seeing Jenna again swept over Septimus; he felt as if he had been given back his future.

"Yep, it's me, Sep. Can't believe it's *you* though!"

"Marcia found my note, didn't she?"

"What note? Come on, let's get out of here while we can."

No one noticed the two serving boys and Princess Esmeralda leave the fray. They left behind them a bevy of Palace servants attending an angry Etheldredda, who was barking at Marcellus Pye, demanding that he "get up this very minute." To the tumultuous sound of the Ballroom in an uproar, they tiptoed out a small door in the paneling at the back of the dais that led to a retiring room for Royal ladies who wished to rest from the effects of eating and drinking too much.

Jenna bolted the door and leaned against it, looking at Septimus in disbelief. The duckling stirred and a small puddle of dampness leaked through her tunic pocket. There was no doubt about it, thought Jenna, the duckling was real—and so, amazingly, was Septimus.

✠ 38 ✠
THE SUMMER HOUSE

That bolt won't last long, Jen," said Septimus, looking at the flimsy filigree bolt designed to grace the Royal Ladies' Retiring Room door. "We'd better get out of here quick."

Jenna nodded. "I know," she said, "but the Palace is stuffed full of people. Sep, you wouldn't believe it, it's *so* different. You can't go anywhere without someone seeing you and curtseying to you and—"

"Bet they wouldn't curtsey to me, Jen," said Septimus, smiling for the first time in one hundred and sixty-nine days and suddenly looking like the Septimus Jenna remembered.

"Not with your hair looking like a rat's nest. What *have* you done to it?"

"Won't comb it. Don't see the point really. And certainly won't let them cut it into that stupid pudding bowl shape. Anyway, it's something to irritate Marcellus with. He's a bit of a fussbudget about things like—*what*, Hugo?" Hugo was tugging at Septimus's sleeve.

"Harken . . ." the boy whispered, eyes bloodshot and face still deathly white from his near strangling. Someone was rattling the door handle.

Sir Hereward barred the door with his battered sword and **Appeared** to Septimus and Hugo, causing the already scared Hugo to leap into the air with fright. "Princess Jenna, I shall protect you and your faithful followers to the end," the knight said gravely.

"Thank you, Sir Hereward," said Jenna. "But we've got to get out of here fast. Sep, you open the window while I make them think we've gone this way." Jenna ran to a small door that led into the Long Walk, opened it and left it swinging.

"Come on," she said, pushing the dazed Hugo toward the window. "Out you go, Hugo." The three of them squeezed out the window and dropped down onto the path that ran around the back of the Palace. Very quietly, Jenna closed the window.

Sir Hereward **Passed Through** the glass and was soon standing next to them. "Whither may I offer thee safe conduct?" inquired the ghost.

"Anywhere away from here," whispered Jenna, "and fast."

"Many use the river for such purposes," Sir Hereward said, pointing to the riverbank, which was lined with an unfamiliar row of cedar trees.

"The river it is," said Jenna.

If anyone from the Ballroom had bothered to look—which no one did, for the guests were all too busy excitedly discussing the happenings of the last few minutes—they would have seen two Palace serving boys and the Princess racing across the long lawns that led down to the river. There were no Spirit-Seers among the guests that night to see the battered old ghost, armor in tatters but his broken sword held high, leading the three at full tilt as if on a battle charge. Protected by a great dark cloud that had drifted in front of the night's full moon and cloaked the lawn in darkness, the battle charge ran as fast as they could.

A sharp frost crackled under their feet and left three sets of dark footprints in the white grass for anyone who wished to see, but they were lucky, for—as yet—no one had thought to look for footprints in the grass. As they reached the river, a search party led by Queen Etheldredda's hasty replacement for the Bumptiouse Barrelle of Larde—a man as short of temper as he was of brains who had had his eye on the Royal Stewardship for many years and could not quite believe his good fortune—was staring at the door and coming to exactly the conclusion that Jenna had wanted them to. The search party threw themselves at the narrow door, each eager to be the first to catch Princess Esmeralda and win favor with the Queen, but the new Steward had the most eagerness—and nastiness. He scratched and kicked his way to the front of the search party and got out the door first. Soon they were rushing after him down the Long Walk, shouting out to anyone to ask if they had "espied the poore deluded Princess." Anxious to oblige the frightening new Steward and his sidekicks, many people gave them completely fictitious directions, and the search party was sent on a wild goose chase.

✳   ✳   ✳

By now Jenna, Septimus, Hugo and Sir Hereward were standing on the landing stage where the Royal Barge was moored.

"The boat will convey us safely hither," said Sir Hereward. " 'Tis a fair, still night and the water runneth slow."

Septimus looked at the Royal Barge and whistled between his teeth, an irritating habit that he had unknowingly picked up from Marcellus Pye. "Don't you think they might notice us in that?" he said.

"Not that one. Sir Hereward means the dinghy, the little rowboat." Jenna pointed to Sir Hereward, who was now hovering above a small, and equally richly painted, rowboat that was tied up behind the Royal Barge and used for ferrying passengers to and from the barge when it could not get to the shore.

Just then the full moon sailed out from behind a cloud and the frosty lawns were bathed in a brilliant white light; it felt as if someone had switched on a searchlight and pointed it straight at them. Sir Hereward knew only too well the dangers of moonlight, for he had entered ghosthood due to a particularly badly timed appearance of a full moon and a well-aimed arrow. The ghost leaped from the boat with the words "We will be discovered—hie we to the summer house!" Dodging between the shadows of the great cedar trees, Sir Hereward shepherded everyone over to the Palace summer house—the very same octagonal building with the golden roof that Jenna knew from her own Time.

From behind the cover of the summer house, Jenna watched the windows of the Palace light up one by one, as each empty room was invaded by the confused search party and a lit candle left to show that the room had been searched.

Suddenly, with a distant crash, the great windows to the Ballroom were thrown open and the new Steward was out on the terrace. Frustrated with his fruitless tour of the Palace, he had left the search party to their bickering and had returned to the Ladies' Retiring Room for a closer inspection. There he had found the window unlatched and his prey gone in quite a different direction. Outside the Ballroom, his hectoring voice carried through the frosty night air as he instructed his new, handpicked search party of thugs.

"Take thee three each to a party. Forsooth, man, art thou an *imbecile*? Ay, thou art. Fool, I didst say *three*. They are but children, surely one each will quell them. Do thee as thou wilt with the serving boys, they matter not, but Esmeralda must be returned to her grieving mama. Now, hie thee to the Great Gates, *thee* to the stables and thou, fools, take thy great flat feet to the river. Tarry not—begone!"

As Jenna, Septimus and Hugo cowered behind the summer house, a yell went up from the large-footed search party. "Behold! 'Tis their imprints upon the frost. I declare, we have them. They are ours!"

The search party, closely followed by the Steward, thundered across the lawns toward them. Frantically, Septimus tried the door of the summer house. It was locked. "I'll break a window, Jen," he said, wrapping his fist in the white serving cloth that had covered the jug of orange sauce.

"No, Sep," hissed Jenna. "They'll hear. Anyway, if you break the window, they'll know we're in here."

"Allow me, young man," said Sir Hereward, still flushed with the earlier success of unlocking Jenna's bedroom door. The knight placed his hand over the lock. They waited anxiously, listening to the search party's arrival at the Royal Barge.

"Please hurry," Jenna whispered urgently.

"My powers are not what they were," said a flustered Sir Hereward. "This lock doth not turn easily."

"Sir Hereward, let me try something," said Jenna. Wishing that she had listened more to the droning of Jillie Djinn, Jenna took the key to the Queen's Room off her belt. With chilled and trembling fingers that were about as much use as a package of frozen sausages, she fumbled and dropped it. It lay on the frosty grass, glinting gold and emerald in the moonlight. Septimus snatched it up, pushed it into the lock and turned it, and the next moment they were all tumbling inside. Septimus locked the door behind them and they stood listening to the hollow thud of footsteps running beneath the cedar trees, and shaking the ground beneath them.

Suddenly Hugo grabbed hold of Septimus's arm—hard.

Two green eyes glinted in the darkness, and a long, low growl began to fill the summer house.

"Ullr?" whispered Jenna into the dark. But then she remembered where she was. How could it be Ullr?

Out of the dark came a voice that Jenna knew. "Kalmm, Ullr. Kalmm," said Snorri, breathless. But Ullr was not calm. The big cat, spooked by the strange smells and sounds of this different Time, had been startled by the shriek of a late-night kitchen maid and had taken off down a warren of passages. Snorri had, to her relief, just caught up with him. Now she held the panther back and stroked his neck where the fur had risen along with his growl.

"It's okay, Sep," Jenna whispered. "It's only Snorri and the NightUllr."

Septimus did not understand a word of what Jenna said, but if a growling panther did not bother Jenna, then he wasn't going to let it bother him either. There were other things to worry about just then, like the harsh voice of the new Steward saying excitedly, "The trail is clear. Our quarry awaits us in the Queen's summer house, men."

A sharp rattling on the door handle was followed by an exclamation, " 'Tis locked and barred, my lord Steward."

"Then batter it down, thou Namby-Pamby Mither of Mischance—*batter it down!*"

A great crash resounded against the flimsy wooden door and the summer house shook. Sir Hereward brandished his sword at the door and declared, "Fear not, they shall not pass." Jenna glanced in panic at Septimus—the Steward's search party would not even notice Sir Hereward; he would be **Passed Through** as if he wasn't there.

"We can escape to the kitchens from here," said Snorri quickly, "but they will follow. I have an idea. Jenna, give me your cloak, please." Any other time Jenna would have been reluctant to give up her beautiful cloak, but as another crash sounded against the door and a thin panel splintered behind her, she tore off the cloak and thrust it into Snorri's hands. Jenna could hardly bear to look as Snorri ripped the cloak from end to end, stamped it into the dirt of the summer house floor and then gave it to Ullr, saying, "Take, Ullr." The panther took Jenna's mangled cloak in his mouth and clamped it between his great white incisors.

"Stay, Ullr. Guard." Ullr obeyed. The great panther stood by the door, his green eyes flashing as another blow sent a shower of dry timber splintering over his broad muscled back.

"Come," whispered Snorri, beckoning to Jenna, Septimus, Hugo and Sir Hereward. "Follow me."

Snorri disappeared into the gloom but the shine of the moonlight on her white-blond hair made it easy to follow her, and soon they were squeezing down a steep flight of spiral stone steps. As they fled, they heard the summer house door finally collapse under the weight of the blows. Then came Ullr's threatening rumble of a growl, followed by a piercing shriek of terror from the Namby-Pamby Mither of Mischance, who had the mischance to be the first through the door.

"Get thee back inside," came the Steward's harsh voice.

"No, no, I pray you, sire. Upon my life I dare not."

"Then, fool, thou art truly cursed, for thou hast no life left to dare upon, unless thee enter and bring out the Princess."

"No—*no, sire, I beg you!*"

"Stand aside, fool. I shall show thee how a man should be—"

At that, a snarl such as no one—not even Snorri—had ever heard from Ullr before filled the narrow stairwell and sent shivers down their spines. A terrified yell pierced the air, and the sound of thudding footsteps could be heard overhead as the Steward's search party ran away, leaving the Steward to show the NightUllr all on his own how a man should be.

The search party arrived back at the Ballroom in disarray, and the few stragglers who had stayed behind to finish their—and their neighbors'—ducklings heard the terrible story of how Princess Esmeralda had been eaten alive by the Black Fiend. No one knew what had become of the new Steward, although they all feared (and hoped—for it greatly improved the story) the worst.

✳   ✳   ✳

With the NightUllr guarding the summer house and possibly eating the Steward (although no one wanted to think about that), Septimus, Jenna, Hugo and Snorri emerged at the bottom of the flight of spiral steps and bumped straight into someone. "Nik!" Septimus yelled in amazement.

At the sound of Septimus's voice, Nicko nearly dropped his candle. A flicker of puzzlement briefly clouded his features as he took in the subtle changes that one hundred and sixty-nine days marooned in a foreign Time had wrought upon Septimus, but it soon cleared, for Nicko could see that underneath the matted hair and the skinny, slightly taller frame, it was the same Septimus, and not only that—behind him was Jenna.

"Come quick," said Snorri, "they may soon send others to defeat Ullr. He will not be able to hold them back forever. We must be gone." Snorri took the candle from Nicko and strode off purposefully. They followed Snorri and the flickering light from her candle along the thoroughfare of the lower kitchens, which was deserted, apart from three tired serving girls disappearing in the distance. The kitchens were filled with the familiar, and to Jenna and Septimus repulsive, smells of the banquet. Glancing about them to check for inquisitive servants, they crept on. They were lucky, these were the few quiet hours of the night when no one but the Palace baker was at work in the kitchens—and he was safely far away on the upper floor.

Jenna knew where they were heading. Not far ahead, she could see the recess that hid the UnderCooks' coat cupboard. She squeezed Septimus's hand and said, "We'll be home soon, Sep—isn't that great?"

"But how?" asked Septimus, puzzled.

Behind him Nicko held up the candle and their shadows were thrown across the old coat cupboard. "That's how," he said. "Don't you recognize it?"

"Recognize what?"

"Where you came in, dillop."

Septimus shook his head. "But this isn't where I came in. I came into the Alchemists' Chamber."

Nicko didn't see why Septimus was being so fussy. "Oh, it doesn't matter, Sep. Let's just go back this way, okay? Getting home is what counts."

Septimus said nothing. He did not see how he could possibly get back home through an old cupboard. At the mention of home, Hugo began to snuffle. Septimus crouched down beside the boy. "What is it, Hugo?" he asked.

Hugo rubbed his tired, sore eyes. "I . . . I want to go home," he mumbled. "See Sally."

"Sally?"

"My dog. See Sally."

"All right, Hugo. Don't worry, I'll take you home."

"Sep!" exclaimed Jenna, horrified. "You *can't*. You've got to come back with us. *Now*. We've got to go before someone catches us."

"But, Jen . . . we can't just leave Hugo here on his own."

Sir Hereward coughed politely. "Princess Jenna. I trust you will allow me to escort the boy back to his household."

"Oh, Sir Hereward," said Jenna, "would you?"

The knight bowed. "It will be an honor, Princess Jenna." The knight extended a rusty-gloved hand to Hugo, who took it and held on tightly to the thin air. "I shall take my leave, fair Princess," said Sir Hereward, bowing low. "Fare thee well, for I shall not see thee again."

"Oh, but you will, Sir Hereward. I will see you tonight and tell you all about it." Jenna grinned.

"I trust not, Princess, for I think you will not be safe here tonight. I wish you and your brave companions Good Speed and a Safe Homecoming. Come, Hugo." With that the ghost walked out the door, Hugo trotting beside him.

" 'Bye, Hugo," said Septimus.

"Good-bye, Apprentice." Hugo turned and smiled. "Perchance I shall see thee tomorrow."

Perchance you will, thought Septimus gloomily.

"Come *on*, Sep," said Jenna impatiently, and she pulled him toward the cupboard.

Snorri took a silver whistle from her pocket and put it to her lips. She blew but no sound came out. "It is for Ullr," she said. "He will come now."

Jenna opened the door to the coat cupboard. "See," she explained to Septimus, "there's a Glass at the back, behind the coats." She threw back the layers of coarse gray wool to reveal the dusty gold frame of the Glass. "There it is!" she said excitedly to Septimus.

"Where?" asked Septimus, as the padding of Ullr's feet came softly toward the four figures crowded around the cupboard.

"*There*," said Jenna, annoyed. Why was Septimus being so awkward?

"It's just an empty frame, Jen," said Septimus. "Just a stupid old empty frame." He kicked it angrily. "That's all."

"No! No, it can't be!" Jenna put her hand up against the Glass, and she saw that Septimus was right. The frame was empty, and of the Glass that had been inside it there was not a trace at all.

"We're *all* trapped in this horrible place now," said Septimus grimly.

Nicko untied the dinghy from the Royal Barge, and under the cover of the giant cedar trees, they slipped away from the Palace landing stage. It was a tight squeeze in the small boat. The NightUllr stood at the prow, his green eyes shining in the dark with Snorri squashed in beside him. In the middle sat Nicko, steadily rowing them upstream, away from the Palace. Jenna and Septimus huddled together in the stern, shivering in the chill that rose from the water, brushing off the fat, lazy snowflakes that were drifting down from the sky. They were all wrapped up in an assortment of UnderCooks' coats, but the cold air easily

found its way through the cheap thin wool—for Palace
UnderCooks did not get paid enough to buy decent outer-
wear.

They were on their way to the Great Chamber of Alchemie
and Physik. Septimus knew it was their only chance to return
to their own Time and he didn't hold out much hope. He was
not in a good mood. "This is not going to be easy," he told
them. "Only Marcellus has the **Keye** to the Great Doors of
Time."

"Well, we will just have to lie in wait in the Chamber and
ambush him when he comes in," said Nicko breezily. "It's
four against one, not bad odds."

"You've forgotten the seven scribes," said Septimus.

"No, *you've* forgotten those, Sep. You didn't say anything
about seven scribes. Oh, well, four against eight then." Nicko
sighed. "Anyway, we've got no choice. Otherwise we're stuck
here forever."

"Do not forget Ullr," murmured Snorri, "if we arrive before
daybreak."

Nicko upped his pace. He'd rather have a panther on his
side than a scraggly orange cat any day. Jenna turned back to
look at the Palace, which was rapidly disappearing behind

them. The fruitless search of the Palace had been completed, and each room now had a candle burning in it; the long, low yellow stone building was ablaze with light, its wide lawns spread out before it with their fresh snowfall like a crisp white cook's apron. Despite knowing that Queen Etheldredda was somewhere within those walls, Jenna could not help but think that it was a wonderful sight to see the Palace so alive, and she decided that if, by some miracle, she ever returned to her Time, she too would light up every room—in celebration.

Jenna looked up at the windows of Esmeralda's—and her—room. "I am glad Esmeralda got away," she said.

"So am I," said Septimus.

Jenna was amazed. "You knew Esmeralda?" she asked.

Septimus nodded. "She only just made it, you know. Marcellus took her through the Queen's way, but they nearly got caught by the Steward. Then—and this is the good part—he threw her cloak into the water just above the Palace on an outgoing tide and made sure one of the footmen fished it out. Everyone thought she had drowned, and Etheldredda was thrilled, seeing as, according to Marcellus, she had been planning to throw Esmerelda into the bottomless whirlpool in Bleak Creek."

"*Marcellus* took her?" asked Jenna.

"Well, he *is* her brother. Esmeralda came to stay with him and she was really nice to me. No one else spoke to me then because they were jealous that I was the Apprentice and they were still just scribes."

Jenna remembered the diary. "So the new Apprentice . . . was *you?*"

Septimus nodded. He lifted up his servant's tunic and showed Jenna his black, red, and gold Alchemie robes underneath. "See? Alchemie Apprentice stuff."

With another pull on the oars, Nicko took them around the next bend, and the Palace was lost from view. They were now approaching a long-forgotten dockyard on the east side of the Castle. The river was deeper here than Nicko was used to in his own Time, the wind was picking up and the current was fast and strong. The little rowboat shot quickly past dozens of tall ships that were moored up for the winter along the shore. The ghostly hum of the wind in the ships' rigging sent even more shivers down the spines of the occupants of the Queen's dinghy, and the long beards of frost that had settled on the complicated traceries of rope and now shone in the moonlight like great silvery cobwebs did nothing to make them feel any warmer.

"Is it much farther, Sep?" Nicko inquired, his breath coming in rapid bursts of warm cloud on the frosty air. He brushed away the snowflakes settling on his eyelashes.

"It can't be far," said Septimus, peering at the piles of rub-
ble and great towers of scaffolding that were springing up from
the riverbank.

"If you've never been down this underground river, how do
you know where it is?" asked Jenna, her teeth chattering.

"The UnderFlow comes out at the Alchemie Arch, Jen.
There's a map on the wall showing where it goes. I've spent
hours with nothing to do but stare at that map. And there's a
gold Alchemie sign above the arch. A circle with a dot in the
middle that's meant to be the Earth going around the sun.
Then there are seven stars around that. Alchemists like sevens—worse luck." Septimus sighed heavily.

"Oh, do cheer up, Sep," said Jenna. "At least we're all in
this together now."

As Nicko rowed, everyone stared at the wall that rose up
from the river, hoping for a sight of the Alchemie sign. But all
they could see was stones, scaffolding and half-finished walls
that reared up into the cloudy night sky. One by one, Jenna,
Nicko and Septimus realized what they were looking at.

"They're building The Ramblings," Jenna said very quietly.

"I know," said Nicko. "It's weird."

"We haven't even been born yet," said Jenna.

"Or Mum, or Dad. It makes my head go funny."

Septimus sighed. "Don't even think about it, Nik. It makes you feel like you're going crazy."

Snorri took no part in the conversation. The Ramblings meant nothing to her and the Castle was as strange to her in this Time as it had been in her own Time. Also Snorri had grown up in a land where many people knew that Time could be long or short, go backward or forward, where Spirits came and went and where all things were possible. She sat quietly and scanned the walls for the Alchemie sign.

"Shh," Nicko suddenly whispered. "There's a boat behind us." Jenna and Septimus turned to look. It was true. If they listened hard, they could hear the splash of the oars of a small rowboat. A voice reached them across the water.

"*Faster*, men. A shilling and a fine cloak to you all if we catch them. *Faster*."

"Nicko," whispered Jenna. "Nicko—*hurry!*"

But Nicko was getting tired. He tried to speed up his pace but found he could row no faster. Jenna and Septimus could do nothing but watch their pursuers draw ever closer until they could clearly see four large shapes precariously perched in a long, narrow rowboat, which was gaining on them quickly.

Snorri paid no attention to the pursuers, but kept her eyes on the wall below the beginnings of The Ramblings. All of a sudden, she said, "I think that the sign that you look for is there."

"Where?" asked Nicko.

"It is there, Nicko," Snorri replied, enjoying saying Nicko's name. "See, it is above the dark archway where the stream runs out into the river. Below the wall with two windows."

"Okay," said Nicko. He did a quick turn and, finding a little extra energy, rowed at top speed into the dark archway, where he stopped to catch his breath. The sound of the approaching rowboat drew nearer, but Nicko dared not pick up his oars for fear of making a telltale noise. Everyone held their breath, watching the small gap in the darkness that showed the empty moonlit river. At lightning speed, their pursuers went past so fast that if anyone had blinked just then, they would have missed it.

"They've gone," breathed Jenna, sinking back into the boat with relief. Nicko picked up the oars reluctantly. He realized that he was going to have to row the boat underground, and was none too happy at the thought. Trying to ignore the beginnings of a panic welling up inside him, he started to row deeper into the darkness.

"That plaque was like the one above the Dragon House, only not so worn away," said Jenna.

"Anything under the Castle or in the walls is old Alchemie stuff, Jen," Septimus said, his face eerily illuminated from below by the light from his Dragon Ring.

"Even the Dragon House?" asked Jenna.

"Especially the Dragon House."

Jenna looked at Septimus. He did not return her glance but stared straight into the dark. He seemed distant, weighed down and much, much older than his extra one hundred and sixty-nine days. For a moment Jenna felt afraid of what Septimus had become while he had been away. "You know a lot of things now, don't you, Sep?" she said rather than asked.

Septimus sighed. "Yeah," he said.

Nicko hated the UnderFlow. The stream smelled odd for a start: kind of musty and rancid as though something had recently died in it, and there were things—soft, squishy things—floating in the water; he could feel the ends of his oars touching them. The tunnel was just not quite wide enough for the stretch of his oars, so with every stroke, the edge of the blades scraped along the side of the wall and a few times brought the boat to a halt. Nicko was forced to pull the oars farther into the boat and row in an awkward rhythm so that the ends did not hit each other.

Nicko could deal with the irritations of rowing, but what he could not stand was the feeling of going ever deeper underground. With every stroke he took, Nicko felt the panic rise higher in his throat. Icy water dripped from the roof of the arched tunnel, which he knew was no more than an arm's length above his head. The whole tunnel was lit only by the dull yellow glow from Septimus's Dragon Ring, and with every pull on the oars, Nicko imagined the walls closing in on him. It was only the presence of Snorri sitting behind him that stopped him from dropping the oars and yelling "Get me out of here." Nicko closed his eyes and tried to imagine he was rowing in the wide-open ocean, for it made no difference whether he could see where he was going or not. There was only one way to go.

About twenty minutes later, which to Nicko had felt more like twenty hours, he knew that even the thought of the ocean and of Snorri sitting behind him could no longer keep his panic at bay. Fortunately Septimus said, "Here we are, Nik, we're in the UnderFlow Pool. You can open your eyes now."

"They *were* open," said Nicko indignantly. He opened his

eyes and saw that they had come to a pool in a huge circular cavern. There was a long stone quay along one side, which was lit by a line of rushlights placed in holders on the walls. The water was inky black with flashes of orange reflecting the flames, and Nicko, who had an instinct for the depth of water, knew that it was very, very deep. But it was not the water Nicko stared at—it was the beautiful lapis lazuli arched roof that spanned the pool.

"The Dragon House," said Jenna, "it's the same as the Dragon House."

"Shh," whispered Septimus. "Someone might hear us, sound carries here." Quietly, Nicko rowed to the quay and held the dinghy steady. Ullr took a flying leap and landed with a soft thud on the smooth stone. He was followed by Snorri, then Jenna and Septimus. Nicko got out and went to tie the boat to a nearby bollard but Septimus stopped him. "No, shove the boat back into the tunnel where no one can see it, Nik, and let's get going."

Very reluctantly, Nicko gave the dinghy a push into the tunnel and watched it float away. "We're burning our boats, Sep," he said. "I hope you know what you're doing."

⊹⊹40⊹⊹
THE GREAT CHAMBER OF ALCHEMIE AND PHYSIK

Three small arches led from the Alchemie Quay. Septimus took a rushlight from one of the holders. "This way," he whispered. "Better get a move on. It's a bit of a trek from the Quay, because the only way to get into the Chamber from here is through the Labyrinth."

"Labyrinth!" exclaimed Jenna. "But . . . do you know the way, Sep?"

"Shh!" whispered Septimus. "You don't need to know the way through a Labyrinth, Jen. It takes you there. You just follow where it leads you and you will find what you look for. We go through the left archway."

"So . . . where do the other ones go?"

"Oh, they'll drop you down into the Great Pitte of Fyre," said Septimus nonchalantly.

"Oh. Fine."

"It'll be all right, Jen." Jenna did not look convinced.

Septimus beckoned to everyone to come closer. Silently they gathered around, a little overawed by the strange, crypt-like feel of the UnderFlow Pool and the flickering, unearthly blue light reflected from the lapis lazuli.

"Let's get going," said Septimus in a low voice. "We've got to keep quiet and stay together. There are other tunnels that run into this one and we don't want anyone to hear us and come looking. Hang on to that panther, Snorri. Don't let it growl, whatever you do. If anyone sees or hears us, we've had it. Got that?"

They all nodded. Ullr's green eyes flashed and Snorri stroked him, saying, "Kalmm, Ullr. Kalmm."

They followed Septimus through the archway and set off in single file with the NightUllr padding behind them. His great

soft paws were silent as they crept through the narrow opening, but there were muted gasps of amazement as they entered
the Labyrinth. In front of them, the flames from Septimus's
rushlight lit up great flashes of blue and gold. The Labyrinth
was lined from top to bottom in finely jointed lapis lazuli
interspersed with strips of gold.

Septimus set a fast pace and they followed behind him,
walking upon the most brilliant hues of blue shot through
with flashes of gold and deep green. The Labyrinth first took
them outward, and then after many turns, Jenna was sure they
had begun to walk toward the center. The deep blue of the
lapis became almost hypnotic, and Jenna found herself feeling
sleepy as she unfocused her eyes and gazed at the smooth blue
walls. Every now and then she was woken from her almost
trancelike state by the interruption of a dark archway, which
signaled an entrance from a tunnel. Here Septimus would
slow his pace and listen for other footsteps but they were
lucky; it was by now the dead of night and even Alchemie
scribes had to sleep sometimes.

Like a small and faithful flock of sheep, Jenna, Nicko,
Snorri and the NightUllr followed Septimus through the blue
haze of light, walking the long, slow curves, doubling back on

themselves and walking the same curves in reverse, until everyone, particularly Nicko, felt dizzy and longed to be out in an open space once more. And then, just as Nicko was despairing of seeing anything but blue walls ever again in his entire life, they reached the center of the Labyrinth, and stepped into the Great Chamber of Alchemie and Physik.

"Whoa-ho." Nicko whistled. "That is *amazing*."

Septimus no longer thought of the Great Chamber as anything like amazing. Every day he had sat in his Siege of the Rose next to Marcellus, whose Siege of the Sunne was at the head of the table set in the middle of the Chamber. Every day had been the same, just another working day for Septimus.

But to Jenna, Nicko and Snorri, the Great Chamber was dazzling. They felt almost blinded by the glinting of the multitude of shiny golden surfaces that caught the light from the dancing flames of Septimus's rushlight. But it was not the small pieces of gold that had caught their attention, it was the two massive chunks of the stuff set into the wall opposite the entrance to the Labyrinth—the Great Doors of Time.

"That's where I came into this place," Septimus whispered, glancing around the Chamber, half afraid that there might be a scribe lurking in the shadows.

On each side of the Doors, standing in a lapis lazuli–lined alcove, was a life-size statue holding a razor-sharp sword.

Jenna stared at the Doors. She thought about what Septimus had told her lay behind them, the True Glass of Time, and she felt a terrible longing to be home in her own Time, with everything back as it should be: Septimus in the Wizard Tower with Marcia, Nicko working down at Jannit Maarten's boatyard. She would be back in her *own* Palace, free of the living Etheldredda, at least, and once again the Palace would be a friendly place, home to Silas and Sarah pottering about and occasionally getting lost.

"We have to get the **Keye**, Sep," she said. "We *have* to."

Nicko, ever practical, was eyeing the Doors with a boat-builder's eye. "I'm sure we could get them open somehow," he said. "Those hinges look a bit weak to me."

"They're not just ordinary doors, Nik," said Septimus. "They're **Locked** with Marcellus's **Keye**." Nicko was not convinced. He took his screwdriver out of his pocket and poked it into one of the hinges. The statues raised their swords and pointed them at Nicko.

"Whoa there," protested Nicko. "No need to get excited."

Ullr growled. "Shh, Ullr." Snorri stroked Ullr's neck and

pulled him close to her, but the NightUllr's orange-tipped tail was fluffed out like that of an irritated house cat, and his hackles were raised.

It is strange how voices carry through a Labyrinth. They find their way along the passageways and appear in the center as clear and bright as if the speaker was standing beside you, particularly if the voice has the penetrating quality of a dentist's drill. Which is why everyone in the Great Chamber of Alchemie and Physik suddenly jumped with fright as the shrill tones of Queen Etheldredda entered the Chamber. "I care not to hear thy troubles, Marcellus. I shall have the Potion *now*. I have tarried long enough. This night did show me not to suffer fools, and I will not suffer *thy* foolishness a moment longer. Oh, for how long does this lamentable Labyrinth wind its tedious way?"

"For as long as it must, Mother."

The sound of Marcellus's exasperated voice spurred Septimus into action. "They're coming," he whispered. "Quick—into the fume cupboard. We'll have to wait until Etheldredda's gone."

Septimus opened the door of a large cupboard in the wall and blew out his rushlight. With only the glow from his

Dragon Ring to light their way, everyone squeezed into the foul-smelling cupboard and Septimus pulled the door closed.

"Oh, rats," muttered Septimus, his ring lighting up what Jenna had assumed was a coil of black rope on the shelf at the back of the cupboard, "I forgot the snake was in here."

"Snake?" whispered Jenna.

"Yeah. It's okay, it's not all that poisonous."

"So how poisonous would 'not all that poisonous' be then, Sep?" asked Nicko, who was fighting a longing to open the door and just get out of there.

But no one heard Septimus's reply. Queen Etheldredda made sure of that.

⊹⊱41⊰⊹
THE PHIAL

The door to the fume cupboard closed just as Queen Ethel-dredda's pointy left foot stepped over the threshold of the Great Chamber of Alchemie and **Physik**. She was closely followed by Marcellus Pye, who did not trust his mother to be alone in the Chamber for even a second. Marcellus looked tired and disheveled after a long night searching the Palace for his Apprentice and the girl his mother insisted was Princess

Esmeralda. He was still wearing his formal Master of Alchemie robes that he had put on for the banquet—which were, to his dismay, now liberally splattered with orange sauce. Around his neck, as ever, hung his **Keye** to the Doors of Time.

Queen Etheldredda marched in, head held high, followed by her Aie-Aie, which clattered behind her, running on its long fingernails. She looked around with her usual expression of disgust. "Forsooth, Marcellus, thou dost a tawdry Chamber keep. So much gold that I hardly know where to rest mine eyes. 'Tis like unto a tinker's bazaar, which is where I trow thou dost buy thy gold trifles and trinkets with which thee doth rattle like a broken cart."

Marcellus Pye looked hurt at his mother's insults.

Queen Etheldredda sniffed disdainfully. "Thou'rt a tender Plant, Marcellus. I shall have my Potion now before thee doth expire from a Fitte of the Vapors."

"No, Mama," came Marcellus's determined voice, "thou shall *not* have it."

"Indeed, I *shall* have it, Marcellus. Do I not see it in its glass cabinet a-waiting me?"

"That is not yours, Mama!"

"Methinks thou art a Laggard with the Truth, Marcellus. Thou wert always a deceitful child. Indeed, I *shall* have it, and I shall have it *now*." Etheldredda's voice rose to a particularly unpleasant note. The Aie-Aie opened its mouth, showing its sharp, long fang, and screeched in sympathy.

Inside the fume cupboard, Ullr whined—the Aie-Aie's screech made his sensitive ears hurt horribly.

"And thou shalt *not* mock me," Etheldredda told Marcellus sharply.

"I mock thee not, Mama."

"Thou doth whine like a baby."

"Indeed, Mama, I do not," said Marcellus sulkily.

"Thou *dost* whine and I will *not* allow it." Etheldredda's voice reached a new pitch and set the Aie-Aie off again. This time the creature did not stop.

Marcellus put his fingers in his ears and yelled, "For pity's sake, Mama, make that creature cease its screaming 'ere my ears do *burst!*"

Etheldredda had no intention of making the Aie-Aie stop. It was upsetting Marcellus and that was fine by her. On and on it yowled like a cat caught in a trap. If the noise was painful for Marcellus, it was unbearable for Ullr. He let out a howl of pain and wrenched himself from Snorri's grasp. The next yell from Etheldredda was one of sheer terror as the fume cupboard door burst open and a panther—hackles raised, claws extended, teeth bared—hurtled out.

Unfortunately for Ullr, he found that instead of escaping the noise, he had run straight into the middle of it, for at the sight of the panther, the Aie-Aie ran up Etheldredda's skirts and continued screeching at panther ear level. The big cat's ears felt as though someone was boring into them. Desperate to get away from the noise, he ran across the chamber and disappeared into the Labyrinth.

"Ullr!" yelled Snorri, bursting out of the cupboard in pursuit of her beloved cat. She raced across the room, unhindered by a shocked Marcellus and a terrified Etheldredda, and disappeared into the Labyrinth, hot on the heels of Ullr.

Septimus felt Nicko's muscles tense, and he knew that his brother wanted to chase after Snorri. He grabbed hold of Nicko before he could move. Inside the fume cupboard there was a terrible hush as the door slowly swung fully open, and the three remaining occupants came face-to-face with Marcellus and Etheldredda.

"Forsooth, thou hast some strange creatures in thy cupboard,

Marcellus," said Etheldredda somewhat hoarsely after her long screech. "But methinks the Princess Esmeralda has played her little game of hide-and-seek once too often. Fetch the child out, Marcellus. She shall vex thee no more."

"She vexes me not, Mama. And if thee didst but know your daughter as a mother should, thou wouldst know that the child is not Esmeralda." Marcellus glowered at his mother.

"Thou'rt a Fool," retorted Etheldredda. "Who but Esmeralda could she be?"

"She will answer for herself, Mama." Marcellus gave Septimus a wry smile. "I trust they paid thee well for thy services at the Palace?"

Sheepishly, Septimus shook his head.

Marcellus ushered them out, saying, "Come thee away now, for the black snake sleepeth there and thou dost discomfit it. Remember, we shall be taking the venom tomorrow—to add to the Tincture."

"Knave!" cried Etheldredda. "Thou wouldst poison thine own mother!"

"As thou hast poisoned thine own poore daughters, Mama? No, indeed, I wouldst not."

Seeing that she was getting nowhere, Etheldredda changed

her tones to a sugary sweetness that fooled no one, least of all Marcellus. "Pray unlock the cabinet, Marcellus, and show me the pretty blue phial, for I do yearn to see at close hand the wonders that my Dearest Son hath wrought."

"Thou hast but one son, Mama," said Marcellus sourly. " 'Twould surely be a strangeness if he were *not* your dearest son, when placed against an absence of other sons, though I doubt he would remain your dearest of *all* were you to include your hunting hounds in the reckoning."

"Thou moans and mithers as well as thee ever did, Marcellus. Pray now, show me the phial that I may gaze upon it, for 'tis a pretty thing with *much* gold upon it."

"Though there may be colloid of gold suspended within, there is no gold upon the phial, Mama," said Marcellus, stung by Etheldredda's sarcastic tone.

Etheldredda lost patience. Like a rat up a drainpipe, she darted across the Chamber and snatched up the phial. "I *shall* have this Potion, Marcellus, before thee defile it with the venom of the black snake. You shall deny me not."

"No, Mama!" Marcellus yelled, horrified at seeing his precious Tincture about to disappear into Etheldredda's gaping mouth. "It is not ready. Who knoweth what it may do!"

But Etheldredda was not about to break the habit of a lifetime and listen to her son. She did not heed the warning in his words. She tipped the sticky contents of the phial into her mouth and choked in disgust, then she doubled up in pain, coughing and retching. The stuff came back up from her stomach and swilled around her mouth, coating her teeth as if with blue tar. Determined, Etheldredda swallowed it again and straightened up, leaning against the bench, pale and weak as a sheet left too long in the bleach by a careless laundress. Unknowing of the effect the Tincture had had on its mistress, the Aie-Aie jumped onto the bench and drained the remaining drops. It licked its lips and ran a long fingernail around the inside of the phial to scrape out the last smears of slime.

Jenna, Septimus, Nicko and Marcellus Pye stared, aghast.

"Thou shouldst not have done that, Mama," Marcellus said quietly.

Etheldredda swayed slightly, took a deep breath and regained her composure, though she still had sticky blue teeth. "I will not be denied, Marcellus," she said as the Tincture began to enter her bloodstream and an exhilarating feeling of power whizzed through her veins. "For I shall rule this Castle *forever*. It is my right and duty. No other Queen shall take my place."

"Thou must not forget thy daughter, Esmeralda, Mama," muttered Marcellus. "For she must take thy place when the Time Is Right."

Fixing Jenna with a poisonous glare, Etheldredda declared, "Esmeralda shall *never* have my crown! Never, never, *never*." With the power of the unfinished Tincture now infusing her whole body, Etheldredda felt invincible. The Chamber began to distort before her eyes, her mealy-mouthed son grew smaller and the tedious Esmeralda became nothing more than un-finished business.

Jenna, transfixed by the sight of her ghastly great-great(and then some)-grandmother's blue teeth and staring eyes, did not react quickly enough when Etheldredda's hand suddenly snaked out and grabbed her arm.

"Let go!" she yelled, twisting away from the vise but suc-ceeding only in hurting her arm even more. The Aie-Aie threw down the phial, leaped onto Etheldredda's skirts and then wrapped its snake-tail around Jenna's neck—once, twice, then three times, until she could barely breathe.

Septimus and Nick rushed to help Jenna but were swatted

away by Etheldredda like a couple of irritating flies.

As Etheldredda and the Aie-Aie disappeared into the Labyrinth, dragging Jenna in their wake, Marcellus sank to his knees in despair at the loss of his Tincture, unseeing as Septimus and Nicko picked themselves up and hurtled into the Labyrinth in pursuit of Jenna.

"We'll get her, Nik," shouted Septimus. "She can't have gotten very far. Can't be more than just around the next bend."

But Jenna wasn't. Nicko and Septimus raced through the endless blue haze of the passageways and found only emptiness.

✛ 42 ✛
THE RIVER

"Thou shalt come with your mama, Esmeralda!" Queen Etheldredda yelled as she pulled Jenna into a small unlit tunnel just off the Labyrinth. "Thou *shalt* come with her, for we have a much-delayed trip to take, do we not?"

With the Aie-Aie's tail curled so tightly around her neck that she barely had breath enough to walk, Jenna could not escape Etheldredda's grip. She was being dragged deeper and deeper into the darkness of the tunnel. The floor beneath Jenna's feet was slippery, and a cold wind blew up through the tunnel, carrying with it the dank smell of river water. The combination of Etheldredda's potion-powered strength and the downward slope of the passage, which was covered in a thin coating of ice, meant that Jenna was almost skating along in Etheldredda's wake.

The darkness did not seem to bother Etheldredda. The Queen knew her way, for it was a route she often took to check up on her son, and she sped along the tunnel like a speed skater on a mission. After what felt like a lifetime, but was no more than fifteen minutes, Jenna thought she could see pale moonlight—or was it the beginnings of dawn?—shining on the icy tunnel floor and beyond that, the blackness of the river. A few moments later, she, Etheldredda and the Aie-Aie were out in the open air, on a small landing platform a few hundred yards upriver from the South Gate. The river swept by in front of them, swift, dark and freezing cold. Jenna pulled back from the water. The landing stage was icy, and she knew it would take only a moment for Etheldredda to push her in.

"Thou art safe for now, Esmeralda," hissed the Queen, keeping her grip on Jenna tight. "I wouldst not have some footman find thee a-bobbing by the Palace on the outflow of the tide this morn. Besides, I wish to show thee one of the

wonders of our land: the bottomless Whirlpool of Bleak
Creek. I shall call our barge and we shall make haste forth-
with, for your mama is not so cruel as to make thee tarry here
a moment longer when such delight awaits." With that,
Queen Etheldredda drew out a golden whistle from a pocket
deep in her rustling silk skins and blew three short, shrill
notes. The piercing noise cut through the icy air and carried
all the way to the Palace landing stage, where it woke the
bargee, who had been sleeping fitfully in his freezing bunk on
board the Royal Barge, his porthole wide open just in case of
such a summons.

But it was not only the Royal bargee that the whistle summoned. In the shadows of the landing stage, the NightUllr
was crouching, waiting for his mistress to find him. As Etheldredda's whistle shrieked, so did Ullr's ears hurt. Almost
deafened with pain, the panther sprang out of the night and
knocked the whistle from Etheldredda's lips. The Queen
screamed out in surprise. The Aie-Aie unwound its tail from
Jenna's neck and leaped to its mistress's aid, leaving Jenna
free to wrench herself from the Queen's clutches and throw
herself clear of the edge of the water.

As Etheldredda slipped on the icy landing stage, her crown

toppled from her head and she fell into the river with a surprisingly small, neat splash. There were no more screams, no
more shrieks, and in a moment she had disappeared below the
water, with nothing but a few black bubbles rising to the surface to show where she had fallen. The Aie-Aie, chattering
with fear, skittered away into the darkness, and the last Jenna
heard of it was a few stones dislodged from the wall as it
climbed to freedom.

Very carefully, Jenna crept to the edge of the landing stage
and peered into the water's depths. It seemed impossible that
Queen Etheldredda could disappear so thoroughly and with
such little fuss. She looked behind to check that Etheldredda
was not creeping up and about to push her in, but there was
nothing there. She was safe. As the sun rose above a small line
of pink clouds on the low horizon above the Farmlands, Jenna
yawned—tired, cold and suddenly remembering that, even
though she was safe from the murderous Etheldredda, she was
still five hundred years away from home.

"Komme, Ullr," said Jenna as she had heard Snorri do.
She turned away from the sunrise, and to her surprise there
was no sign of the panther anywhere. Thinking that he must
have padded back up the tunnel, Jenna turned wearily into

the tunnel entrance to retrace her steps back to the Chamber, for where else could she go?

"Meow . . . *meow*." A strange orange cat with a black-tipped tail rubbed itself against Jenna's leg.

"Hello, puss," said Jenna, bending down to stroke the cat. "How did you get here?"

"Meow." The cat seemed a little impatient with her. "*Meow*."

And then Jenna remembered. "Ullr," she murmured.

"Meow," responded Ullr. The orange cat set off back up the dark and slippery tunnel. Tired and cold, Jenna trudged after him.

As Jenna left the landing stage, the Royal Barge—with eight sleepy oarsmen creaking at their places and the frozen bargee, teeth chattering and hand sticking to the ice on the tiller—rounded the bend. The barge was a beautiful sight in the winter's dawn: candles hastily lit and burning bright at the portholes, the Royal Red canopy moving gently with the motion of the barge and the swirls of golden paintwork glinting in the long, low rays of the rising winter sun. Inside the cabin, a table was set with a jug of hot mulled wine and a plate of savory biscuits; around the table were comfortable seats covered in Royal Red rugs and cushions. In the middle of the cabin, a small stove was glowing with a blaze of seasoned apple logs and aromatic herbs, which filled the cabin with a warming and welcoming fragrance.

But there was no one left to welcome aboard. As the Royal Barge drew up to the deserted landing stage, the bargee and the oarsmen had no idea that far below the keel, weighed down by her great black skirts, the body of Queen Etheldredda floated a few inches above the muddy bottom of the river.

✠43✠
THE GREAT DOORS OF TIME

A small orange cat sauntered out of the tunnel that led to the Royal landing stage.

"Ullr!" gasped Nicko.

"Shh," warned Septimus.

Nicko picked up Ullr. "Snorri?" he whispered into the tunnel. "Snorri?" But it was Jenna who came out of the darkness, not Snorri.

* * *

In the Great Chamber of Alchemie and Physik, Marcellus Pye was alone. He was sitting in his Siege of the Sunne at the head of the table, head in his hands. At the sound of approaching footsteps in the Labyrinth he panicked. He jumped up, ran into the fume cupboard and closed the door, trembling. He could not face his mother, not right now.

"What do you mean, she just fell in the water, Jen?" Nicko's whisper carried into the Great Chamber. "Didn't she try to get out?"

"No, she just went sort of *plop* and disappeared. It was weird. Like . . . like she couldn't be bothered to do anything about it. It was as if she thought it didn't really matter."

"Well, it wouldn't, would it, if you thought you were going to live forever?" Septimus pointed out.

Inside the fume cupboard Marcellus heard every whispered word and the realization began to dawn on him that they were talking about his mother.

Jenna was still shaken from seeing her great-great(and then some)-grandmother drown. "But I didn't wish her dead. Really I didn't—"

Marcellus gasped and clutched at a shelf for support. Dead? Mama was *dead*?

"Aargh!" There was a sudden yell from inside the fume cupboard and the door crashed open. The cupboard's previous occupants leaped with shock as Marcellus Pye rushed out, clasping a long black snake just behind its head between his thumb and forefinger. The snake's mouth was open and its white fangs dripped venom down the front of Marcellus's black tunic. "Forsooth, 'tis a vicious brute," Marcellus gasped. He sped over to the bench where the phial of his Tincture had until recently been resident, pulled the top from a large glass jar, threw the snake in and slammed the top back on.

Then, carefully wiping the venom from his tunic—which had produced an interesting effect on the orange sauce—he surveyed his stunned audience. "Pray, Septimus," he said quickly, "do not run from Here."

Septimus sighed. So much for their ambush. Marcellus had ambushed *them*. Wearily, he pulled out his chair at the Siege of the Rose and made Jenna sit down. She looked pale and had red marks around her neck from the Aie-Aie's tail. Still feeling shaken, Jenna scooped up Ullr and hugged the cat close for comfort. Suspicious of Marcellus, Nicko hung back; but Septimus, as was his habit when he had nothing to do in the Chamber, perched on one of the scribes' stools and yawned. It would not be long before the working day in the Chamber of Alchemie and Physik started and the early-morning scribes began to arrive.

Marcellus caught Septimus's yawn. It had been a long and difficult night. He sat down in his great high-backed chair at the head of the table and regarded Jenna and Septimus with a thoughtful air. There was something he wanted to discuss.

Nicko hung back from the table. He was having none of this cozy conversation with the man he regarded as Septimus's kidnapper. It seemed to him that it would be easy to take Marcellus unawares. Nicko figured that with the muscles he had recently acquired working in the boatyard, he was a match for anyone, especially a lanky Alchemist who looked as if he had inhaled too many mercury fumes. The only thing that held Nicko back was Snorri. Where *was* she? What should he do? Nicko hovered, so enmeshed in his thoughts that he did not hear the offer that Marcellus Pye was making Septimus.

At the end of their conversation both Marcellus and Septimus were smiling. The decision made, Marcellus leaned back in his chair.

Nicko meanwhile had also made a decision. He would get the **Keye**. It was now or never. With skills learned from Rupert Gringe, he lunged at Marcellus from behind and grabbed him by the throat.

"Take the **Keye**, Sep—quick!" he yelled.

"Aargh!" Marcellus gurgled, half strangled as Nicko wrenched at the thick chain from which the **Keye** dangled.

"No, Nik!" shouted Septimus as Marcellus began to turn a nasty purple.

"We gotta do it now." *Tug.* "It's our last chance." *Yank.* "Come on, Sep, help me." *Wrench.* Marcellus's eyes started to bulge, and he began to resemble some of the pickled purple frogs on the top shelf of the fume cupboard.

"*No*, Nik!" Septimus pulled Nicko away, and Marcellus collapsed, gasping, back into his chair.

Nicko was furious. "What did you do *that* for?" he demanded. "You idiot!"

"He's just *offered* us the **Keye**, you dillop," said Septimus. "He's going to let us go—or he *was*."

Jenna poured Marcellus a glass of water from a jug on the table. He took it with a shaking hand and drank it down. "Thank you, Esmeral—er, Jenna. Prithee take some for yourself, for I do believe you have as much need as I do." Marcellus turned to Septimus. "Now, Apprentice, dost thou still wish to go through the Great Doors? Perchance thee might find less violent friends in thine own Time."

"I do still wish," said Septimus, "and I wish my friends to go with me."

"Very well, if thy Friends so wish it—though 'tis an Unknown Danger to go forward to a Time not your own. All who have gone have never Returned. Which is why these Doors are Guarded at all times." Marcellus got to his feet and regarded Septimus gravely. "So we are agreed?" he asked.

"Yes," replied Septimus.

"I trust thee," said Marcellus, "as I have never trusted any Person before. Not even my dearest Broda. My Life is in your hands, Apprentice."

Septimus nodded.

"What's going on, Sep?" Nicko hissed, who didn't like the sound of this.

"The Conjunction of the Seven Planets," Septimus told him.

"The *what*?"

"Marcellus can't make another Tincture—one that will

work—until the same Conjunction of the Planets happens."

"So? Hard luck for Marcellus and all that, but what's it to do with us?"

"Well, it happens tomorrow."

"Good for them."

"It happens tomorrow—*in our Time*."

Nicko shrugged. He didn't see what the planets had to do with going home.

"I have promised to make the Tincture in our Time, Nik. Tomorrow at the time of the Conjunction. I can make it so that Marcellus can be young in our Time, too. I am sure I can."

"He's coming with us?" asked Nicko, shocked. "But he *kidnapped* you."

"No, he's not coming with us. He's there already, just really old and sick. I'm going to try and make him okay. Now, stop asking questions, Nik. Don't you want to go home?"

The truth was that Nicko wanted desperately to—but not without Snorri. He kept glancing at the entrance to the Great Chamber in the hope that she would suddenly rush in, pale hair flying, eyes shining, and he could tell her that they were all going home.

Marcellus took the **Keye** from around his neck, inspecting the misshapen links on the chain that Nicko had very nearly succeeded in breaking. He went over to the Doors and began to make preparations for their opening. The statues sheathed their swords and bowed their heads as Marcellus placed his **Keye** into its mirror-image indentation in the center of the Great Doors. And then, deep within the Doors, Septimus heard a sound that made the hairs on the back of his neck prickle—the rumble of the bar inside moving, a sound that he had last heard when the Great Doors had closed behind him one hundred and seventy days before.

Slowly, silently, the Great Doors of Time swung open, the gold flashing in the candlelight as they moved apart to reveal the dark surface of the Glass, which stood patiently waiting beneath them. Septimus had forgotten how deep the Glass looked, and as he gazed into its depths he felt as if he were standing on the edge of a precipice. A familiar feeling of vertigo swept up from his feet and made him sway.

"Fare thee well, Septimus," said Marcellus, "and thank you."

"Thank you, too, for all you taught me about **Physik**," replied Septimus.

"Now take thee this," said Marcellus, to Septimus's surprise, handing him the **Keye**. "It will open the Glass at the top of the lapis steps, which is where thee must Go Out. It is thine to keep, I shall make another for myself. I shall place thy **Physik** Chest sub rosa in the cloaks cupboard at the top of the steps to the Wizard Tower. Use it well, thou hast the makings of a great Physician."

"I will," Septimus promised. He took the **Keye** and placed it around his neck. It felt heavy and was still warm from Marcellus's touch. "But how," he asked, "shall I get the Tincture to you?"

"Fear not, I wouldst not ask thee to bring it through the Glass, for I know the horror thou hast of such a thing. Place the tincture, pray, in a gold Box marked with the Symbol of the Sunne and throw it into the Moat beside my House. I will find it."

"How will I know that *you* have found it?" Septimus asked.

"Thou shalt know by the presence of the Golden Arrow of **Flyte**, which I didst see upon my Ancient Person. I shall place it in the Box by return. Art thou a fisherman?"

"No," replied Septimus, puzzled.

"Methinks thou wilt become one," Marcellus chuckled.

"The Golden Arrow of Flyte will be my thanks to you and will bring you great freedom."

"It already has," muttered Septimus, "until *you* took it."

Marcellus did not hear; he had turned his attention to Jenna.

"Fear not that my mother should continue to Haunt thee in thine own Time," he told her. "Although she hath drunk of my Tincture which, while incomplete, may give her Spirit some Substance, she shall not trouble thee. The ExtraOrdinary Wizard and I shall Entrance her into her portrait. Methinks I shall also hunt down the Aie-Aie, for did it not too drink of my Tincture? It truly is a most Poisonous Creature and doth carry a Pestilence in its bite, which Mama hath used to terrify all who displease her. So, Jenna, it is decided: I shall Entrance them both into the portrait and Seal them in a room that None shall find."

"But Dad Unsealed it," Jenna gasped.

Marcellus did not reply. Something in the Glass had caught his attention.

"Dad did *what?*" asked Septimus.

"He and Gringe Unsealed Etheldredda's portrait. You remember. It was hanging in the Long Walk—"

Marcellus's voice interrupted Jenna. With an unmistakable note of panic, he said, "Pray do not tarry, this Glass hath become Unstable. I can see cracks appearing deep within. It will not hold for long, I fear. Go you now—or never!"

Deep within the Glass Septimus saw what Marcellus had seen. Beyond long, lazy swirls of Time moving within it, fissures were materializing around the edges of the Glass. It was indeed now or never.

"We've got to go!" yelled Septimus. "Now!" He grabbed hold of Jenna with one hand and Nicko with the other and ran at the Glass.

At the very last moment, Nicko wrenched away. "I'm not going without Snorri," he said.

"Nik—you must come, you *must*," said Septimus desperately.

"The Glass will not wait," said Marcellus, urgently. "Begone, begone before it is too late."

"Go!" yelled Nicko. "I'll see you later. I promise!" With that, Nicko ran from the Great Chamber of Alchemie and **Physik**.

"No, Nicko. No!" Jenna yelled.

"Come on, Jen," said Septimus. "We've gotta go."

Jenna nodded and together, with a small orange cat, they stepped into the Glass and walked into the liquid cold of Time.

✢44✢
THE FIND

The Great Doors of Time swung silently closed behind them.

"Nicko," sobbed Jenna. "*Nicko!*"

"It's no good, Jen," said Septimus wearily. "He's five hundred years away now."

Jenna looked at Septimus in disbelief. She had expected to walk straight out into the Castle—not find herself in a dingy tunnel lit with weird glass globes. "What . . . you mean we're already back—back in our own Time?"

Septimus nodded. "We're home now, Jen. This is the Old Way. It's really, *really* old. It runs far below even the Ice Tunnels."

"So where's the old Marcellus?" Jenna asked wearily. "You'd think he'd be waiting for us, since he knows we're coming."

"Five hundred years is a long time to remember stuff, Jen. I don't think he knows what's going on anymore, really. He'll be around somewhere. Come on, let's get out of here."

With the air of a seasoned traveler, Septimus set off along the Old Way, with Jenna, clutching Ullr to her, trudging behind. They walked along in silence, each deep in their own thoughts about Nicko.

After a while Jenna said, "If Nicko ever does **Come Through**, how will he find his way back?"

"Nicko will find a way, Jen. He always does," replied Septimus, sounding more hopeful than he really was, for it was not long since Nicko had mistaken an ant for a footpath and gotten them both lost in the Forest.

"And Snorri . . ." said Jenna. "I really liked Snorri."

"Yeah. So did Nik. That was the trouble." Septimus sounded mad.

All the time, Ullr made no sound. The small orange cat
with the black-tipped tail sat quietly in Jenna's arms, his spirit
elsewhere—with his mistress in a distant Time.

Five hundred years away, Snorri Snorrelssen was sitting
lost and miserable on a riverbank. But, as she gazed into the
distance, she **Saw** the Old Way and the long lines of globes of
Everlasting Fyre, and though she did not understand what it
was she was **Seeing**, she knew that she was **Seeing** through
Ullr's eyes.

It was bitterly cold in the Old Way. Jenna and Septimus pulled
their UnderCooks' coats around them, but still the chill
worked its way through and made them shiver. The rough
fabric of the coats brushed along the wide, smooth pavement,
and the faint rustling sounds filled the air like the flapping of
bats' wings at twilight.

Marcellus was waiting for them at the foot of the lapis
steps, slumped against the stone with his deep-set eyes closed.
Jenna jumped at the sight of the ancient man and squeezed
Ullr tightly to her—so tightly that far away, Snorri gasped at
the sudden pain around her ribs.

"He . . . he's not *dead*, is he?" Jenna whispered.

"Not yet," came a quavery voice. "Though there is not much difference, 'tis true." Old Marcellus licked his dry lips and stared at Septimus as if trying to remember something. "You are the boy with the Tincture?" he asked, looking at them with his rheumy eyes. Septimus thought he could still see something of the young Marcellus's expression in those eyes.

"I am going to make it tomorrow at the Conjunction," said Septimus. "Don't you remember? You told me to drop it in the Moat inside a gold box marked with the sun?"

The old man snorted. "What care I for the sun?"

"I shall put it in the box, just as I said I would," said Septimus patiently. "And then—do you remember?—you will let me know you have it by returning the **Flyte Charm**."

Marcellus smiled and his tombstone teeth glowed red in the flames of the globes. "I remember now, Septimus. I do not forget my promises. Be you a fisherman?"

Septimus shook his head.

"Methinks you will become one." Marcellus chuckled.

"Good-bye, Marcellus," said Septimus.

"Fare thee well, Septimus. Thou wert a good Apprentice. Fare thee well, my dear . . . Esmeralda." The ancient man closed his eyes once more.

"Good-bye, Marcellus," said Jenna.

At last they reached the top of the long, winding lapis steps and came face to face with the Glass. Septimus remembered the last time he had stood there, and could hardly believe that this time he would be able to go through it. He looked at the Glass, hardly daring to place the **Keye** into the indentation above it. He could see that this Glass was not the same as the True Glass of Time. Gone were the heady sense of depth and the intricate swirling patterns of Time—this Glass looked dull and empty, seeming to be nothing more than a poorly silvered glass.

"Time to go home," whispered Septimus.

"So . . . we just go through here and come out into the Robing Room?" asked Jenna.

"I guess so. Come on, let's go." Septimus took hold of Jenna's hand, but Jenna resisted, glancing behind her one last time. "Nik hasn't **Come Through**, Jen," Septimus said quietly. "I've been listening for him all along, and he's not here. There is no human heartbeat in the Old Way apart from you and me and—about every five minutes—Marcellus."

Septimus tentatively placed his hand against the Glass. It went through as easily as putting his hand into an icy bowl of water. "Come on, Jen," he said, gently.

Taking Septimus's hand, Jenna followed him into the Glass—and out to the world where they belonged.

They were welcomed by an ear-splitting shriek. Marcia leaped up from her place at the table in the Hermetic Chamber and dropped a huge book of calculation charts on her foot. Jillie Djinn came running.

"What *is* it, Marcia?" gasped Jillie, emerging from the seven-cornered passage into the Hermetic Chamber. "The mouse catcher caught them all yesterday, he *promised*. There can't be any more—oh, my goodness, the *Glass!*"

"Septimus!" yelled Marcia, kicking the calculation charts away in abandon and rushing to the Glass. "Oh, Septimus, Septimus!" She swept up the emerging Septimus into her arms and swung him around, much to his complete amazement, for Marcia did not do hugs.

Jenna watched, happy that at last that she had put right the harm she had done Septimus. And then she remembered Nicko and burst into tears.

In the Manuscriptorium, twenty-one pale faces looked up as the tearful Princess, carrying a scraggy orange cat, and a disheveled boy, who looked a lot like the ExtraOrdinary Apprentice—but could not possibly be, because everyone knew that the ExtraOrdinary Wizard would never have allowed him to have his hair like *that*—came quietly out of the Hermetic Chamber with the ExtraOrdinary Wizard. No one had seen them go in, but some of the older scribes were used to that. People who went into the Hermetic Chamber did not always come out, and people who came out had not always gone in. It was just the way things were. The scribes also noticed that the ExtraOrdinary Wizard was smiling, which she most certainly had not been the day before when she had gone into the Chamber. Most scribes had, in fact, thought that, as part of her job, the ExtraOrdinary Wizard was not *allowed* to smile and were quite shocked. But whatever any of the scribes happened to be thinking at that moment, they all suddenly stopped when a loud *crash* shattered the pin-drop silence of the Manuscriptorium—and the front window.

Foxy, who had taken over from Beetle after he had been rushed to the Infirmary with the Sickenesse, threw himself through the flimsy door that separated the front office from the Manuscriptorium, white-faced and yelling, "Help, help! There's a dragon in the office!" Then he fainted.

There was indeed a dragon in the office—and not much else. The window was in a million pieces, the desk was firewood and the teetering stacks of pamphlets, papers, booklets and manuscripts were either trampled to the floor and covered in muddy dragon prints or were blowing down Wizard Way in the brisk early-morning breeze.

"Spit Fyre!" gasped Septimus, rubbing the dragon's nose. "How did you know I'd be here?"

"We did a **Seek**," said Jenna happily. "And it worked. Kind of."

Jillie Djinn surveyed the wreckage. She was not happy. "I would ask you to keep your dragon under control, Marcia," she said, "but it is obviously too late."

"It is not *my* dragon, Miss Djinn," snapped Marcia, her smile rapidly evaporating. "It belongs to my Apprentice here, who is a skilled and careful dragon keeper."

Jillie Djinn snorted dismissively. "Not quite skilled enough, apparently, Madam Marcia. I shall be sending you the bill for the window and the multitude of lost and destroyed papers."

"You may send as many bills as you wish, Miss Djinn. The nights are drawing in, and I shall take great pleasure in lighting the fire with them. Good day to you. Come, Jenna and

Septimus, time to go home." Marcia stepped disdainfully over the chaos and swept out the door. Once safely in Wizard Way, Marcia clicked her fingers at Spit Fyre, who jumped obediently through the smashed window, for there was something about Marcia that still made Spit Fyre think *Dragon Mother*.

Barely able to believe that his dream had come true, Septimus wandered onto Wizard Way—*his* Wizard Way. He stopped and breathed in the air—the air of *his* Time, which smelled of wood smoke and baked pies from the meat pie and sausage cart that was approaching the Manuscriptorium just in time for the mid-morning break. He looked down the broad expanse of the Way, with the long, low Palace—*Jenna's* Palace—in the distance, and he could not stop smiling. This, thought Septimus, is where I belong.

But while Septimus was feeling glad to be alive and, after six months of near silence could not stop talking, Jenna was exhausted. "You are to come back with us and get some sleep," Marcia told her. "I will send a message to the Palace."

They walked through the Great Arch, Septimus closely tailed by Spit Fyre, who was suspiciously sniffing his strange-smelling tunic. "Ouch!" yelped Septimus as the dragon trod on the backs of his heels in an effort to keep as close as possible to his Imprintor.

"Goodness," said Marcia, "what *have* you got on your feet, Septimus?"

Septimus felt quite silly enough in his shoes without explaining them to Marcia. He quickly changed the subject. "I wish Beetle had seen Spit Fyre come in through the window. He'll be really sorry to have missed that. I wonder where he was?"

"Ah, yes," Marcia sighed. "Beetle. Oh, dear. Septimus, there's something you ought to know . . ."

⊹⊹45⊹⊹
THE PHYSIK CHEST

Ａnd another thing, *Septimus*," said Marcia, sounding as stern as she could manage while they watched Catchpole, inexpertly wielding a large crowbar, try to lever up a dusty floorboard in the broom closet. "You are *not* to stay out at night on your own *ever* again."

"What, *never*?" Septimus looked up, saw the smile in Marcia's eyes and ventured, "Not even when I'm really old . . . like when I'm *thirty*?"

"Not while you're my Apprentice you're not—*oh for good-ness sake, Catchpole, give me the crowbar and I'll do it*—and don't think that going out with an irresponsible old ghost will be all right either, because it won't. Anyway—*oof, whoever nailed this board down made a good job of it*—I sincerely hope that by the time you're thirty—*aha, I think it's moving*—you will have an Apprentice of your own, and then it will be your turn to worry." Marcia's smile faded as she remembered. She straightened up and looked Septimus in the eye. "But I hope you never find a letter from them written five hundred years ago the way I found yours. *Never.*"

"No. I hope not too," said Septimus quietly.

Marcia set to with the crowbar again, and a few moments later there was a loud *crack* as the nails finally gave up their struggle against the determined ExtraOrdinary Wizard. Septimus helped Marcia lift the board.

"I had no idea that this rose was here," said Marcia, closely inspecting the intricate rose that was carved deep into the wood. It was much worn away by hundreds of years of feet tramping over it—for the broom closet had previously been used as a cloakroom—but the delicate curves of its petals were still clearly visible.

"It was my symbol," said Septimus almost proudly. Now that he was back safe in his own Time, Septimus was beginning to enjoy thinking about his time with Marcellus Pye. "It's the old sign for a seventh son. Marcellus had it carved into his table years before I got there."

"Wicked man," said Marcia. "I'd like to tell him a thing or two."

"He was okay really," Septimus ventured.

"We'll agree to differ on that subject, Septimus," said Marcia huffily. "I am just about prepared to dig out this chest full of quackery, since even a remote chance of curing the Sickenesse is worth a try, but you will never find me agreeing that that man was 'okay really.' *Never*."

Septimus and Marcia knelt down and peered into the dusty void under the floor. Gingerly, Septimus put his hand into the space and the glow from his Dragon Ring found an answering shine in the depths.

"I can see it," he said, amazed. "Here it is, just like Marcellus said it would be—*sub rosa*. Hidden beneath the rose."

"Oh, twaddle and tripe," Marcia huffed. "Now come on, Catchpole, don't just stand there gawking, we could do with a hand to get this thing out."

It took more than the weedy Catchpole's help to lift out the chest. It needed the combined efforts of five Ordinary Wizards—without Catchpole, who suddenly felt dizzy—to drag the chest onto the spiral stairs.

At the top of the Tower Marcia, Septimus and the five Wizards heaved the chest and dragged it along the landing. The great purple door to Marcia's rooms swung open, and everyone pushed and pulled the small but amazingly heavy chest inside. Marcia stood up with a groan and rubbed her back. "Are you sure this thing isn't just full of bricks?" she said. "What could it possibly have in it to make it so *heavy?*"

"Gold. It's lined with really thick slabs of the stuff," said Septimus.

"What on earth for?" asked Marcia indignantly.

"Because it's the purest, most perfect metal. And **Physik** is all about that too, sort of trying to reach perfection with ourselves . . ." Septimus trailed off, noticing Marcia's exasperated expression. It was not lost on the Ordinary Wizards either, who quickly scuttled away.

Marcia sighed. She looked down at the blackened old chest with its scraped gold corners and unbroken golden bands, and she just *knew* that it was going to be trouble. Not to mention the fact that it was making horrible dents in her best Chinese carpet. "It's all very well, Septimus," she said somewhat grumpily, "but how on earth do you intend to open this thing?"

"Easy," said Septimus. He knelt beside the chest and took the **Keye** from around his neck. Marcia watched as he pressed it into its mirror image on the front of the chest, and slowly the lid silently opened.

Septimus looked inside and smiled. Everything was as he remembered, neatly laid out, clean and tidy. Lines of gleaming gold instruments lay in a tray; bottles of tinctures and mixes, remedies and fusions lay just as he had left them. And, at the bottom of the chest was what Septimus was looking for: his carefully written formula for the antidote to the Sickenesse.

"Here it is," he said, triumphantly pulling out a ragged piece of much-folded vellum. "*Look.*" Septimus handed it to Marcia, who put her spectacles on. The hours of perusing Jillie Djinn's prediction tables and calculations had done her eyesight no good at all, and she peered at the fine brown-ink scrawl that covered the vellum. Her face brightened; at least she recognized what it was: an example of late Etheldredda/

early Esmeralda variant script with the typical reverse scrawl used by the Physicians of those days.

"Right, Septimus," said Marcia briskly, glad at last to be able to take charge. "Get yourself down to the Manuscriptorium and have the Ancient Script Scribe write you an immediate translation—*immediate*, mind. No messing about. There's no time to lose. Off you go. Well, go *on*."

Septimus shook his head. "But I don't need to do that—I wrote this myself."

Marcia felt very odd. She had to go and sit down.

Some hours later, Septimus was carefully drawing up a colloid of silver with his pipette and dropping it into a large flask. Marcia, feeling rather unnecessary, sat watching her Apprentice finding his way around the old **Physik** Chest with an ease that amazed her.

Despite Septimus's long tangled hair, which she really *must* get him to do something about, and the fact that he was definitely a little taller and thinner, she found it hard to believe that he had really been away for nearly six months of his life, while only two days had passed at the Castle. And something else was different about Septimus too. He was more assured and—this was what Marcia found really strange—now he knew and believed things that she did not. *That* took a bit of getting used to.

"Do I add the valerian to this or add this to the valerian? What do you think?" Septimus's voice broke into Marcia's thoughts.

"You're the expert, Septimus," said Marcia, trying to get used to her new role. "But as a general rule I would say add light to dark."

"Okay." Septimus added the greenish oil to the contents of his flask. "Now, could you pass me the balance, please?" he asked. Getting into her role of lab assistant, Marcia handed Septimus a small set of gold scales complete with tiny gold weights. She watched him pick up the smallest weight with a long-nosed pair of tweezers and place it on the balance. Then, taking out a tiny, round-bowled gold spoon, Septimus measured out a fine blue powder and poured it onto the other side of the scales until the two sides were delicately balanced, and then something caught his eye. He looked at the spoon more closely and frowned.

"What's wrong?" asked Marcia.

Septimus passed her the spoon. He pointed his blue-stained finger to some marks underneath the handle.

Marcia fished out her spectacles from her pocket and peered at the scratches on the spoon. "Sep . . . tim . . . us," she read slowly.

"I remember writing that," said Septimus. "It was the day after I . . . arrived. I wrote my name everywhere for a while. It was like writing messages forward to our own Time."

Marcia folded up her spectacles and dabbed at her eyes with her purple silk handkerchief. "That powder stings," she said. "You should put the lid back on."

Several hours later, when the mixture had cooled, Septimus went back to complete the serum. He removed the large crystal that had formed, crushed it in a mortar and pestle and returned the powdered crystal to the flask. He put a stopper in the flask, shook the mixture for thirteen seconds until it became clear and poured it into a tall clear glass medicine bottle. Now Septimus lit a candle. Then he took his diving rod from the **Physik** chest, dipped it into the mixture, turned it seven times and held it up to the candle flame. It looked good. Septimus placed a clean piece of silk over the open top and pushed a cork down onto it, creating a tight seal.

"It's finished!" he called up the stairs. Marcia hurried down.

"Now for the final test," said Septimus, a little nervously. Marcia watched her Apprentice pick up the bottle and hold it up to the light of the little arched window, turning it so that it caught a ray of sunlight. The sunlight struck the glass, traveled through the liquid and emerged as a blindingly blue streak of light. "It works—it *works!*" Septimus shouted.

"No more than I would expect." Marcia smiled. "Now, get your cloak, Septimus, we have to get this to where it's needed. There is no time to lose."

As Marcia and her Apprentice quickly crossed the Wizard Tower courtyard, the dragon kennel shook as Spit Fyre hurled himself at the door. Septimus ran up to the door and said, "I'll be back soon, Spit Fyre. Really, I will. Then you can come out. I *promise.* See you later, Spit Fyre!"

"Jenna will have to **UnDo** the **Seek**," Marcia told him. "He'll be a complete pest until then. He won't leave you alone."

"I know," said Septimus, clutching the bottle of Antidote close and running to catch up as Marcia took the side gate out into a small alley. They were on their way to the Infirmary. Knowing Septimus's dislike of heights, Marcia ignored the shortcut along the Castle walls and instead took the winding streets below. Septimus thought that he had never been so happy as he was now, except perhaps when he had returned to the Wizard Tower from the Manuscriptorium the previous day and the writing across the floor had said, WELCOME BACK TO YOUR TIME, APPRENTICE. WE HAVE MISSED YOU. That had been a good moment, a very good moment. Septimus loved the fact that once again he was wearing the green robes of the ExtraOrdinary Apprentice, rather than the black and red robes of an Alchemie Apprentice, and it was *his* friends that called out and said hello, with no weird accents and strange words that you always had to think twice about.

Soon they reached the North Gate.

"Afternoon, your ExtraOrdinariness," said Gringe, blocking their path.

"Oh. Good afternoon, Gringe," said Marcia, a little curtly.

"You going anywhere nice?" asked Gringe as Marcia tried to squeeze around him and get onto the drawbridge.

"No. Would you mind getting out of the way, please, Gringe?"

"Oh. Sorry, Your ExtraOrdinariness. Of course." Gringe squeezed himself against the gatehouse wall to allow Marcia and Septimus to pass. "Oh, hello," said Gringe, noticing Septimus. "You gave your poor dad a couple of sleepless nights, you did."

Suddenly Septimus remembered. Dad . . . Gringe . . . *Etheldredda's portrait.* "Gringe—you have to go down to the Palace *right now,* and you have to tell Dad to put that picture back exactly where you found it. Then he's got to **ReSeal** the room. Properly!"

Gringe's eyes widened in surprise. "What?" he said.

"Put that portrait back *exactly* where you found it. The one of Queen Etheldredda."

"Well, I'm not surprised he don't like lookin' at it—she's a scary old bird, no mistake about it—but just in case you 'adn't noticed, I got a gatehouse to run 'ere and I can't just drop everythin' an' go rearrangin' someone's pictures for 'em." Gringe turned away abruptly to take a silver penny from a returning Infirmary nurse.

Marcia saw Septimus's look of dismay. She had no idea what it was about, but she had learned enough over the past few months to know that if something was bothering Septimus, she should take notice of it. She swept onto the drawbridge where Gringe was now passing time with a couple of boys coming back from the Forest with bunches of kindling.

"Gringe," she said, towering over the Gatekeeper, her winter cloak blowing in the breeze and making Gringe sneeze, because he was allergic to fur. "You will do as you are asked, *now*. You and Silas Heap are to move that portrait and *I* will come and **ReSeal** the room. Mark my words, there will be trouble if I do not find that portrait exactly where it should be."

"Atchooo! Can't—atchooo—leave the Gate—atchooo, atchooo, *atchooooo*—unattended."

"Mrs. Gringe can step in."

"Mrs. Gringe is visiting her sister in the Infirmary. Got bit yesterday."

"Oh. I'm very sorry. Well, Lucy then."

"Lucy, in case you didn't know, has run off after that nogood brother of your Apprentice, much good may it do her," snapped Gringe. "But if it's so important, I'll go an' do the picture after sunset once I got the bridge up. Awright?"

"No, Gringe, that will not be *all right*. You will just have to close the North Gate for the afternoon."

Gringe looked horrified. "I can't do that," he protested. "That has never been done in my time as a Gatekeeper. *Never*."

"There's always a first time for everything, Gringe," Marcia said in a steely voice. "Just as there will be a first time for a Gatekeeper being sent to the lock-up while still on duty."

"Eh? You wouldn't . . ."

"I would. Indeed, I *will*."

"Very well then. Excuse me for a moment, Madam Marcia." Gringe went over to the gatehouse door and yelled into the shadows of the drawbridge winding room. "Hey! Bridge Boy!" bawled Gringe. "Wake up, yer lazy lummox!"

The Bridge Boy appeared, bleary-eyed. "What?" he said grumpily.

"Promotion for you," Gringe told him. "You're taking over until Mrs. Gringe gets back. No pocketing the money, mind, be polite to the customers and don't let no one over without paying, especially your good-for-nothing friends. Got that?"

The Bridge Boy, who was staring openmouthed at the sight of the ExtraOrdinary Wizard standing no more than a few feet away, nodded slowly.

"Good," snapped Gringe, "because I am on an important mission for the ExtraOrdinary and I don't want to be worrying about the bridge while I'm away on such a delicate matter." Gringe handed the Bridge Boy his money bag along with the warning "An' I know *exactly* how much is in there, so don't try any funny business." Then he turned and set off from the North Gate gatehouse with a sigh. *More* Heap trouble, he thought. Didn't he have enough already?

⊹⊦46⊹⊦
The Infirmary

The Infirmary was a bleak place, despite the best efforts of
the healers who worked there. It was a long, low wooden
building, hidden under the outlying trees of the Forest, covered with moss and mold after years of water dripping from
the trees above and mists seeping up from the Moat below.
The Infirmary was not often used, except for cases of sickness
that were thought to be contagious, but there were now so

many Castle inhabitants who had become ill that no one was taking any chances.

Marcia and Septimus approached the Infirmary along the now well-worn path on the far bank of the Moat. The afternoon light was fading, and as they approached, they could see the flicker of the first candles being placed in the tiny windows. The door was open, and with some trepidation, Marcia and Septimus went inside.

"Septimus! Is that you? What are *you* doing here?" Sarah Heap leaped up from her work. She had been sitting at a small table by the door, measuring out doses of ground-up leaves into rows of tiny pots neatly lined up in front of her. Sarah had not been out of the Infirmary since she had arrived and Silas had decided not to worry her about Septimus's disappearance and just hope for the best, which, for once, had been the right thing to do.

Sarah looked at her youngest son. "What have you done to your hair?" she asked. "It's a terrible mess. Really, Marcia, I know he's getting to that awkward age, but you should make him comb his hair once in a while."

"We haven't come to discuss Septimus's hairstyle, Sarah," said Marcia, who guessed, with some relief, that Sarah knew nothing of what had happened. "We have come on urgent business."

Sarah took no notice of the ExtraOrdinary Wizard. She had not taken her eyes off Septimus and wore a puzzled frown. "You look . . . different, Septimus," she said. "Have you been ill? Is there something you haven't told me?" she asked, beginning to get suspicious.

"No," said Marcia, far too quickly.

"I'm fine, Mum," said Septimus. "Really fine. Look, I've made an Antidote to this Sickenesse."

Sarah looked at Septimus fondly. "That's very sweet of you, love," she said, "but lots of people have tried and it's no good, nothing seems to work."

"But this *will* work, Mum—I know it will."

"Oh, Septimus," said Sarah gently, "I know how worried you must be about Beetle, I know how much you liked him—"

"Liked?" asked Septimus, suddenly scared. "What do you mean *liked*? I *still* like Beetle—lots. H-He's okay . . . isn't he?"

Sarah looked serious. "He's not well, Septimus. He . . . oh, dear. He is very ill and we don't have much hope. Would you like to see him?"

Septimus nodded. He and Marcia followed Sarah through

some swinging doors into the Infirmary ward, a long room that occupied the entire building. A row of narrow beds lined each side of the ward. The beds were crowded close together and every single one was occupied. The figures lay still and deathly pale in their beds, some had their eyes closed and some gazed at the ceiling, seeing nothing. The ward was hushed and still, full of late-afternoon shadows, which were slowly being dispersed by a young helper, who moved down the ward carrying a tray of candles, placing one in each window to keep the night at bay a little longer, as well as any stray Forest creatures. Septimus found it strange that for so many people crammed together in such a small space, there was very little noise; in fact, the only sound that he could hear was the occasional metallic *ping* as a drip of water found its way through the rotten shingles on the roof and hit one of the assortment of metal buckets placed at strategic points.

"Beetle's over here," whispered Sarah, putting her hand on her son's shoulder and guiding him toward a nearby bed. "He's near the door so that we can keep an eye on him."

If Sarah had not taken them to Beetle's very bedside, Septimus would never have found his best friend. The only thing that was recognizable was Beetle's shock of thick black hair, which his mother, who had only just left, had lovingly combed flat in a particular way that Septimus just knew Beetle would hate. The rest of Beetle was a pale white rag of a boy with wide staring eyes that saw nothing.

Sarah looked with concern at Septimus. "I'm so sorry, love," she said. "Would you like to sit with Beetle for a while? His mother will be back soon with his father, but you'll have a little time with him before they get here." Sarah brought an extra chair for Marcia, and she and Septimus sat down at Beetle's bedside. "I must get on now, Septimus," said Sarah. "I'll come back in a few minutes."

Septimus was suddenly horribly afraid that the Antidote would not work. He glanced nervously at Marcia, who whispered, "It *will* work, Septimus. You *must* believe in it."

"**Physik** isn't like **Magyk**," said Septimus unhappily. "It doesn't matter whether you expect it to work or not. Either it does or it doesn't."

"I doubt that very much," said Marcia. "A little belief in something always helps. Anyway, you *know* this works, don't you?"

Septimus nodded. He put the bottle on the rickety little table beside Beetle's bed and took out a pipette from the pocket inside his Apprentice cloak. He drew up a small amount of the Antidote into the pipette and dropped three drops of the clear liquid into Beetle's half-open mouth. And then, sitting on the edge of their seats, he and Marcia waited.

The last lit candle was just being placed in the window at the far end of the ward when Beetle blinked. And then he blinked again, frowned as if wondering where he was and suddenly sat up, wide-eyed, hair sticking up on end like it always did.

"Wotcha, Sep," croaked Beetle.

"Wotcha, Beetle," laughed Septimus. "Wotcha!"

"Shh . . ." Sarah shushed. "Beetle's family is here now, Septimus. They'd like a little time alone with him before . . . you know . . . oh, my goodness."

"It works, Mum!" Septimus laughed. "My mixture *works*."

"You mean . . . *you* did this?" asked Sarah, incredulous. Sarah, with all her knowledge of herbs and healing, had tried endless remedies for the Sickenesse, and nothing had had the slightest effect.

"Where am I?" asked Beetle, looking around him.

"You're in the Infirmary," Septimus told him. "You got the Sickenesse, remember?"

"Nope. Don't remember anything. Well, not after Princess

Jenna came to see me. . . . I remember *that*. Hey—she was looking for *you*."

Septimus smiled. "Well, she came and found me, Beetle. You wouldn't believe where she found me though."

"Where, Sep?"

"Tell you later, Beetle. Get lots of FizzFroot, you'll need it. Here's your mum."

There was still some of the Antidote left even after Septimus had dropped three drops into every mouth on the ward, so he left the bottle with Sarah for any new arrivals. To the accompaniment of an excited hubbub of chatter, and the celebration of relatives who had just arrived on the ferry for their evening visit, Septimus carefully wrote out a label—just as Marcellus had taught him—for Sarah to stick on the bottle:

> *Rx The Antidote*
> *sig: iii drops p.o.*
> *ut dict.*

"Your writing's gotten worse, Septimus," Sarah commented as she proudly took the bottle from her son and placed it in a cupboard behind her table. "It looks just like a real Physician's."

Septimus smiled. At that moment, he *felt* just like a real Physician.

✦47✦
PALACE RATS

Hildegarde *was on duty at* the Palace door when Gringe arrived, breathless and frazzled.

"I've come on important business on be'alf of the ExtraOrdinary," puffed Gringe. "I need to see Silas 'Eap."

"I'm afraid no one knows where he is, Mr. Gringe," said Hildegarde apologetically. "The Princess was looking for him earlier and could not find him."

" 'E'll be with the Counters, miss. Up in the attic."

Hildegarde smiled at Gringe. "Well, you are welcome to go in, Mr. Gringe, and try your luck."

"Thank you, miss." Gringe, still a little overawed by the Palace, hurried past and disappeared into the shadows of the Long Walk. Minutes later he drew back a ragged curtain hanging in a dark alcove and took a long flight of dusty stairs up to the attic. At the top Gringe pushed open the creaky door and peered in; at the far end of the long, beamed loft space, he saw the flickering light of a candle. Silas Heap was exactly where Gringe had expected—in the **UnSealed** room tending his Counter Colony.

The Counters were doing well, and at Gringe's approach Silas looked up, pleased to see his friend. "Look at this little fellow, Gringe. He's going to be a perfect Tunneler. I'm training him, getting him used to wriggling through things. Look at him go."

"Yeah, very nice, Silas, I'm sure. But I ain't come to watch your precious Counters."

Silas did not reply. He was down on his hands and knees, squinting into recesses under the floorboards. "Darn. He's gone. He's tunneled off."

"Yeah, well, that's the trouble with Tunnelers, Silas. Now look 'ere, I've had the ExtraOrdinary on at me and I've 'ad to leave the good-for-nothing Bridge Boy on the Gate—and Mrs. Gringe'll have my guts for garters when she finds that out, make no mistake—but we've got to put that painting back up 'ere an' *you* got to **Seal** the room again. Pronto."

"What are you going on about, Gringe? What painting? Here, boy, come on, boy, that's it . . . oh, he's gone again. Darn."

"The portrait of the crazy old bird in the crown. Pointy nose and scary look in 'er eyes."

"I'm not putting that thing back here, it'll unsettle the Counters. It can go somewhere else in the attic if they don't want it downstairs."

Gringe shook his head. "It's got to go back in 'ere, Silas—back to where it was before. And you've got to **Seal** it in like it was before an' all. Matter of Life or Death, your boy said."

Silas looked up. Gringe had his full attention now. "Which boy?" he asked, hardly daring to hope.

"Your Apprentice boy. Septimus."

"*Septimus*? When did he say that?"

"'Bout 'alf an hour ago. He was with the ExtraOrdinary. She's got scary eyes, an' all, 'asn't she?"

In a flurry of dust, Silas leaped to his feet. "He's back—
Septimus is back! Is he all right, Gringe?"

Gringe shrugged. "Looked all right to me. Bit scruffy, I suppose."

"And Jenna, is she back too?"

"I dunno, Silas, do I? No one tells me anything—except to
move pictures around or get shoved in the lock-up," Gringe
said grumpily.

"I must get to the Wizard Tower and see him," said Silas,
gathering his dusty Ordinary Wizard robes around him and,
candle held high, setting off toward the little door at the far
end of the attic.

"He ain't there, Silas," said Gringe, running after him.
"He's gone to the Infirmary. Got some cure for the Sickenesse
or something. Silas, we gotta take care of that portrait or I'm
in big trouble."

Silas ignored Gringe. He rushed off, stumbling over the
uneven floor, picking his way around the broken and rotten
boards. Suddenly Gringe said something Silas had never heard
him say before.

"You've got to take care of that picture, Silas—*please.*"

Silas stopped. "*What* did you say, Gringe?"

"You heard."

"Well, it *must* be serious. All right, come on, Gringe. We'll fix the picture."

It was a struggle getting Etheldredda's portrait off the wall. Silas got the impression that the picture had a mind of its own and did not want to be moved. Eventually a vicious tug from Gringe pulled the painting, along with a great lump of plaster and the picture nail, away from the wall and sent Gringe flying with it. Then, with a fair amount of what Sarah Heap called "*language*," Silas and Gringe began the awkward task of manhandling the disapproving portrait up the attic stairs.

"You'd think this thing 'ad arms," muttered Gringe after squeezing around a particularly tight corner. "Feels like it's 'olding on to the banisters."

"Ouch!" gasped Silas suddenly. "Stop kicking my shins, Gringe. That *hurt*."

"Weren't me, Silas. In fact—*ouch*—you can stop kicking my ankles."

"Don't be silly, Gringe. I've got better things to do than kick your stubby little ankles. Hey! That was my knee. You try that one more time, Gringe, and I'll—"

"You'll *what*, Silas 'Eap? Huh, *huh*?"

Both Silas and Gringe were battered and bruised and very near coming to blows by the time they reached the landing outside the attic door. They leaned the portrait against the wall and glared at each other, while the portrait glared at *them*.

"It's 'er, isn't it?" muttered Gringe after a while. "I dunno how she's done it, but it's been 'er that's been kicking us."

"Wouldn't be surprised," said Silas, accepting Gringe's peace offering. "Come on, Gringe, let's have a rest, we'll do this later. Fancy a game of Counter-Feet?"

"Deluxe version?" asked Gringe.

"Deluxe version," agreed Silas.

"And no mini-crocodiles?"

"No mini-crocodiles."

On the floor below, Jenna and Sir Hereward were listening to the bumps and thumps above their heads. Jenna had returned to the Palace and, unable to find Silas or Sarah, had gone to see Sir Hereward. He was at his usual post, half hidden in the shadows, leaning against a long tapestry that hung down beside the doors.

"Good morning, fair Princess. The Palace rats do grow ever

bolder, I declare," said the knight, pointing his broken sword up to the ceiling, where, immediately above them, Silas had got his foot stuck between two rotten floorboards.

"Good morning, Sir Hereward," said Jenna, who had become used to noises in the attic ever since Silas had started cultivating his Counter Colony. "They sound like two-legged rats with boots on to me."

Sir Hereward looked at Jenna as if searching for an answer to something that was bothering him. "You are safely returned after your absence?" he asked. "For as I recall you were not here last night, nor the night before—two long nights indeed, for none knew where to find you. 'Tis good to see you, and with a little orange rug as a keepsake from your travels. How very charming."

"It's a cat, Sir Hereward," said Jenna, holding Ullr up to show the knight.

Sir Hereward peered at the scrap of orange fur. Ullr stared vacantly at the ghost, seeing only a Time five hundred years ago. "'Tis a poor kind of cat," observed the knight.

"I know," said Jenna. "It's like he's not here anymore."

"Perchance your cat has the Sickenesse," said Sir Hereward.

Jenna shook her head. "I think he's missing someone," she said. "Just like I am."

"Ah, you are strangely melancholy this morning, Princess, but here is something to raise your spirits. What is the difference between an elephant and a tangerine?"

"One's big and gray and has a trunk, and the other is small and orange."

"Oh." Sir Hereward looked crestfallen.

"Just joking. I don't know, what *is* the difference between an elephant and a tangerine?"

"Well, I won't send you out to do *my* shopping then. Hur hur."

"Ho, ho. Sir Hereward . . . you know where I went away to, don't you?"

The knight seemed unwilling to answer. He poked his sword at his foot and fiddled with a loose plate of armor. "Only you can know that, Princess. Where, pray tell me?"

"I was *here*, Sir Hereward. And so were you."

"Ah."

"I was here *five hundred years ago*."

Sir Hereward, who as an old ghost was on the transparent side already, nearly faded away. But he recovered himself enough to say, "And you are back. *Safe*. And only two days gone. It is a wonder, Princess Jenna, and it is a burden lifted from my old shoulders. Ever since you told me your name was Jenna, I have worried that one day you would disappear and never be seen again."

"You never said."

"I thought that it was not something you would wish to know, Princess. It is best not to know what the future holds for us." Jenna thought of Marcellus Pye knowing that he had at least five hundred cold, dark years to spend alone in the Old Way, and she nodded.

"I have so many questions to ask you about what happened in the past, Sir Hereward."

"One at a time, Princess. I'm an old ghost now, and my memory tires easily."

"Just one today then: Did Hugo get home safely?"

Sir Hereward looked puzzled. "Hugo?" he asked.

"You remember Hugo," said Jenna. "He was with us. Well, with Septimus really. Wore a Palace Servant's uniform that was far too big for him."

Sir Hereward smiled. "Ah yes, I remember Hugo. And very pleased his mother was to see him too."

"I'm glad. Hugo was sweet."

"Yes. He became a wonderful Physician later, due to young Septimus Heap, he always said. But I shall cause you to tarry no longer. You will be wanting to go to your Chamber and rest."

Jenna shook her head, the memory of the little Princesses' crying behind the wainscoting was still fresh. "No, not just yet, thank you, Sir Hereward. I am going to sit by the river."

The autumn sun had warmed the old planks of the landing stage, and Jenna—comfortably upwind from Billy Pot's piles of dragon dung—was sitting with Ullr on her lap, dangling her feet into the surprisingly warm water of the sluggish river. Beside her was a blue and white saucer full of mashed corn, and nibbling at the corn was a small, naked duckling. As Jenna watched the corn steadily disappear into the duckling, her eyes grew heavy, and the blankets and cushion that she had brought down from Sarah Heap's living room seemed irresistible.

Which is why, when the Chief Customs Officer's launch drew up alongside the Palace landing stage, Alice Nettles and Alther Mella found a steadily breathing pile of crocheted blankets with an orange cat with a black-tipped tail and a small, stubbly duckling asleep on top of it.

"It's Jenna!" Alice gasped, recognizing Jenna's dark hair and the golden circlet. "How did she get *here*?"

"Are you sure?" asked the ghost, hardly daring to believe it. Alther and Alice had come to the Palace to break the terrible news of Jenna's and Nicko's disappearance to their parents. Alther had been ready to fly off alone, but Alice had insisted on going with him, and so Alther had followed the Customs Launch on its long journey upriver, all the while dreading what he was going to have to say.

"See for yourself." Alice smiled. "She's fast asleep."

Gently, Alther blew the covers back from Jenna's face and saw for himself. Jenna stirred at the ghost's warm touch but slept on, exhausted.

"Best to leave her sleeping," said Alice. "It's a warm after-noon, and she'll come to no harm."

"Funny ducklings they have around here," said Alther as he and Alice wandered across the sunlit lawns toward the Palace. "Must be a fancy new breed, I suppose."

✠ 48 ✠
THE SEND

The shadows over the lawns were lengthening, and still Jenna slept on, curled up under her blankets. From a distance Alther and Alice, who had searched the Palace for Silas and Sarah Heap and found neither, sat together on the lawn, watching the river from afar and chatting quietly.

On the other side of the Palace, walking briskly up the drive, were Marcia and Septimus, closely followed by Spit Fyre. Septimus was bringing Spit Fyre to see Jenna so that she could **UnDo** the **Seek**. Spit Fyre was dogging his every step and it was beginning to get extremely irritating.

"What I don't understand, Septimus," Marcia was saying, "is how a ghost of some kind of rat thingy—"

"It's an Aie-Aie," Septimus corrected. "Spit Fyre, *please* don't breathe down my neck like that."

"Aie-Aie, rat, elephant, whatever it is doesn't matter—the point is that it is still a *ghost*. And ghosts don't bite. Granted they can sometimes **Cause** a window to blow open or a door to slam shut, but they don't bite. *Mind my cloak, you idiot dragon.*"

"Ouch. That was my heel, Spit Fyre. I know, but this isn't just a ghost, it's a Substantial Spirit."

"Those don't exist, Septimus," said Marcia. "You've been reading the Witches' Apparition Almanac again, haven't you?"

"No, I haven't. I know it's a Substantial Spirit because Marcellus said—"

"I am getting just a little tired of hearing what Marcellus said," snapped Marcia.

"But you see, the Aie-Aie drank the same thing that Etheldredda drank. It was the Tincture that Marcellus made—" Marcia heaved a loud sigh at Marcellus's name but said nothing.

Septimus continued. "He was going to drink it himself but

it wasn't ready and then Etheldredda snatched it and drank it. Marcellus was really upset. And then Etheldredda grabbed Jen and took her to the river but it was icy and she—Etheldredda—fell in and drowned, which served her right, so then Marcellus said he was going to **Entrance** her ghost into her official portrait and **Seal** it into a room, as he knew that she would become a Substantial Spirit and that soon it would be just the same as if she were alive anyway except that she would be able to live forever, which is what she wanted in the first place and—"

"Stop!" said Marcia. "I can feel another headache coming on."

"So the Aie-Aie is a Substantial Spirit too and that's why it's biting people," Septimus finished in a rush before Marcia could stop him.

By now they had reached the little wooden bridge that spanned the Palace Moat. Marcia stopped for a moment to collect her thoughts. She had, despite appearances to the contrary, listened to every word that Septimus had said. "So who knows what the Substantial Spirit of Etheldredda is capable of by now?" she muttered. "We've got to get her **Sealed** fast, Septimus."

The wooden bridge over the Palace Moat sagged alarmingly under Spit Fyre's weight as they approached the Palace doors. Hildegarde, the sub-Wizard on door duty, looked worried.

"Silas Heap, please, Hildegarde," snapped Marcia. "At once."

"I believe he is in the attic, Madam Marcia," said Hildegarde, eyeing Spit Fyre warily. Hildegarde did not like reptiles very much and the Palace already had far too many for her liking, what with the snapping turtles in the Moat and Billy Pot's multitude of Lawn Lizards.

"Good," said Marcia. "Maybe he's doing something right for once, though somehow I doubt it." To Hildegarde's relief she turned to Septimus and said, "Septimus, *do not* bring that dragon in here. Take it around to the back. I'm sure Mr. Pot would be grateful for some more contributions." With that, Marcia rushed off into the shadows of the Long Walk, where there was a loud *crash* as she collided with the Palace cleaner and knocked over his bucket.

Leaving Marcia to tell the unfortunate cleaner where to put his bucket in the future, Septimus took the path around to the back of the Palace while Spit Fyre trotted after him, as if attached by a very short piece of invisible string.

✳ ✳ ✳

After getting lost several times, Marcia finally made it up to the attic. She arrived to the sounds of an argument.

"Look, Gringe. I cannot be held responsible if you are unable to control your Counters. *My* Kicker would *never* have Kicked everything off the board."

"It *was* your Kicker," muttered Gringe. "Mine was just goin' about 'is business and then he gets sent flyin' across the room. Dunno *where* he's gone."

"Don't know where *any* of them have gone," said Silas grumpily, getting down on his hands and knees and peering between the floorboards. "Probably never see them again. *Huh.*"

"Silas Heap, what *are* you doing?" Marcia's voice rang out as she strode down the long, empty attic toward the Counter-Feet players at the far end. Guiltily Silas jumped up and hit his head on a low rafter.

"*Ouch!*"

At the sight of the ExtraOrdinary Wizard approaching, cloak flying, eyes flashing and a look of fury on her face, Gringe went pale. "We were just about to put the painting back," he said. "Honest."

"Honest is not a word I automatically associate with *you*, Gringe," snapped Marcia, a trifle unfairly.

"Keep your hair on, Marcia," said Silas. "We're *doing* it. I don't see what the fuss is all about anyway."

"That, Silas Heap, is why you are only an Ordinary Wizard. This room was **Sealed** for a reason: to keep the ghost of Queen Etheldredda **Sealed** inside—and her disgusting pet whatever-it-is, which has been running around the Castle biting people and spreading the Sickenesse."

"Oh, come off it, Marcia," Silas objected. "You can't blame me for the Sickenesse too."

"You let it out, Silas. No one else did. Ever since you stupidly **UnSealed** that portrait it is no coincidence that we have had the Sickenesse, and even worse, we've had Queen Etheldredda let loose."

"She's only a *ghost*, Marcia," Silas protested. "There's no need to get so worked up about it. There are loads of ghosts around here, and some of them are a real pain—much worse than her. I mean, there's that one with the irritating whistle and then there's—"

"Be quiet, Silas. Etheldredda is no ordinary ghost. She is dangerous, Silas. She was **Sealed** in by her son—her own *son*, no less—who knew what she was capable of."

"What do you mean, capable of?" asked Silas, beginning to get a bad feeling about the whole business.

"Murdering her children. Princesses. Rightful heirs to the Castle. And now she is let loose here, in our Time, and she is intent on doing the same."

"What?" asked Silas. "You don't mean ... Jenna?"

"I mean just that. And now Jenna has returned—"

"Jenna's back!" gasped Silas. "Is she all right?"

"For the moment. She and Septimus are—"

"*Septimus*. So it's true, they're both safe?" Silas felt as though a weight had been lifted from him. Suddenly he felt far less like arguing with Marcia. "Give us a hand then, Marcia," he said. "We'll get this picture **Sealed** up in no time, won't we, Gringe?"

Gringe shrugged. As far as he was concerned, it was just another game of Counter-Feet brought to an untimely end by Silas Heap.

As the portrait moved slowly down the attic, Queen Etheldredda's Royal Barge was **Passing Through** the anti-Sickenesse blockade below Raven's Rock. The fishermen manning the boats on the blockade shivered as a chill breeze blew through the ships' rigging and set the ropes eerily humming. Queen Etheldredda sat alone on her ghostly seat—the Aie-Aie was skulking outside the Manuscriptorium, waiting to bite a few soft-skinned scribes as they left work. As the Royal Barge progressed through the blockade and headed upriver to the Palace landing stage, the smile on Queen Etheldredda's thin lips grew wider, for in her hands she cradled Jenna's silver pistol.

And in the silver pistol she had placed Jenna's Named bullet: I.P. for Infant Princess.

Up in the attic, Queen Etheldredda's portrait was not going quietly. Silas was sure it had bit him, and Gringe's arms felt like they were being pinched by a large crab as they struggled down the length of the attic toward the **UnSealed** room. About halfway there Gringe let out a loud yelp and dropped the painting. It landed on Silas's toe, and Marcia finally lost the remaining shreds of her patience.

"Stand back!" she yelled. "I will **Send** it to the room."

Silas was aghast. "You can't do that," he said. "You don't know *where* it will end up."

"Don't go telling me my job, Silas Heap," snapped Marcia. "It will **Go** where I **Send** it."

"Don't bank on it, Marcia," muttered Silas.

Marcia did not reply. She was already summoning up the **Magyk** she needed for the **Send**—and she needed a lot of it. Silas watched the **Magykal** haze—a flickering, purplish mist—appear around Marcia until it was hard to see where Marcia ended and the attic began. Gringe just watched, open-mouthed, as Marcia, staring intently at the portrait, began to chant slowly,

> "Go You where I Send
> Tarry not until the End
> Stay You where I Tell
> Mark You This and Mark it Well:
> *Go You to your Room!*"

At once Marcia had the horrible feeling she had done something wrong. Alther's wise words came back to her—*Be specific, Marcia. Say exactly what you mean*—but too late. The **Magykal** haze enveloped the portrait, as it was meant to. Queen Etheldredda's portrait rose, as it was meant to. Then it hurled itself through the window, as it was most definitively *not* meant to.

Marcia leaned out the window to see what had happened. She watched the portrait fly through the air and disappear into the wall of the turret—straight into the Queen's Room.

Marcia waited for Silas's scathing comment but it did not materialize. Silas had gone.

A ghostly barge makes no noise and so, as it drew up to the Palace landing stage, Jenna heard nothing. She slept peacefully on, but the duckling woke up. There was something in the air that reminded it of somewhere horrible—somewhere that smelled of oranges.

In a distant Time, Snorri Snorrelssen, no longer alone, sat on Snake Slipway with Nicko Heap and watched the water flow by. As she gazed unfocussed into the Moat, once again Snorri **Saw** *through Ullr's eyes. She* **Saw** *the Royal Barge come to rest at the landing stage. She* **Saw** *Queen Etheldredda stand up, pistol in hand, and she* **Saw** *the winter sun glint off the polished silver of the weapon as Etheldredda raised the pistol and aimed it at the sleeping Jenna.*

✳ ✳ ✳

Even though they were separated by five hundred years of Time, Ullr was still Snorri's cat, and he still did what his mistress asked. Which is why Ullr suddenly sprang to life and hurled himself at the ghost. But this time, Etheldredda, who was more Substantial, fought back and hit the small orange cat a swinging blow with the pistol. Ullr fell to the ground, but not before he had woken Jenna with his screech.

Jenna sat up with a jolt, still full of sleep. She could not make sense of what she saw—Ullr sprawled across the landing stage and a naked duckling running around in circles, cheeping like a tiny alarm clock.

On the lawn by the Palace, Alice had heard Ullr's screech and seen the flash of sun off the silver pistol. "That's odd," she said to Alther, who was dozing. "There's something going on down on the landing stage."

Alther opened his eyes and saw what Alice could not see. In a streak of panic, the ghost hurled himself across the lawn toward the river.

"Alther!" said Alice, following at top speed. "Alther, what *is* it?"

As Queen Etheldredda stepped daintily from the Royal

Barge, Jenna felt a chill envelop her and, as though doused with a bucket of cold water, her head suddenly cleared. There was a *pistol* hovering in the air. *Her* pistol. The one the Hunter had used to hunt her. The one that Aunt Zelda was keeping safe for her. So what was it doing *pointing at her?*"

Queen Etheldredda raised the silver pistol and took aim at Jenna just as Alther arrived like a whirlwind. "Go!" he yelled to Jenna. He threw himself at Etheldredda, but she **Passed Through** Alther like a knife through butter. Alther collapsed, poleaxed by the **Substantial Spirit**'s malice.

Jenna hesitated.

Etheldredda pulled the trigger.

There was a loud *crack* of the pistol shot, Alice Nettles threw herself at Jenna, and the silver bullet found its target.

The bullet went into Alice's heart —and there it stayed. A small silver ball with the letters I.P. scribed into the metal. Alice Nettles—named Iona at birth by her mother, Betty Pot—had been brought up by her aunt, Mary Nettles, who had always liked the name Alice. But there is no fooling a silver bullet.

✛49✛
THE BONEFYRE

There was no hope for Alice. Pale and still, she lay on the landing stage with a peaceful smile on her lips. Around her knelt Silas and Marcia, who had come running at the sound of the shot, and Alther and Jenna, who held the unconscious Ullr in her arms.

Beside Alther lay the silver pistol, which

Etheldredda had thrown down in disgust. As Alther gently stroked Alice's hair he began to realize that at last—at long last—he and Alice would be together. He could not help but wonder if Alice had been thinking of that when she had thrown herself in the path of the bullet—and if that was why she looked so peaceful now.

Marcia broke the shocked silence that surrounded Alice. "Jenna," she said, "I want you to stay close to me from now on. You are not safe while Etheldredda remains **UnSealed**. Now where is that wretched dragon? I think for once we may have a use for him."

Jenna nodded. Wishing that Snorri were there to help, she glanced around for any sight of Etheldredda. She saw nothing, but Jenna realized that nothing was exactly what Etheldredda wanted her to see. Warily she got up and laid Ullr on her blankets. The orange cat stirred, opened his eyes and gazed at Jenna with his faraway, unfocused look.

Jenna scooped up the little duckling, which was shivering, and settled it in between Ullr's paws for warmth. Then she and Marcia went to find Spit Fyre. The dragon was in the kitchen garden gulping down cooking apples with enthusiastic snorting noises. Septimus had heard the pistol shot, but he had assumed it to be some part of the dragon's digestive process. He was waiting impatiently while Spit Fyre sucked up the last of the windfalls and did not notice Marcia and Jenna's arrival. Neither did he see that right behind Jenna lurked Queen Etheldredda, though if he had looked closely Septimus might have seen a murkiness in the air, for Etheldredda was becoming increasingly **Substantial**.

But through Ullr's eyes, Snorri **Saw** *Etheldredda stalking Jenna as a tiger stalks its prey.*

Marcia marched up to Septimus. "Get that dragon organized, Septimus," she said. "We need **Fyre**—right now."

"He can't do **Fyre**," said Septimus.

"Yes he can," corrected Jenna.

"No he can't."

"He can. Look at his eyes. He's got the red ring of **Fyre**."

Septimus stood on tiptoe and stared into Spit Fyre's unblinking dragon eyes. Sure enough, the bright green iris was ringed with a thin red circle. "How did he get that?" Septimus asked suspiciously.

"I had to do the **Ignite**," Jenna explained.

"But he's *my* dragon," Septimus said, annoyed that he had not been there at such an important time.

"Enough of that," said Marcia. "It doesn't matter whose dragon he is. Follow me." She strode out of the kitchen garden. Spit Fyre, at the sight of his **Seek** rapidly disappearing, gulped down the last cooking apple, emitted a cider-smelling belch and rushed off after Septimus. He very nearly trampled Queen Etheldredda into the ground, but to Snorri's dismay, she sidestepped the dragon just in time and carried on stalking Jenna.

Etheldredda was not about to give up. She might have missed her chance with the pistol, but she would *not* be thwarted—from now on she would **Follow** Jenna wherever she went. She had all the time in the world and her chance would surely come. Jenna only had to step too near the edge of a parapet, stand too close to a running horse, warm her hands beside a blazing fire . . . and she, Etheldredda, rightful Queen, would be there—*ready*.

As Jenna followed Marcia across the Palace lawn, she shivered and rubbed the back of her neck —it felt strangely cold. She glanced behind her but saw nothing.

Marcia stopped in the middle of the lawn between the

Palace and the river. "Here will do," she said. "Septimus, I need Fyre—now."

"I don't know how," said Septimus, a little sulkily.

"I'll show you, Sep," Jenna said, fishing her Navigator Tin from her tunic pocket. She prised it open and offered Septimus the **Ignite**. Septimus did not look impressed, but he took the piece of dragon skin and examined it carefully. "Is that all you have to say?' he asked. "Just **Ignite**?"

Jenna nodded.

"You sure there's not something missing, Jen?"

Jenna sighed. "Of course I'm sure," she said, suppressing another shiver. "I did *do* it, you know."

Septimus did not look convinced, but he took a deep breath, looked Spit Fyre in his red-ringed eye, and said in a loud voice, **"Ignite!"**

With plenty of fuel—the dragon's fire stomach was still uncomfortably crammed with the Sacred Herd of Sarn—Spit Fyre was only too happy to oblige. Deep in his fire stomach a rumble began; it grew and grew, shaking the ground and filling the air with low, unsettling reverberations as the gases built up until they reached an unbearable pressure—and the fire valve opened. With a rush that shocked Spit Fyre as much as anyone else, the gases shot from the dragon's flared nostrils, hit the air and **Ignited** into a roaring jet of flame.

Everyone jumped back. Queen Etheldredda rubbed her hands together with glee; she had not expected an opportunity to present itself quite so soon. What could be better than a quick stumble into the path of a dragon's **Fyre**? No one would be able to save Jenna in time. Not with flames like that. Who would have thought that the interfering Marcia Overstrand would have so thoughtfully provided her with such an early opportunity? Etheldredda hovered, waiting impatiently for Jenna to get just a little closer—just enough for one tiny push. . . .

Far away, across Time, Snorri was frantic. She **Saw** *Etheldredda, she* **Saw** *the* **Fyre** *and* **Called** *to Ullr, but the orange cat, still stunned, did nothing.*

"Keep the **Fyre** going, Septimus!" Marcia yelled above the roar of the gases and flames. "And *now* for the **BoneFyre**. Stand back, everyone."

Once again the **Magykal** haze surrounded Marcia. When the ExtraOrdinary Wizard was sure that her **Magyk** was complete and she was fully protected, she went up to Spit Fyre, the **Fyre** still pouring from his nostrils. The dragon looked at her warily through his red-ringed eyes, but he did not move. Then, to the amazement of Septimus and Jenna, Marcia put her hand into the jet of flame and **Took** a handful of **Fyre**. She rolled it between her hands until it looked like a great ball of red-hot dough, threw it high into the air and chanted:

> "Pure Fyre
> Burn higher
> Make a Pyre,
> A True BoneFyre"

Marcia's handful of **Fyre** exploded into a great fireball. With intense concentration Marcia guided the roaring ball of fire down until it was a few feet off the ground. There it hovered, burning with a brilliant orange flame and a deep purple center, casting long, dancing shadows across the lawn. The **BoneFyre** was ready.

Spit Fyre, his fire stomach exhausted, **Ceased** his own **Fyre**. As the roaring from the **BoneFyre** settled down,

Septimus and Jenna drew closer to the flames to watch as
Marcia began the second part of her plan—the **Fetch**. **Un-
Seen** by anyone, even Alther—who was too taken with his
Alice to notice—Etheldredda's pointy features lit up with
excitement. Jenna was once again within stumbling distance
of the fire. Etheldredda stepped behind Jenna, her vicious
hand hovering no more than a finger's breadth above Jenna's
back, waiting for the right moment for that one final push.

*Only Snorri **Saw** the danger. "Ullr will not **Hear** me," she told
Nicko. "But maybe there is once last thing. . . . I do not know if I
can do it, but I have to try." And then Snorri did something she had
never dared to do before. She **Summoned** a Spirit across Time. In
the Hole in the Wall Tavern, the bemused ghost of Olaf Snorrelssen
found himself being picked up, dragged through the throng of ghosts
and, breaking all the rules of ghosthood, hurtling toward the Palace.
And Snorri **Saw** her father for the very first time.*

Now, Etheldredda decided, was the time to send Jenna into
the flames. *Now.* Etheldredda extended her hands—and Olaf
Snorrelssen grabbed her wrists. He did not know why, but he
did it anyway.

"Unhand me, vile oaf!" screamed Etheldredda. Nothing would have pleased Olaf Snorrelssen more than to let go of the sharp and bony Spirit, but he couldn't. *Something* would not let him. Jenna felt a strange prickling at the back of her neck. Again she glanced around, but she saw nothing of the battle being fought over her by the two ghosts. Despite the heat from the flames, she shivered and turned back to watch Marcia.

Marcia was now well into the **Fetch**. Through the purple light of the flames and the **Magykal** haze, Jenna saw the portrait of Queen Etheldredda and the Aie-Aie emerge through the walls of the turret. Marcia reeled it in like a protesting fish— twisting, flapping, flailing—drawing it unrelentingly toward the **BoneFyre**.

Etheldredda saw it too and, knowing exactly what was in store, she redoubled her efforts to break free of Olaf Snorrelssen's grasp. If she was going into the **BoneFyre**, she was not going alone—she would take Jenna with her. But Olaf Snorrelssen, who had been strong and wiry in his Lifetime, hung on to Queen Etheldredda's arms and not once did the queen get her chance to give Jenna that great shove she so longed to.

Now the portrait was hovering above the flames, resisting
to the last. The purple haze around Marcia deepened, and suddenly a resounding *crack* echoed around the Palace walls—
Marcia had won. The portrait gave up its fight, and with a
great *whoosh* it was sucked into the **BoneFyre**. It exploded
with a searing black flame. With a terrible shriek, Etheldredda
joined it and was consumed by the **Fyre**.

Etheldredda the Awful was no more.

*Snorri laughed with relief. Reluctantly—for she would have liked
to have* **Seen** *her father longer—she let Olaf Snorrelssen* **Return**
*to the safety of the Hole in the Wall Tavern, where he sat bemused
for many hours, nursing his beer and wondering why he had such a
strong image in his head of a young girl who looked so much like
his own dear Alfrún.*

But the **Fetch** was not finished. A small speck appeared in the
sky above the Palace and a terrible wail pierced the air: "Aie
aie aie aie!" Twisting and resisting, snake tail flailing, its red
saucer eyes popping with panic, Etheldredda's Aie-Aie hurtled
toward the **BoneFyre** and, with a terrible scream, joined its
mistress in the flames.

Deep within the **BoneFyre**, something was happening. An intense golden glow could be seen in the center of the purple flames. Entranced, Jenna and Septimus watched until it was so bright that neither could look at it further. As they turned away, something rolled out of the Fyre. It landed in the grass with a soft thud and, to their amazement, they saw Ethel-dredda's crown bounce along the scorched grass and roll down the slope toward the river. Jenna raced after it, grabbed at the crown, missed—and the crown fell into the river with a great hiss of steam. Throwing herself to the ground, Jenna plunged her arms into the freezing water and caught the crown as it slowly sank to the riverbed.

Triumphant and dripping, holding the True Crown in her hands for the first time, Jenna went and sat beside Silas, Alther, and Alice—who lay pale and peaceful on the landing stage. Nursing the crown, which felt surprisingly heavy in her hands, Jenna murmured, "Thank you, Alice. Thank you for saving me. I will always think of you when I put on this crown."

"Alice did a wonderful thing," said Silas, still shaken by what had happened. "But, er, maybe best not to tell your mother everything just yet?"

"She'll find out soon enough, Silas," said Alther. "It will be all over the Castle by the morning."

"That's what worries me," said Silas gloomily. Then he smiled at Jenna. "But you're back safe, that's all that matters."

Jenna said nothing. Suddenly she knew how Silas felt. She couldn't tell him now. Not about Nicko. Not yet.

Marcia **Ceased** the **BoneFyre**. The strange purple glow of the flames subsided and twilight began to take its place. Marcia, Septimus, and Spit Fyre joined the somber group on the landing stage. Marcia took off her heavy winter cloak with its indigo fur lining, folded it and placed it gently under Alice's head.

"How are you, Alther?" she asked.

Alther shook his head and did not reply.

Jenna sat quietly and looked at her crown. Even though it had spent years sitting on top of the disapproving head of Queen Etheldredda, the True Crown felt good in her hands— and as Jenna held it, the last ray of light from the setting sun caught the pure gold and the crown glowed as it never had when perched on Queen Etheldredda's angry head.

"It is yours now, Jenna," said Marcia. "You have the True Crown—the one that Etheldredda stole from her descendants."

✳ ✳ ✳

Darkness fell and, unnoticed by anyone, the black from the tip of the DayUllr's tail spread slowly across the orange and changed him to the night creature that he really was. The NightUllr sat like the Sphinx, his green eyes seeing only what Snorri asked him to see.

Far away, in another Time, Snorri Snorrelssen **Saw** *Jenna holding her crown and knew that all was well. She released Ullr. "Go, Ullr," she whispered. "Go with Jenna until the day I will return."*

The NightUllr got up, padded out of the shadows and took his place beside Jenna. "Hello, Ullr, welcome back." Jenna smiled, stroking the panther and scratching his ears. "Come with me, there's something I want to do."

As the Palace clock struck Midnight and the lights from a hundred and one candles—Jenna had placed one in every window of the Palace—lit up the night, they all stood on the landing stage and waved farewell to Alice, who had been placed in her Leaving Boat and was drifting slowly away. Alther sat quietly beside the new ghost of Alice Nettles, as he would continue to do for the next year and a day at that very spot—for under the Rules of Ghosthood, ghosts must spend a year and a day in the very place where they entered their ghosthood, and Alther had no intention of leaving Alice to do that on her own.

"Well," Marcia sighed, as Alice's Leaving Boat disappeared into the night, beginning its long journey to the Beyond. "What a day. . . . I hope you don't have anything quite so exciting planned for tomorrow, Septimus."

Septimus shook his head. It was not strictly true; he did have something exciting planned—but he figured that just then Marcia would not appreciate being told the details of how he was going to save Marcellus Pye from his fate worse than death and get his **Flyte** Charm back.

He kept it simple. He smiled at Marcia. "I'm going fishing," he said.

THINGS
YOU MIGHT LIKE TO
KNOW ABOUT . . .

QUEEN ETHELDREDDA
AND THE PORTRAIT IN THE ATTIC

After Queen Etheldredda fell in the river she did not bother to try to save herself—why should she? She was keen to embark on eternal life right away. She lay gazing up to the surface of the water, and soon she began to wonder why she felt so strange: kind of hollow and not quite there. Increasingly impatient, she watched the bottom of the Royal Barge as the bargee waited for hours, not daring to leave in case he missed her.

Slowly it began to dawn on Etheldredda that Marcellus's potion had not worked—she was nothing more than a common ghost. Unaware that the potion had worked to some extent and that she was in fact a **Substantial Spirit**—for it is hard to tell the difference at first—Etheldredda lay under the water, watching the shifting surface, and working up a temper.

Etheldredda's temper was at the boiling point when Marcellus Pye at last located his mother. And so it was that, thirteen days after she had slipped into the river and drowned, Queen Etheldredda was **Called Up** by her son at midnight. Like a cork out of a bottle, Etheldredda burst from the black waters of the river and, kicking and screaming, she flew through the freezing night air, giant snowflakes **Passing Through** her and turning her watery insides to ice. Still protesting, she was pulled into the small room hidden under the eaves at the far end of the Palace attic, where Marcellus Pye and Julius Pike, the ExtraOrdinary Wizard, were waiting for her. There, between the black and red robes of the Alchemist and the purple cloak of the Wizard, she saw the life-size portrait of herself and her Aie-Aie.

Etheldredda knew enough about **Magyk** to know what was about to happen, but there was nothing she could do. Despite her kicking and biting, punching and scratching, Julius Pike and Marcellus Pye dragged the **Substantial Spirit** of Etheldredda into her likeness, where she joined the Aie-Aie, which Marcellus had captured and killed the previous day.

They propped the portrait up against the wall and **Sealed** the room. And there she and the Aie-Aie stayed, until Silas Heap **UnSealed** the room five hundred years later.

PRINCESS ESMERALDA

After Marcellus had **Sealed** Etheldredda into the portrait and was sure that her Spirit could do Esmeralda no harm, he went through the Queen's Way and told Esmeralda the news. At first Esmeralda was pleased that she was no longer in danger from her mother, until it dawned on her that her mother was actu-ally dead. After that Esmeralda spent a long time wandering the Marram Marshes, thinking about her mother and her lost sis-ters. She refused to come back to the Castle and spent her teenage years living with Broda. But, when the Time was Right, Esmeralda did return and take her rightful place as Queen.

Esmeralda did her best to rule well, although she never quite got rid of the nervousness brought about by having Queen Etheldredda as a mother. She married a handsome and very steady farmer from the apple farm just across the One-

Way Bridge and had two daughters, Daisy and Boo, who both became Queens in their turn, for Daisy had five sons but no daughters.

After the Great Alchemie disaster—when for seven days and nights she helped Marcellus with the **Sealing** of the Ice Tunnels—Esmeralda developed a headache and spent most of her time in the small sitting room at the back of the Palace with the curtains closed, while the very capable Princess Daisy took over the Palace.

The Crowns

For as long as there had been Queens in the Castle, the True Crown had graced their heads. It was reputed to have been made from the finest and most **Magykal** gold ever known— the golden thread spun by the Spiders of Aurum. It certainly predated Hotep-Ra, who had founded the Wizard Tower. But, with the demise of Etheldredda, the True Crown was lost and Etheldredda's prediction came true—Esmeralda never did wear the True Crown.

But Esmeralda didn't care about that. The True Crown was

gone, and good riddance to it. Esmeralda wanted a brand-new sparkly crown all her own and in the fashion of the day, which was rather overwrought. Esmeralda was her mother's daughter, and what Esmeralda wanted, Esmeralda got. She was crowned in the throne room of the Palace on a rainy Mid-Summer's day, and then, resplendent in her new Crown, went to see the Dragon Boat. The dragon raised an eyebrow at the sight of so many diamonds and gems but said nothing. For some time Esmeralda would not be parted from her crown and wore it everywhere, until she got a stiff neck and reluctantly took it off when she went to sleep.

It was this crown that, many hundreds of years later, the Supreme Custodian ran off with, leaving Jenna with no crown of her own—until the True Crown rolled out of the **Bone-Fyre** and found its rightful owner once more.

THE AIE-AIE

Etheldredda found the Aie-Aie in the Palace gardens when she was a little girl. The creature had jumped ship after realizing that the ship's cook was planning to boil it for supper in revenge for a nasty nip on the ankle the Aie-Aie had given him that morning. Later that night the cook became delirious, and the ship's crew went without supper. Three weeks later the cook died—for the Aie-Aie carried the Sickenesse in its bite.

But Etheldredda soon realized this and found the Aie-Aie to be a most useful weapon. Her mother was terrified of her new pet but dared do nothing, for Etheldredda (or Ethel-Dreadful, as she was known) wanted the Aie-Aie, and even when she was only nine years old, what Etheldredda wanted, Etheldredda got.

The Aie-Aie was a long-lived creature despite many surreptitious attempts on its life by numerous Palace servants. It was said that Etheldredda cared more for the Aie-Aie than she did for her own daughters—which was, of course, true.

The Bumptious Barrelle of Larde

Although the Bumptious Barrelle of Larde was not called that as a child, his own name was almost as bad: Aloysius Umbrella! Tyresius Dupont. His second name was a mistake on the part of the Registrar at the naming ceremony, in response to a barked instruction from the infant Aloysius's father to his wife to take the umbrella off his foot.

The young Aloysius Umbrella! was an only child who always knew best. When he was ten his mother, tired of being told how to darn his socks properly, secured a job at the Palace for him as an UnderMessenger to the Fourth Secretary of the Keeper of the Royal Doorstop. There was no stopping Aloysius Umbrella! after that—he worked his way up through the complicated Palace hierarchy until he was himself the Keeper of the Royal Doorstop at the tender age of fourteen.

At the age of twenty, Aloysius Umbrella! stepped in as deputy Steward to Queen Etheldredda after the actual Steward had been laid low by a mysterious bout of food poisoning— one of many he had suffered since Aloysius Umbrella! had begun to sit next to him at the weekly Servants' Supper. The Steward never fully recovered and Aloysius Umbrella! was offered the post full-time. Although Aloysius Umbrella! was by then known as Bumptious, he did not acquire his full nickname until he had spent a further three years overindulging in Palace food.

After he fled the Palace in terror, having slapped Queen Etheldredda, Aloysius Umbrella! took the night boat to the

Port and left on the first ship he could find. He spent the rest of his days in a small town in a very hot Far Country, where he worked as a drain inspector during the day and spent his evenings carefully ironing the tattered remains of his Palace ribbons.

THE TRUE GLASS OF TIME

In Ancient Times there were many True Glasses of Time, but over the centuries they became lost, destroyed or—like Marcellus's Glass—they disintegrated under the opposing forces of Time. By the time Marcellus Pye was a promising young Alchemist, all were lost.

Marcellus read all he could find about the Glasses of Time. He discovered many things: that you needed a linked pair, and that whatever happens to one will happen to the other. He also discovered that when you walk through one you find yourself in a place that has no Time, and to go into another Time you *must* go through the other of the pair. But nowhere could he discover the secret formula of Time.

Marcellus became obsessed with discovering the formula,

and after three years of searching he had a stroke of luck. One wet winter's afternoon, when he was meant to be visiting his mother, he stumbled across it in an ancient text buried under a dingy stack of books at the back of the Manuscriptorium. Marcellus memorized the formula and immediately burned it in the flame of his candle, for he wanted no one else to discover the secret. He soon regretted this, for the first two Glasses he made did not work properly. They merely transported him through a solid wall, which, though marvellous in itself, was not enough for Marcellus, whose ambition was to move freely through Time.

Marcellus decided that even so, these Glasses could be useful. He **Locked** each Glass so that only his **Keye** could control it and put them in ornate gilded frames. He gave one to his mother as a peace offering after one of their frequent arguments. Etheldredda did not care for it; she put the Glass in her Robing Room and promptly forgot about it. It was this Glass that Septimus was dragged through.

Marcellus gave the other to the Chief Scribe of the Manuscriptorium, who was a vain man and was thrilled to have his own looking glass—an incredibly expensive item in those times. He did not realize that Marcellus was using it to secretly gain access to the Hermetic Chamber. This was the Glass through which Jenna, Ullr, and Septimus returned to their own Time.

After these two disappointments, Marcellus locked himself in his room and hypnotized himself until he remembered every last nuance of the formula for the True Glass of Time—or so he thought. In a daring innovation, Marcellus fused the pair of Glasses together, and they worked. The True Glass of Time was huge, immensely fragile—and dangerous. After Marcellus installed it in the Great Chamber of Physik he sent a number of scribes through but none returned. After his best friend disappeared through it, Marcellus decided not to risk using it himself and **Locked** the doors.

Now Marcellus was getting confident. He started to experiment. He wanted something light and transportable that he could use to gather secrets from the **Darke** Alchemists in the Lands of the Long Nights. After the passage of an auspicious number of days—one hundred and sixty-nine (thirteen times thirteen)—Marcellus successfully made a matched pair of Glasses. Keeping one at the Castle, he secretly sent the other through the Queen's Way to his wife, Broda Pye, with instructions for Broda to get it to the Port. Marcellus traveled to the port and supervised the Glass being loaded onto his ship—but while he slept, his first night on board, the Glass was promptly unloaded by the unscrupulous, debt-ridden captain and sold to Drago Mills as a Luxury Novelty Glass. Unaware that he had been double crossed, Marcellus traveled all the way to the Lands of the Long Nights and did not discover the deception until the hold was emptied. Furious, he returned to the Port, intent on reclaiming his property, only to find that it was impounded in Warehouse Number Nine. Try as he might, Marcellus could not get it back. This was the Glass that Jenna, Nicko, Snorri, and Ullr went into—and Spit Fyre smashed.

The other Glass from the matched pair, which Marcellus had kept in the Great Chamber of Alchemie and Physik, ready to take him to any Time in the Land of the Long Nights, was of no use to him. Marcellus put it away in a cupboard in disgust. Years later the cupboard found its way to the Palace, where it was used as the UnderCooks' coat cupboard. It was this Glass that Jenna, Nicko, Snorri, and Ullr came out of and stepped into Marcellus's Time.

After this Marcellus made no more Glasses. He decided he preferred gold—at least you knew where you were with gold.

Hugo Tenderfoot

Hugo never forgot Septimus and the time Septimus had spent patiently teaching him all he had learned about **Physik**. After Sir Hereward had taken him home and his mother had been so relieved to see him, Hugo realized that his family did care for him after all, and he became much more confident. When Marcellus Pye found Hugo reading a **Physik** book when he was meant to be on door duty, instead of being angry he took Hugo on as his Apprentice. Hugo did indeed become a talented Physician—although he never managed to cure Esmeralda's headaches.

Snorri's Mother

Alfrún Snorrelssen came from a long line of Traders and so she was used to the yearly exodus of ships and Traders to the Small Wet Country Across the Sea. Every year after the first frost—and frost came early in those dark northern latitudes—the Trader's barges would set off laden with furs, spices, wool, tar, trinkets and trifles. They would not return until well after

MidWinter Feast Day. Alfrún Snorrelssen always knew when
her Olaf would return, and as the time drew near her friends
would begin to ask, "Alfrún, Alfrún, can you **See** the ships
yet?" And Alfrún always could. But the year that Olaf Snorrelssen went away for the last time, when Alfrún's friends asked,
"Alfrún, Alfrún, can you **See** the ships yet?" Alfrún shook her
head. Even when the fleet of Trader's barges had appeared on
the gray wintry horizon, still Alfrún shook her head, but this
time in despair, for she knew that her Olaf was never coming
back.

Alfrún gave her baby daughter the name that Olaf had chosen and named in his Letter of Charters. No matter that Olaf
had been convinced that his child would be a boy; Alfrún honored his wishes and called the baby Snorri.

Snorri grew up surrounded by various aunts, uncles, grand-
mothers and cousins. She was a happy, bubbly child, and it
was only when, at the age of thirteen, she found her father's
Letters of Charter naming Snorri as his Successor to Trade
that she became dissatisfied. Snorri had never given her father
much thought before, but now she longed to sail in his path,
tread in his footsteps through the Castle of the Small Wet
Country Across the Sea and, most of all, drink Springo Special

in the fabled Sally Mullin's Tea and Ale House. And as a Spirit-Seer, she also longed to see his ghost.

When Snorri told her mother of her intention to Trade in the coming season, Alfrún Snorrelssen was aghast. She told her daughter of the dangers of the sea, she told her she was too young to Trade, that she was a girl and girls did not Trade, and besides, what did Snorri know about the price of fur and the quality of woolen cloth?

Snorri knew nothing, but she could learn. And when her mother found her stack of Traders' Manuals shoved under her bed and threw them into the tiled stove, Snorri took Ullr and stormed out of their little wooden house on the harbor and went to the *Alfrún*. Her mother guessed where she was and let her be, thinking that spending a cold night on an uncomfortable barge would bring Snorri to her senses and she would be back in the morning. But by morning Snorri was sailing out on the ebbing tide. She caught the southerly wind and was soon heading down the coast to pick up her very first cargo as a Trader. Alfrún Snorrelssen was distraught—she sent a fast pilot gig after Snorri, but there was a brisk wind that morning, and although the rowers of the gig had sight of the barge, they had no chance of catching up with

it. Her daughter was gone, and Alfrún Snorrelssen blamed no
one but herself.

SNORRI'S FATHER

When Olaf Snorrelssen knew that he and Alfrún were expecting
their first child he was thrilled. He took his Letters of Charter to
the League Office and insisted that they name his first child,
Snorri, as his Successor. And then, promising Alfrún that this
would be his last trip until the child was old enough to go with
him, with a heavy heart, Olaf Snorrelssen set off to Trade.

He arrived late at the Castle of the Small, Wet Country
Across the Sea and did not get a good pitch at the Traders'
Market. That night Olaf went to the Grateful Turbot (one of
the Traders' favorite hostelries just outside the Castle) to drown
his sorrows in the way that Northern Traders traditionally did,
and as a consequence were banned from most Castle hostelries.
Returning alone across the One-Way Bridge, Olaf Snorrelssen
stumbled and hit his head on the parapet. He was found, dead
and frozen, the next morning by a farmer on his way to market.

The ghost of Olaf Snorrelssen lingered at the bridge for a
year and a day, as all ghosts must do at the scene of their entry

into ghosthood. He chose not to **Appear** to anyone, but a nasty chill settled over the bridge, and many people claimed to feel quite depressed after crossing it. The Grateful Turbot Tavern nearly went out of business, as people became reluctant to cross the One-Way Bridge after dark. As soon as his year and a day was completed, Olaf Snorrelssen wafted away to the Hole in the Wall Tavern, and there he stayed.

THE *ALFRÚN*

The *Alfrún* languished at the Quarantine Dock all through the long winter months, where she acquired the forlorn air and the damp smell of neglected boats. When Jenna found out where the barge was she asked Jannit Maarten to bring her to the Castle boatyard. But before Jannit had got around to doing it, the *Alfrún* was gone.

WOLF BOY

When Wolf Boy left the *Alfrún*, he paddled across the river and found Sam Heap laughing at the sight of him frantically turning the paddles of the pink paddleboat. He got a warm welcome at Camp Heap, where the other Heap brothers lived, and despite the endless variety of jokes about his taste in boats, Wolf Boy was pleased to be back. However, he was disappointed that he could persuade none of the Heap brothers to help him find Septimus. Knowing that his own skills as a tracker were not going to help him find his old friend 412, for there had been no trail to pick up, Wolf Boy decided that Aunt Zelda would have the answer. He took his much-derided pink paddleboat down the river to the Port and then set off along the Causeway, which led to the Marram Marshes. Here Wolf Boy's tracking skills came in useful. He followed the trail of the Boggart and arrived safely at Aunt Zelda's, where he discovered Jenna, who had just come through the Queen's Way to return the silver pistol to Aunt Zelda.

Wolf Boy stayed with Aunt Zelda. She stopped trying to teach him to read and began telling him about the things he really wanted to know—about the moon and stars, herbs and potions, and everything to do with White Witch lore. Wolf Boy was an eager and talented pupil, and it was not long before Aunt Zelda began to wonder if it would be possible to break with tradition and nominate Wolf Boy as her successor as Keeper.

LUCY GRINGE

Lucy Gringe arrived safely at the Port in Nicko's row boat. It was nearly midnight, and she tied the boat up to the harbor wall, curled up in Simon's cloak and tried to sleep.

The next morning, Lucy bought a pie from the Harbor and Dock Pie Shop. Maureen, who owned the shop, noticed how pale and cold Lucy looked and offered her a place by the fire in the kitchen to sit and eat her pie. Lucy was ravenous, and bought two more pies in quick succession plus three mugs of hot chocolate, downed everything, then fell asleep by the fire. Maureen left her to sleep, and later that day Lucy returned the favor by washing the pie dishes and serving in the shop. Maureen liked Lucy and was grateful for the help. She offered Lucy a bed in the corner of the kitchen and her keep in return for her efforts. Lucy accepted, glad of somewhere warm and friendly to stay with a steady supply of customers to ask if they had seen Simon.

To Lucy's disappointment, none of the customers had seen Simon, but late one night when she was sitting by the dying embers of the fire, Lucy saw a rat in the corner nibbling at the crumbs that her broom had missed. Lucy liked rats and did not chase it away as she knew Maureen would want her to.

She watched the rat for a few minutes and then whispered, "Stanley?"

The rat looked shocked. "What?" it said.

"Stanley. You're Stanley, aren't you?" asked Lucy. "Remember, I fed you biscuits after Dad locked me up—you're a bit fatter than you were then."

"You're none too thin yourself, Lucy Gringe," Stanley retorted—and this was true, for Lucy did not hold herself back on the pies.

And this was how, at long last, Lucy Gringe found her way to Simon Heap. For Stanley, ex-Message Rat and member of the Secret Rat Service, knew where Simon was—although it took many talks at cross-purposes and many long hours of listening to Stanley's reminiscences before Lucy discovered exactly what Stanley knew. The Big Freeze had already set in when Stanley at last agreed to take Lucy to the Badlands, and it was not until the spring of the following year that they actually set off. By late spring, Lucy and Simon were reunited at last.

ANGIE SAGE was born in London and grew up in the Thames Valley, London, and Kent. She now lives beside a creek in Cornwall, which is a Magykal place. She is the author-illustrator of many picture books, and is also the author of the Araminta Spookie series. The first two books in the Septimus Heap series are international bestsellers. You can visit Ms. Sage online at www.septimusheap.com.

MARK ZUG has loved fantasy novels since he was a teenager. He has illustrated many collectible card games, including *Magic: The Gathering* and *Dune*, as well as books and magazines. He lives in Pennsylvania.